# THE LOWEST DEPTHS OF LUST

Lisa thought she knew what to expect when the pirate chieftain Hawk summoned her. Once again she would have to feign arousal as he publicly fondled her breasts, her thighs.

*But tonight Hawk had different plans. Before Lisa realized what was happening, he stripped away her dress as she stood in a circle of grinning men.*

"You deserve a prize," Hawk roared at a dark French seaman who stood gaping at this vision. "I'm loaning you the wench until morning!" As Lisa was led by this eager man to a cave a short distance away, she knew this was just the beginning. From now on, Hawk would use her to reward any man he chose. She didn't care what happened to her body tonight, because it was no longer her own.

*Once she had been Lady Lisa Saunders, proud wife of a great British admiral, adored mistress of Jeremy Beaufort, and hated rival of Jeremy's wife, Sarah. Now she was a woman who wanted only one thing more than death. She lusted for revenge. . . .*

## SIGNET Bestsellers You'll Want to Read

If you wish to order these titles,
please see the coupon in the
back of this book.

# MISTRESS
# OF OAKHURST

### (Second in the Oakhurst series)

By
*Walter Reed Johnson*

A SIGNET BOOK
NEW AMERICAN LIBRARY
TIMES MIRROR

COPYRIGHT © 1978 BY BOOK CREATIONS, INC.

All rights reserved

Produced by Lyle Kenyon Engel

SIGNET TRADEMARK REG. U.S. PAT. OFF. AND FOREIGN COUNTRIES
REGISTERED TRADEMARK—MARCA REGISTRADA
HECHO EN CHICAGO, U.S.A.

SIGNET, SIGNET CLASSICS, MENTOR, PLUME AND MERIDIAN BOOKS
are published by The New American Library, Inc.,
1301 Avenue of the Americas, New York, New York 10019

FIRST SIGNET PRINTING, SEPTEMBER, 1978

1 2 3 4 5 6 7 8 9

PRINTED IN THE UNITED STATES OF AMERICA

# MISTRESS
# OF
# OAKHURST

# Chapter 1

Sarah Benton Beaufort, mistress of Oakhurst Manor, faced the worst crisis of her life. Within twenty-four hours at the most, perhaps this very day, she would learn whether the happiness for which she had fought so hard would be destroyed for all time.

She had created the situation herself, but there had been no alternative. Not only was her own future at stake, but that of her little son was threatened, and the fate of the great plantation she had struggled so hard to save was hanging in the balance too.

Sarah had created the confrontation herself, forcing another meeting between her husband, Jeremy, and the ravishing, mysterious beauty who had appeared out of his past. That meeting would take place here at Oakhurst Manor, her own home, and the stakes for which she was gambling were so high she felt dizzy.

Fight fire with fire, she told herself. Fight fire with fire; it's the only way. As she had done so often in past times of stress, she leaned against one of the great white columns on the portico of the South Carolina mansion, gaining strength from it as she looked out across the manicured lawns toward the fields where more than four hundred slaves grew the cotton and tobacco responsible for the prosperity of Oakhurst Manor.

On the surface, Sarah had everything a young woman living in the United States in 1817 could want. Tall and slender, with a figure that a girl of seventeen might envy, she had wheat-blond hair that cascaded in waves down her back, and only her enormous green eyes, fringed by dark lashes, sometimes indicated all that she had suffered.

Life, as she had learned, was astonishing. A scant four years earlier she had been a Boston innocent, daughter of a prominent attorney and passionately devoted to the abolition of slavery in the South. The night her betrothed, Jeremy Beaufort, had disappeared—not until years later had she learned he had been impressed into the British Navy—her own life had changed.

She and her younger sister, Margot, had come to Oakhurst Manor on a visit, and in South Carolina they had stayed. Here at Oakhurst Manor Sarah's son, Jerry, had been born. Margot had married Jeremy's younger brother, Tom, and after a stormy beginning they were making a success together at nearby Trelawney, a plantation that Jeremy had purchased for them from the family's closest friends, the Emersons.

But so much had happened before Jeremy had reappeared out of nowhere, wealthy, self-assured, and worldly. Sarah's father, Isaiah Benton, a widower, had married Lorene Small, the aunt of the young Emersons, and had settled in nearby Charleston. Paul Wellington Beaufort, the master of Oakhurst Manor and the father of Jeremy and Tom, whom Sarah had adored, had died of the Sickness, an epidemic that later would be known as cholera. Most of the slaves had died, too, and a desperate Sarah had been on the verge of selling the plantation. Because she had no choice.

But she had fought grimly against seemingly overwhelming odds, and her faith in Jeremy had been justified. He had returned to her and their child after suffering of his own. Life before the mast in the Royal Navy had been a nightmare, but his courage and intellect had impressed his commanding officer, Captain Viscount Saunders, and he had won a commission.

Almost drowning in a hurricane, he had been picked up by

a slave ship and carried to equatorial Africa, where he had saved the life of the king of the powerful Bantu, and that incident had marked a sharp change in his fortunes. Jeremy had returned home with several hundred slaves, Watusi enemies of the Bantu who had been conquered in battle. A necklace of rough-cut diamonds presented to him by the Bantu monarch had made him wealthy, and the largest of those stones, now fashioned into a brilliant ring, graced Sarah's finger.

Accompanying Jeremy had been a strange couple. M'Bwana, second son of the Bantu king, was Jeremy's blood brother, a free black who was now the overseer at Oakhurst Manor, the first of his race to hold such a post anywhere in the South. With him was his wife, Kai, a lovely young creature, an Algerian girl who was white, or seemingly white.

Also in the party had been the little son of M'Bwana and Kai, a child named Lance. Just looking at the boy, Sarah had known he had been sired by Jeremy, not M'Bwana. His resemblance to Jerry, her own son, was startling. Sarah didn't know what had happened, particularly as it was obvious that Kai and M'Bwana were deeply in love with each other, but she had been content to wait for the explanation that her husband still had not summoned the courage to offer her.

Jeremy loved her, Sarah knew, as much as she loved him, and that was good enough. A man's sexual urges were more primitive, more demanding than those of a woman, and she could overlook his affair with Kai, whatever it might have been. It sufficed for her that M'Bwana, as resourceful and brave as Jeremy himself, was devoted to Kai and that the shy girl felt the same toward him. Lance was recognized as M'Bwana's son, and Sarah was confident that, sooner or later, Jeremy would tell her the truth about his past.

Until a few days earlier, Sarah could have asked no more than what she had in life. A steadfast, loving husband. A healthy little son who worshiped his father and was loved in return. Mistress of Oakhurst Manor, a social position second to none anywhere in America. Complete financial security. Jewels, clothes, and material comforts beyond the dreams— much less the reach—of most women. A system of slavery so sensible and humane that it made many neighbors uneasy, a system that didn't tolerate physical punishment on a plantation where slaves were taught to read and write.

Cleo, the two-hundred-and-fifty-pound black housekeeper who ruled the domestic staff and in many ways was the real mistress of Oakhurst Manor, joined Sarah on the portico and glowered at her. "Breakfast on table," she said. "Jeremy eating, Jerry eating. Missy come now. Eat, too."

Sarah shook her head. "Not this morning, Cleo," she said. "I'm not hungry today. I'll come out to the kitchen shortly to discuss tonight's menu with you. Dinner this evening will be special."

Cleo studied her and realized that everything about today appeared to be special. Mistress Beaufort was wearing a full-skirted gown of powder-blue silk trimmed in eyelet lace, with a low, square-cut neckline, the sort of dress she ordinarily wore only in the evening, when she was giving a party. Her eyes were rimmed with kohl, there was a shiny green substance on her lids, and she wore rouge on her cheeks and lips; in Cleo's opinion she needed no cosmetics to emphasize her delicate beauty. Certainly it was unusual for her to make up her face in the morning, when her normal routine consisted of a visit to every household department, a tour of the slave quarters to attend the sick and hear complaints and problems, and then a long session in the library, where she kept the plantation's ledgers. Clearly this was a day unlike any other.

Cleo could intimidate virtually everyone, including Jeremy and his brother, Tom, having supervised their upbringing after their mother had died while giving birth to her younger son. But Missy Sarah was different: no one could scare her, no situation could frighten her. Cleo muttered under her breath and vanished into the mansion.

Sarah had read her mind, and smiled wearily. The truth of the matter was that she was more frightened than she had ever been in all her life. Soon the guests would arrive, and her whole world well might crash in ruins around her.

She heard footsteps behind her on the marble floor of the foyer, and recognized them without turning.

Jeremy Beaufort, the master of Oakhurst Manor, came onto the portico, young Jerry perched on his shoulder. And even now, after all this time, Sarah's pulse raced when she saw him. He was tall and lean, a perfect physical specimen in prime condition, muscles rippling beneath his shirt of fine lawn. There were flecks of gray at his temples and in his full, trimmed beard, indications that he had not lived an easy life, even though still in his twenties. His hazel eyes were wise and compassionate, but this morning Sarah saw—or thought she saw—something new in them, something alien to his nature. A hint of uneasiness, perhaps.

"Jerry and I missed you at breakfast," Jeremy said as he kissed her.

Sarah clung to him for a moment. "I ate too much last night and had to compensate this morning." All women told white lies on occasion, she thought.

"Well, we're on our way. M'Bwana is waiting for me, with Lance. We're checking on the fall harvest, and we decided the boys could ride with us."

"I going with Papa," Jerry announced proudly.

"Don't go off to the far ends of the plantation, please," Sarah said. "Our company will be arriving at any time, and you'll want to be on hand to greet them."

"What company?" Jeremy asked, and seemed genuinely puzzled.

Surely he couldn't have forgotten! "Admiral Lord Saunders and his lady!"

"Oh, yes. I hadn't realized it was today they were coming."

Sarah saw his eyes cloud, and she felt a sinking sensation in the pit of her stomach.

"I've been meaning to ask you, Sarah. Whatever possessed you to invite them here?"

She was prepared for the question. "You've told me yourself that it was Lord Saunders who taught you seamanship and navigation, then granted you a commission. If it hadn't been for him, you'd have spent the entire War of 1812 as a common seaman in the British Navy. You owe him a great deal."

"You're right, my dear, as always," he said, and grinned.

"Besides, Lady Saunders is so beautiful and charming, I'd like to know her better, and I should think you would, too." The remark was deliberately provocative.

Sarah was sure she wasn't imagining things when she saw her husband stiffen and watched his face go blank. He shrugged and moved off down the steps to the driveway, where a groom waited with his horse. "There's no telling when they'll arrive, so send someone to fetch me," he said.

She watched him as he mounted, Jerry still clinging to him; then he settled the boy in front of him on the saddle.

M'Bwana was waiting for him in front of his own house, the comfortable two-story overseer's house, newly enlarged for him and his family. The Bantu was as tall as Jeremy but huskier. The bond between them was something special, and both shouted greetings.

Lance was perched on M'Bwana's saddle, and Sarah never ceased to marvel when she saw the child. In fact, she wondered how she could have been blind for so long. The resemblance between Jerry and Lance was remarkable, and anyone looking at the boys would know that both were Jeremy's sons.

But Sarah literally didn't care, at least not all that much. Not with the threat that faced her now.

Never, as long as she lived, would she forget the moment in the Charleston drawing room of her father and stepmother when Jeremy and Lady Saunders had come face to face. Both had accepted introductions, as though they were total strangers, but Sarah had been positive both had dissembled.

The very air had crackled with electricity. The magnetic attraction of Jeremy and Lady Saunders to each other had been so powerful it had sent shivers through Sarah. She had marveled that no one else had been aware of that intense, overwhelming sense of intimacy.

Now she was making the experiment of bringing them together again, and she wondered if she had gone mad. She was curious, of course, wondering when and where and under what circumstances they had met during Jeremy's long years of travel and suffering. Such details were unimportant. What mattered was that they had been lovers; she was positive of it, and when two people were drawn to each other that strongly, there was no way of predicting what might happen.

Sarah stood on the portico for a long time, and did not rouse herself until she saw a carriage pulled by a team of her father's matched grays appear at the far end of the long driveway and approach between the towering trees that lined the road.

She had an opportunity to study her rival at leisure, and she knew the invitation had been a mistake, but it was too late now to rectify it. She herself was young, but Lisa, Lady Saunders, was younger by at least a year or two. Sarah took justifiable pride in her own figure, but that of Lady Saunders was superior to it: Sarah was tall, Lisa was taller, with an even tinier waist, high breasts, and firm, gently rounded hips. Sarah knew she herself was exceptionally attractive, but Lisa's beauty was breathtaking. Her chiseled features were flawless; her burnished copper hair gleamed in the autumn sunlight. And only a woman who was very sure of herself would dare to wear a flimsy Empire dress, out of style since Napoleon Bonaparte had been sent in exile to St. Helena.

It was something of a shock when Sarah realized that Lady Saunders' eyes were the same shade of green as her own. It was almost like looking in a mirror.

Admiral Lord Saunders, attired in his dress uniform of gold, blue, and white, used a walking stick as he descended from the carriage. He was suffering from an attack of gout, he explained, but would allow nothing to interfere with this visit.

Sarah's feeling of unaccustomed inferiority swept over her again as she and Lady Saunders exchanged token curtsies. The other girl was so poised, so completely in command of herself and her surroundings.

A servant was sent off at a gallop for Jeremy, and Sarah accompanied the guests into the mansion, first showing them to the suite they would occupy, then giving them a tour of Oakhurst Manor's principal rooms. The admiral was handicapped by his gout, but insisted on seeing everything, and displayed a lively interest in Oakhurst Manor's antiques as well as the flower garden that Sarah tended herself.

Lady Saunders said very little, but her manner was not aloof. On the contrary, there was an expression of warmth and sympathy in her face whenever her eyes and Sarah's met.

Sarah had the uncanny feeling that, under different circumstances, she and this lovely girl with the clipped English accent could become close friends.

They sat down to tiffin in the breakfast room overlooking Sarah's gardens, and were enjoying a light meal of beef tea, Cleo's hot biscuits, and a honey butter she made from a secret recipe when Jeremy arrived, dust on his boots, with a grubby Jerry in tow.

The master of Oakhurst Manor and the British admiral greeted each other as they had in Charleston, pounding each other on the back like a pair of exuberant schoolboys.

Then Jeremy bowed to Lady Saunders. "Your servant, milady," he said.

"Your servant, sir," she murmured, curtsying low.

Their fingertips barely touched, but Sarah felt precisely as she had when they had met in Charleston. Bolts of lightning seemed to shoot through the room, the walls quivered, and the air seethed and was filled with unfathomable tensions.

Ordinarily a servant would have taken Jerry elsewhere, but Sarah allowed him to remain for a short time. His presence, as she well knew, was a direct reminder to Lady Saunders that Jeremy was a family man, that the future of many people became threatened if they renewed their affair. Eventually the child had to be removed, but his presence had served its purpose.

Jeremy and Lord Saunders became engrossed in a discussion of a new type of merchant ship that was being built to Jeremy's specifications in Savannah. It would be as swift as a sloop of war, he explained, and almost as large as a frigate.

"Surely you won't carry a crew of two or three hundred, as a frigate does," the admiral said.

"No, I intend to utilize most of the space for cargo. Now that we're at peace again with England, our trade with the West Indian islands is expanding at a tremendous rate."

Sarah had heard his plans on many occasions, and her mind wandered. In fact, she was so nervous it was almost impossible for her to concentrate.

But Lisa made the effort. "Who will sail your ship, Master Beaufort?"

"I intend to act as my own captain, at least initially, milady."

"As a natural-born sailor you should!" the admiral declared.

Lisa was not satisfied, however. "But won't you be neglecting this marvelous plantation, sir?"

"Luckily," Jeremy said, "I have a wife who is competent to run Oakhurst Manor, as she did before I came home."

"I envy you, Mistress Beaufort," Lisa said.

As Sarah accepted the compliment with a graceful nod, she wondered if there was a double meaning in Lady Saunders' words.

"I don't intend to stay at sea indefinitely," Jeremy said. "My Bantu brother, M'Bwana, acted as my mate when we sailed here from Africa, and with a bit more experience he'll be able to sail the merchant vessel alone."

He and the admiral became involved in a maze of highly technical details that neither of the women understood.

It was impossible for Sarah and Lisa to exchange more than a few polite words, however. A barrier stood between them, making a flow of easy conversation impossible.

The chiming of a clock in the adjacent dining room impelled Sarah to take positive action. "Jeremy," she suggested, "why don't you take our guests for an inspection of the plantation? You'll have ample time before we dine."

There was nothing her husband enjoyed more than showing off Oakhurst Manor, and he was on his feet instantly.

But Lord Saunders demurred. "If you don't mind," he said, "take Lisa with you, but I'll beg off until tomorrow. This blasted foot won't let me do more than peek at Mistress Beaufort's flower garden."

As Lisa went off to change into riding clothes, Sarah told herself she had known what would happen, the admiral's gout preventing him from going out for a long ride. She really was insane, deliberately sending Jeremy and Lady Saunders off together.

Kill or cure. There was no in-between.

She had to admire Lady Saunders' independence, her refusal to abide by conventions. She appeared in a man's shirt, riding breeches, and boots, all made to order for her, and refusing to ride sidesaddle, as other ladies did, she mounted her mare with practiced ease.

Sarah watched Jeremy ride off with her, and wondered if her own marriage would be shattered by the time they returned.

They rode in silence for the better part of a half-hour down paths that led through fields of cotton and tobacco, ripening corn and rye. They passed rows of vegetables, melon and squash and cucumbers bulging on vines, purple grape arbors, and paddies of rice.

At last Jeremy could stand the strain no longer. "Twice I returned to Kingston," he said, "and rode up to the Liguanea Hills. On both occasions I saw Mistress Ferguson at the Star Apple, but she claimed not to know what had become of you."

"So she told me," Lisa said.

"I knew she lied to me."

"At my direction," Lisa said. "I told you when we parted in Jamaica that it was best if we never saw each other again."

"I wish to God I could have forgotten you," Jeremy said bitterly. "I envy your ability to have forgotten me."

Lisa halted her mare, unbuttoned a cuff, and turned up her sleeve. On her wrist was the unadorned gold bracelet Jeremy had sent her after the last night they had spent together.

He halted his horse, too, and stared at the bracelet, then at the copper-haired girl.

"Forget you?" Lisa's laugh was harsh and shrill. "From the day I received this bracelet it has never been taken from my wrist."

Their eyes met for a moment, but their pain was as great as the surging excitement that gripped them, and they looked away again.

"What does Dickie Saunders know of your past?" Jeremy asked abruptly.

"Only what I've felt it necessary to tell him. There has been no need for him to know that I was compelled by financial need to work as a voluntary inmate of the most exclusive bordello in the West Indian islands."

He flushed beneath his heavy tan. "That isn't what I meant. I refer to . . . you and me."

There was no humor in Lisa's smile. "He regards you as his protégé and friend. I saw no point in hurting him by telling him that you and I met at the Star Apple and became involved. Beyond our ability to control."

"I've assumed he didn't know. Any more than Sarah knows."

"Oh, but she does." Lisa spoke calmly.

Jeremy gaped at her.

"Your Sarah is all you told me about her. And more. She's incomparably lovely. She's strong. She's wise. And she has the instinct of a woman in love. She looks at you and me together, and she *knows* what has passed between us."

"I've tried to spare her," Jeremy said. "I can't explain to her what I don't understand myself. I just wish we hadn't met again in Charleston at the Benton house. For your sake. For Sarah's sake. It was the greatest shock I've ever known."

"I was warned, fortunately, or I'd have fainted. Your father-in-law told us you and Sarah were coming to Charleston for the party in our honor. I would have escaped it if I could, and I thought of feigning illness. But I had to see you again." Her voice fell to a whisper. "I had no choice."

"I know. I feel the same way."

They sat in their saddles, several feet apart, unmindful of the hot sun beating down on them, unaware of the ripening tobacco plants around them, unable to summon the courage to look at each other without flinching.

"This is none of my business," Jeremy said, his voice metallic. "But do you love Lord Saunders?"

"No." As always, Lisa was blunt. "I've never pretended to love him. He's kind and thoughtful and attentive. He's given me the social station and the security I've always craved. In return I'm a decorative wife, a charming hostess, a competent housekeeper at our home in Barbados."

He nodded, not surprised.

"Above all," Lisa said, "I give him fidelity."

"Which is what I give Sarah."

"I never knew I was capable of loving any man," Lisa said. "Then it happened, when I least expected it. I've learned to live with my feelings, because I must. But I'll never love another."

"You're more fortunate than I am," Jeremy said, and forced himself to look steadily at her. "I love Sarah with all my heart. She performed miracles during the years I was away. No woman could have been more loyal, more steadfast."

"I knew the instant I saw her that your description of her was accurate, and I ached for her, knowing how lonely she had been during all the years she didn't know where you were or what had become of you."

"What I feel for you," Jeremy said, squaring his shoulders, "is also love. For a time I tried to convince myself that it was just a yearning to bed you. Well, it's that, too, but it's far more."

"Stop, please." Lisa shivered, and her voice was ragged. Sarah would have been astonished by her lack of poise. "You're torturing both of us."

"I'm speaking out because I must," Jeremy said. "At times I've wondered how I could have such deep feelings for two women. I've spent some time in the Muslim world, and I can see why Muhammad allows the faithful to take more than one wife."

She tried in vain to smile. "It wouldn't be a satisfactory arrangement in our world. For the wives."

"I know. That's why I can't speak of all this to Sarah. Because . . . what I feel for you doesn't cause me to love her any the less. Just as my love for her doesn't stop me from dreaming of you. I'm a successful planter, an expert ship's captain, a man of means, and a respected citizen in my community. But in my own opinion I'm despicable."

"I don't agree," Lisa said. "Because I *can* understand the way you feel, where Sarah couldn't. That's a part of my hell."

"Ever since I saw you in Charleston I've had only one thought in my mind. What can we do about this situation? I'm afraid I've found no answer."

"There is none," Lisa told him. "If you insisted, and you wouldn't have to insist very hard, you could make love to me right here, on the ground. I want it as badly as you do. All that holds me back is the knowledge that we'd crush Sarah, do great harm to Dickie . . . and—above all—we'd hate ourselves."

"As much as I want you, I couldn't make love to you," Jeremy said. "I owe Sarah fidelity. I can't be untrue to my friendship with Dickie. And I can't cheapen the feelings I have for you, feelings that refuse to dissipate."

Lisa's sigh was tremulous. "I was right when I said we shouldn't meet again. But we have, and the damage is done."

It was unfair to let her carry the brunt of the burden, and Jeremy's jaw jutted forward. "Then we must undo it as best we can," he said. "I can't guarantee that we won't meet again—"

"Neither can I," Lisa interrupted. "Dickie's squadron is visiting a number of American ports. Boston, New York, Philadelphia, Baltimore. On a goodwill mission. And before we sail for home he's been charged with a diplomatic errand. All I know is that we're scheduled to pay a visit to your President Monroe in Washington City. And we may put into Charleston again, too. I have no voice in such matters. All I know is that we'll be spending several more months in the United States, so our paths might cross again."

"If we do, I promise you I'll remember you're the wife of the man who saved me from a life of degradation and possible death."

"I assure you," she replied, "that I won't forget you're Sarah Beaufort's husband."

"Then we'll meet as friends?"

"My dear," Lisa said, her expression stony, "after what you and I have meant to each other—and still mean—we can never be just friends."

Admiral Lord Saunders leaned on his walking stick as he examined each of the many varieties of roses in the garden that extended around two sides of the great mansion. He knew as much about flowers as his hostess, and his questions were penetrating.

Sarah made a tremendous effort to play the role that was expected of her, but her mind was elsewhere—on the ride to the far reaches of the plantation. If Jeremy preferred Lisa, she would surrender him to the other woman, no matter what the cost. True marriage meant that one held one's beloved with open hands, never grasping tightly, never resorting to trickery.

Other women might scheme and connive to preserve their marriages, as she had seen her sister, Margot, do on occasion. But she simply wasn't built that way. Her pride demanded that if Jeremy truly loved her, he would remain with her voluntarily. Because he wanted her more than he wanted anyone else, because he freely elected to spend the rest of his days with her.

Sarah stiffened when she heard the sound of approaching

horses, and out of the corner of an eye she saw Jeremy and Lady Saunders coming up the driveway. Their eyes were bleak, their faces drained of all expression. Lisa dismounted quickly, leaping to the ground before Jeremy could assist her, and she went straight to her suite to change for dinner. It was apparent to Sarah that she was avoiding Jeremy's physical touch.

Jeremy went off to change quickly, too, so he could rejoin the admiral, who would wear his uniform for the rest of the day.

Sarah soon excused herself and went upstairs. She had already selected the gown she would wear, an off-the-shoulder, full-skirted dress of ivory satin. The maid who had been with her since she had lived in Boston, Amanda, helped her to change, and they chatted like the old friends they were.

Amanda was married to Willie, Cleo's son, a gifted cabinetmaker whom Jeremy had recently given his freedom from slavery. The subject paramount in Amanda's mind was whether she and her husband should remain at Oakhurst Manor, as Cleo wanted, or start a new life together in Boston, as Amanda wished.

Sarah could not devote her mind to the problem. Not today, when her whole future was in jeopardy.

As she began to repair her makeup, Amanda drifted away, and a few moments later Jeremy came into the dressing room on his way downstairs. His smile was forced and his manner was strained.

Sarah invited him to sit in the room's only comfortable chair.

"I've got to go down and join Dickie Saunders," he said. "I don't want to leave him there alone too long." In spite of his statement, however, he continued to linger.

She glanced at his reflection in her dressing-table mirror, and saw there was something he wanted to say to her. She turned, encouraging him by taking his hand.

Twice he opened his mouth to speak, twice he closed it again, then bolted from the room.

Sarah had no way of knowing what he had wanted to tell her. Was it his intention to clear the slate by revealing his past relations with Lisa Saunders? Or was his news more ominous? She didn't know, and a sigh welled up from deep within her.

Miraculously, her hand remained steady as she completed her task at the dressing table, and her step was firm as she went down to join the men.

The first guests to arrive were her red-haired sister, Margot, and her husband, Tom Beaufort. This was their first social appearance since the recent birth of their daughter, Alison, and both were in high spirits. They were accompanied by their good friend Scott Emerson, from whom Jeremy had purchased the Trelawney plantation for Tom and Margot.

Just looking at Scott gave Sarah greater hope for the future. He was recklessly handsome, and his only interests for years had been hunting and women, liquor and gambling. Now, however, he was a lawyer associated with her father's firm in Charleston, and had become sober, hard-working, and responsible. She wished there were more young men like him.

Other guests began to arrive from neighboring plantations, and soon the entire company was assembled, with one notable exception. Lisa, Lady Saunders, timed her entrance to perfection.

Looking at her convinced Sarah that her own cause was hopeless. Sarah's blond hair was piled high on her head in an intricate arrangement; Lisa's copper-colored hair fell in seemingly casual waves. Sarah had applied her makeup artfully; Lisa appeared to be wearing no makeup, and only another woman could recognize the delicacy of her touch. Sarah's dress was lovely; Lisa's gown of copper-colored silk, precisely matching her hair, was figure-hugging yet ladylike, emphasizing her perfect body.

It was plain that every man in the room wanted her, every woman envied her. Sarah wondered how she could compete with such a dazzling beauty.

Dinner was announced, and it was Jeremy's duty to escort Lisa to the table. As Sarah took Admiral Lord Saunders' arm and they fell in behind her husband, she noted that Lisa's touch on his arm was feather-light, her fingertips barely grazing the fabric of his swallow-tailed coat.

A shipment of champagne had arrived recently, and a number of bottles had been cooling all morning in the creek that ran behind the kitchen outbuilding. Jeremy offered the first toast, saluting Admiral and Lady Saunders, the guests of honor.

Lord Saunders replied, gracefully toasting the Beauforts and their home.

Ordinarily it would have been Tom Beaufort's place to offer the next toast. Before he could push back his chair, however, Lisa Saunders demonstrated her independence, her flair for the unexpected, by rising to her feet.

"I know it isn't customary," she said, "but I wonder, in this free America, if a woman is permitted to offer a toast."

The admiral was amused by her audacity, and chuckled aloud.

"Certainly," Jeremy said, but looked as mystified as all the rest.

"I drink to the happiness and health of our hostess," Lisa said, raising her glass and looking directly at Sarah. "May Sarah Beaufort enjoy a long and contented life with her loving husband in her wonderful home."

Sarah knew, as the others raised their glasses and drank to her, that Lisa's words conveyed more than was apparent on the surface. What the other girl actually was saying was: regardless of what my feelings for your husband may be, regardless of what we may have meant to each other in the past, I won't disrupt your life. I won't interfere. I won't try to take him away from you.

The immediate battle was won, and a sense of relief flooded Sarah. But her instinct told her the victory was only temporary, that a long war remained to be waged. Regardless of Lisa's good intentions and Jeremy's high sense of honor, the intensity of what lay between them was too powerful a force to be ignored. The long-term issue was not resolved.

# Chapter 2

A warm, late-autumn sun shone down on Charleston harbor from a cloudless sky, and the breeze was reminiscent of midsummer. A large crowd was gathered at the dock, and a special grandstand had been constructed for what was a very special occasion. A merchantman unlike any vessel ever before seen was tied to the pilings, and those who came to attend the ceremony gaped at her.

Her prow was sharp, like that of a sloop of war, and her silhouette was almost as narrow. But she was almost as long and heavy as a navy frigate, and had more than double the cargo space that was customary on even the larger merchant brigs. She was triple-masted, too, with a high mainmast, and at first glance resembled an oversized schooner. Thanks to the ingenuity of Jeremy Beaufort, who had designed the ship himself, a third deck had been built beneath the quarterdeck and main deck for the sake of greater ease in moving cargo on and off the vessel. Veterans of the War of 1812 who had served in the U.S. Navy were quick to note the innovation, and remarked that, in case of need, this deck could be converted into a gun deck where cannon as heavy as twelve-pounders could be emplaced.

The ship had other unique features, unknown to those who had not toured her interior. For the comfort of the ship's master and his first mate, their respective living quarters were exceptionally large and handsomely furnished. In one corner of the captain's cabin, cleverly concealed behind a bulkhead, was a secret compartment, carved of hard teakwood by Willie as a gift to Jeremy, that could be used for the storage of private papers and valuables. And set into the quarterdeck railing was yet another of Willie's triumphs, a hollowed section, hidden by a removable panel, in which a brace of pistols could be placed, out of sight.

Sarah Beaufort's father and stepmother, Isaiah and Lorene Benton, were the first to take seats in the first row of the grandstand. Isaiah, gray-haired and distinguished, not only was one of South Carolina's most distinguished attorneys, but looked the part, and the beautifully gowned Lorene, in her mid-forties, appeared to be at least a decade younger. With them was her nephew Scott Emerson, to whom Isaiah was already turning over portions of his law practice.

They were soon joined by Margot and Tom Beaufort, the former fetching in a fur-trimmed cape and matching gown of brocaded silk. The day was so warm that Margot soon shed her cape.

There was a stir when Sarah Beaufort made her appearance, radiant in a full-skirted dress of watered silk; it was white, and many in the crowd thought she looked like a bride. Accompanying her was Kai, the pretty, delicate Algerian girl who was universally regarded in South Carolina as unorthodox and mysterious. All that was known about her was that, seemingly white, she was married to M'Bwana, Jeremy's Bantu overseer and the first mate of his ship. Their child, Lance, supposedly was M'Bwana's son, but anyone who looked at the boy knew at a glance that Jeremy had sired him.

No one, including Sarah, was aware of Kai's background. No one realized there was black somewhere in her ancestry, that she had been reared as a slave and given to Jeremy in Africa, where she and M'Bwana had saved his life after she had given herself to him for a night, an opportunity he had not been able to resist. Thereafter, when he had recovered from his wounds and discovered she had borne a child, and simultaneously had learned that she and M'Bwana had fallen in love, he had immediately set her free, enabling her to marry M'Bwana.

Now, with her command of English increasing daily, Kai at last felt at home at Oakhurst Manor. Devoted to her husband and child, grateful to Jeremy for his friendship, she had everything she wanted in life and was content.

Still a trifle withdrawn, she was no longer as shy as she had been. Certainly no one looking at her in her gown of yellow lawn, with a plunging neckline and a full skirt over her many petticoats, would have guessed she was slightly ill-at-ease. Others might think it strange that she was married to a black man, but Kai was indifferent to the opinions of outsiders. She and M'Bwana loved each other, and nothing else mattered.

Sarah and Kai took their places together, and their arrival was a signal to begin the ceremonies.

The crew of the ship filed onto the main deck, all in blue uniforms with white piping. The majority were white, and included in their number were several immigrants from England and Scotland who had seen Royal Navy service during the long wars with Bonaparte. Seven of the forty-one sailors were black, members of the Watusi tribe who had worked as field hands at Oakhurst Manor and whom Jeremy had freed when he had learned they had lived on the seacoast in their native Africa and were expert seamen. Mixed crews were no novelty in the Northern states, but were still regarded as unusual in the South.

A fife-and-drum corps that occupied a portion of the grandstand struck up a lively air, and two lieutenants, the ship's young junior officers, climbed to the quarterdeck. They were followed by M'Bwana, wearing a bicorn and a gold-trimmed blue-and-white uniform. With him were Sarah's and Kai's sons, Jerry and Lance, and both mothers smiled as M'Bwana shepherded them to a corner of the quarterdeck, where they would be out of harm's way. The boys had received strict orders, their roles had been rehearsed, and they did not stray from their assigned places.

Jerry could not resist waving to Sarah.

Lance's gravity suited the occasion, however, and the small child stood erect, his sober expression a copy of M'Bwana's.

The first mate called the ship's company to attention, and

Jeremy Beaufort appeared on the quarterdeck, the silver epaulets on his shoulders proclaiming his rank. He stood the men at ease, and a clergyman in the front row of the grandstand prayed for the safety of the ship's company.

Isaiah Benton had been asked by his son-in-law to deliver a few remarks, and the lawyer wasted no words. This ship, he said, inaugurated a new era in American trade. She could carry as much cargo as any three ships currently at sea, and she was destined to revolutionize America's relations with the islands of the West Indies.

Now the solemn portion of the ceremony began. "Mate," Jeremy said in a voice that carried to the spectators on shore, "you may raise the national pennant."

"Very good, sir!" M'Bwana replied. "Fly the ensign!"

The Stars and Stripes, the American flag, began to inch up the yardarm.

The fife-and-drum corps began to play a song that had become popular during the latter stages of the War of 1812, "The Star-Spangled Banner."

Now it was Sarah's turn. She rose and walked to the prow of the ship, accompanied by her father, who handed her a bottle of wine securely wrapped in burlap cloth.

Her eyes met Jeremy's, and as always, her heart skipped a beat.

He looked down at her from the quarterdeck, his love shining in his eyes.

She returned that love.

"I christen thee *Elizabeth*," she said, and smashed the bottle against the prow.

"Mate, you may cut your lines and set your jib," Jeremy said.

M'Bwana gave the order, and with the fife-and-drum corps still playing, the ship moved slowly to the far side of the harbor, where she would drop anchor.

Sarah shivered and told herself she was being disloyal, that this was the wrong time for the suspicions that flooded her mind. Jeremy had told her he was naming the vessel after his grandmother, and perhaps he had been telling her the truth. But she couldn't put Lisa, Lady Saunders, out of her thoughts. The name Lisa was a diminutive of the name Elizabeth. Was it possible that Jeremy was naming the vessel for the lovely girl with whom he had so obviously been intimate somewhere in the Caribbean?

Sarah realized she might never learn the truth, that she would be wise not to torture herself and to accept his word. Perhaps her vanity was wounded because Jeremy hadn't named the ship for her, but it was wrong of her to expect him to demonstrate his love for her in new ways. It had to be enough that he had stayed with her, while Lisa had sailed off from Charleston with her own husband.

As a wife Sarah could ask for no more. Certainly she would be miserable if she spent the rest of her days wondering, questioning, probing. Surely she would create a hell on earth for herself if she dissected the motives behind everything Jeremy did. Rest easy, her conscience told her, or you'll drive him away.

As the *Elizabeth* moved away from the dock, the ceremony came to an end. The guests climbed into their carriages, and the entire party adjourned to the Benton house. There tents had been erected on the lawn, and the company was served a buffet that included hams, turkeys, smoked wild goose, and larded beef stuffed with truffles, as well as a variety of hot breads, jams and Italian salads. Beverages included a potent rum concoction and another with a brandywine base, but Sarah, Kai, and a number of the other ladies elected to drink a fruit punch that lacked an alcoholic base.

Eventually the officers arrived, bringing Jerry and Lance with them. In honor of the occasion Jeremy had presented both children with gold-trimmed bicorns and miniature blunt-edged swords of their own, and the excitement had made the boys so weary that a nursemaid had to take them off to bed.

Jeremy and M'Bwana circulated through the crowd, accepting the congratulations and good wishes of the company, and the better part of an hour passed before the master of the *Elizabeth* could join his wife in a corner of the garden.

"May I get you a drink?" he asked.

"Thank you, dear, but I'm not thirsty."

"A plate of Lorene's special chicken, jellied in wine aspic, then. It looks delicious."

"I'm not really hungry, either."

"This is a festive occasion, but you aren't very happy today," Jeremy said.

"I don't often give in to my moods. I'm sorry."

"What's wrong, Sarah?"

She shrugged.

"I've given you my word that I won't spend more than four weeks at sea on the maiden voyage. And you know my long-range plans. For each day I'm away, I'll spend two days at Oakhurst Manor. As soon as M'Bwana is able to handle the *Elizabeth* himself, I'll turn the ship over to him. Kai may not be too happy for a time, but she's stronger than she looks, and she'll acclimate to his new way of life."

Sarah felt a stab of jealousy. He spoke so knowledgeably about Kai, and she couldn't forget he was actually the father of her child.

"Something very definitely is upsetting you." Jeremy became firm.

She took a deep breath. "I suppose I'm still thinking about Lisa Saunders."

Neither his expression nor his manner changed, and whatever the relationship may have been, he appeared to have put Lisa behind him. "What about her?"

Again Sarah shrugged, and couldn't help being evasive. "She's so lovely that I . . . I suppose I envy her."

Jeremy laughed aloud. It was astonishing that this woman who had fought so gallantly, alone, to save Oakhurst Manor during its darkest days could sound so childish. Never would he understand her. "Lisa," he said, "told me in so many words that you're the most beautiful girl she's ever seen. She envies you."

Sarah forced a smile. Lisa's intentions might be good, but no woman could resist a prize as attractive as Jeremy.

"Come along and meet Lester Howard," he urged her.

"Who?"

"The new overseer I've hired, now that M'Bwana will be spending most of his time at sea. He's a splendid person, a real gentleman, and I'm sure you'll like him."

"I'll have plenty of opportunity back home to get acquainted with him." Sarah knew she was behaving badly, but felt too lethargic to care.

"Most of the guests are leaving," Jeremy said with a sudden grin. "I'll tell your father and Lorene that we're going too, and we'll sneak away."

Sarah stared at him, convinced he had taken leave of his senses. "Where do you think we're going?"

"I know," he replied with a chuckle. "I'm taking you out to the *Elizabeth*, and we won't come back until it's time for breakfast. I don't pretend to know what you're feeling, or why, but I do know the cure. Mistress Beaufort, you're going to be alone with your husband, totally isolated with him, and he fully intends to spend the whole night making love to you."

Late the following morning the *Elizabeth* sailed on her maiden voyage to the West Indian islands, fully provisioned, her holds bulging with merchandise. Sarah and Kai saw the ship off, and both were silent on the short drive back to the Benton house, although their children maintained a shrill jabber, both boys insisting they would be sea captains when they grew up.

Sarah knew she was indulging a whim of Jeremy's, that he would have heeded her advice had she insisted he remain on shore. Thanks to the funds he had provided when he had returned home from Africa, Oakhurst Manor was solidly based, its future prosperity assured, and there had been no real need for her husband to leave her again. She supposed it had to be true, as he had told her, that saltwater was in his blood now, and he couldn't find complete contentment if he spent the rest of his life on land. Some aspects of a man's temperament were beyond her comprehension.

It was enough for her, at least for the present, that Jeremy had kept his word last night, making love to her until dawn, and she felt deliciously weary. No matter what Lisa had meant to him in the past, he couldn't really care for her now. And whatever the relationship he had enjoyed with Kai, that was buried in the past, too. Sarah couldn't remember a time when she had felt so wonderfully satiated. Jeremy was her man and she was his woman. They belonged to each other.

Lorene asked Sarah and Kai to stay for dinner, but they demurred. The children would be calmer at home, and Sarah didn't want to absent herself from the plantation for too long, particularly with Jeremy away. The luggage was strapped to the roof, and with Jerry and Lance insisting on riding with the coachman, the two young women had the interior of the luxurious carriage to themselves for the two-hour drive.

Kai spoke English slowly, always choosing her words with care. "It will be very strange to live for a time without M'Bwana," she said. "I miss him already."

"I'm sure you do," Sarah replied.

The Algerian girl smiled. "How selfish I sound! You and Jeremy were separated for many years, but you did not complain, ever."

"How do you know that?"

"Many people have told me. Also, I know much about Jeremy's feelings in that time."

Sarah stiffened. "I daresay."

Kai became shy and hesitated. "He has not yet told you about . . . life in the village of the Bantu?"

Sarah shook her head.

"It is his place to tell, not mine," Kai said, gaining courage. "But if he does not, I shall."

Sarah could hear Lance shouting exuberantly on the buckboard. Kai's son. Jeremy's son. She supposed the pain would always be with her.

"Nothing," Kai said, "was what you might think. When you hear, then you will understand."

"I hope so." Sarah tried not to be unyielding.

"This much I will tell you," the Algerian girl said earnestly. "Jeremy almost died when a greedy Portuguese slave trader tried to kill him and steal the diamonds M'Bwana's father had given him. For almost a year M'Bwana and I took care of him. For all of that time he was out of his mind. In all of that time he spoke only of you. Sarah, Sarah, Sarah. When I gave him food or bathed his head, when I changed the dressing on his wound or covered him when he had a fever, always he called me Sarah."

Tears came to Sarah's eyes.

"Never has any man had so much love for any woman," the Algerian girl said.

Sarah knew she was right, that she herself had been wrong to doubt Jeremy, to question their relationship. Their faith had been tested in a crucible, and had been reaffirmed last night. "Sometimes," she said, "I become . . . a bit confused."

Kai was grave. "It is easy to see how that can be, Sarah. I hope you will believe that Jeremy and I have never cared for each other. He is my friend, my great benefactor, as you will learn when you hear the story. But . . . just as he has loved only you, I have loved no man except M'Bwana."

Sarah reached impulsively for the other girl's small hand. "Thank you for telling me that much, Kai. You make it easier for me to bear the next month, until Jeremy returns to me."

The last remaining tensions vanished. They were friends now, and even though Sarah still couldn't understand how Jeremy could have sired Lance if he hadn't had a true bond of intimacy with Kai, she was willing to wait still longer for the riddle to be solved. It was a mistake, as she had learned during the years she had been alone, to brood too much, to let imagination overcome common sense.

When they arrived at Oakhurst Manor, Cleo took charge of the children, giving them a light meal and taking them off for their naps. Sarah and Kai changed from their voluminous traveling clothes into more comfortable dresses, and then they dined together, chatting and laughing throughout the meal as though neither had a care in the world.

Old habits were easy to resume, and after dinner Sarah retired to the library to work on the ever-present ledgers. Throughout Jeremy's long absence she had never failed in the task, and since his return from the seeming dead she had kept the responsibility. She liked the job, she thought, because it enabled her to keep a finger on the pulse of the plantation.

She became immersed in columns of figures, checking on the funds paid out, the income received, and the amounts still due from the merchants who bought Oakhurst Manor's agricultural products. All at once it dawned on her that someone had come into the room, and she looked up, to see the patient Cleo standing in front of her desk.

"New overseer here," the housekeeper said. "Want to see missy." Her manner indicated that she approved of the man.

Sarah was relieved. Cleo's attitude was vitally important, and if she disliked the overseer it wouldn't be long before he would be forced to go elsewhere. He would learn, as did everyone else who was new here, that Cleo was the power behind the throne. "Ask him to come in, please."

Lester Howard was tall but slightly built, a careworn man in his late thirties with dark blond, receding hair, mild blue eyes, and regular features. He conveyed an air of gentility, and at first glance he appeared soft, but something that lurked behind his eyes, or perhaps the way he carried himself, indicated to Sarah that he was a man of conviction endowed with hidden strength. Jeremy, who knew character, gave him a hearty endorsement, and that was reassuring.

"I hope I'm not disturbing you, Mistress Beaufort," he said, his voice surprisingly mellow.

"Not at all. Please sit down, Master Howard. And always feel free to come in here without announcing yourself. We despise formality at Oakhurst Manor."

"So I gathered when your husband insisted I call him by his Christian name." Howard's light laugh was both genuine and contagious. "I've only been here a few hours, but I've never seen a place like it. Comfortable houses and school-rooms for slaves, even a medical dispensary for them. Extraordinary!"

She felt he had challenged her. "You don't approve, Master Howard?"

His eyes seemed to grow paler, and looked like steel. "My vocation is that of a farmer, Mistress Beaufort. By conviction I'm an abolitionist. I'm also enough of a realist to know that slavery is going to exist in this country through your lifetime and mine. So I believe in treating slaves like people, not animals or inanimate objects. I had a long discussion of all this with your husband. He's one of the few plantation owners I've ever met who approves of my methods. I don't use whips, I don't put rebels in chains. I expect slaves to obey the same laws we obey, and when they don't, I see to it they're given the same punishments. Does that satisfy you, ma'am?"

"More than I can tell you, sir. I don't know if Jeremy mentioned this to you, but back in Boston, where I grew up, I was an abolitionist too. I like to think I'm primarily responsible for the new system being used at Oakhurst Manor. Some of our neighbors criticize us, but we have a better health record than any of them, with no insurrections or revolts, and our production average is thirty percent higher than the best of them can boast." Sarah's smile was warm.

Howard grinned in return. "It looks like we talk the same language, ma'am."

"Obviously." All at once it occurred to Sarah that he was not looking at her the way an employee normally looked at a plantation owner. His gaze was that of a man admiring a woman, appreciating her beauty, relishing her personality. She could detect no lust in his eyes, no covetousness, merely a lively, full sense of enjoyment.

She supposed she should be upset, but instead she discovered she was relishing the unusual experience. Because she liked him, too. Continuing to smile, she met his gaze, and their eyes locked.

Suddenly the atmosphere changed, and Sarah felt as though a bolt of electricity was passing through her. Her mind was numb, her whole body tingled.

She was having the same effect on Lester Howard. He grew pale beneath his deep tan, a film of perspiration appeared on his upper lip, and he tried to look away, but could not.

This is insane, she thought. Not only do I feel as though I've known this total stranger all my life, but I want him to hold me close. I'm a respectable matron, a woman completely in love with my husband, but I'm willing this man I've never before met to make love to me. And I know he feels the same way.

Howard wrenched himself to his feet. "I . . . I'd best be going now, ma'am."

"Wait!" she commanded, then tried desperately to think of something to say. "What quarters have you been given?"

"Nothing permanent. My belongings haven't arrived yet, so any cottage not being used by field hands will be fine with me."

"No, that isn't right." She made a swift decision. "M'Bwana and Kai have been living in the house that the overseer traditionally has used here. In fact, we had it enlarged for them. But he'll be away most of the time now, so I'm sure she'll be happy to move into the big house with her baby."

"I don't want to inconvenience anyone," Howard said.

"You won't," Sarah assured him. "It will be best all around that way."

He thanked her, bowed slightly, and took his leave.

Even after he was gone, the spell was not broken, and Sarah dabbed at the moist palms of her hands with a handkerchief. Never had she experienced such an odd sensation. She felt as though an irresistible force was drawing her to Lester Howard, and her instinct told her he felt the same toward her.

Only today had Jeremy gone to sea, but instead of thinking about him, she was yearning for a man she had met a scant quarter of an hour earlier. No, that wasn't quite true. She not only missed Jeremy, but she loved him with all her being. Nothing in their relationship was changed, and she doubted that it could be. Yet that didn't prevent her from feeling a wild, surging sense of excitement over Lester Howard. Was she being an adolescent, an abandoned hussy, or both?

A thunderclap sounded in Sarah's mind and staggered her. This extraordinary attraction she and Howard felt for each other, this mysterious force that defied reason, wasn't of her deliberate making, any more than it was logical. It was there, however, a force with which she had to contend.

Perhaps this was what had happened to Jeremy and Lisa Saunders. Her new, unnerving reaction to Howard and his to her put Jeremy's and Lisa's relationship in a new light. Not that she could understand it, not that she could sympathize with it. But, she thought miserably, she appeared to have been dropped into the same boat.

Enough. Instead of mooning like a lovesick schoolgirl over a man about whom she knew literally nothing, she forced herself to go back to work. Yet thoughts of Howard kept intruding.

Shortly before supper Kai and Lance moved into a spacious suite in the manor house, with servants bringing the belongings that Kai wanted. Most of the basic furnishings she left behind in the overseer's house.

Sarah made a point of greeting Kai and installing her in her new quarters. But she needed all of her strength to refrain from visiting the overseer's house to see if all was well with Howard. Stop making a fool of yourself, she thought.

She had little appetite for supper, which Kai attributed to loneliness for Jeremy. Sarah retired early, but it took her a long time to drop off to sleep, and she awakened before dawn. The night had been warm, but she was in a cold sweat, and she felt alarmed when she realized she had actually been dreaming about Lester Howard.

Not until she had bathed in a tub Amanda brought her and was seated at her dressing table, a steaming mug of tea beside her, did she decide she had to take firm action to halt the nonsense in which she was indulging. Daydreams were as dangerous as they were absurd, and if she continued to drift, she well might find herself in serious trouble.

If she was trying to even the score with Jeremy, which she doubted, there were different standards for women than those that existed for men. Someone in Jeremy's position could have affairs with virtual impunity. Other men would not only refrain from condemning him, but would envy him. Women might pretend to be shocked, and a few would sympathize with his unfortunate wife, but many would wish, privately, that Jeremy would make advances to them.

If Sarah were stupid enough to engage in an affair, however, she would be ruined. Her reputation would be shattered, her friends would shun her, and no one would blame her husband if he threw her out of the house. A man could behave like a tomcat, but a lady was required to act like a lady, and that was that.

Sarah could see only one way to rid herself of her strange attraction to Lester Howard. They had met for only a few minutes, so she would spend more time with him, and familiarity would breed inevitable contempt. No man was in Jeremy's class, and when she saw the difference, in specifics, she would soon lose interest in the overseer.

In spite of her good intentions, however, she donned a new, pretty dress with a laced bodice and nipped-in waist, and contrary to her custom, she made up with care. When she went down to the dining room for breakfast, she had no appetite and merely pretended to eat, and when she chatted with Kai, her mind was elsewhere.

Soon thereafter she left the house, a sunbonnet hanging by a ribbon from her wrist, and headed in the direction of the slave quarters for her regular morning visit. Surely it was a coincidence that, at this very moment, Lester Howard emerged from the overseer's house in boots, breeches, and open-throated shirt. It was no accident, however, that he waited for her.

Sarah could feel his eyes devouring her as she approached him at a saunter.

" 'Morning, ma'am," he said. "You're out early today."

"I always visit the slave cottages at this same hour. Would you care to come with me?" She wondered what had possessed her to be so brazen.

"Delighted. I make the same practice." He fell in beside her.

"Is everything in your house to your liking?"

"It couldn't be better, ma'am."

"Do stop calling me ma'am. My name is Sarah, and I believe you're called Lester." Now she had the audacity to encourage a greater intimacy between them, and she told herself she deserved the problems she appeared to be seeking.

Howard, however, was not the type to take advantage of a lady. "Thank you, Sarah," he said gravely.

His sensitivity was so acute she wanted to scream. This gentle, unassuming man seemed to know exactly what was taking place inside her, and she knew he not only was aware of her turmoil but also was trying to find some way to ease it.

Lester Howard became crisp when they began their tour of the slaves' cottages. He made certain the ailing went without delay to the dispensary, where a young physician, new to the area, spent several hours each morning. He lavished praise on those whose homes were neat, and he dealt firmly with those who left food in the open, lecturing them on disease. In one dwelling a youth in his late teens had overslept, and Howard promptly teased him into fleeing to his appointed place in the field. At no time did the new overseer lose his sense of balance, and the slaves, who had been apprehensive, responded to him happily.

"We're going to start bringing in the tobacco crop this morning," he told Sarah as they headed back in the direction of the mansion. "Would you like to see the start of the operation?"

She had a hundred things to do at the house, but instead she found herself nodding brightly. "There's nothing I'd like better," she said, and had to admit that, at least, she was being honest.

His horse was already saddled, a mare was saddled for Sarah, and when he helped her into the saddle she thrilled to his touch. He was impersonal, doing only what any gentleman would do to assist a lady, yet she felt as though she had been seared by fire.

And glancing at Howard as he clamped his broad-brimmed hat on his head, she realized he was shaken by the experience too.

They rode in a tense silence, but gradually the highly charged air changed, and it occurred to Sarah as she tied the ribbons of her sunbonnet under her chin that she was now at peace. Just being in the presence of this man made her joyful, and unexpectedly she laughed aloud.

There was no need for Lester Howard to ask her why she laughed. He simply looked at her without comment and grinned broadly, his tanned face creasing.

She knew he shared this strange sensation of tranquillity, and she couldn't help laughing again.

The next couple of hours passed swiftly, without incident, and later Sarah found it impossible to reconstruct that time in her mind. She had memories only of a pleasant blur. She stayed in the background as Howard demonstrated the way he wanted the tobacco leaves cut, and she neither commented nor intruded as he supervised the work. Only when he was satisfied that the operation was proceeding smoothly did he turn to escort her back to the house.

Inasmuch as they were on Oakhurst Manor property, there was no real need for him to accompany her, of course, but Sarah did not protest. On the contrary, she began to realize that her plan to see more of the overseer wasn't working out as she had hoped. Every moment she spent in his company was precious, and she glowed.

As they approached the house, she saw Jerry and Lance rolling on the ground in front of the portico, pummeling each other and shouting. A nursemaid stood nearby, but the two little boys ignored her remonstrances. Lance, who was younger, nevertheless was very sturdy and gave as good as he received.

Sarah climbed down from her mare as rapidly as she could.

Before she could act, however, Lester Howard scooped up the children, separated them, and set one on each shoulder. "Well," he said, "it looks to me like we have a couple of ferocious lion cubs here."

The boys began to hurl accusations at each other.

"Enough," Howard told them, and although he spoke gently, there was a note of command in his voice that they heeded. He placed them on the ground, his manner quiet but firm. "No tattling. Now, shake hands. Like men."

The sheepish children obeyed.

"You know," he said, "I was aiming to take you youngsters out to the fields to watch the tobacco cutting this afternoon. But I can't do it unless you're friends. Good friends."

"We friends," Jerry assured him.

Lance nodded, assenting eagerly.

Both boys were docile as they went off with the nursemaid, their differences forgotten.

Sarah laughed in relief. Lester Howard handled the children so deftly, with such seeming ease, that she could dismiss the incident from her mind. Then, as she turned to the overseer, intending to thank him, her laughter suddenly faded. He was looking at her with such tenderness, such depth of feeling, that chills raced up and down her spine.

He had fallen in love with her; there could be no doubt of it. And as nearly as she could judge, she returned his affection, even though she still loved Jeremy. All she knew, in her torment and confusion, was that here was a problem she couldn't solve in an hour or a day.

# Chapter 3

Lorene Benton arrived unexpectedly at Oakhurst Manor late one morning after making the two-hour carriage drive alone. Sarah, who was working in her garden, immediately saw the gravity of her stepmother's expression, and they adjourned to the private sitting room of the mansion's master suite.

"I don't want to burden you, my dear, especially when Jeremy is away," Lorene said. "But a problem has come up that I simply can't handle alone. Isaiah and I have been discussing it for days, and we've talked with Scott Emerson about it, too. All of us are bewildered." She paused, then added, "My niece has come home from New Orleans."

"Alicia Emerson?"

Lorene nodded. "With a baby daughter whom she calls Carolyn."

"I didn't know Alicia was married," Sarah said.

"To the best of our knowledge she isn't, although she refuses to say a word about it. Scott and I have tried, separately and together, but she just smiles at us."

"Oh, dear."

"Alicia merely said that the baby has the last name of Emerson through choice. So we simply don't know if there

33

was a marriage, followed by a separation or divorce, or whether the baby is illegitimate. When we try to question Alicia, she just smiles."

"Where is she staying?"

"With us, for the moment. Scott and your father have offered to rent a house of her own for her and to help her financially, but she refuses."

"Why?"

Lorene shrugged. "All we can figure out—and we admit we're groping—is that when Tom bought Trelawney from Scott and Alicia, she felt as though her roots had been chopped off. She's made it very clear to us, though, that she has no desire to go back to Trelawney. I'm sure Margot and Tom would welcome her, but she says it would be too painful for her there."

"How odd."

"In more ways than you realize. Carrie, as the baby is known, is adorable. I don't think I've ever seen a prettier infant. But Alicia is so changed that we scarcely recognized her when she appeared."

"Changed in what way?"

Lorene hesitated. "This is so nasty I hate to say it. But the way she dresses and piles makeup on her face, the way she wears gaudy jewelry—well, Scott and your father say she looks like a trollop. And I must admit she does remind me of those girls we sometimes see going in and out of Mrs. Hayden's fancy bordello in Charleston."

"How awful!" Sarah was shocked, but in a moment she recovered and shook her head. "Alicia was giddy and too flirtatious for her own good, but I can't imagine she could have become a . . . a prostitute."

"That's what I've said," Lorene replied. "But I can't deny her appearance is terribly bold. And then there's little Carrie. Alicia flatly refuses to identify the baby's father. Scott became very angry the other night, but she clammed up and he couldn't drag a word out of her."

"What are Alicia's plans?"

Lorene shrugged. "She has none, as nearly as we can tell. Yesterday she ordered a couple of new dresses made—rather daring dresses—and paid for them in advance. So she seems to have all the money she needs, although we're none too sure of that, either."

"Would it help if I invited her to come to Oakhurst Manor with her baby and stay as long as she pleases?" Sarah wanted to know.

"That would be an imposition on you," Lorene said.

"Nonsense!" Sarah was firm. "The Beaufort and Emerson families have been the closest of friends for generations. It's the very least I can do, and I'm positive that Jeremy will feel just as I do. If Margot was in trouble of some kind or if I was in trouble, Scott Emerson would do anything and everything in his power to help us. I don't know if we can offer Alicia any solace or help, and from what you tell me, she may not want either. But I can provide her and her baby with a comfortable home as long as she might want to stay. I have Jerry, and Kai has Lance, and with our husbands off at sea, our situations, at least on the surface, wouldn't appear too different from Alicia's. So she might feel at home here."

"Strangely, that's precisely how she does feel. As we've been casting about for a solution, we mentioned the idea of living here, and she sparked to it. In fact, she said you're the only person she knows who is capable of understanding her position."

"I'm flattered, although I don't know what she means."

"I think I do, vaguely. You may recall, several years ago, when she flirted with Tom and came between him and Margot, just for the sake of creating mischief, both the Emerson and Beaufort families turned against her. You said she was high-spirited and meant no real harm, and you were the only one who showed her any sympathy. Obviously she hasn't forgotten."

"If I can do Alicia any good, I'm delighted to have her at Oakhurst Manor," Sarah said. "So that's settled!"

A warm breeze filled the sails of the *Elizabeth,* and she cut through the almost transparent blue-green waters of the Caribbean Sea on an even keel. Never had Jeremy sailed a more sensitive ship, and he was elated by her performance. Before undertaking this voyage he had suffered occasional doubts because she was so much larger and heavier than most merchant vessels, but she handled as easily as a sloop. He was delighted that he had ordered a second, slightly smaller version ship built on the same lines, and he hoped it would be ready to go to sea by the time he returned home.

The voyage was a resounding success. He had called at Fort de France, Kingston, and several other ports, where not only had he obtained high prices for his cargo, but also he was returning with a full hold of West Indian produce, and his profits would be substantial. The Jamaican logwood that comprised the better part of his cargo was highly prized because it provided the best of all bases for the making of black dyes, and would earn him a small fortune. In fact, his net income from this one voyage would be almost a quarter of what he made each year from his beloved Oakhurst Manor.

He was already well off, but he saw no reason why he wouldn't become one of the wealthiest men in South Carolina. Not that he was greedy or wanted anything he didn't already own. But it was good to know that he and Sarah would never face another serious financial crisis, and Jerry would have no worries when he grew to manhood. In fact, Jeremy was already casting about in his mind for some way to leave Lance a small fortune too.

The problem was delicate. He never lost sight of the fact that Lance was actually his son, even though, under the law, the boy was legally the offspring of M'Bwana. For all practical purposes, in day-to-day living the Bantu was the child's father, and acted accordingly. Yet Jeremy felt compelled to provide Lance with financial security for the rest of the boy's life. That was the least he could do.

He had to accomplish that goal in subtle ways, to be sure. M'Bwana was indifferent to material possessions because he was just becoming acclimated to the Western world. Above all, M'Bwana was Jeremy's friend, and under no circumstances could he insult the Bantu by doing anything that would even intimate that M'Bwana was shirking his own duties as a father.

Fortunately there was no need to solve the problem today or tomorrow. They were young men in the prime of life, enjoying the best of robust health, and the solution could wait for a long time. Jerry and Lance were still little children.

M'Bwana had the current watch, and Jeremy stood at one side of the quarterdeck, watching in silent approval as his first mate sailed the *Elizabeth*. It was astonishing how rapidly M'Bwana learned; he was already an expert navigator, completely at home with compass and sextant, and his seamanship improved each day. Jeremy had allowed him to remain in charge during several squalls, and the Bantu prince had given a good account of himself. It wouldn't be long, perhaps no more than another year, before he would be qualified to become the master of his own ship.

M'Bwana became aware of the captain's presence, and grinned at him. "This sea is like glass today," he said. "What a life this is!"

"You're like me, I'm afraid," Jeremy said. "We have saltwater in our veins."

"I would rather sail a ship than do anything else in this world," M'Bwana replied, becoming solemn. "I love my wife and I love my son. I enjoy the comforts of life on land, but I need the sea more than food or drink or rest. I must be descended from one of the sea gods who make their homes off the African coast."

Jeremy felt a little sorry for Kai, as he did for Sarah. No man who felt as he did or as M'Bwana did about the sea could give himself wholly to his wife, to any woman. Once a yearning for the sea crept into a man's bloodstream, it stayed there as long as he lived.

Alicia Emerson arrived at Oakhurst Manor in one of the Benton carriages, a nursemaid who rode beside her holding her infant. Behind the coach came a cart piled high with Alicia's belongings. Most were leather boxes of the type used only for clothes, so it appeared they contained her expensive wardrobe.

Sarah stood on the portico, and watching the carriage move up the driveway, was glad that Lorene had warned her. Alicia had been a pretty, vivacious girl when Trelawney had been sold and she had gone off to live in New Orleans. Now she was a sophisticated woman, and her appearance was startling.

She wore no hat, and her gleaming blue-black hair fell to her waist in a style—or lack of style—that ladies always avoided. Her gown of black silk hugged her voluptuous figure, its white trim emphasizing her shockingly low neckline.

As if that effect were not enough, Alicia also had pasted a small black beauty patch at one side of her cleavage to call further attention to her full, pointed breasts.

Her dark eyes were rimmed in black, and something on her lashes made them seem even longer and fuller than they were. She had used rouge on her cheekbones with a heavy hand; her sensuous, pouting mouth was a scarlet slash, its color matching her long, painted fingernails. Most of all, it was her eyes that were different. They were wise and un-smiling, the eyes of a worldly woman who had experienced much and knew precisely how to utilize her assets in dealing with men.

Sarah felt a twinge of discomfort, and knew Lorene had been right. There was something about Alicia reminiscent of the overdressed—or were they underdressed?—young women one sometimes glimpsed entering or leaving Mrs. Hayden's bordello in Charleston, reputedly the most expensive and exclusive establishment of its kind in the whole South.

But an even greater surprise awaited Sarah. When Alicia left the carriage and embraced her, she was totally without affectation. Her attitude belied her appearance, and she was impulsive, lighthearted, and ingenuous, seemingly the same person she had been before going off to New Orleans.

She clung to Sarah, and for a moment tears appeared in her eyes as she said, "I've dreamed of Oakhurst Manor. You don't know how happy I am to be here, or how grateful I am to you for letting me come."

A few seconds later she was giggling like a schoolgirl.

Carrie, her baby, was gorgeous, the most beautiful infant Sarah had ever seen. Lorene had not exaggerated.

A short time later, at dinner, Alicia met Kai for the first time, and they established an immediate rapport. Soon they were chatting like old friends, even though they discussed nothing of consequence. They were alike in many ways, Sarah thought. They were simple, pleasure-loving girls who trusted people, lived in the present, and had limited senses of responsibility.

Nevertheless, it occurred to Sarah, they were sophisticated in ways that she herself was naive. Kai was married to one man after giving birth to another's child, yet was able to live with a clear conscience in the home of the man who had sired her son. Alicia, making no mention of her past, was not worrying about the legitimacy of her baby.

Sarah couldn't help wondering whether her own attitudes were hopelessly old-fashioned. Her standards were high, her scruples unyielding. It would be so easy to give in to her desires and have an affair with Lester Howard, yet she held off and waged a never-ending fight against her urges. Certainly she was clever enough to conceal an affair so that Jeremy would never learn of it. But that wasn't good enough. Because she'd still have to live with herself. Perhaps Alicia and Kai could break moral laws with impunity and never suffer pangs of conscience, but she was a Bostonian, not a South Carolina belle or an Algerian, and that made the difference. She had to live with herself before she could live with anyone else.

An unexpected incident occurred as they were finishing dinner that caused Sarah to see Alicia Emerson in a somewhat different light.

Fifty wagonloads of cotton were ready to be shipped off to a buyer in Charleston, and Lester Howard came up to the house to discuss the problems of transportation with the mistress of Oakhurst Manor. Sarah automatically and unthinkingly invited him into the dining room for a cup of coffee.

The changes in Alicia were immediate. Her voice dropped a half-octave and became husky. Her manner became sultry, she fluttered her eyelashes, and she flirted brazenly with the overseer. The mere presence of a man compelled her to test her powers of attraction, and she was transformed from a naive girl into a sophisticated woman who was daring a male to ignore her.

Sarah's first reaction was one of outraged jealousy.

But Howard quickly demonstrated that her fears were ungrounded. He was scrupulously polite to Alicia, as he was to all ladies, but her charms left him cold. He had come to the mansion to discuss a professional problem with Sarah, and this he did, undeterred by Alicia's frequent interruptions of the conversation. He appreciated the humor of the situation too, and whenever Alicia became persistent in her attempts to monopolize his attention, there were lights dancing in his eyes as he glanced at Sarah.

She responded in kind, glorying in their ability to communicate without the use of words. Alicia might think of herself as a femme fatale, but the Lester Howards of the world were oblivious of her many and obvious charms. Sarah felt a sense of triumph, but it was short-lived. What, after all, had she won?

Her inhibitions still prevented her from allowing Lester Howard to make love to her. His morals were equally high, which was one of the principal reasons she was drawn to him. But he was a man, after all, and she was afraid that ultimately he might give in to the temptation of the delights that Alicia seemed to be offering him.

Those portions of the president's house that had been destroyed in the fires set by the British when they had invaded Washington City during the War of 1812 had been rebuilt. There had been no way to repair the charred surfaces of the remaining portions of the establishment, however, so President James Madison had ordered the entire mansion painted white. Now that his successor, James Monroe, had taken office, residents of the nation's capital were calling his office-home the White House.

President Monroe and his wife, Elizabeth, lived simply and without ostentation, as they did at their Virginia estate, even though he had served as Madison's secretary of state and previously had been the American minister to France. They gave quiet dinner parties, with the meals prepared and served by a few members of their own staff who had accompanied them to Washington City, and they avoided pomp, keeping ceremonies to a minimum.

Visitors were received informally, regardless of whether they were old family friends, leaders of Congress, or foreign dignitaries. No exception was made when Rear Admiral Viscount Saunders of the British navy came to the White House, even though the admiral was making an official call. Mrs. Monroe took Lisa, Lady Saunders, off to the family living room for tea, and the men settled down in front of a blazing fire in the president's office.

Lord Saunders offered his host a West Indian *cigarro*.

President Monroe declined with a chuckle. "Thank you, Admiral, but they're too strong for me and make me hiccup.

The best I can manage is my pipe, and I'm careful to use only the light tobacco I grow on my own Virginia property."

They chatted about inconsequentials for a short time, but Saunders soon came to the point of his visit. "I'm here to discuss a rather delicate matter with you, Mr. President. His Majesty's government could have approached you through normal diplomatic channels, but it hasn't been all that long since our two countries were at war, so London decided it might save embarrassment all around if I came to you privately."

The president stretched, and his long, lean body seemed even longer. "Makes sense," he said, careful to make no commitment.

"I daresay, sir, that there's little I can tell you about the damage being done to your merchant shipping—as well as to ours—by the new breed of buccaneers who are on the prowl through the West Indian islands."

"They're a nuisance, a danger, and an expense," Monroe said with a frown. "We've lost three merchant ships in the past month. Two were sunk, with twenty-seven sailors drowned, and the third simply vanished. There are new incidents every month."

"The same is happening to us, sir," Admiral Saunders said. "Since I have the honor to command our West Indies squadron, London has asked for my advice. I've recommended a joint Anglo-American expedition to wipe out the scum. London has approved, and I'm here now to sound you out."

"You've already touched on one problem," Monroe said. "Our war ended only two years ago, so I'm not sure our public is yet ready for a formal venture in which the U.S. Navy and the Royal Navy join hands. What's more, this country is just getting on its feet again financially, and I'm afraid Congress would be in no mood to appropriate a large sum of money for such an enterprise. Even though something badly needs to be done to halt the raids of the sea robbers. I agree with your goals, Admiral, but in today's political atmosphere it won't be easy to achieve them."

"I've thought about the problem for months, Mr. President, and so have some of my superiors in London. We may have found a solution you'll find satisfactory."

James Monroe stuffed his pipe with tobacco.

"Suppose, Mr. President, you could find some patriotic American shipowners who know the West Indies and would be willing to contribute their own services and those of their ships. All you'd need to do would be to grant temporary U.S. Navy status to them and their crews, and to pay the sailors, which would be negligible expense."

"The Congress would be delighted, and so would I," President Monroe said. "But where am I to find men willing to undertake this task?"

"I'm well-acquainted with such a man. Jeremy Beaufort of South Carolina, who should be returning any day from a trade voyage to the West Indies, and who has a second ship ready to go to sea. He knows the islands intimately, he's a first-rate commander and a great sailor. I'd have no hesitation in giving him a commission as a commodore in my fleet."

"A strong recommendation, Admiral. I'll look into his credentials. Unfortunately, there's one more stumbling block. Guns and ammunition. We'd need to strip armaments from our present navy, which—as you know—we're just building, and I'm afraid Congress would balk."

"I believe that difficulty can be overcome, too, Mr. President," Lord Saunders said. "At my arsenal in Barbados I have more than enough spare cannon, ammunition, and gunpowder to equip your squadron."

"It seems to me," Monroe said with a wry smile, "that the Royal Navy could launch an expedition against the West Indian buccaneers without any help whatever from the United States."

"I believe we could, sir," the admiral said. "But it wouldn't be the same. Your country is rapidly becoming the biggest power in the Western Hemisphere. These pirates are persistent bastards, if you'll pardon my language, and they won't quit permanently until they're convinced that the United States and Great Britain, acting together, are determined to put them out of business."

The president nodded. "From all I've been told about the situation, Admiral Saunders, your analysis is correct. So be it. I'll see how things stand with this fellow Beaufort you've recommended, and then I'll be in touch with you."

Routines interspersed with minor crises had kept Sarah

busier than usual, and after supper she preferred to head for bed rather than spend an hour listening to Alicia and Kai giggle at each other. She retired to her suite, changed into an old, comfortable cotton nightgown, and scrubbed makeup from her face. She was wearing more of it than she had in the past because she wanted to look her best at all times for Lester Howard, but at least she could get rid of it at night, and she worked until her face shone.

Then she began the dreary chore of putting her hair in pigtails, which she did only when she was alone, and the task kept her busy for more than a half-hour. Her arms ached and her fingers felt stiff by the time she was finishing.

Hoofbeats sounded on the driveway, and she heard the deep sound of men's voices. She couldn't imagine who might be dropping in this late, but it didn't matter. Cleo would tell visitors that she had retired.

The dressing-room door burst open, and Jeremy stood in the frame.

Sarah wanted to weep. Never had she looked so unattractive.

"My God, you're beautiful!" he said, and swept her off her feet and into his arms.

Not until he had kissed her repeatedly did he put her down. "M'Bwana and I landed early this evening," he said, "and rather than wait until morning, we came straight home."

She wanted to remove the pigtails and use some lip rouge, but he continued to hug and kiss her, giving her no opportunity.

Cleo brought him a sandwich, a slab of peach pie, and a hot toddy.

Sarah retired to their bedchamber with him, at last realizing that, in his eyes, she did look beautiful.

"We made a small fortune on this voyage," he told her as he ate, "and we'll do even better on the next. I'm hiring Ned Slocum as captain of the *Louise*, which should be ready to go to sea, and we'll sail the two ships together, which will offer us greater protection against the buccaneers who are infesting West Indian waters these days."

Sarah brought him up-to-date on life at Oakhurst Manor. Jerry was in the best of health. Kai and Lance had moved into the manor house so Lester Howard could take possession of the overseer's house.

"How is Lester making out?" Jeremy asked, interrupting her recital.

"He's wonderful, the perfect overseer in every way," she replied, and felt guilty.

"I knew it when I hired him. My only fear was that you might not get along with him."

"Why wouldn't I?" She wondered if he had guessed or in some way divined her compulsive interest in Howard.

Jeremy shrugged. "One never knows how a woman will react."

She changed the subject by telling him that Alicia and her baby were living at Oakhurst Manor.

Jeremy was surprised, but made no comment until she finished the entire story. "You did the right thing by taking her in, of course," he said. "I'm proud of you for it, and certainly she can stay as long as she pleases. But. . . surely she didn't become a strumpet in New Orleans?"

"I find it impossible to believe myself," Sarah said. "But her behavior is rather odd. She's natural and unaffected when she's with Kai and me, or with any other woman. But let a man appear—Tom or Lester Howard or whoever—and she tries to overwhelm him. You can judge for yourself at breakfast."

"So I shall. Now, then, suppose I wake up Jerry to tell him I'm home and give him some of the gifts I brought him—"

"You'll do no such thing, Master Beaufort! Jerry would get so excited it would take him hours to go off to sleep again, and tomorrow he'd be so cross he'd fight with Lance all day."

Jeremy chuckled, went into the dressing room for a sea bag he had dropped there, and returned to the bedchamber with it. "In that case, Mistress Beaufort, we'll start with the trinkets I've brought you. Here's a bolt of cloth from Martinique . . ."

"It's like gauze. It's exquisite!"

"This ivory bracelet and the earrings to match it were carved by a retired seaman who lives in St. Kitts."

"You're too extravagant."

"And here's a little something I picked up for you in San Juan."

Sarah hesitantly took a small box from him, opened it, and stared at a sapphire ring, surrounded by a circle of diamonds. Tears came to her eyes.

Jeremy slipped the ring onto her finger. "I reckon that a wife who attends to the drudgery at home deserves something from a husband who goes off gallivanting on the high seas."

Too overcome to speak, she pulled down his head and kissed him.

Almost instantly they were making love, gently yet with the vehemence of a couple who had been abstinent for several months.

Sarah knew, after they reached a climax but continued to cling to each other, that she hadn't been fooling herself all this time. In spite of the strange, unrequited yearning for Lester Howard that she couldn't put out of her mind, Jeremy was the man she loved. He belonged to her as much as she belonged to him, and she could forgive him anything, even his attraction to Lisa Saunders.

They fell asleep in each other's arms.

In the morning they were awakened by an exuberant Jerry, who had just learned from Amanda that his father had returned. Jeremy romped with him and gave him gifts, and only after the child was taken off to the nursery for breakfast could the master of Oakhurst Manor get dressed.

By the time Sarah was ready for the day, and felt nervous about the meeting between her husband and the overseer. She didn't want to be present for that encounter, but told herself she would be a coward if she avoided it. Perhaps, when she saw them together, her desire for Howard would vanish into the mists from which it had materialized.

The meeting took place unexpectedly, and sooner than she had anticipated. When she and Jeremy went downstairs, he wanted to step outdoors before they went to the dining room, so she accompanied him onto the lawn.

Lester Howard was just leaving his house. He caught sight of Jeremy and hurried to the mansion. For an instant he glanced at Sarah, and she felt as she always did when he looked at her, as though she had been struck a physical blow.

Then he and Jeremy were clasping hands, each genuinely pleased to see each other.

"I hear you're doing splendidly," Jeremy said.

"Well enough," the overseer replied. "But I'd be worthless if it weren't for Sarah."

"I'll tell you a secret," Jeremy said. "So would I."

"Most days there's no real need for an overseer on this plantation. She can do just about everything here."

Jeremy slipped an arm around his wife's shoulders. "Well, Lester, next time I go to sea, put her to work for you."

The overseer grinned and looked at Sarah again.

Even at this moment, with Jeremy's strong hand gripping her shoulder, Sarah felt familiar chills. Jeremy was her husband and lover, but Howard still had the power to mesmerize her. And something in his expression told her that she continued to have the same impact on him.

She scarcely heard the two men arranging to meet again later in the morning.

Jeremy led her back into the house, and they went to the dining room, where Kai and M'Bwana were already eating breakfast. Sarah and the Bantu greeted each other warmly, and Jeremy, as always, was pleasantly polite to Kai, as she was to him. It was a never-ending mystery to Sarah that her husband and this girl who had borne him a son were friendly yet almost impersonal in their relations. They shared no sense of intimacy, and there was no hint in their attitudes that they had been lovers. What compounded the puzzle was that their approaches to each other were genuine, in no way feigned for the benefit of others. It was obvious that Jeremy thought of Kai only as the wife of his friend, and that was that, while Kai looked at him as a benefactor as well as her husband's closest associate.

Someday, Sarah hoped, her husband would solve the conundrum for her. Until then, however, no strains were apparent, and she had learned to live with a potentially explosive situation that, in ways she could not understand, had been defused.

All four chatted amiably through breakfast. M'Bwana, free of responsibilities at the plantation, planned to spend the morning fishing and intended to take Lance with him. He extended an invitation to Jerry, too, but Jeremy preferred that the child accompany him when he inspected the plantation with Lester Howard.

Soon after M'Bwana and Kai left the table, Alicia Emerson made her appearance. Her snug-fitting silk gown with a plunging neckline, her heavy makeup and oversized gold-hoop earrings were totally inappropriate for this early hour of the day. Certainly she knew better; at least she had been taught propriety in the home of her parents during her formative years. But she seemed oblivious of what was right or wrong. She had developed her own style, her own approach to life, and plainly intended to pursue it.

Her attitude toward Jeremy was startling, however. He greeted her with a kiss on the cheek, as befitted a close family friend whom he had known since earliest childhood. Alicia quietly thanked him for his hospitality in offering a home to her and to Carrie. In spite of her flamboyant appearance, she was demure, her manner sedate, and she made no attempt to flirt with him. Ever since she had come to Oakhurst Manor she had thrown herself at every man whose path she had crossed, but today she was behaving like a lady.

Jeremy's years of experience and suffering, beginning with his impressment into the British navy prior to the outbreak of the War of 1812, made him intolerant of the diplomatic niceties that other people practiced. Alicia was a guest in his home, so he thought he and Sarah had a right to know more about her past than she had volunteered to anyone.

Eating some of the smoked ham that was cured on the premises, he spoke casually. "I gather you didn't care much for New Orleans."

"I loved it for a time," Alicia replied as she nibbled a hot biscuit.

"What happened to change your mind?"

"Life there became too complicated for me." She was adept in the art of giving evasive replies to direct questions.

But Jeremy persisted. "In what way?"

Alicia laughed as she glanced at Sarah, then looked at her host. "You're unique, Jeremy. No one else, including my brother and Aunt Lorene, had the courage to come out in the open. Well, I suppose you have a right to know."

All at once Sarah felt sorry for her. In spite of her flashy appearance, she seemed very young and vulnerable.

"My story isn't all that unusual," Alicia said. "I fell in love with a married man. His wife had been an invalid for a long time. He told me she was dying, and he promised to marry me when he became free. Well, she's an invalid, all right, but she'll live for many years. I changed my appearance to please him, and the way I look now is part of me, the way I am. He took good care of me financially, and of Carrie too. In fact, he's even offered to make her his legal ward."

Sarah couldn't remain silent any longer. "But you refused?"

Alicia raised her head proudly. "I have no intention of allowing him to recognize our child unless he also recognizes me as his wife. I don't enjoy being treated like an outcast."

Jeremy sipped the small mug of ale that he always drank with his breakfast. "Don't you owe it to your child—?"

"No!" Suddenly Alicia became strident. "I owe nothing to anyone in this world. Other than to you and Sarah. I've been feeling bruised, so I've been licking my wounds here. But one day I'll feel strong again, ready to face the world, and I shall. I've learned a great deal about myself. I enjoy the company of men, while most women bore me. If one man in New Orleans could fall in love with me, there will be others. I'll be in a position to choose, and I promise you he'll be wealthy enough to look after me, and Carrie too."

Obviously she meant what she said, and her attitude was cynical: at the right time and with the right person she was intending to barter her favors for financial security. At the same time, however, as Sarah realized, she was still in love with the New Orleans lover who had betrayed her.

What mattered now was what she did in the immediate future. Jeremy was impressed by her candor, as Sarah could plainly see, and perhaps it was no accident or coincidence that Alicia had revealed so much to him. She had known him for a long time, so she understood that honesty appealed to him.

Sarah realized with a shock that Alicia might be thinking in terms of seeking Jeremy's long-range protection for herself and her baby. He was wealthy, well able to afford giving such assistance. He was enormously attractive, and Alicia's slyly demure behavior, combined with her frank discussion of her past, indicated that she might be angling for him, hoping he would establish her in a home of her own in Savannah or some other city.

A warning flare had been lighted, and Sarah knew she had to be on her guard.

# Chapter 4

A special courier carried the letter to Oakhurst Manor, and the communication bore the wax seal of the United States secretary of state. The letter itself, signed by the secretary, John Quincy Adams, was succinct. President Monroe wanted to discuss a matter of national importance with Jeremy Beaufort, and hoped that Mr. Beaufort would call upon him at his earliest convenience.

Jeremy left for Washington City early the next morning. He and Sarah had never visited the nation's capital together, so she accompanied him. They traveled by carriage, and changing horses twice daily, reached Washington City in a week.

Fortunately Congress was not in session, so accommodations were available in the crowded, growing metropolis, and the Beauforts were able to engage a small suite at O'Neale's Inn and Tavern, which Secretary of War John C. Calhoun of South Carolina had advised them was the most comfortable establishment in town. Even before Sarah could unpack their belongings, Jeremy sent a note to the White House, informing the president of his arrival.

A marine corps officer came to O'Neale's Tavern a short

time later with an invitation to the Beauforts to dine at the White House the following day. Both were flattered, and it was evident that President Monroe had something important in mind.

There were so few places to eat in the town that Jeremy and Sarah had supper at O'Neale's, and retired early. The next morning they went for a walk, and were surprised to discover that the capital of the United States was still in a primitive state. Most streets were rutted dirt roads, and only Pennsylvania Avenue, which ran a mile and a half from the president's mansion to the Capitol, was being paved. The Treasury and War Department headquarters, which had been destroyed by the British during the War of 1812, had been rebuilt, and other new government structures were in one stage or another of construction. All were made of wood.

A few private homes, most occupied by members of the Cabinet, had been erected on K Street, but most senior government officials lived in nearby Georgetown, a half-hour horseback ride from their offices. Other than government buildings, Washington City was filled with rooming houses and inns used by members of the Senate and House of Representatives when Congress was in session, and by other visitors. There were few shops in town other than several general stores and a large, dry-goods house, and there was a complete lack of theaters or other places of entertainment. Sarah could understand why the wives of senators and congressmen rarely accompanied their husbands to Washington, and why few people lingered there when their official business was done.

Sarah dressed with care in a sedate mulberry gown of crushed velvet, and deciding her diamond-and-sapphire rings were too ostentatious, did not wear them for the occasion. They walked the short distance to the White House, avoiding mud puddles in the road, and Jeremy presented his invitation to the two army sentries stationed at the main entrance. One of them rang a bell, and a butler conducted the guests inside.

Elizabeth Monroe, a plain woman who wore an old-fashioned dress of black taffeta, greeted the visitors in a small sitting room and took Sarah off to the family quarters. A male secretary conducted Jeremy to the president's office, where a large portrait of George Washington adorned one wall, and smaller pictures of his other predecessors—John Adams, Thomas Jefferson, and James Madison—were hanging on another.

President Monroe, sitting in his shirtsleeves in front of an open fire, was reading a document when Jeremy was ushered in, and putting his papers aside, stood and extended a bony hand. His cuffs were slightly frayed, his waistcoat was unbuttoned, and completely lacking in airs, he resembled the frontier planter he had been.

"Mr. Beaufort," he said as they took seats in front of the fire, "I've heard good things about you from many people. The first to call you to my attention was Admiral Lord Saunders of the Royal Navy, and I've subsequently made some exhaustive inquiries about you. It appears you're just the man we need for a difficult task, one that will bring you little glory, cost you money, and subject you to danger."

Jeremy appreciated his irony, and grinned.

"As a shipowner and master, you're familiar with the problems caused these days by buccaneers in the West Indies."

"I sure am, Mr. President. They're the scum of the earth, and I'd like to hang all of them."

Monroe explained the purpose of the Anglo-American mission to rid the Caribbean Sea of pirates. He emphasized the need for the United States to participate in the venture, but made it clear that American funds for the venture were limited.

Jeremy anticipated his request. "I have two ships, Mr. President. The *Elizabeth,* which I sail myself, and the *Louise,* which has just been launched. I've hired a retired navy officer, Ned Slocum, as her master, and I have no doubt he'll be eager to join me. I volunteer both my ships for the expedition, and although I can't speak for my crews, I'm sure most of the men will want to sail with us."

The president was greatly relieved. "The country is grateful for your generosity, Mr. Beaufort, and so am I. The navy will find you as many replacements as you need to fill your crews. I can also provide you with two small brigs that can be converted into sloops of war, so you'll have a squadron of four ships, in all."

"That should be enough, Mr. President, especially if we're going to sail with the British."

Monroe explained that cannon, ammunition, and powder would be supplied by Lord Saunders, and they spent the next half-hour discussing the expedition in detail. "You'll be granted a temporary commission as a commodore," the president said, "and you'll operate under navy supervision. Submit a list of your officers and ratings to the Navy Department, and they'll be approved. I hope you can spend the better part of tomorrow at the Navy Department to settle the questions of provisions and other matters."

"Of course, sir. How soon do you want this operation to begin?"

"Well, Lord Saunders has already returned to the West Indies, and is making his preparations. The sooner you can put to sea, the sooner the scourge of piracy can be ended, but I prefer thoroughness to rush. You're being given a free hand to deal with the situation as you see fit, and you're being given only one order. Commodore Beaufort, clear the West Indian waters of buccaneers!"

The secretaries of state, war, and the navy and their wives were dinner guests at the White House, so Jeremy had no chance to tell Sarah in detail about his mission until they returned to the O'Neale Tavern.

Sarah listened in silence, her face devoid of expression.

Jeremy gleaned that she disapproved. "I couldn't refuse a direct request by the president, and I wouldn't want to."

"I wouldn't want you to," she said.

He was relieved. "One of the key factors in my decision was that I'm one of the few qualified men in the country who is wealthy enough to accept the assignment. Another is that I loathe the buccaneers."

"Forgive my ignorance," she said, "but I've always thought of them as rather romantic."

"The pirates of a couple of hundred years ago, even a hundred years ago, were a different breed," he explained. "They were soldiers of fortune, adventurers, even patriots. Sir Henry Morgan, the most renowned of them, became lieutenant governor of Jamaica. Today's buccaneers are criminals, every last one of them. Robbers, murderers, men totally lacking in honor. I'm going to enjoy playing a role in exterminating them!"

"How soon will you leave?"

"I won't know for certain until my meetings at the Navy Department tomorrow. The two small ships joining my squadron will sail to Charleston from Baltimore, and then we'll have to get our crews ready, put in provisions, and so forth. I'd guess, roughly, that we'll be set to sail to Barbados in about six weeks."

"Barbados?" Sarah's voice was weak.

"Dickie Saunders is giving us cannon and munitions from his arsenal there," he said.

It was bad enough that Jeremy was going to sea again, months earlier than he had anticipated, and that he would be risking his life in his encounters with the buccaneers. But these dangers were of little consequence.

Jeremy would be seeing Admiral Lord Saunders, which meant he would be meeting Lisa again. In her own world, quite probably in her own home.

Sarah knew from her own experience with Lester Howard that the attraction Jeremy and Lisa felt for each other was too powerful for either of them to resist. It was stronger by far than her own almost overwhelming desire for Howard. It was so potent that even she, the outsider, had been aware of it.

So the real danger she faced now was that of losing her husband to a ravishingly beautiful woman with whom she could not compete.

Preparations for the expedition were made at breakneck pace. Jeremy had to move to Charleston, and as he was spending most of his time ashore, he accepted the invitation of Sarah's father and stepmother to live at their house. Having been sworn into the navy as a temporary commodore, he always appeared in public in his new uniform, with a broad gold band on each sleeve and a pair of full silver epaulets on his shoulders. Having decided to keep personal command of the *Elizabeth* as well as of the whole squadron, he granted a commission as a commander to M'Bwana, who would become first lieutenant of the flagship. The lean, ascetic Ned Slocum was made a captain and immediately assumed command of the new ship, the *Louise.*

The smaller vessels of the squadron, the *Marilyn* and the

*Jane*, soon arrived at Charleston, and their masters were commissioned as commanders. Crew members of all four vessels who volunteered for the expedition were enlisted in the navy, and arrangements had been made to fill any vacancies that might occur. But there were none. American seamen, many of them War of 1812 veterans, were as one in their eagerness to rid the West Indian seas of the buccaneers who robbed and sank merchant ships and were merciless in their treatment of conquered foes and captives.

Once again Sarah took charge at Oakhurst Manor, assisted by Lester Howard, but her personal situation was not yet as tense as it had been when Jeremy had been at sea. She joined him in Charleston every weekend, often bringing Jerry with her, just as Kai and Lance visited M'Bwana, who was already living in his quarters on board the *Elizabeth*. She felt temptations in her relations with Howard, but the knowledge that she would be joining Jeremy in Charleston in a few days helped her maintain her balance.

Never had Jeremy been so busy. He supervised the gunnery practice his crews conducted daily on a small island off the Charleston coast that belonged to the navy. He took personal charge of the purchase of food, naval stores, medical supplies, and other provisions, and he inspected the spare uniforms his quartermaster received from the Navy Department. He spent at least a portion of each day with his officers, studying maps and charts of the Caribbean provided by the Navy and War departments, and he had to confer regularly with officers sent from Washington City to assist him. He wrote weekly to Lord Saunders too, keeping his colleague and friend apprised of his progress.

His work was far from finished at the end of the normal work day. While his subordinates relaxed in the evenings, he returned to his labors after eating supper at the Benton house, retiring either to the library or his own bedchamber to read the most recent, secret reports sent him by the Navy Department on the day-to-day activities of the buccaneers.

After bearing down for a month, he could see the end in sight, and estimated that he would be ready to put to sea in another three weeks, slightly longer than he had first guessed. He would miss Sarah and their life together at Oakhurst Manor, it was true, but he was eager to attend to the mission

President Monroe had given him. The United States was depending on him, and he could not let his country down.

One evening in midweek, after a particularly hectic day, Jeremy felt weary when he came ashore following an inspection of all four vessels in his squadron. A young officer awaited him at the navy wharf with a thick folder of secret documents just received from Washington City, so he knew there would be no respite that night. Instead, hours of concentrated reading awaited him.

It was just as well, he thought as he rode to the Benton house in a navy carriage, that Isaiah and Lorene had left earlier in the day for a visit to Tom and Margot at Trelawney. He actually looked forward to a quiet dinner alone before settling down to a long night of reading.

As the carriage approached the Benton house, Jeremy noted that lamps were burning behind the drawn blinds in the small parlor where he usually joined Lorene and Isaiah for a predinner drink. Perhaps they had changed their minds about going to Trelawney today.

A servant admitted him to the house, and he headed for the parlor, then stopped short. Sitting in an easy chair facing the entrance was Alicia Emerson, and it was her appearance even more than her presence that startled him. She was wearing a gown of thin, pale silk, its tiny sleeves pulled down from her shoulders, and never had he seen such a low neckline. It was obvious, too, that she wore no breast supports under her dress.

Alicia stood and extended a hand in greeting. "You needn't look so astonished, Jeremy. I always stay here at Aunt Lorene's when I come to Charleston, and I have some fittings with my dressmaker in the next couple of days."

Jeremy murmured a greeting and felt a trifle uncomfortable when she held his hand longer than politeness required. He realized, too, that she had doused herself with a pungent, clinging scent.

"I didn't know until I arrived that Aunt Lorene and Isaiah had gone off to the country," she said.

She sounded too glib, and it occurred to him that she had indeed known the Bentons would not be at home. Perhaps she was up to some mischief, but he preferred not to speculate on what it might be.

"This is the first time I've seen you in your navy uniform," Alicia said. "Oh, you do look handsome."

He was embarrassed, and muttered his thanks.

She was too shrewd to dwell on the matter, and immediately changed the subject. "I hope your drinking habits haven't changed since you left Oakhurst Manor, because I've prepared you a drink." She handed him a glass of whiskey and water.

He would have preferred something milder tonight, like sack, because of the reading that awaited him. But it would have been ungracious to refuse, so he took the glass, thanked her, and sat on the divan.

Alicia picked up a glass too, and raised it in a silent toast.

Jeremy responded, then sipped, and wanted to tell her she made far too strong a drink. But it would be much easier to leave the better part of it. "Did you bring me any messages from Sarah?"

"Actually," she said, "I didn't see her before I left, so I just left her a note saying I'd be away for a few days."

The thought crossed his mind that, either by accident or design, neither Sarah nor anyone else knew that Alicia had come here. It was almost as though she had set up a rendezvous with him on purpose.

As she roamed around the parlor, sipping her drink, he realized that she too was drinking whiskey, and he was amazed. A lady who had been reared at Trelawney normally would drink nothing stronger than sack or a mild wine.

At last Alicia dropped onto the divan near Jeremy, and as she curled up beside him, her snug-fitting skirt somehow became shorter, revealing her calves.

Perhaps he was being absurd, but she reminded him of the flashily attractive young women he had seen, years earlier, at the house of assignation in Jamaica when he had been searching for Lisa. Perhaps it was her scarlet, pouting mouth, or the thick black substance that coated her lashes. Most of all it was her provocative attire and the way she held her body, shifting her shoulders and allowing her neckline to drop still lower as she made herself comfortable.

"I assume you left your baby with one of the nursemaids at Oakhurst Manor," he said.

"Of course." Her shrug indicated that she wasn't thinking of Carrie. "May I tell you a secret, Jeremy?"

"Certainly." He realized he was consuming more of his drink than he had intended, but nevertheless he took another gulp.

"As much as I love it in the country, and I really do enjoy myself at Oakhurst Manor, I sometimes need a touch of city life. Maybe growing up on a plantation is responsible, but I get bored unless there's a little excitement in my life."

"Charleston isn't the most exciting of cities, you know." He remembered that she had been approximately her own daughter's age when he had first seen her, and she had been ever-present in the background as he himself had grown up. Scott's sister and Tom's friend, she had climbed trees and gone fishing with the boys, making scenes when she hadn't been permitted to accompany them when they went hunting.

Now she was a stranger, a heavily perfumed and made-up woman, scantily clad, who gave off a persistent aura of sensuality. Sarah had indicated that Alicia chased after men, regarding herself as irresistible, but he had scoffed at the notion because her conduct in his presence had been so circumspect. Tonight was different, however, and he began to suspect that Sarah was right, as she so often was.

"I can't believe you aren't having a wonderful time in Charleston. You're a commodore now, the commander of a whole fleet—"

"A squadron."

"Whatever you want to call it. Every pretty girl in town must be throwing herself at you."

"In the first place," Jeremy said firmly, "I'm a married man—"

Alicia's giggle interrupted him. "You may have traveled all over the world, but you're still naive." She offered no further explanation.

"In the second place," he continued, "I don't have the time to seek excitement, even if I had the desire."

Her sigh was exaggerated as she rose, and not asking if he wanted more whiskey, she refilled both of their glasses.

It occurred to him when she resumed her place on the divan that she had moved still closer to him. As a girl she had been an innocent flirt, but she was a woman now, and was playing a dangerous and complex game. "I leave the house shortly after dawn every morning," he persisted, "and I'm on the run every minute of the day. And night." Perhaps she could accept a subtle hint, so he tapped the folder he had just received from Washington City. "I've got to spend three or four hours this very night reading some dispatches from the Navy Department."

Alicia looked amused. "What would happen if you didn't read them?"

"I'd have that much more to do tomorrow night," he said, and was irritated.

"Sometimes delays are well worth a person's time," Alicia said, inclining toward him, her bright red lips parting slightly.

Jeremy knew beyond all doubt now that she was inviting him to kiss her, to take her. For a fleeting moment he was tempted. Her air of sexuality was enticing, and she was an exceptionally attractive young woman.

But there were too many barriers. Above all the others loomed Sarah. Even if his wife did not exist, however, he could not seduce this woman whom he had known all of his life, whose brother was his friend. Putting it more correctly, he thought, he could not permit himself to be seduced by her.

Alicia obviously thought she had won an advantage, that he was weakening. A hand crept toward him.

He was momentarily fascinated by her long, painted nails. Then he shook off his lethargy and acted before it was too late, deliberately moving away from her so he could pick up his glass. The next instant he was on his feet, standing with his legs apart, as though weathering a storm on his quarter-deck. Although he didn't really understand women, he knew enough to refrain from rejecting her openly or lecturing her on her abandoned ways.

"One reason I was made a commodore," he said, "is that my superiors know I'll do the work that's necessary without any prompting or outside pressure." He walked to a small desk, took a sheet of paper from a cubbyhole, and dipping a quill pen into a jar of ink, scribbled something on it.

Alicia was disappointed, but hadn't yet given up, and she continued to smile at him, her black-rimmed eyes inviting him to return to a place beside her.

Jeremy sanded the wet ink, then pulled a bell rope and went to the entrance.

A butler appeared.

Jeremy conferred with him in a low tone, then turned back into the room after handing him the folded paper.

Alicia took a long swallow of her fresh drink and waited for his explanation.

His best defense in this situation, he decided, was a pose of masculine ingenuousness. "Since I'm going to be busy tonight—and have no real choice—I don't want you to be completely deprived of the excitement you craved in the city. So I've just sent off a note to your brother."

She was incredulous. "You've written to Scott?"

Jeremy continued to play the role of the innocent. "Of course. His house is only a five-minute walk from here, so I've asked him to join us for dinner. And later, if you feel like it, I'm sure he'll be pleased to take you to an inn for coffee."

Alicia stared at him; disbelief mingled with contempt in her eyes.

Jeremy relaxed. There was more than one way to win a battle, and there was more than one way to avoid a designing woman too. It didn't bother him that he had made an enemy of Alicia. There was nothing she could do to harm him or his immediate family, and by the time he returned from the West Indies, she would have forgotten the incident. If not, she would no longer be welcome at Oakhurst Manor.

At last the squadron was almost ready to go to sea. The crews of all four ships were granted final shore leaves, and barges made their way back and forth across the Charleston harbor, carrying last-minute supplies of fresh fruit, vegetables, and water.

Officer's wives and children were permitted to visit the ships, and on the afternoon prior to the squadron's departure, Jeremy held a reception in the officers' wardroom on board the *Elizabeth*. A mild punch and tea biscuits were served, and Sarah stood with her husband at the head of the reception line, the other captains and their wives beside them. The dour Captain Slocum was a widower, and hating social functions, muttered at such length under his breath that Sarah, who was standing next to him, couldn't help giggling.

After the last of the officers and their wives had gone through the receiving line, he leaned behind Sarah and spoke to Jeremy. "Now, Commodore?"

"Now, Captain." Jeremy offered Sarah his arm, and let her out of the wardroom.

They were followed by the three captains, as well as M'Bwana and Kai.

"This is their last party for many weeks," Jeremy explained to his bewildered wife, "and they can't really relax in the presence of senior officers, so we got out."

The captains' gigs were waiting for them, and they left the flagship without delay. A boat was waiting to take M'Bwana and Kai ashore for their last night together too, and the flag lieutenant bent over Sarah's hand, bidding her farewell.

"May God sail with you," she told him.

To her astonishment, Jeremy's good-bye to Kai was far more personal. He held her by the waist, she placed her hands on his shoulders, and they kissed, delicately but with feeling. It was the first time Sarah had seen them indulge in an intimate gesture, and she was stunned.

She stood unmoving outside Jeremy's cabin after Kai and M'Bwana departed. "You and Kai . . ." she began, but could not finish her sentence.

"We have a special friendship."

"I know. There's Lance."

Jeremy knew he had procrastinated long enough. He should have offered her a full explanation much earlier, and the eve of his departure on a long voyage was not the ideal time, but he had no real choice. He motioned her into the cabin and closed the door behind them.

Sarah sank into the nearest chair, her turmoil so great that she could scarcely think.

"I should have come to you long ago," Jeremy said, bracing himself, "but I didn't want to hurt you. Obviously I was wrong, and for whatever good it may do, I'm desperately sorry."

She fought back her tears. "Everyone who has seen Lance knows he's your son."

His faint smile was tight. "He is . . . and he isn't."

"How can that be?"

"What I'm going to tell you now must remain between us, for reasons you'll soon understand. You'll recall that I saved the life of M'Bwana's father in the African bush, and he was so grateful he couldn't give me enough gifts. The necklace of rough-cut diamonds that became the base of our great fortune. The lifelong companionship of M'Bwana, his second son. The Watusi enemies the Bantu had taken in battle—who would have been killed if I hadn't brought them home to Oakhurst Manor."

"I know all that." She found it difficult to control her impatience.

"There was one other gift," Jeremy said, speaking slowly. "A young Algerian slave girl, born into slavery, who had been reared for one purpose, her master's physical pleasure."

Sarah gasped. "Kai was a slave?"

He nodded. "She insisted on giving herself to me because she believed it was expected of her." He hesitated, then plunged on. "I weakened . . . and I took her. That same night, the attempt was made on my life that almost succeeded, and for the next year I was out of my mind. Kai and M'Bwana nursed me back to health, and they tell me that in my delirium I called her by your name."

At least she was admitting he had gone to bed with Kai, and Sarah felt numb.

"When I came to my senses," Jeremy went on, his voice strained, "I realized at once that Kai and M'Bwana had fallen in love. I freed her from bondage immediately, which I would have done in any event if I hadn't been wounded by a thief. Not until later did I even learn that Lance had been born, and then I discovered that M'Bwana was already treating him like a son."

The first rays of understanding began to penetrate.

"Kai and M'Bwana were married, and he adopted Lance. I'll never forget what he told me. 'The son of my friend is my son,' he said, and that's the way things have been from that day to this."

Sarah digested what he had told her, and finally found her voice. "Then you . . . you weren't really interested in Kai as a mistress?"

"At no time," he replied firmly. "I hadn't been with a

woman—any woman—for a very long time. A pretty girl who was doing what she regarded as her duty offered herself to me in the nude, and I didn't have the strength to resist her. I didn't know her, she didn't know me . . . and we spent a very short time together before I was almost murdered. No more than a half-hour, perhaps." He searched for some way to convey the spirit of that brief encounter. "It was a meeting of two strangers."

Sarah's tensions began to subside somewhat, and she found herself sympathizing deeply with Kai, who had since demonstrated her fundamental decency and who had been in a position that any honorable woman would find deplorable. But one aspect of the situation continued to rankle. "I can see how difficult it must have been for her, and I had no idea she had been a slave—"

"That's why I've stressed secrecy," Jeremy interrupted. "Her life here would be ruined if it ever became public knowledge."

"I'd never betray her," Sarah replied. "And I'm thankful that you've admitted the truth. You and Kai were caught in a painful situation, and I realize how difficult it has been for you to tell me the story." In spite of her words, she remained reserved.

"It appears," he said, "that you still aren't forgiving me. M'Bwana has become my closest associate, and I trust him as I trust no other man, not even my own brother. So I can't even think in terms of sending him and his family away. I'm too much in M'Bwana's debt ever to desert him, just as I know he'd never turn against me."

"I wouldn't ask it of you." She closed her eyes for a moment.

"What, then?"

"I don't regard myself as being a particularly jealous woman. I pitied Alicia Emerson after you told me about your miserable encounter with her a couple of weeks ago. But this is different. After you kissed Kai a few minutes ago, you spoke of your special relationship with her."

The lines vanished from Jeremy's forehead, and he laughed. "Think in her terms and mine. This has nothing to do with her love for M'Bwana and has no connection with Lance either. She'll always remember that I granted her freedom from slavery and made it possible for her to lead a far different life. As for me, I'll never forget that she devoted a full year to helping me regain my health, and that—at the time—she had no idea she might have anything personal to gain."

At last Sarah understood.

"The ties that bind Kai and me," Jeremy continued, "are unique. They're irrelevant to my love for you and her love for M'Bwana. Even if you and M'Bwana didn't exist, she would never be more than a friend, but that is something she'll always be."

Sarah stood and went to him. "I promise you I'll never be jealous of you and Kai again, and I admire both of you for the way you've dealt with the circumstances that are delicate and unfortunate."

Jeremy kissed her, and the breach was healed.

They went to the main deck, and with sailors standing at attention, Jeremy climbed down a rope ladder to his waiting gig. Sarah seated herself in a basketlike contraption and was lowered to the boat.

As the oarsmen rowed them ashore for their last night together, she knew that one concern was lifted from her mind. But a far deeper worry remained, one that she couldn't bring herself to mention to her husband. How would he and Lisa Saunders react when they met again?

For that matter, she would have to watch her own step. In another twenty-four hours she would return to Oakhurst Manor and the ever-present possibility that she might lose her own way and stray when she saw Lester Howard again.

The families of officers and men lined the navy wharf, and Jeremy, looking through his glass, quickly found Sarah, who was waving a scarf. With her free hand she was holding Jerry, who was jumping up and down in such excitement that he was in danger of falling into the harbor. The tide had turned and was going out, so the moment to depart had come, and Jeremy raised a hand to his bicorn in a farewell salute to his wife and son.

"Flag Lieutenant," he said crisply, "you may inform the squadron to raise distinguishing pennants."

"Aye, aye, sir!" M'Bwana gave an order, and signal flags fluttered as they climbed the yardarm.

All four ships simultaneously showed the United States flag, and a fife-and-drum corps on shore began to play.

"You may notify the squadron to weigh anchor and hoist sails."

"Aye, aye, sir."

The crowd on shore cheered as the ships edged their way out of the harbor, with the *Elizabeth* in the lead.

Jeremy turned away from the crowd on the dock and looked out toward the sea. The time had come for him to put Oakhurst Manor out of his mind and leave its concerns to Sarah and his overseer. From this hour forward he had to concentrate on his mission, ridding the Caribbean of buccaneers.

# Chapter 5

Life at Oakhurst Manor would never be the same without Amanda and Willie. Carrying a generous farewell gift Jeremy had given them before he had gone to sea, a sum large enough to support them for a year while Willie established himself as a cabinetmaker in Boston, they left the plantation after an early breakfast. Amanda wore a frilly, elaborate dress that concealed her pregnancy, and the slender Willie was attired in the same black suit he had worn years earlier on his one visit to New England.

Every precaution was taken to guard against untoward incident before they reached the North. Amanda carried documents proving she was a free-born citizen of Massachusetts, and Willie was armed with a number of notarized papers, among them copies of the court order granting him freedom.

Sarah was still worried, however, that they might encounter some bigot who would create complications for them, particularly as escaped slaves faced severe penalties everywhere in the South. So Lester Howard obtained the assistance of his nephew, a young man in his early twenties, who agreed to provide the couple with a white escort as far as the Pennsylvania border.

Cleo was convinced she would never see her son and daughter-in-law again, in spite of their reassurances that they would return to Oakhurst Manor for a visit every year. But she remained dry-eyed as their carriage moved off down the driveway, and stood unmoving, her heavy arms folded, until they disappeared from sight. Members of the household staff took care to avoid her for the rest of the day.

Sarah felt depressed when she returned to the house after seeing the couple off, and habit rather than inclination sent her to the dining room for breakfast. She and Amanda had been close for many years, and she couldn't rid herself of the feeling that she had lost a dear friend.

Other matters weighed on her mind, too. Yesterday Lester Howard had escorted her to a dinner party at Trelawney, and the affair had been disastrous. Alicia, who appeared to be sleeping late this morning, had consumed more liquor than was good for her, and had flirted outrageously with every man at the party. Tom had taken pains to avoid her, but Margot had been annoyed, and Scott Emerson had been so upset by his sister's conduct that Margot had been forced to calm him.

But Sarah was not as concerned about Alicia's behavior as she was about her own. She had grown careless, and she felt certain she had allowed her interest in Lester Howard to show. He, in return, had been sparked by her warmth, and by this morning she was afraid she had become the center of gossip on every plantation in the neighborhood. She wasn't merely the victim of her own imagination, either. It would be a long time before she would forget the moment she had impulsively placed a hand on Lester's arm and smiled up at him. That moment had been electric, and she had caught a glimpse of Tom and Margot exchanging a prolonged, significant glance.

Kai was already seated at the breakfast table, and was in a strange mood too. She was smiling, although she seemed near tears, and she toyed with her hominy grits, ordinarily her favorite morning dish. "America is an astonishing country, a wonderful country," she said.

Sarah nodded, but didn't know what she meant.

"Anywhere else in the world Amanda would have been captured by a slave dealer and sold into bondage, even though she was born free. And only here could Willie begin a new, independent life for himself after being granted his freedom."

"I suppose you're right," Sarah said.

Kai was fervent. "I know I'm right! Something like this couldn't have happened in my native land. The bey of Algiers would have intervened personally to prevent it." Suddenly it occurred to her that she was saying too much, and she halted in confusion.

In spite of her own problems, Sarah realized this was the right moment to reveal what she had learned. "Before Jeremy went to sea, he told me about . . . you and him."

"I'm glad," Kai said simply. "I wanted you to know." She drew a deep breath. "You bear me no grudge for what happened between us?"

Sarah lowered her voice so no servant loitering in the pantry beyond the dining room could hear her. "How could I? You were a slave and you had no choice."

"I owe everything to Jeremy," Kai replied. "My marriage to M'Bwana, my whole life. If it weren't for Jeremy, I would still be a concubine, living in the harem of one master until he grew tired of me, then being sold to another. And another, until I became old and went to work as a serving woman for another generation of concubines." She saw the horror in Sarah's face, and smiled gently. "You've never seen a harem."

"No, thank God."

"I was born in the harem of a great noble in Algiers, and knew no other life until Jeremy freed me. Forgive me if I say too much, but even though M'Bwana is my son's father, I am secretly happy that Lance has Jeremy's blood in his veins."

Sarah reached out and took her hand. "I couldn't have said this a few days ago, I couldn't even have dreamed of saying it. But so am I."

Suddenly both regained their appetites and began to eat. "You and I are fortunate because we have husbands who love us," Kai said. "But in America even the woman who has no husband is lucky. Even though some do not realize it. That Alicia," she added, "is disgusting."

Sarah was forced to agree.

"In Algiers no lord would keep such a woman in his harem. He would sell her to one of the terrible places where any man may have a woman, provided he pays the right price."

"I don't think Alicia is all that bad." Sarah wondered why she was defending her, especially after the attempt Alicia had made to seduce Jeremy. "Her attitudes are childish, and her only standard is whether she can conquer a man."

"No." Kai was firm. "She cares nothing for anyone but herself, and even her lovely child means nothing to her. I have seen others like her in the harem. You are so good, Sarah, that you recognize evil in no one. But I tell you that Alicia is wicked, and will let no one stand in her path. She hates you, just as she hates me, because we have so much in life that she wants and doesn't have. Beware of her, Sarah."

They were interrupted when Scott Emerson came into the dining room, the dust thick on his boots.

Sarah was embarrassed, and hoped he hadn't overheard them talking about his sister.

"Good morning, ladies," he said. "I hope I'm not disturbing you."

Sarah insisted he join them for coffee.

"I stayed overnight at Trelawney with Tom and Margot," Scott said, "and I'm glad I decided to drop over here early this morning. I saw Willie and Amanda on the road, and I'd have been sorry if I hadn't had the chance to wish them well in their new life. Willie is just about the best friend Tom and I ever had."

"It is astonishing that in America slaves can be the friends of freemen," Kai said.

Scott grinned. "Tom and Willie and I grew up together."

Sarah felt compelled to explain. "The Beaufort and Emerson families," she said, "take an unusual approach to the institution of slavery. There aren't many as enlightened."

"There will be someday," Scott said as he sipped his coffee, and then he changed the subject. "I gather my sister hasn't made an appearance this morning."

"Not yet," Sarah said.

"Well, I'm anxious to see her before I head back to

Charleston, and I'm pleading a case in circuit court this afternoon, so I'll be obliged if you'll send for her."

Sarah immediately sent a servant to Alicia's suite.

A quarter of an hour passed before Alicia came downstairs. She was wearing nothing but a dressing gown of thin
silk, carelessly sashed, her blue-black hair was uncombed, and
the previous evening's makeup was still thick on her face.
Greeting the others with a surly nod, she helped herself to
coffee.

Scott asked if he could confer with her in private, and
Sarah offered him the use of the library. He stalked out, his
sister reluctantly following him.

The fireworks began immediately, and although neither
Sarah nor Kai could make out the words, it was apparent
that Scott was delivering a lecture. Whenever he paused for
breath, Alicia's sultry voice was raised in a defensive whine.

Suddenly Scott's roar echoed through the mansion. "You've
got to mend your ways. You forget that you're an Emerson."

Alicia was shouting too. "What's so special about being an
Emerson?" she demanded, her tone derisive.

"You ought to marry and settle down!"

"There's no man I want as a husband, thank you. I'll get
whatever I want. Without marriage."

Sarah wanted to leave the table, and Kai was embarrassed
too, but both felt it would be wrong to absent themselves
when Scott might emerge at any moment. A feeling of inertia
set in, and it was easier to sit rigidly, avoid looking at each
other, and pretend, even though it was absurd, that they
heard nothing.

Again Scott's voice rang out. "I tell you, Alicia, you're
nothing but a goddamn slut!"

Kai stirred, unable to keep silent any longer. She turned to
Sarah, the wisdom of her upbringing in her eyes, in spite of
her own limited experience with men. "What he says is true,
Sarah," she whispered, "all too true."

A feeling of helpless weariness enveloped Sarah. "I can't
let her drift from bad to worse. I can't send her away . . .
because she has no place to go."

Kingston Town, the capital and principal city of the crown
colony of Jamaica, was the first port of call. Royal Navy offi-

cials arranged for the American squadron's clearance, and after Jeremy made the necessary arrangements for the purchase of fruits, vegetables, and fresh water, he was ready to go ashore.

As he rode across the harbor in his gig, he looked up at the mountains behind the city, their tops hidden by clouds, and for a time he stared at the closer, rolling hills of Liguanea. It was there he had met Lisa and enjoyed his idyll with her, and he would never forget those days. A gentle breeze cooled him; his nostrils were filled with the heavy scent of the tropics, which was compounded of growing things and rotting vegetation, and everything conspired to remind him of Lisa.

Dammit, he was a senior officer in the United States Navy, employed on a mission given him by the president himself. It was high time he stopped mooning like a lovesick schoolboy.

A carriage took him to the home of the rear admiral who commanded the local Royal Navy station, and Jeremy dined with the admiral and his staff. Little was known of the whereabouts of the buccaneers, they told him. The pirates had acquired a fleet of several ships, but accounts of their number differed.

"All we know for certain," the admiral said, "is that they're increasingly bold, Commodore Beaufort. They find an isolated merchantman, steal everything on board, and then sink her, usually with her entire crew on board. There are a few survivors."

"We guess," an aide added, "that they're making their headquarters in the wild interior of Hispaniola."

"It may be a good guess," Jeremy said. "Hispaniola has been the home lair of buccaneers for two hundred years. I believe the earliest pirates in these parts lived on the wild cattle they slaughtered and roasted."

"I'm inclined to believe they're still doing it," the admiral said.

"What do you learn from the governments of Haiti and Santo Domingo?" Haiti, which had declared its independence from France, and Santo Domingo, a Spanish colony, occupied the island of Hispaniola, and were separated by the highest mountains in the West Indies.

"We've learned nothing, Commodore," the admiral said.

"The Haitians are too busy fighting among themselves as they try to set up a viable government, and the Spanish administrators of the colony rarely venture far from Santo Domingo City. There are parts of the interior that no one has ever seen, that have never been explored, and it might take years to locate the pirates there."

"Surely they can't hide their ships, Admiral."

"Unfortunately, they can. There are hundreds of small bays, coves, and inlets, many of them hidden, and we'd have to search every last one to find ships at anchor in one or another." The admiral smiled. "I'm not trying to discourage you, Beaufort. On the contrary, I'm attempting to give you a realistic idea of the odds that you and Dickie Saunders face."

"We'll do our best, sir." It occurred to Jeremy that the admiral's nose was out of joint because he hadn't been given command of the expedition. The Royal Navy officer who brought an end to the buccaneer raids in the Caribbean was certain to win a promotion.

Like many Englishmen on overseas duty, the admiral made no concessions to tropical living, and the dinner consisted of a hearty soup, two kinds of fish, roasted chicken, and a joint of beef served with potatoes and vegetables. Even the dessert was the kind of pudding ordinarily served in winter in England.

Jeremy felt uncomfortably full after the meal, and declining a carriage ride back to the wharf where his gig awaited him, he decided to walk. He started out briskly, but the heat of the tropics was too much for him in his gold-trimmed uniform, so he slowed his pace to a saunter.

He was amused to note, in a community ever conscious of naval ranks, that his presence on Duke Street created quite a stir. The last time he had been here he had been an insignificant junior officer in the Royal Navy. Now his epaulets and the broad gold band on his cuffs called immediate attention to him. Shopkeepers hurried to the doors of their establishments, hoping he would come in, and ordinary citizens moved respectfully out of his path. Even the harlots who infested the streets were too much in awe to address him, afraid he would summon the constabulary and have them sent to jail.

Jeremy slowed his pace as he approached the shop where

he had bought Lisa a gold bracelet with the first pay he had earned as an officer after the nightmare of serving before the mast as an enlisted man. He had to resist the urge to pay the shop another visit.

Suddenly someone crashed into him, almost knocking him off his feet.

A burly man of about forty, hatless and balding, brandished a fist under the American's nose, and the first thing Jeremy noticed was that his clothes were worn and frayed.

"Bloody senior officers think you own the world, don't ye?" he roared. "And you're not even Royal Navy! You're a bloody Yank!"

Jeremy would have known that voice anywhere, even if he needed a moment to recognize the man himself. Boatswain Talbot had been responsible for his abduction from Boston and his impressment in the Royal Navy. Boatswain Talbot's cat-o'-nine-tails had permanently scarred his back when he had been court-martialed and punished. He and Talbot had fought a grim battle with their fists less than a quarter of a mile from this spot, and after getting royally drunk together had become fast friends. Jeremy had not set eyes on the man since being transferred to another ship early in the War of 1812.

"The trouble with boatswains," he said, "is that they never learn to keep civil tongues in their heads."

Talbot stared at him for a moment, then emitted a wild whoop that caused two horseback riders and a lady in a carriage to halt and look at him in amazement. "Jeremy! My God, it's really you! Steal that uniform, did you?"

"How are you, Harry?" Jeremy pumped his hand.

Talbot's pleasure quickly evaporated. "I been better, I been worse."

On close inspection his clothes were even more disreputable than Jeremy had at first realized. "If you have nothing better to do, come out to my flagship for a chat. I believe I can produce a decanter of the brandywine I recall you liked."

"We'll talk, all right, but there'll be no brandywine for me. Liquor was my undoing." Talbot fell in beside him. "The last I heard, ye went down in the Atlantic when all hands on your bomb ketch was drowned. I should have known ye had as many lives as a cat."

Jeremy quickly brought him up-to-date, but asked no questions of a man who obviously had seen better days.

The crew of the gig stood at attention when Jeremy approached the boat, and he and Talbot were rowed across the harbor in silence. Then a boatswain's mate piped Jeremy aboard his flagship, and his personal pennant was immediately hoisted to the *Elizabeth*'s yardarm.

Talbot was impressed in spite of himself. "Just think," he said. "If it wasn't for me kidnapping you all them years ago, you wouldn't be his high-and-mighty magnificence today."

The man was still a rogue, Jeremy thought, and couldn't help laughing aloud as he conducted the visitor to his spacious cabin. "You're sure you won't have a drink, Harry?"

"As sure as ever I've been of anything in this world. But if your cook has a bite to spare, I might find the appetite to eat it."

At Jeremy's direction a yeoman brought the visitor a plate heaped with cold meats and another with fruit just taken on board.

Conversation was suspended while Talbot wolfed down the food. Then he sat back in his chair, wiped his mouth on his worn sleeve, and belched in satisfaction. "You Yanks eat better than we ever did in our navy," he said.

"What are you doing in Jamaica?"

"Making a bloody fool of myself, that's what!" Talbot retorted. "I wasn't satisfied with my pension and a cottage in Cornwall when I was mustered out at the end of the war. Oh, no, not me! I worked my passage to Jamaica, and what with gaming, liquor, and women, I've spent every last farthing of my year's pension."

"How do you live?"

"I beg for pennies," Talbot said candidly, "mostly from Royal Navy folk who are ashamed to see one of their own on the streets. When I don't get enough, I go into the countryside and steal bananas, coconuts, and such."

Jeremy felt sorry for him, although he wanted no pity. "Can't you reenlist?"

"The lords of the Admiralty wind themselves in so much red tape it would sink a man-o'-war," the former boatswain said, his voice becoming bitter. "Seeing as I'm a Royal Navy pensioner, they won't have me back, even if I give up my pension, which I've offered. As for merchantmen, the brigs that come to Kingston already have their crews and do no local hiring."

His predicament was obvious.

He grinned, showing a missing front tooth. "My next pension payment is due in about eight months, and if I don't starve before then, I'll use every last ha'penny to get me back to England, where I can find a berth on some sort of ship, even if she be one of the tubs that sails back and forth across the Channel."

As always, Jeremy thought, Talbot was not lacking in courage.

"What brings the Yank commodore to these warm waters?"

Jeremy explained his mission.

The former boatswain's eyes gleamed.

"We intend to operate with a British squadron headed by Lord Saunders."

Talbot slapped his leg. "Dickie Saunders was the best captain I ever had. He should be a great admiral. Damn, old friend, maybe you could persuade him to cut through London's red tape for me and give me work I know how to do."

"I may be able to do even better than that." Jeremy's mind was racing. "My crews are first-rate seamen, and my veterans are expert gunners. Perhaps the best in the world."

"We found that to be true in the war. It surprised me, it did, that Yanks could shoot so well."

"Well, Harry, some of my younger sailors, those who have gone to sea for the first time since the war, lack one element. They've never known proper naval discipline. I've been wondering how I can best handle the problem, and now I see a solution, particularly as President Monroe has authorized me to take on anyone I believe can be of help to us. How would you like to be a chief boatswain in the United States Navy?"

Talbot almost leaped out of his chair. "You're joking, Jeremy!"

"Indeed I'm not. What I have in mind is a roving assignment. You'll serve on each of my ships in turn, and you'll be responsible only to me, my second in command, and my flag lieutenant. When you're stationed on other ships, of course, you'll report to their captains."

Tears of joy appeared in Talbot's eyes. "I'm your man. You won't regret this!"

"I'm sure I won't. How long will it take you to go ashore and pack your gear?"

"Everything I own is on my back, and fit only for the sharks. And that's the truth."

"You'll fill out a form that one of my lieutenants will help you prepare, and we'll find you a set of uniforms. I'll swear you in this afternoon. You're just what I've needed."

Talbot stood, stiffened to attention, and saluted. "Chief Boatswain Talbot reports for duty, sir," he said.

Jeremy returned his salute, then extended his hand. "Welcome aboard, Boatswain. We made a great team in the past, and now we'll do it again."

"May the Lord have mercy on them buccaneers," Talbot said.

The field workers built two new silos at the far end of the plantation for the storage of corn, rye, and other grains grown at Oakhurst Manor. When the work was done, Sarah rode out with Lester Howard to inspect the project, and enjoyed herself thoroughly. She was wearing a new winter dress of red-and-yellow wool, with lace collars and cuffs. Her mirror had told her she looked even prettier than usual, and she was in a gay mood.

Her happiness was contagious. She and the overseer laughed at each other's little jokes, and when she flirted subtly with him, he returned the compliment. She felt as giddy, light-headed, and irresponsible as she had when she had been a pupil at Mistress Allen's Seminary for Young Ladies in Boston, and for a short time she could almost pretend to herself that she had no duties, no husband, and no child.

The whole experience was refreshing, and she felt like dancing when she left Howard at the entrance to his house. Instead, still smiling, she rode at a sedate pace to the mansion.

Someone was standing on the portico, watching her, and Sarah assumed it was Kai. Then she caught a glimpse of her sister's red hair beneath a broad-brimmed hat, and wondered what had brought Margot here on a Wednesday. Ordinarily Sarah had supper at Trelawney with Margot and Tom on

Tuesdays, and the younger Beauforts came to Oakhurst Manor on Fridays.

"I hope you haven't been waiting long," Sarah called as she dismounted.

"No, I just arrived about a half-hour ago," Margot replied. "I've had a chat with Kai, and then I visited with Cleo."

"Did she tell you we've heard from Amanda and Willie?" Sarah asked as they walked into the house and started up the broad staircase together. "They've arrived safely in Boston, and they've been lucky enough to rent a little house right off Beacon Street."

"Yes, Cleo said Willie will have his workshop there, too."

They went to the master-bedroom suite, and as they made themselves comfortable in the sitting room, a housemaid brought them tea.

"I don't suppose you happened to see Alicia?" Sarah asked.

"From a distance, but she didn't see me, and I certainly made no attempt to call myself to her attention."

"Poor Scott is so worried about her. They had a frightful argument here the other morning."

"That's what Scott told us before he left for Charleston," Margot said.

"He can't do anything to persuade her to change her ways, and neither can Lorene. She makes such a fuss over every man she sees that I'm embarrassed whenever we have guests." Sarah sighed as she added lemon to her tea. "I just don't know where Alicia is headed."

Margot, whose habitual expression was buoyant, even impish, looked very solemn. "It's far more important to know where Sarah Benton Beaufort is headed," she said.

Her remark was so unexpected, so out of character, that Sarah gaped at her.

"Tom and I have been thinking and talking about you ever since our party the other evening." Margot was distressed, but it was plain she intended to speak her mind. "Tom told me to stay out of your business and keep my mouth shut, and when I left Trelawney to come over here, I wasn't quite sure what I'd do, even though you and I have always been honest with each other, as Papa taught us to be. Then, when I was waiting for you just now, I saw you with Lester Howard again, and I simply can't keep silent any longer."

Color drained from Sarah's face, and she stiffened.

"Everyone at the party the other evening saw the way you were carrying on with him. No, that's too strong. I make you sound like Alicia, but you're not that bad. Not yet."

Sarah found it difficult to speak. "What did I do that was so . . . objectionable?"

"Your conduct wasn't objectionable, dear. It was painful. You and Lester spent the entire evening together, and I don't believe you addressed ten remarks to other people. You constantly had your heads together, whispering and giggling. Everyone noticed it, and I'm dead certain everyone in the neighborhood is talking."

"If you paid that much attention," Sarah replied defensively, "then you know Lester and I never touched, not once. So what could people say?"

Margot grimaced. "That you looked like a young girl. In love for the first time in her life. And the way he was mooning over you was just as adolescent."

Sarah didn't know what to reply. It would be such a feeble explanation to say that some strong, mysterious force kept drawing her and Lester toward each other. That a feeling of warmth and happiness flooded her when she was in his presence. That she felt at peace with him.

"You were making an exhibition of yourself again, just now, when you were riding with him. Your indiscretion and lack of self-control astonish me, Sarah."

"You exaggerate, Margot." Sarah's indignation was feeble.

Her younger sister shook herself. "Fool yourself, if you wish, and try to fool other people. But you can't fool me. You remind me of the way you looked and acted when you and Jeremy first started to see each other regularly."

Sarah gasped, and a hand flew to her mouth.

"Tell me to shut up, but there's a question I'm going to ask you." Margot took a deep breath, then plunged ahead. "Are you having an affair with Lester Howard?"

"Certainly not!" Sarah refrained from adding that she dreamed of Lester and sometimes imagined they were making love.

"Do you intend to have an affair with him?" her sister persisted.

"I do not!"

"Then I don't understand the game you're playing. Sarah, you're not just another wife and mother. You're a symbol. You're the mistress of Oakhurst Manor, so you've got to be more pure, more careful than most."

"I've done nothing I'm ashamed of," Sarah said.

Margot shook her head in wonder. "I'm surprised you didn't see some of the good ladies exchanging looks at Trelawney the other evening. Their eyebrows were shooting up to the tops of their foreheads."

"I have no control over what people may think or say!"

"But you do have control of your own conduct. Jeremy would—"

"Leave Jeremy out of this, if you please," Sarah said. "I love him. As much as I've ever loved him. As much as he loves me, which I know he does."

"You'll have to forgive me for seeming to pry, which I'm not doing. But Tom and I have been wondering whether . . . well, whether you've chosen your association with Lester Howard, whatever it may be, as a way of evening the score with Jeremy."

Surely Margot and Tom didn't know about Lisa Saunders! Sarah became cool. "I hope you'll be good enough to explain."

Margot was red-faced. "Because of . . . Kai's baby."

It was odd to feel relieved. "I know all there is to be known on that subject," Sarah said. "From Jeremy, and from Kai, too. It's a matter I don't intend to discuss with anyone, not even you or Lorene. Now or ever. I'll just say this much. I'm not upset in any way over Kai's son, and I have no reason to be upset."

"Very well," Margot said with a shrug. "That takes us right back to the beginning of the maze."

"Don't speak in riddles."

"Lester Howard. I realize he's a good-looking, charming, hard-working man, and that he'll make a good husband to the woman fortunate enough to marry him. That doesn't in any way make it appropriate for the mistress of Oakhurst Manor to carry on such a blatant flirtation with him that she becomes the number-one subject of gossip in all of South Carolina!"

Sarah clenched her fists. "I've never been concerned about gossip, and neither has Jeremy."

"I know you don't want my advice," Margot said, "but I'm going to give it to you anyway. Dismiss Lester Howard and hire another overseer for Oakhurst Manor."

"I can't believe you're serious!"

"I mean it. Get rid of him," Margot said earnestly. "Perhaps you're just amusing yourself while Jeremy is off at sea, and perhaps Lester is just passing the time, too. You're an exceptionally attractive woman, Sarah. As Tom says, every man who sees you immediately thinks how much he'd like to take you to bed."

Sarah felt her face grow hot.

"What's more, Lester is a dynamic man. And he has a sensual quality that every woman recognizes. I'm aware of it myself. Spend too much time with him, smiling at him, whispering and giggling, and you're asking for trouble. Both of you."

"Are you implying we'll drift into an affair in spite of our intentions and sense of honor?"

"You wouldn't be the first," Margot said. "I'm begging you to be practical. We don't live here as we did in Boston, where thousands of people are strangers. Go anywhere in South Carolina—Charleston or Greenville or wherever—and every person who sees you knows you're Sarah Benton Beaufort, the wife of the great Jeremy Beaufort and the mistress of the most successful plantation in the state. Not only do you live under a magnifying glass, so that every move you make is exaggerated and distorted, but the moment you make a mistake, it becomes common knowledge."

"I don't see why Lester should be made to suffer because the Beauforts are well-known."

"Because you and Lester aren't invisible." Margot was losing patience.

"Point number one," Sarah said, enumerating on her fingers, "Lester Howard was hired by Jeremy, who had complete confidence in him, as I have, and it would be inappropriate for anyone other than Jeremy to dismiss him."

"Now you're rationalizing."

"Point number two," Sarah continued, ignoring the remark, "Lester is a wonderful overseer, the best in the business. He's done marvelous things here, and Jeremy is so pleased that, before he sailed, he arranged to give Lester a share of the profits. I'd be mad to discharge him. Oakhurst Manor would suffer."

"His reputation as an overseer is splendid. I'm sure he'd be deluged with offers of new positions if he left Oakhurst Manor."

"Oh, indeed, and I have no doubt that you and Tom would love to have him at Trelawney, but you're not going to get him. Nor is anyone else. Lester Howard is going to stay right here, for the rest of our natural lives, I hope—and that's final!"

# Chapter 6

Barbados, easternmost of all the West Indian islands, was unique. Its hills were low and undulating, and even its highest "mountain" stood only 1,100 feet above sea level. Discovered and settled by British explorers early in the seventeenth century, it had never been occupied by any other power. The newcomers soon discovered that climate and soil were perfect for the growing of sugarcane, and by the middle of the century the island had become "one vast plantation," as Lord Saunders sometimes told visitors.

But large tracts of jungle had not been cleared away, and the island boasted more flowers of various kinds than any of the other islands. "What's more," Lisa, Lady Saunders, sometimes remarked, "their scents are delicious. Elsewhere in the Caribbean most flowers have no odor, but every one of them here has a lovely smell."

Bridgetown, the capital, which was located on the broad sweep of Carlisle Bay, was one of the busiest ports in the New World, and certainly one of the most attractive. Many of its principal buildings, among them St. Michael's Cathedral, Government House, and the colonial offices on Trafalgar Square, were solid edifices of coral rock. Even a number of the shops on Broad Street were fashioned of coral rock.

Coral played a major role in the life of Barbados. Much of the island was surrounded by reefs, some of them extending as far as two and a half miles to sea, and this natural protection long had discouraged invaders. Incoming ships had to thread their way carefully, and Commodore Jeremy Beaufort was in command of his flagship himself, with Chief Boatswain Talbot close beside him. The *Marilyn* and the *Jane* followed the *Elizabeth*, and the *Louise* brought up the rear.

American flags were flying from all four vessels, and when they were sighted from the fort, the highest point of land in Bridgetown, cannon boomed a welcome. Jeremy was pleased when he was greeted by an eleven-gun salute, which befitted his rank, the first time he had been given that honor.

A Royal Navy pilot boat guided the American ships to their anchorage, and while they were dropping anchor Boatswain Talbot addressed his superior. "Admiral's barge approaching, sir!"

"Have him piped aboard with due ceremony, Boatswain, if you please."

Twenty white-gloved sailors carrying muskets presented arms, and the pipes of a boatswain's mate played shrilly as Rear Admiral Lord Saunders climbed the ladder to the main deck, followed by his aides.

The solemnity of the moment was interrupted when the admiral recognized Talbot, and paused to shake the hand of his old shipmate.

M'Bwana, acting in his capacity as flag lieutenant, escorted the British commander to the quarterdeck, where Jeremy and his staff were waiting; salutes were exchanged, and the junior officers were presented to the admiral.

Jeremy and Lord Saunders adjourned to the former's cabin, where they awaited the other American captains, who were being rowed to the *Elizabeth* in their gigs, and the friends had a chance for a private conversation.

"I have you to thank for this assignment, Dickie," Jeremy said, "and I'm grateful to you."

"You may change your mind after we've played hide and seek with the buccaneers. I have five sloops searching West Indian waters for them, and I'm hoping we'll soon receive a report on their whereabouts. I must say, old chap, I envy you Talbot. I wish I had him on board the *Porpoise,* I can tell you."

Jeremy grinned, but refrained from saying that the British loss of the boatswain was his and America's gain. "What's our schedule?"

"We'll start fitting your ships with cannon at once, which is why I've had you anchored as close to shore as you could sail."

"How long do you reckon it'll take to arm us?"

"Three days, with luck, and another to bring your munitions on board."

"Fair enough. Captain Slocum has the full list of provisions, water, and the like that we'll need, and will give the details to your chief of staff."

"We'll attend to such matters at the joint meeting I've called at the fort in an hour. Bring all of your officers."

"I will, thank you."

"And while you're here, Jeremy, we want you to stay with us, of course."

Jeremy had known the invitation would be extended, and had dreaded this moment. It would be torture to spend several days, perhaps even longer, under Lisa's roof. "I don't want to impose on you—"

"Nonsense!" Saunders was hearty, tolerating no dissent. "I'd be insulted if you went elsewhere, and so would Lisa. Matter of fact, we're giving a dinner party in your honor this afternoon. We'll expect your captains, of course, and that remarkable M'Bwana. Lisa has been arranging this party for days," he added with a chuckle, "and you've never seen such an eye for detail. She's even invited some unmarried ladies as partners for the bachelors."

There was no escape, Jeremy knew, and he would have to submit to the torment.

His captains arrived and were presented to the admiral, token toasts were exchanged, and the entire party went ashore, with Jeremy accompanying Lord Saunders in his barge. Soon the officers of all the American ships followed.

A far larger group of British officers awaited them at the fort, and the meeting was convened in the mess hall, the only chamber large enough to hold so many. The seconds in command discussed the provisioning of the ships and the schedule for arming the American vessels, and the flag lieutenants made out the personnel assignments for the tasks. No time was being wasted, and the operations would begin in two hours.

Then Lord Saunders called the meeting to order. "We'll have no long speeches today, and no flag-waving," he said. "It's enough that this joint venture is unique in the history of our two countries. Come to know each other, gentlemen. You're going to dine together in the days ahead, and I want you to spend as much time together as you can. Commodore Beaufort, would you care to add a few words?"

"Thank you, sir," Jeremy said. "Gentlemen, our countries have been fighting each other, on and off, for the past forty years and more. But we're engaged in a common cause now, so be good enough to remember we're fighting on the same side. Make it your first order of business to get along with each other. Our own lives and the future of our joint merchant shipping in the West Indies depend on our ability to work together in harmony."

He and the admiral left the podium, and the officers of both nations stood at attention until they went through the door. Never had members of either navy attended such a short meeting, and it was apparent that both commanders preferred action to words.

Lord Saunders insisted that Jeremy accompany him on an inspection tour of his flagship, *HMS Porpoise*. They were piped aboard with due ceremony, crew members standing at rigid attention, and Jeremy was reminded of his own years in the Royal Navy. He had traveled far and risen high since that time, yet he felt much the same in many ways. He was still ambitious, still eager to achieve, even though he had already accomplished a great deal, and he was still young enough and vigorous enough to enjoy life to the full.

The contrast between the American and British navies was sharp. Discipline was tighter on board the *Porpoise* than on his own ships, although the addition of Chief Boatswain Talbot to his staff was already bearing fruit. What he realized, more clearly than ever, was the difference in attitudes: American sailors were taken into their officers' confidence and were told the reasons a campaign was being waged, while British seamen were expected to obey orders blindly. It didn't matter whether they knew why they were being told to risk their lives.

The Royal Navy, to be sure, was still the most powerful on earth, its many fleets providing the cement that held the great British Empire together. But the United States was growing stronger, and Jeremy could envisage the day when the American navy would achieve supremacy, in part because of the enlightened attitudes that reflected the great experiment in self-government that his nation was conducting.

When they went ashore again, they tarried long enough to watch the first of the cannon that would arm the *Elizabeth* being loaded onto barges. Some were twelve-pounders, powerful enough to smash gaping holes in the hull of a freebooter; others were the all-purpose nine-pounders that American gunners had learned to use with such deadly accuracy in the War of 1812 and the campaign against the pirate states of North Africa that had followed it. A few were six-pounders, useless at long range but highly effective when a warship fought an enemy at close quarters prior to launching a boarding operation. In all, the American squadron would be well able to look after itself.

Saddled horses and an escort of green-clad Royal marines were waiting, and the meeting Jeremy dreaded could not be postponed any longer. "We live in the section still known as Indian Bridge," Lord Saunders said as they rode through the town, then took a road that followed the seashore. "It wasn't so long ago that the whole city was known by that name."

There were fewer coral reefs here, so the waves that swept in toward the shore were stronger, and hills rose abruptly behind high dunes dotted with sea grass that acted as a binding. There was no protection from the sun on the road, but the breeze that swept in from the Caribbean kept the area cool.

"A number of plantation owners live in the neighborhood, and so do the proprietors of the local rum factories," Lord Saunders said. "Until the war ended, there were few aristocrats here, but in recent years a number of wealthy nobles have built winter homes for themselves. Lisa and I find the pace of their social life a trifle too hectic for our taste, but I must say that Barbados is becoming a little London."

The predominant odor on the ride along the coast had

been the tang of salt air. Now, however, the scent of flowers crept in and soon became almost overpowering. Every estate was surrounded by hedges and bushes ablaze with color, and even Jeremy, accustomed to Sarah's gardens at Oakhurst Manor, was impressed.

At last they came to a property completely hidden by poinsettia bushes that rose twelve feet high; and bushes laden with other flowers in shades of pink, yellow, and purple bordered the driveway. The house itself, set high on a cliff overlooking the sea, was fashioned of Georgian brick, its only concession to the tropics being the wide jalousies that substituted for glass windows in several of the chambers.

The Royal Navy long had been the paramount influence in Viscount Saunders' life, but its atmosphere was missing in his home. A groom in a white linen jacket and black trousers took the horses, and a serving maid in a long, flounced dress, her hair tied in a West Indian kerchief, greeted her master and the guest. Another servant in civilian attire attended to the visitor's luggage.

Lisa, who was already dressed for the dinner party, stood in the dining room, where she was conferring with her butler and cook, a long list in one hand. Her copper hair fell loosely over her shoulders, she had made up with her usual, scrupulous care, emphasizing her liquid, green eyes, and her silk gown of pale yellow ignored the new styles. As always, she chose to emphasize the contours of her perfect figure.

Just the sight of her caused Jeremy to break out in a cold sweat. It was beyond credence how much he wanted this woman who was the wife of his mentor, colleague, and friend, even though she herself had made it plain to him that he had to put her out of his mind and heart for the sake of the wife he truly loved.

He felt certain she could read the desire in his eyes as he bent over her hand. "Your servant, ma'am."

But Lisa was cool, pleasantly polite, as she would be to any guest under her roof, yet remote. "Your servant, sir," she said as she curtsied, then turned to her husband. "We're putting Commodore Beaufort in the blue suite. Will you have his luggage taken there, my dear?"

"I've already attended to it," the admiral said, and chuckled. "My good wife is always absentminded on the day she gives a party. I make it my business to stay out of her way, and I advise you to do the same. In my humble opinion, you and I need a stiff drink."

Lisa was already reabsorbed in her discussion with the members of the household staff.

Jeremy felt rebuffed yet strangely relieved as he accompanied his host to an expanse of beautifully groomed lawn behind the house. There were similarities between West Indian living and the style he knew so well at Oakhurst Manor. In a huge pit at the far side of the lawn a quarter of beef was being roasted on one spit, hogs were crackling on another, and a cook in a white dress and kerchief was stirring a brew in a huge kettle.

A butler stood behind a table on which several large cut-glass bowls were resting, and without prompting he handed the admiral and the American officer cut-glass cups that he filled with the darkest of the concoctions.

"To you, sir, and to our victory," Jeremy said.

Lord Saunders raised his cup in return. "To the same."

Almost choking on his first swallow, Jeremy knew he had never tasted such a strong rum punch.

Dickie Saunders grinned at his discomfort. "I felt as you do when I first settled here, but this Barbadian rum is habit-forming."

Soon the guests began to arrive, among the first being the ever-prompt American and British captains and flag lieutenants, who were followed by large numbers of local residents, most of them English. A number of prominent Barbadians came too, and Jeremy thought their presence curious. Slavery still existed on the island, although there was serious talk of its abolition, yet well-to-do natives of color were accepted as equals by the British.

Lisa kept her distance from Jeremy, greeting the new arrivals at the far end of the garden. It was impossible for him to determine whether she was avoiding him by accident or design, but he suspected it was the latter.

The last to arrive were Lord and Lady Muirhead, the governor-general of the colony and his wife. Officers stood at attention and saluted the personal representative of the crown, civilian gentlemen bowed low, and ladies lowered themselves to the ground as they curtsied. There could be no doubt that this was indeed an outpost of the British Empire.

It proved to be true that Lisa had invited a number of single women to act as the partners of the officers who had come alone. Jeremy, taking care not to drink too much of the potent rum punch, found himself in conversation with a pretty blond whose hair reminded him of Sarah's. She was a widow named Angela St. Clair, the daughter of a baronet who had come to Barbados to marry a planter, and when he had died two years later, she had elected to remain on the island.

She was pleasant company, and it was easy to converse with her, but she was as vapid as she was pretty, and Jeremy soon became a trifle bored. Out of the corner of his eye he kept track of Lisa's whereabouts, and was surprised when she swooped down on him and his companion, with Ned Slocum in tow.

"Mistress St. Clair," she said, "I discover that Captain Slocum is a freshwater fishing enthusiast, and I've told him you own the only stocked pond on the island. Do tell him about your fish."

Without further ado she placed her hand on Jeremy's arm and whisked him away, waiting until they were out of earshot near a bush bursting with flowers before she said, "You're being rude to me."

He was too astonished to say more than, "I am?"

"If you choose to ignore me, that's your privilege, of course, although you're showing precious little respect for your hostess. What I do resent is the way you're falling all over Angela St. Clair. I would think that a man in your position would know better than to melt so openly when she flutters her silly lashes at you!"

Jeremy stared at her for another moment, then laughed aloud.

Lisa's green eyes flashed, and he thought she intended to slap him across the face.

"If you please," he said hastily, "I'd like to set the record straight. You're the one who has done the avoiding, not I. You've taken care to station yourself at the greatest distance from me that you've been able to achieve. And since nothing between us is changed . . ."

"It isn't?" she breathed.

He was uncertain whether she voiced it as a statement or a question. "It isn't," he repeated firmly. "Therefore I've congratulated you on your wisdom. As for the widow St. Clair, the world is filled with such pretty, innocuous women, and I'll thank you not to trouble me with such people again."

It was Lisa's turn to laugh, and her voice sounded like the tinkling of tiny silver bells. "I could kiss you for that," she said.

"If you do, you'll regret it. And so will I. Because we'll make confounded spectacles of ourselves."

Lisa sobered and met his candid gaze. "I'm sorry, Jeremy. I behaved stupidly just now. It was ridiculous of me to become jealous of poor Angela."

He had no desire for small talk, and cut to the heart of the matter. "I would have preferred to stay elsewhere while I'm here," he said, "but Dickie wouldn't hear of it."

"Neither would I," she replied. "In the first place, you're his friend. What's more, the time has come for you and me to become friends too."

"I'm not sure that's possible."

"Neither am I, to be honest with you," Lisa said, and for a fleeting moment there was pain in her eyes. "But we must try. For Dickie's sake, for your sake, and for mine. And for the sake of Sarah, who isn't here to protect her own interests."

Jeremy wanted her desperately, and he knew that in spite of her words she wanted him just as badly. "I'll do my best," he said, "but if it becomes too much for me, I'll find some excuse to return to my flagship. I've hoped we could stop acting like lovesick adolescents and become adults, but the instant I saw you, I turned to jelly."

Lisa looked at him hard, and as she did, her eyes became opaque, her face masklike. Then she turned abruptly, suddenly, and went off to make certain the governor-general had enough punch.

Jeremy decided he needed another cup himself, and went back to the table where it was being served. There Angela St. Clair scooped him up again, and he reconciled himself to the fact that he would not be rid of her until they went into the house for dinner.

But Lisa was too clever to serve a formal meal, knowing

that protocol would require her to place Lord Muirhead on her right and Jeremy on her left. She had no intention of subjecting herself to the torture of such prolonged proximity to the American, so servants appeared carrying many small tables and chairs.

Before Jeremy quite realized what was happening, he and Angela were seated with Lord and Lady Muirhead, the latter a silent woman who ate and drank steadily. If the widow St. Clair was dull, the governor-general was a crashing bore. His great passion in life was salmon fishing in Scotland, which he discussed in detail. He had been a member of the Duke of Wellington's staff during the peninsular campaign in Iberia, and Jeremy, who cared nothing about land warfare, had to follow him from Lisbon to Madrid. Then, it developed, he had commanded a division at the Battle of Waterloo, which he described at great length.

At least it wasn't necessary to talk much, and Jeremy merely nodded, smiled, and asked an occasional question. And the meal was delicious, making it apparent that Lisa had not lost her knack as a hostess. The first dish was a cold crayfish, prepared with a West Indian hot sauce that included spices, herbs, and pickled fruits. Next came a favorite in all the islands, a pumpkin soup made with a beef stock and thick with vegetables. It was followed by a flaky white fish that had been baked in clay, and then came mounds of beef and roasted pork, each served with fresh, locally grown vegetables, among them a kind of cauliflower that tasted like cucumber, and tiny, succulent green beans.

A sherbert cleared the palates, and Jeremy was stunned when the dessert proved to be star apples, a delicious purple-colored fruit that grew only in Jamaica. He and Lisa had eaten it before going to bed together for the first time, and he knew she had had an order sent from Kingston Town strictly for his sake.

He looked at her, sitting several small tables away, and for an instant their eyes met. She realized he had received her subtle message, and that was enough for her, so she glanced away again. No one seeing them would have recognized the significance of that swift exchange.

A variety of wines had been served, and the meal ended with a selection of cheeses, eaten with the hard, flaky-crusted bread that was a Barbadian specialty. Then champagne was poured.

Jeremy was mindful of his obligations and offered a toast to the king.

Lord Muirhead responded with a toast to the president of the United States.

Thereafter glasses were raised to the expedition's commanders, their captains, their officers, and their crews. The formalities ended, and a string quartet appeared and played selections from *The Beggar's Opera* and other musical plays.

Night had fallen, and the Caribbean sky was filled with stars. The air was balmy and the atmosphere romantic, but Jeremy kept his distance from Lisa, and she took care to avoid him too. It was obvious to both of them that they could take no chances if they hoped to remain true to their respective trusts.

Lord and Lady Muirhead were the first to leave, protocol dictating that no one else could go until the governor-general and his wife departed. Thereafter the exodus was general, and while the household staff began to clean up in the garden, Lord Saunders took Jeremy to a little pavilion on the grounds, overlooking the sea, for a final glass of brandywine.

There Lisa found them. "Parties exhaust me, I'm afraid, so I'm going to bed." She still looked ravishing.

"I'll be along shortly," her husband told her.

Jeremy swallowed hard. "Good night, Lisa," he said.

She smiled at him, and as though acting on impulse, kissed him lightly on the cheek while her husband beamed. "Good night, Jeremy. I hope you'll be comfortable here."

The place on his face that her lips had touched seemed to be burning, and his whole body was aflame. Lisa had given in to a small temptation, innocent enough in itself, but it left him craving more and yet more, and he was shaken.

It was hard for him to concentrate, but Dickie Saunders was just making small talk, and a quarter of an hour later they strolled back to the house.

The jalousies in Jeremy's bedchamber were closed, but ribbons of moonlight seeped in through the cracks, and in spite of the long day he was alert, wide-awake, as though his head had been plunged in ice water. He poured himself another small glass of brandywine from a decanter, lighted a *cigarro*, and lowered himself into an easy chair.

It was almost impossible for him to cope with the complexities of life, he decided. Certainly he loved Sarah; there was no doubt of that in his mind, and in no way could he find fault with her as a wife, mistress, or companion. Why, then, was he overwhelmed by a desire for Lisa? If all he felt for her was a sex urge, he could understand it, but far more was at stake. He realized that she, like Sarah, was a woman with whom he could find contentment for the rest of his days. His feelings defied reason, and all he really knew was that he had to keep them under control until he left Barbados. Once he went to sea again and left Lisa behind him, it would be infinitely easier to deal with his incomprehensible yearnings.

Sleep still would not come, so he opened his jalousies and looked down the cliff at the beach, where a coral breakwater formed a small, placid lagoon. Perhaps a vigorous swim would tire him and enable him to obtain a few hours of rest. He stripped, donned a dressing gown, and silently walking down the corridors in bare feet, left the house and climbed down the side of the dune to the water.

The sea was cool but not too chilly, and Jeremy swam for at least a half-hour, making his way out to the breakwater and back, until his muscles told him he was tiring. In his haste he had forgotten to bring a towel with him, so he let the cool night breeze dry him. Then, as he reached for the dressing gown he had dropped on the sand, he happened to glance down the beach.

At the far end, walking toward the water, was an unclad woman, every line of her superb figure clearly outlined in the moonlight. He would have recognized Lisa instantly, even if he hadn't known that she too had a penchant for swimming in the nude.

It was impossible for him to determine or even guess whether she had seen him too, and was resolutely ignoring his presence.

All he knew was that if he went to her now, they would make love. No exercise of mutual self-control, no power on earth would be strong enough to prevent them from coming together.

Jeremy gave himself no chance to ponder or weigh the

consequences. He pulled on his robe, climbed the dune, and hurried toward the house, sprinting as he crossed the lawn. It was irrelevant that Lisa obviously had felt as he had, and had gone for a swim because she hadn't been able to sleep. He would be taking unfair advantage of her if he joined her, and he couldn't—wouldn't—permit himself to do it.

When he finally reached his suite, he discovered that he was trembling uncontrollably.

The next two days were among the busiest Jeremy had known in a long time. He and Dickie Saunders left the estate in Indian Bridge early both mornings and did not return until after sundown. Crews of laborers, aided by American and British seamen, carried the cannon to the ships of the American squadron, where they were hauled on board, carried on squat contraptions with wheels to their permanent locations, and then emplaced. Jeremy's gig carried him back and forth incessantly from the fort to his vessels.

Chief Boatswain Talbot was worth every penny of his pay. He thundered and roared, cursed and cajoled, and the work crews responded to him, doubling and redoubling their efforts. Even so, the work did not proceed on schedule. A heavy twelve-pounder cannon fell overboard from a barge, and a dozen men spent the better part of a day retrieving it from the waters of the harbor and carrying it to the *Elizabeth*. A British sailor caught his hand between a nine-pounder and the deck of the *Louise*, and had to be rushed to the hospital.

As Jeremy and Dickie Saunders rode back to the estate at the end of their second full day, they discussed the progress to date in detail, and agreed that, even with crews working around the clock, it would be another two and a half days before the ships of the American squadron would be fully armed and ready to go to sea.

Lisa awaited her husband and their guest in the pavilion, a stone structure with a floor and a roof supported by four columns, which was open on all sides. She had prepared a bowl of the dark, potent rum punch for them herself, and was dressed in a gauzelike gown that made no secret of her physical charms.

Jeremy wished she would dress less seductively, but realized her style was her own.

They had scarcely tasted their punch when a Royal Navy lieutenant who wasted no time on the formality of having himself announced raced across the lawn to the pavilion, skidded to a halt, and saluted.

"Captain Markham's compliments, sir," he said, badly out of breath. "The *Gull* has just put into port. We and the *Albatross* sighted four ships of the buccaneer fleet only eighteen hours ago, and Captain Markham is convinced they're on their way to a rendezvous with the rest of their fleet."

Jeremy and Lord Saunders jumped to their feet.

"Where is the *Albatross*?" the admiral demanded.

"Keeping the enemy under surveillance, milord. The enemy could annihilate a single sloop of war, of course, so her captain is keeping a healthy distance between his ship and the enemy."

"In what direction were they sailing when you last sighted them?" Jeremy asked.

"Northwest by west, sir."

Jeremy and Saunders exchanged glances. It was no secret that a large convoy of merchant ships was sailing from island to island in the West Indies, taking on cargo for delivery to American and British ports. So it seemed likely that the pirates were assembling their entire strength and intended to attack the helpless brigs in full force.

"The commander of the fort has requested me to notify you, milord, that the alert has been given," the lieutenant said. "All officers and crews are being assembled."

"Good," Saunders said. "We can sail on the evening tide. My sea chest is already on board the *Porpoise*, so I'll ride into town with you, Lieutenant, as soon as I pick up a few personal belongings to take with me."

Jeremy groaned. "We've got to sail with you, even though our armaments aren't settled yet."

"You can't," the admiral said firmly, "and you damned well know it."

Jeremy felt frustrated. "You're right, unfortunately. There's no point in going into battle unless I'm ready to fight it."

Saunders understood how he felt. "I'll send the *Gull* or the *Albatross* back with information. Let's see. This is Wednesday evening, and you should be ready to sail on the late tide Friday morning. So I promise you that a sloop will be on hand by then to bring you up-to-date and tell you where to locate me, so we can join forces."

Jeremy thanked him, knowing this was the best that could be managed under the circumstances, and then, not daring to glance at Lisa, felt a wave of apprehension. "I think it might be best if I ride into town with you and move into my quarters on my flagship."

"Rubbish," Dickie Saunders said. "There's literally nothing you can do to speed the work that's already being done. It's enough that you're spending your days in the harbor. I absolutely insist that you stay here until you're ready to sail, and so does my wife."

"Of course," Lisa said, her face and tone devoid of all expression.

Jeremy had no real choice without convincing an old friend that he was being deliberately rude, so he was trapped.

Saunders shook hands with him. "The next time we meet," he said, "we'll go hunting together for freebooters. I truly don't think your delay will spoil any of the fun for you. The buccaneers are sure to play hide and seek for some days."

He headed toward the house, with Lisa accompanying him. The lieutenant tagged along behind, and Jeremy was alone in the pavilion.

He paced up and down, angry because circumstances made it impossible for him to go to sea immediately, and deeply disturbed because only he and Lisa would remain in the house for the next two nights. He drained his cup and helped himself to more punch, even though he knew it was essential to keep his faculties under tight control.

After a time he saw Dickie Saunders and the Royal Navy lieutenant galloping off down the road toward Bridgetown. This, he told himself fiercely, is the home of a friend who trusts me, and no matter how much I want his wife, I cannot dishonor our friendship.

It seemed like an eternity before Lisa returned. "We'll be called to supper in a few minutes," she said.

As he nodded, he couldn't help wishing she had changed into a gown less revealing, something that made her movements seem less provocative.

She rarely drank hard liquor, but now she poured herself a glass of punch and downed it in a few swift gulps. "You and I," she said, her voice husky, "seem destined to be thrown together."

"So it seems."

"I watched your face when that young officer was telling you and Dickie the news. You were terribly disappointed because you'll have to wait two more days before you go off to fight the buccaneers. That's the way of a man, I guess, although I wouldn't know about such matters. Then, gradually, something else dawned on you, something that occurred to me instantly, and from that moment to this you've been fighting it."

"I'll continue to fight," Jeremy said, tight-lipped.

"So shall I," Lisa replied, "and at this moment I don't know if we'll win or lose. At least we'll be doing it together." Her smile was strained as she put her hand on his arm. "Shall we go to supper?"

As they walked slowly to the house, he realized that this was the first time they had been alone with each other since they had been lovers in the Liguanea Hills of Jamaica. "I reckon we're being tested, although I can't imagine why."

Lisa's eyes were old and pained. "A very long time ago," she said, "I stopped questioning fate. I learned to spend each day as best I can, snatching what little happiness is available and trying hard not to hurt anyone else. Happiness is almost always bought at someone else's expense, and that's something I don't pretend to understand."

They sat at opposite ends of the long dining-room table, and had circumstances been different, the lapping of waves at the base of the cliff, the flickering candlelight indoors, and the glow of the moon on the lawn might have been romantic. Both were miserable, and neither ate more than token quantities of the splendid five-course dinner the staff had prepared.

Jeremy discovered he was drinking more wine than was his custom, and Lisa repeatedly allowed the butler to refill her glass too. Their conversation was unnatural, and not until they were ready to leave the table did it take a different turn.

"I'd like to have coffee and liqueur in the pavilion," Lisa said. "Will you join me?"

"Do you think that's wise?" Jeremy countered.

She laughed without humor. "Dickie promised to send up a pair of red and green flares as a signal to me when he sails, and I want to be outdoors where I can see them."

"In that case," Jeremy said, "I'll be pleased to accompany you."

They seated themselves at opposite ends of the pavilion, and one of the servants brought them large cups of black coffee, which they laced with liberal quantities of rum. Jeremy lighted a *cigarro*, then unconsciously held it in front of him as though it were a sword with which to defend himself.

Lisa recognized the gesture and was amused by it, but made no comment. "May I have a *cigarro* too?" she asked at last.

"Certainly, and forgive me. I'd completely forgotten you like them on occasion." Perhaps it was her unorthodoxy that was responsible for her taste, he thought, or perhaps it was her part-West Indian heritage. He lighted one for her, crossed the pavilion, and handed it to her.

She made certain their hands did not touch as she took the *cigarro* from him, and he retreated to his own wicker chair. "I take care never to smoke in front of Dickie," she said. "He's marvelously liberal and advanced, having been stationed in all parts of the world, but in his dealings with ladies he's very old-fashioned."

Under no circumstances, Jeremy reflected, would Lord Saunders be able to forgive a wife who had intimate relations with his good friend.

Lisa seemed to sense his thoughts, as she so often did. "I find it strange," she said, her face momentarily hidden behind a cloud of blue-gray smoke, "that you and I should be taking such care to hurt no one but ourselves. If Sarah ever learned you and I were here—without Dickie—she'd be certain we slept together, no matter what you told her."

"I wouldn't mention the whole subject to her," Jeremy said.

"Precisely the point I'm trying to make, my dear," Lisa replied. "Regardless of whether we resumed our affair or not, you wouldn't tell Sarah about this period because you wouldn't want to hurt her. She might guess, of course, just as she's already guessed a great deal about the past, but there's a vast difference between guessing and knowing."

He knew she was being realistic, as always, and wasn't suggesting they lower their guard.

"May I say something about me?"

He nodded, bracing himself.

"When we last met, in South Carolina," she said, "I told you I've never loved Dickie, but that I'm grateful to him for giving me his name, his station in life, and all this luxury."

"I haven't forgotten."

"What I refrained from mentioning is that Dickie knows the way I feel, and accepts our situation. He doesn't love me, either, you see. I'm an ornament to him, even more glittering than his gold epaulets. I'm a first-rate hostess, a social credit to him, and if we decide to go to England after he retires from the navy, I'll be a help to him there, as well."

"Please, that's enough."

"There's one thing more I want you to know," Lisa said. "Three months after we were married, Dickie was ill for a long time with a fever. It left him impotent."

Jeremy gripped the arms of his chair until his knuckles turned white. "Must you?"

"Yes. I see no reason to spare you when I can't spare myself. Since that time," she went on, her voice becoming ragged, "he's urged me—for my own sake—to become . . . friendly with others."

"But hardly with a friend whom he trusts," Jeremy said, almost shouting.

"On the few occasions he's mentioned it, he's insisted he doesn't want to know. I've never pursued the subject with him because I've never followed his advice."

"Dickie is an honorable man . . . and a gentleman."

"As well as the most considerate person I've ever encountered. I . . . I just wanted you to know," Lisa said, and fell silent.

Jeremy cursed her under his breath for telling him her husband could no longer have relations with her and had suggested she find release elsewhere. The revelation made his own position almost unbearable. In all fairness to her, however, the struggle now became as difficult for him as it was for her.

The butler returned with more coffee and rum.

They drank and smoked in silence, and the tension that enveloped them was alive.

Suddenly Lisa jumped to her feet and pointed to the sky. "There they are!" she cried.

Jeremy looked and saw two flares, one red and one green, rising high above the sea off Bridgetown. After the lights reached their apex and began to drop, they faded swiftly, then disappeared from sight.

"Dickie has gone to sea now," she said.

"May the Almighty sail with him," he replied somberly.

Lisa turned abruptly on the high heel of a sandal. "Good night," she said. "Since you leave so early to go down to the harbor, I doubt if I'll see you in the morning, but please remember I'll be expecting you to join me tomorrow evening for supper."

He watched her as she walked across the lawn to the house, her hips swaying. Damn her, even the unconscious way she walked was loaded with an explosive charge of gunpowder. He closed his eyes and did not open them again until he was certain Lisa had vanished from sight.

Sleep was a goal even more difficult to achieve than it had been the previous night. Pacing did no good, brandywine didn't help, and a second *cigarro* tasted bitter, so Jeremy stubbed it out. But under no circumstances would he give in to the temptation of going to the door of Lisa's suite and tapping on it.

Instead, acting as though demons were pursuing him, he fled to the beach, threw off his dressing gown, and plunged into the sea. Even the water failed to cool him, however, so he swam with all the speed and strength he could muster as far as the breakwater, then decided to see how far he could swim underwater on his return without rising to the surface.

He swam until he thought his lungs would burst, and when he finally came to the top, he discovered he was standing in waist-high water. As he blinked his eyes, he realized he was not alone.

Lisa stood near him. She too was nude, and drops of seawater sparkled on her bare, perfectly formed breasts.

For a long moment they stood motionless, looking at each other in the moonlight.

It was impossible now for them to remain apart, no matter what the consequences, and with one accord they came together, kissing as though starved for kisses. His hands roamed her body, her long fingernails dug furrows in his scarred back, and they threw aside all caution.

They had waited so long they could hold off no longer. Moving into slightly deeper water, Jeremy stood with his feet braced on the sandy bottom, Lisa hooked her legs around his hips, and they became one, unmindful of their surroundings, aware only of their terrible, desperate need for each other.

When they found release, the moon seemd to spin on its axis and the whole sky appeared to be filled with shooting stars. Lisa screamed aloud without realizing it, and Jeremy's deep groan echoed against the dunes.

At last they drew apart, breathing hard, greedily sucking in air, then began to walk ashore, hand in hand.

For the first time now they saw each other's entire bodies, and the flame of their desire was rekindled. Hastily they spread their robes on the hard-packed sand and made love a second time, their thirst insatiable. They could not devour enough of each other with hands and lips and tongues, and the consummation was even more explosive than had been the first. Years had passed since they had first taken each other, but the years suddenly disappeared, and their mutual yearning was overwhelming. Even after they achieved a prolonged, simultaneous climax, they were not completely satiated.

Lost in the wonder of their tumultous reunion, they donned their dressing gowns and slowly climbed the dune. Then, rather than go to the house, they halted with one accord, and together turned away from it. The house was the domain of Dickie Saunders, and neither was yet ready to invade it.

Instead they went to the pavilion. Both knew they were evading an issue, that the pavilion was as much the admiral's property as his house, but they were in no state of mind to think clearly. Somehow it seemed preferable to be out here together rather than in a bedchamber.

Slowly lowering themselves to the thick straw mat in the

center of the pavilion, Jeremy and Lisa made love for the third time. Now they were in no hurry and savored every touch. Time stood still as they lingered, toying and teasing and playing, relishing every sensation, loving each thrill for its own sake.

Ultimately, however, their passions overwhelmed them again, and their desire was at least as great as it had been earlier. They came explosively, reached a fiery climax, and then, still locked in each other's arms, drifted off to sleep.

Jeremy awakened when dawn broke. Lisa was still sleeping soundly, so he stole off to the house, pausing for a quick swim first, then shaved and dressed rapidly. A cup of coffee and a slab of fresh bread sufficed for breakfast, and his horse was already saddled.

Not until he was on the road to Bridgetown, still suffused with the wonder of the previous night, did it suddenly occur to him that not once in their long, ardent encounter had he and Lisa exchanged a single word.

There had been no need for words.

Jeremy worked all day like a man possessed, and by sundown the gun-emplacement crews had made considerable progress. Leaving nothing to chance, he ordered fresh foodstuffs, water, and other supplies delivered that same evening. The next day was Friday, and he intended to put out to sea on the late-morning tide, permitting nothing to delay him.

At odd moments during the day he debated whether to send to the Saunders estate in Indian Bridge for his belongings, but decided that would be absurd. Not only did he urgently want to see Lisa again, but what was done could not be undone, and he could imagine nothing that could be gained by making such a theatrical gesture.

A feeling of guilt crept over him as he rode out to the estate, but, as he told himself wryly, it did not prevent him from going there. Even though Lisa's husband was impotent and had told her to take a lover, he himself was not relieved from the burden of trust that his friendship with Dickie Saunders imposed on him. What was even more important, nothing could erase the fact that he had been unfaithful to Sarah.

Lisa awaited him in the pavilion, as he had anticipated. She was wearing a snug-fitting gown of pale green silk that aroused him as soon as he saw her in it, and her eyes were luminous as she smiled at him.

They met, embraced, and kissed in the center of the pavilion.

Lisa eased the spell by handing him a cup of punch. "You'll find this hard to believe," she said, "but I slept out here until ten this morning."

Jeremy joined in her laugh, but felt uncomfortable. Nevertheless, tonight they sat near each other.

"I've accepted my fate," Lisa said.

"So have I, because I have no choice."

"Whatever has happened to us happened long ago and was meant to be," she said. "I don't pretend to understand the chemistry that draws us together. All I know is that it exists and that it can't be fought."

"We tried hard. At least we have that much to our credit."

She studied him for a moment, and was characteristically blunt. "You're unhappy," she said, "because we're adulterers."

"Frankly . . . yes."

"I don't expect you to tell Dickie about us, not when you're going off tomorrow to fight side by side with him. That would be too much for both of you. If you wish, I'll speak to him after he comes home, even though he's indicated to me very specifically that he'd rather not know."

"No," Jeremy said. "It would be wrong of me to try to expiate my guilt by making him unhappy. That would be just compounding my selfishness."

"I agree. That leaves Sarah."

He faced her squarely. "When you and I had our first affair all those years ago," he said, "Sarah and I were betrothed, not married. Now she's my wife. The difference may be technical, but it exists."

"Sarah," Lisa said, "is well aware of the attraction you and I feel for each other. In fact, she and I have even discussed it."

"You have?" Jeremy was astonished.

"She's aware of how hard both of us have fought against it, and she sympathizes with us. It wouldn't surprise her in the least to learn what happened last night."

"Maybe not, but she'd be badly hurt."

"Precisely. This isn't sophistry, but if your only reason for telling her is to make yourself feel better, spare her. If there's something to be gained, tell her."

"I can't imagine what anyone would gain," Jeremy said.

"Neither can I." Lisa sipped her punch and looked for a long time into her cup. "Tell me truthfully, do you love Sarah any less because of what's between us?"

"No, I don't," Jeremy said. "Just as I love you no less—and want you no less—because of what I feel for her. I . . . I wish I were two people."

"Well, you aren't," she said, and smiled.

"Sarah gives me peace, serenity, a sense of tranquillity," Jeremy said. "You don't. You fill me with excitement, with a sense of almost superhuman energy. I don't mean to be crude, but after Sarah and I have made love, I'm satisfied, often for days at a time. You don't have that effect on me. I want you more . . . and more . . . and more."

"So I've noticed," Lisa said, and looked demure.

"If I could forget you, I would. If I could put you out of my life forever, I would."

"I know, because I feel the same way about you. But I can't simply drop you from my life, any more than you can drop me." Lisa paused. "May I tell you what went through your mind when you approached this pavilion tonight and saw me waiting for you? You told yourself this is the way it would be . . . if we were married."

"You're right, I'm afraid. But you have a husband and I have a wife. We can't hurt them by asking to be released from our vows, and we can't be childish by running away together."

"Of course not, for the simple reason that we couldn't hide from ourselves," Lisa said.

"Then what do we do?" His torment overwhelmed him.

"My dear," Lisa said gently, "we stop fighting our destiny. We accept this extraordinary affinity, enjoy it, and appreciate it. After we part tomorrow morning, our paths may cross again, or they may not. I can't pretend to see what lies in the future, and neither can you. I've come to the belief that we should cherish what we have together, for however long it may last."

"For me," he said, "the feeling will last as long as I live.

Even if I didn't see you for ten years—twenty years, whatever—I'd feel the same way the moment I saw you again."

"I hope you would," Lisa said, "because I'd feel that exact same way. I'm glad," she added, "that you're married to Sarah. I'd be jealous of some other woman, but I can't be jealous of her, knowing how lovely she is and how contented she makes you."

He was too bewildered to know what to reply.

Lisa smiled, stood, and taking his head in her hands, pressed his face to her breasts. "Commodore Beaufort," she said, "in matters of business and the sea, you're a man of integrity and decision. In matters of the heart, you think too much. Stop using your mind and enjoy what we have together."

Jeremy responded by putting his arms around her and trying to draw her closer.

Lisa managed to disentangle herself, however, and surprised him again by giggling. "That isn't quite what I meant. Touch me again, and supper will be ruined. We're going in now."

She placed her hand on his arm, and they looked like the most decorous of couples as they walked sedately to the house.

Later neither could remember what they discussed at the supper table, but both were reminded of an idyllic hour they had spent in the Jamaican hills. All that mattered was that they were together.

After the meal they adjourned to a small drawing room, where they refused rum in their coffee. They continued to chat with great animation about nothing, about everything. Jeremy found himself telling Lisa the full story of his brief affair with Kai, her subsequent romance with M'Bwana, and the birth of Lance.

Lisa responded by telling him a far more harrowing tale. Some months earlier, at a reception, she had met a Royal Navy captain who had been one of her lovers at the Jamaican house of assignation in which she had resided. "I was petrified," she said, "but he didn't recognize me."

"Ah, he was a gentleman."

"No, he wasn't, which is why I broke off my relationship

with him. He simply didn't connect Lady Saunders with Lisa, the trollop he had known in Jamaica."

"Never were you a trollop!" Jeremy said fiercely. "You had to get out of an untenable situation and improve yourself, so you took the only road open to you, but you were always a lady, long before you acquired a title."

Her eyes became misty. "It's no wonder I love you," she said, and all at once her mood changed. "Come along."

He rose to his feet when she stood. "Where are we going?"

"Upstairs, of course."

Jeremy hesitated.

"I've had quite enough of sandy beaches and pavilion mats," Lisa said. "We may or may not want to go for a swim later, but that's beside the point."

He felt uncomfortable as she took his hand and led him up the stairs.

"I know what you're thinking," she told him, "but it isn't as horrendous as you think. You'll soon see."

She proved to be right. To his surprise and relief, he discovered she had her own bedchamber in the master suite, separated from Lord Saunder's bedroom by a spacious living room. The mere fact that it was Lisa's alone relieved him, precisely as she had known it would.

It was incredible how well she knew him, how quickly she divined his moods, how thoroughly she understood his needs. Now he could see a difference between Sarah and Lisa. Sarah leaned on him, depended on him. But he depended on Lisa, all-wise, all-knowing, all-loving.

Tonight they undressed without undue haste, and for a time their initial lovemaking was almost chaste. Ultimately, however, when their passions rose, they became increasingly wild, and their release was only temporary.

They made love a second time, then went for a swim and repeated their previous night's experimental frolic in the water. By the time they returned to the house, their bodies craved a respite, but their minds remained active, and although they rested, they talked through the better part of the night. Then, after dropping off to sleep for a short time, they made love once again.

Jeremy went off to his own suite to prepare for his departure, and soon thereafter a seemingly demure Lisa met him for breakfast in the dining room, where the presence of the household staff made it necessary for them to maintain at least a facade of decorum.

"I've rarely had less sleep," Jeremy said, "but I've never felt better or more energetic."

"Me too," Lisa replied. "We pump new life into each other in some miraculous way."

Although their parting was imminent, they were in no way sad, and conversation bubbled through the early-morning meal.

Two of Jeremy's junior officers arrived to escort him into town, so he and Lisa said their farewell in private. They kissed passionately, their attraction for each other making it impossible for either to exercise restraint, and then they stood apart.

"The next time we meet," Jeremy said, "everything will be different."

Lisa shook her head. "No, we may have to behave differently, but the bond we've forged is permanent. I'm sure we'll be together again, truly together, although I have no idea how or when it will happen. When a man and a woman feel as we do, in spite of all the obstacles that come between them, nothing can possibly separate them forever."

He suspected that she was right. They asked nothing of each other. Neither made a commitment of any kind because it was impossible for them to offer promises they could not fulfill. Yet the bond was firm, even though it seemed fragile.

Jeremy grinned when they parted, and Lisa smiled. Their mutual reaction seemed appropriate, and was the only way they knew.

Riding into Bridgetown at a canter, Jeremy found his gig waiting for him at the wharf near the fort. His officers and crews were on board the ships, provisioning had been completed, and all that remained was the receipt of Admiral Lord Saunders' message.

As the commodore was being rowed to his flagship, *HMS Gull* sailed into the harbor, and the captains of the American vessels hurried to the *Elizabeth* without waiting to be summoned. The tired captain of the *Gull* joined them as soon as the sloop of war dropped anchor, and a meeting was held in Jeremy's cabin.

"The admiral has picked up the trail of the buccaneer fleet," the Royal Navy officer told the Americans. "The enemy has been joined by a fifth ship, and his lordship inclines toward the view that others will be appearing from Hispaniola too, so we should be seeing action before too many days have passed."

They studied charts, with each of the commanders pinpointing the last-known positions of both the British and freebooter fleets.

"The admiral," the Royal Navy officer said, "has directed me to lead you to him, Commodore. He doubled eastward again late yesterday afternoon after sailing due west, so we may be able to rendezvous with him in about thirty-six hours after we sail. With luck."

"Fair enough." Jeremy was all business now. "Gentlemen," he told his subordinates before they dispersed to their own ships, "there's no need for speeches. The president and the Navy Department have ordered us to rid these seas of a vicious company of criminals, and we'll do it. Keep your powder dry."

He made a thorough inspection of his flagship, then went to the quarterdeck, where M'Bwana awaited him. Shortly before eleven A.M. anchors were weighed and the squadron sailed out of the harbor, with the *Elizabeth* close behind the *Gull.* They moved beyond the coral reef and for a time stayed close to the shoreline as they started westward.

Within a short time the Indian Bridge section came within view, and Jeremy raised his glass.

As he had hoped, he saw Lisa standing on the beach, the breeze rippling her soft dress. Even though she could not see him clearly, she raised an arm high over her head.

Jeremy had no idea whether she could read signal-flag messages, but he nevertheless ordered a set of pennants sent up the yardarm. "Hail and farewell," he told her, and he did not lower his glass until she disappeared from view.

# Chapter 7

The squadron sailed toward the northwest, with Jeremy elect-
ing to give the islands of the Leeward and Windward chains
as wide a berth as possible. It was reasonable to assume that
the buccaneers had agents scattered throughout the West Indies to keep track of merchant shipping, and he hoped the
presence in these waters of his own heavily armed vessels
would be undetected. The element of surprise could be important in determining the outcome of the forthcoming action.

For two days and nights the squadron continued under
forced sail, and early on the third morning the *Elizabeth*'s
lookout saw a ship on the horizon. Soon several others appeared, and Jeremy, uncertain whether he was approaching
friend or foe, alerted all of his vessels. Then, with the aid of
his glass, he made out the silhouette of a Royal Navy frigate,
and ran up his own colors.

An hour later he and his captains boarded the *Porpoise* for
a breakfast meeting with the admiral. The American commodore was piped aboard with due ceremony, and found
Lord Saunders awaiting him, obviously delighted to see him.

As they shook hands, Jeremy felt overwhelmed by a sense

of guilt. This was his friend, the man he had made a cuckold, and it didn't matter that Saunders had urged his wife to live her own life because of his own inability to satisfy her. The friendship was altered, and Jeremy knew he could never completely recover his own sense of honor, no matter what might develop in the future.

"I told you I'd wait for you before closing with the enemy," Dickie Saunders said. "That's because I want to make a private wager with you. We'll sink more of the pirates than you will."

"You have your wager, sir," Jeremy replied as they repaired to the fleet commander's spacious cabin.

"How was Lisa when you last saw her?" The question was innocent, totally lacking in hidden meanings.

"I had breakfast with her before I sailed," Jeremy replied truthfully, "and as we sailed past Indian Bridge, she did us the honor of coming down to the beach to wave good-bye."

"Splendid," Dickie said.

Rarely had Jeremy felt less proud of himself.

Soon all of the American and British captains were assembled, yeomen served them plates of pickled beef, smoked fish, and hardtack, which they washed down with ale, a typical meal for men at sea. Everyone present was long accustomed to such food, and all ate without hesitation.

"The *Albatross* is still on a scouting mission," Lord Saunders said, "and at last report the buccaneer fleet held a rendezvous off the northern coast of Puerto Rico. At last count they had assembled thirteen ships."

A number of the captains looked solemn. The British fleet numbered five ships, not including the sloops of war that were best suited for courier service, and there were four more in the American squadron.

"Looks like we're going to be outnumbered," Captain Ned Slocum observed.

"There's no doubt of it," the admiral replied, "and we'll be operating under other handicaps too. From all I've been told, the buccaneer gunnery is as good as their seamanship, which is superb."

"There's still another factor we must take into consideration," Jeremy added. "Certainly the freebooters know by now that a concerted effort is being made to exterminate them. They'll be even more startled when they discover that an American squadron has joined the British fleet. They must realize that with the record they've established, we intend to send every last one of their ships to the bottom. So men who know that no mercy will be shown them are going to be desperate. They'll take risks that no sensible sailor would dream of taking."

"Now," the admiral said, "let's look at the other side of the ledger. Both the *Porpoise* and the *Elizabeth* are armed with twelve-pounder cannon, guns that are larger and have a greater range than anything the buccaneers carry. Our ketches and converted brigs may be roughly the same size as most of their ships, but our seamanship is disciplined, while they're forced to rely on individual heroics."

"I must concur with Lord Saunders' judgment," Jeremy said. "I'll grant that we're outnumbered, but the scales are tipped in our direction, provided we utilize our strengths."

"I prefer to establish no plan of battle until we meet the enemy," the admiral said. "I believe circumstances should determine our strategy. Do you agree, Commodore?"

"I do, sir, basically," Jeremy replied. "But I think there's one factor that all of us should take into consideration. This is more true of our larger ships than our smaller. Considering the nature of our enemy, we can't take the fundamental approach of a Horatio Nelson or a John Paul Jones. For the past half-century, fleet commanders and their captains have tended to engage in a slugging contest with their foes. The temptation will be particularly great for the *Porpoise* and the *Elizabeth*, but I believe we'll be subjecting ourselves to needless punishment."

The admiral frowned. "I'm not sure I understand the point you're making, Commodore."

"Just this, sir. A stationary target is much easier to hit than a moving target. It seems to me that we should adopt fluid tactics. No matter what approach we take when the time comes, we should keep in constant motion. A favorite buccaneer trick, for example, is to pretend to be disabled and then cripple an enemy beyond repair when she casts anchor or otherwise tries to end the encounter. I strongly suggest that we stay under sail at all times. Until we send every last one of the bastards to the bottom."

There was a hearty chorus of approval.

"Very well, gentlemen," the admiral said. "So be it. We divide naturally into two units, mine and Commodore Beaufort's. I'll be responsible for my own internal organization, and the commodore will establish the American order of battle. I'll communicate overall orders only to him for the American squadron, and he'll dispose of his ships as he sees fit. Does anyone wish to comment?"

The question was rhetorical, and everyone present knew it. No captain in his right mind would argue with an admiral or question his authority.

As the various officers returned to their ships, Lord Saunders drew Jeremy aside. "We haven't settled the terms of our wager. I suggest that the loser gives a banquet for the winner, to be held either at Oakhurst Manor or at Indian Bridge, as the case may be."

Jeremy felt ill, but had no alternative. "Agreed," he said. He was not afraid to meet enemy gunfire, but dreaded the prospect of once again facing Sarah and Lisa at the same time.

The combined units threaded through the waters that separated Puerto Rico and the Virgin Islands, then headed westward again. This time it was the *Gull* that brought them news. The buccaneer flotilla had been sighted, and was moving under reduced speed until two other ships that appeared to have sailed from Hispaniola joined them.

"Full speed ahead," the admiral signaled, and the warships crowded on sail.

Twenty hours later the enemy was sighted, and Lord Saunders ordered a pursuit. The freebooters had fifteen ships now, so Jeremy thought they would stand and fight. They surprised him by fleeing, but he and the admiral had no intention of allowing them to escape, and the Anglo-American force followed.

Both fleets were compelled to slow their pace when night came, but the *Albatross* and the *Gull* closed the gap and gave the freebooters no opportunity to slip away in the dark. The chase went on.

In the morning a tropical sun rose in a cloudless sky, and a warm but brisk breeze blew from the northwest. It would have been a perfect day for swimming or lazing on a beach.

Suddenly, as the buccaneer fleet approached the Mona Passage, the broad strip of water that separated Puerto Rico and Hispaniola, the pirate commander elected to fight. His vessels slowed to a crawl, then moved into a double line, with the larger ships in the center.

"Now we will fight," Lord Saunders signaled to Jeremy from the *Porpoise*. "I will approach on portside, you will take starboard positions."

Jeremy acknowledged the directive, then arranged his own order of battle. He placed the reliable Ned Slocum's *Louise* in the vanguard, followed by the *Marilyn* and the *Jane*, and himself assumed the anchor position in the *Elizabeth*.

M'Bwana, who was facing his first actual sea engagement, was ecstatic, and offended protocol by anticipating an order. "Shouldn't we strip for action?"

It was difficult for Jeremy to keep a straight face. "A good idea," he said. "Please proceed."

Signals were flown, and gunports were lowered on all four of the American ships. Unnecessary objects were removed from the decks, fires were lighted for the heating of shot, and large buckets of sand were placed at strategic points on the decks so fires started by the enemy could be extinguished. Surgeons and pharmacists' mates retired to their dispensaries, and experienced hands tied bandannas around their heads as protection from flying splinters.

Chief Boatswain Talbot's calm matched that of the commodore as he came to the quarterdeck of the *Elizabeth*. "The ship is stripped, sir."

"Good. You may want to distribute tots of rum to the crew, Boatswain."

Talbot's smile revealed the gaps between his remaining teeth. "Hell, Commodore, that's the first thing I did!"

Jeremy couldn't help laughing, then sobered. "How are the men's spirits?"

"The young ones don't know no better, sir, so they can't wait for the shooting to start. The old ones, like me, are scared out of their wits."

"So am I." Jeremy glanced obliquely at the expectant

M'Bwana, who was watching the enemy through his glass. "Inspect your battle stations, Boatswain."

"I done that too." Talbot looked and sounded complacent. "Who begins this brawl, sir, them or us?"

"That depends on the admiral."

The chief boatswain moved to his own battle station at the aft quarterdeck rail.

The buccaneer flagship hoisted its identifying pennant, a black banner with a yellow border, and the other fourteen ships of the flotilla promptly did the same. Sir Henry Morgan had utilized such an insignia when he had lost his own flags on a march through the jungles of Panama, and ever since his day freebooters had followed his example.

"You may request the squadron to hoist the colors," Jeremy told M'Bwana.

Within moments the Stars and Stripes flew from the yardarms of all four ships. Meantime, the Union Jack was raised on the ships of the British fleet. Now, at last, the buccaneers knew they faced professionals whose skill and determination matched their own.

The British approached the enemy from the left, sailing in single file, while the Americans, utilizing the same formation, drew nearer on the right.

"You may stand by for action," Jeremy said.

Again the order was transmitted.

The commodore motioned to Talbot, who came to him at once. "Boatswain," he said, "this may be slightly irregular, but I want you to take charge of the gun crews. The gunnery officer will direct the actual fire, but I want you to make certain that cannon are reloaded as soon as they're fired, that barrels are swabbed after each round, and that crews stand clear after a fuse has been lighted."

"Aye, aye, sir." Talbot completely understood the order. Only a veteran remembered to take such precautions in the heat of battle, and as many of the Americans were going into combat for the first time, lives would be saved. He saluted, then loped off to the gun deck.

Within moments his loud voice could be heard all over the flagship.

Jeremy couldn't help grinning. If he closed his eyes, he could imagine himself a gunner in the Royal Navy again, writhing under Talbot's abuse. But he was far more now, responsible for the lives of hundreds of fellow Americans and the safety of four ships. For an instant a sense of panic flooded him, and then he became icily calm, as he always did just before a fight began.

The buccaneer flagship opened the engagement by firing a salvo at the *Louise*. The heated iron cannonballs fell short of the target by at least 150 yards, but Jeremy was impressed. It simply hadn't occurred to him that the freebooters might be using twelve-pounders.

"Engage at will," Admiral Lord Saunders signaled.

"Acknowledge," Jeremy snapped, and took direct command of the *Elizabeth*. "Portside heavy guns, prepare to fire." He waited for a moment, giving the gunnery lieutenant time to set his sights. "You may fire a salvo!"

Twelve-pounders roared, and the *Elizabeth* shuddered. The shots were about fifty feet short.

Again Jeremy paused. "Fire a second salvo!"

This time the guns were on target, and no fewer than five or six shots struck the freebooter flagship, at least two crashing into her hull.

"Fire at will!" Jeremy directed, then devoted his attention to the rest of his squadron, leaving the *Elizabeth* under M'Bwana's direction.

The *Louise* was drawing close enough to the foe for her nine-pounder cannon to become effective, and Jeremy sent a signal to Captain Slocum, granting him permission to open fire when he wished. The smaller ships would be required to wait until the squadron closed with the foe.

Meanwhile Admiral Lord Saunders was ready to do his part, and the twelve-pounders on the *Porpoise* opened her attack. The buccaneers were caught in a crossfire as the two columns sailed past their foe, tacked, and returned to the fray, still moving in single lines.

The fire was devastating, but the pirates had no intention of submitting meekly, and all of their ships unleashed salvo after salvo at both the Americans and the British.

Jeremy ordered his squadron to move still closer, so the smaller cannon on the *Jane* and the *Marilyn* could be utilized. The danger was greater, to be sure, but so was the effectiveness of his own cannon. The gunfire on both sides was incessant now, the thunder so loud that every order had to be repeated to make certain it was understood.

The first casualty was a buccaneer vessel, a captured brig that had been converted into a warship. One moment it seemed to be intact; an instant later it was enveloped in flames, with crew members leaping overboard into the sea in a futile attempt to save themselves. Jeremy watched the destruction of the pirate vessel with a sense of detachment, feeling neither pleasure nor pity. He could not determine whether British or American gunners were responsible, and he didn't really care. All that mattered was that one enemy ship was gone, while fourteen still remained as targets.

Suddenly a heated twelve-pounder shot landed on the main deck of the *Elizabeth*, cut a deep furrow in the hard wood, and carried away a section of railing as it skidded into the sea. One sailor was killed and two others wounded.

The battle raged through the better part of the day, and occasionally the cannon on board one or another ship had to be allowed to fall silent so they would grow cooler. The *Albatross*, coming to the aid of a small British bomb ketch, lost her mainmast and appeared to be a helpless target. But a new mast was jury-rigged and she limped out of range, unable to return to active combat.

The *Jane* was battered unmercifully and lost a major portion of her effectiveness, but refused to withdraw. A British schooner also took a heavy beating, but remained in the thick of the fight.

The buccaneer losses were far more severe, thanks to the tactics that Lord Saunders and Jeremy utilized. A second freebooter was set on fire, a third was sunk, and a fourth, after being reduced to a helpless hulk, exploded when a fire unseen from afar exploded in her gunpowder reserves.

By nightfall the buccaneer commander had had enough, and gathering his battered forces, sailed toward the south through the Mona Passage under the cover of darkness. The British and Americans wanted to pursue their vanquished enemy, but were too tired. The *Gull* and the *Marilyn* made the attempt to follow, but were driven off by heavy nine-pounder fire, and had to abandon the effort.

A weary Jeremy, his hands, face, and uniform blackened by smoke, was rowed to the *Porpoise* in his gig. The first task, which he and Lord Saunders performed with dispatch, was the regrouping of their forces. The *Albatross*, the damaged British schooner, and the *Jane* were sent to Jamaica for repairs, with the *Louise* and a small British frigate acting as escorts. The wounded were transferred to the other smaller ships, all of which were sent back to Barbados, where adequate medical facilities were available.

Then Jeremy and Dickie Saunders compared notes. The Americans had suffered eleven killed and thirty-two wounded; British casualties were slightly higher. Both flagships had suffered only minor damage and were virtually intact.

"I suppose," Dickie Saunders said as he poured generous quantities of rum into two glasses, "that we can congratulate ourselves on winning a victory. We sent four of the devils to the bottom without losing a ship."

"We didn't do too badly," Jeremy said, "but eleven of the bastards got away. I'll grant you that two of those ships are hulks, and I very much doubt that they can be repaired."

"A toll of six enemy ships will please London and Washington City." Saunders sighed as he opened the collar of his tunic.

"But it doesn't satisfy you or me, Dickie." Jeremy took a swallow of his rum. "Nine of the buccaneer ships will return to robbery on the high seas one of these days."

"I know." The admiral was silent for a time. "We've got to do something more."

"They couldn't be sailing very far," Jeremy said, deep in thought. "Those hulks aren't seaworthy enough to make a long voyage."

"Our flagships are still intact, and neither has suffered more than minimal losses." Dickie smiled grimly.

"Right." It was apparent they were thinking along similar lines, and Jeremy grinned. "How I'd like to hunt the bastards down and sink the rest of their fleet!"

The admiral hauled himself to his feet and went to the bookshelves built into a bulkhead, returning with a large map. He handed it to his colleague without comment.

"Hispaniola," Jeremy said.

"According to every account that either of us has heard, the home base of the buccaneers."

"Easier said than done," Jeremy said. "There are hundreds

of miles of wilderness, not to mention mountains ten thousand feet high. We could spend the next year searching Hispaniola without finding the freebooters."

"What's more, the Spaniards wouldn't appreciate our efforts. You can bet Madrid would complain to Washington and London."

"Aha!" Jeremy sat upright, his fatigue forgotten, and drained his glass.

The admiral poured more rum as he awaited an explanation.

"Suppose we sail both flagships to Santo Domingo City first thing in the morning. We'll give our crews shore leave and pick up supplies while you and I call on the Spanish governor. He can't enjoy having the buccaneers cavorting on what is supposedly his domain, thumbing their noses at him. I should think he'd welcome an expedition that would rid him of the nuisance—and the menace—once and for all."

"By God, we'll do it!" Saunders said, slapping his knee. "We have a great deal to gain—damned little to lose!"

Hispaniola had been discovered by Columbus in 1492, and Santo Domingo City was the oldest community in the New World. It resembled no other port in the West Indian islands; the flavor of the Caribbean was lacking, and it was totally Spanish in appearance, atmosphere, and approach. The principal headquarters of Spanish colonial administrators in the Americas since the city had been founded by Bartolomé Columbus in 1496, it bore a striking resemblance to Seville. Its narrow streets were straight and laid out at right angles, most homes were sturdy two-story buildings made of stone brought down from the mountains, and most had slanting tile roofs of red, green, pink, or yellow.

Government buildings, which were clustered in the area of the protected deep-water port, were massive edifices of stone, and so were the buildings of the oldest institution of higher education in the New World, St. Thomas Aquinas University. Towering over every other structure in town was the great cathedral, reminiscent of some of the great churches in Madrid, and it was believed that Christopher Columbus himself was buried there, although definite proof of the allegation was lacking.

Shops, inns, and taverns were neat, the streets were clean, and virtually all of the merchandise offered for sale had been made in Spain. Unlike the other powers that had established bases in the West Indies and encouraged international trade, Spain still clung to the policy of forcing her American colonies to trade exclusively with the mother country.

Most of the inhabitants were well-dressed, and appeared to be either aristocrats or members of the middle class. If there was poverty, it was hidden on the great estates located beyond the limits of the capital. As in Spain itself, soldiers were everywhere, walking the streets in pairs in their spotted, dusty uniforms, with muskets slung over their shoulders. The water-front prisons were large, at most times well-populated, and no one paused in the vicinity of the soldiers.

The institution of slavery still existed, at least in theory, but many blacks had bought their freedom and had prospered. Racial intermarriage was common, and Santo Domingo was unique because no color bar of any kind existed in the colony.

Admiral Lord Saunders and Commodore Beaufort registered with the port authorities on their arrival, were made welcome by a Spanish admiral, and resplendent in their dress uniforms, were provided with a carriage and a military escort for the short drive to the palace of the governor, Don Hector de Medillo López.

They absorbed the unique atmosphere of Santo Domingo on the ride, and a brief exchange of glances indicated their consciousness of another aspect of the city's culture that members of their crews were already discovering. The streets of Santo Domingo were teeming with prostitutes, black and white, and respectable citizens seemed to take their presence for granted.

Don Hector de Medillo López, who greeted his visitors in a high-ceilinged chamber filled with paintings, statues, and bric-a-brac, seemed to be a survivor of another era. He wore knee breeches with diamond buckles, a ruffled silk shirt, and an embroidered silk coat; there were diamonds on the tongues of his pumps, and diamond rings on his fingers. His white, powdered wig had gone out of style in the previous century, and so had the beauty patch of black velvet that was pasted to one cheekbone. His manner was slightly effeminate, but his voice was deep, his handshake was firm, and it was a surprise to discover he was in his early thirties. Spanish nobles, as Jeremy had learned on his travels through the West Indian islands, were a breed apart.

A servant whose uniform resembled his master's attire came in with an exquisite wine decanter and glasses of paper-thin crystal, and toasts were offered to the kings of Great Britain and Spain and the president of the United States. Formalities having been completed, Don Hector sank into a chair and unbuttoned his ornately embroidered waistcoat.

"It has come to my attention this morning," he said in almost unaccented English, "that you gentlemen waged a good fight with the buccaneers yesterday only a few miles off our coasts."

"Your Excellency keeps well-informed," Lord Saunders said.

The governor bared his teeth when he smiled. "One of my own ships was present at the encounter as an observer, remaining a discreet distance from the line of fire. I only regret you did not sink all of the swine. They are the scourge of the Americas, and whenever I have the good fortune to capture one of them, I have him tortured to death in a delicate process that lasts for many days. It is one of my greatest pleasures."

Jeremy had to ignore his distaste for the man. "We've come to you, your Excellency," he said, "because our victory yesterday wasn't complete. We suspect the freebooters came ashore somewhere in this colony."

"I would assume they did. Our mountains crawl with the vermin."

"We're prepared to pursue them," Lord Saunders said, "and hope you can tell us where to find them."

"Ah, would that I could." Don Hector sniffed a perfumed lace handkerchief, inhaling deeply. "If I knew where to locate them, I would send an expedition against them. Better still, I would lead it myself." He paused, then grimaced. "No, gentlemen, I fool myself. Many of my troops are young Spanish peasants who have been conscripted into our army. They hate King Ferdinand because he took them from their homes, and they hate me because I represent the king here. Take them into the mountains, and they would not only desert and join the ranks of the buccaneers, but they would roast me on a spit in the same way the buccaneers roast their sides of wild beef." To the astonishment of his guests, he spat on the thick cream-colored Ottoman rug beneath his feet.

Lord Saunders was so stunned he didn't know what to say.

The more resilient Jeremy was the first to recover. "Is there any way you can help us in our mission, your Excellency? I need scarcely remind you that Spain loses more shipping to the freebooters than any other nation. We've been given the mission of hunting them down, and we won't rest until we've exterminated them."

Don Hector refilled their glasses with the pale sack that was one of Spain's remaining glories. Her great empire was crumbling, her trade had declined drastically, and Ferdinand VII had instituted a domestic reign of terror reminiscent of the Middle Ages, but Spanish wines were still incomparable.

"I gladly offer you my blessings, gentlemen," he said, "and I shall provide you with a permit, on which I shall place my seal as viceroy, that will grant you the right to travel with your companies of armed men anywhere you wish in my domain. I know it is a small boon that I grant you, but I'm afraid it is the best I can offer."

Jeremy and the admiral drank their wine, accepted the permit, and left the palace, both bitterly disappointed. Wanting to talk, they declined a ride back to the harbor and instead walked, to the astonishment of local residents, who had never seen high-ranking officers go anywhere on their own feet.

"A stinking kettle of fish," a fuming Dickie Saunders said. "His Excellency gives us a scrap of paper, puts his seal on it, and dismisses us. My God, your government or mine would send thousands of men to hunt down the scoundrel freebooters and hang them."

"Don Hector knows his own troops, I imagine. He wasn't joking when he said they'd desert and join the buccaneers. He's helpless."

"And so are we!" The admiral rarely lost his temper, but now he cursed at length without repeating himself.

"We do have his permit," Jeremy said. "So that grants us the right to search his coastline for the buccaneer fleet."

"If you'll take the trouble to study maps of Hispaniola, as

I have, you'll discover that what you're proposing is impossible."

"Why?"

"Because thére are more harbors, coves, sounds, bays, and inlets in Hispaniola than anyone has ever counted. Scores of them, perhaps hundreds, are hidden by cliffs, bluffs, and the like. We could spend years hunting for the hiding place of the buccaneer fleet and never find it."

"I refuse to give up and sail for home," Jeremy said.

"So do I, but I'm damned if I know of a viable alternative."

They had come to the center of town, where the streets were crowded, so they gave up conversation, preferring to wait until they could talk privately, and instead they trudged side by side in gloomy silence.

A sudden whoop startled them. "Commodore Beaufort, Milord Admiral! You be just in time!"

Blocking their path was a grinning Boatswain Talbot, who was not alone. Clinging to his arm was a young strumpet, her long hair flowing freely and makeup thick on her face. She was wearing what appeared to be the national costume of prostitutes in Santo Domingo, a sleazy blouse with a neckline that plunged to her small waist, a tight-fitting skirt slit high on one thigh, and absurdly high-heeled shoes.

"I've got it all arranged," the boatswain said. "For a couple of hundred Spanish *dólares*, Dolores here will give ye what ye want most."

Lord Saunders was outraged. "You've gone too far, Talbot!"

"Sir, I mean it! I ain't saying what ye think I'm saying!"

As nearly as Jeremy could judge, the man appeared to be cold sober, and his expression was serious. All the same, a busy street in Santo Domingo was not the appropriate place for the commanders of the Anglo-American expedition to be seen chatting with a local harlot. "The admiral and I are dining on board the *Elizabeth*," he said. "If you have anything of consequence to report to us, you'll find us there."

He made a detour around the girl, who was flirting impartially with him and with the admiral, and they made their way to the wharf, where Saunders' launch awaited them.

"I don't object to an occasional prank," Dickie Saunders

said as they were rowed to the American flagship, "but I cannot tolerate a lack of respect for rank. I hope you'll deal with the fellow as he deserves, Jeremy. He should be given a summary court-martial and dismissed from your navy."

"I'll grant you his conduct was odd, and certainly he knows better than to play a cheap joke on us." Jeremy preferred to reserve judgment.

When they reached the *Elizabeth* they were joined in Jeremy's cabin by M'Bwana, and all three quickly became involved in an informal council of war.

They had no sooner started their discussion, however, when they were interrupted by a tap at the door, and Boatswain Talbot came in, one brawny arm curled around the waist of the strumpet.

Jeremy stiffened. It was a criminal offense to bring such a woman on board an American warship.

Talbot wasted no time. "Commodore," he said, "Dolores here can take us to the buccaneers' hideout!"

All three officers stared at him.

The boatswain continued to maintain his hold on the girl, whose poise had deserted her and who looked apprehensive in these strange and martial surroundings. "Like I told you, sir, we got to pay her a couple of hundred *dólares*."

Jeremy was the first to recover from his astonishment. "If this is legitimate," he said, "I see no trouble in meeting the young woman's price."

"Very strange," the admiral murmured.

"How is it possible for her to know such things?" M'Bwana demanded.

Talbot and Dolores conversed in Spanish before the boatswain replied. "She lived there for near a half-year," he said. "One of the buccaneer lieutenants was her lover, but he got tired of her, and she had to come back to the city alone. It took her a long time to get here, and she hates him so much she wants to even the score with him."

Revenge, Jeremy thought, was one of the most powerful of human motives. He went to his strongbox and took out one hundred American dollars in the new paper money that the Monroe administration had recently authorized.

"If she can deliver what she promises," Jeremy said, "we're buying a bargain. Talbot, tell her this is a first payment.

She'll get another, equal amount when she's shown us the freebooter headquarters."

The boatswain translated his remarks and handed her the money.

The girl counted the bills, her eyes gleaming, then folded them and stuffed them inside her blouse. Her manner changed now, and she flirted impartially with everyone in the cabin.

Talbot became a trifle uncomfortable. "She'll have to sail with us, Commodore, so she can show us the harbor the buccaneers use, and then she'll have to travel inland with us."

"I'll make you responsible for her, Boatswain," Jeremy told him. "I don't want her practicing her trade on board this ship. And while we're about it, take her ashore again and buy her some clothes that won't take the minds of the crew away from their duty!" He handed Talbot some additional money.

Dolores was delighted when the boatswain again translated for her, and happily went off with him.

"The longer I live," Lord Saunders said after the pair departed, "the more I realize that the ways of the world are strange. I can only say I'm relieved that the wench will be sailing on your ship, Jeremy, not on mine!"

The *Elizabeth* and the *Porpoise* sailed westward along the southern coastline of Hispaniola after leaving Santo Domingo City, with the American ship in the lead. The voyage started at dawn, and when the sun rose high overhead several hours later, Talbot brought Dolores to the quarterdeck.

At Jeremy's insistence her face was scrubbed clean of cosmetics, and even though the day was warm she was covered from her neck to her ankles by a voluminous cape. In spite of these precautions, however, the sailors gaped at her and the helmsman found it difficult to concentrate on his work at the wheel.

It was the girl's nature to smile provocatively at every man she encountered, and although she meant no harm, she was a disruptive influence. Jeremy and M'Bwana would be relieved when she directed them to the lair of the buccaneers and they could be rid of her.

After distributing smiles and winks to every officer and

seaman on the quarterdeck, the girl spoke at length to Talbot in rapid-fire Spanish.

"She's saying that we're coming near to the harbor, Commodore," the boatswain said, "and she guesses there will be a freebooter ship or two hiding there."

"Thank her for me," Jeremy replied, and turned to M'Bwana. "You may strip for action, and be good enough to alert Lord Saunders."

Gunports were lowered on both ships, and the crews moved to their battle stations.

Dolores, thoroughly enjoying the limelight, continued to offer advice for the next quarter of an hour, then raised an arm and pointed dramatically.

Jeremy could see no harbor, but felt he had no alternative, so he tacked, then headed cautiously toward the shore under vastly reduced sail.

Suddenly, almost miraculously, a narrow channel became visible between two cliffs, their jungle foliage concealing the opening until the *Elizabeth* drew near it.

"I hope we can clear the passage," M'Bwana said, and turned to Dolores for confirmation.

She spoke volubly.

"Dolores swears we'll get through, sir," Talbot interpreted.

If she was wrong, Jeremy thought, or if she was deliberately playing a trick on behalf of the freebooters, he would run aground and suffer permanent disgrace. But he continued to inch forward, and the *Porpoise*, close behind him, did the same.

Both ships squeezed through the channel, tree branches and long, drooping weeds actually brushing against the hulls of both vessels as they threaded the narrows.

All at once they entered the placid waters of a lagoon. Directly ahead, riding at anchor, were four of the buccaneer ships, one of them the large vessel that had mounted twelve-pounder cannon, another a converted brig that had been reduced to a near-hulk.

"Open fire!" Jeremy ordered. "Send them to the bottom!"

The guns roared, with twelve-pounders, nine-pounders, and six-pounders all going into action simultaneously. Lord Saunders needed no urging, and the *Porpoise* quickly opened fire too.

Dolores screamed and covered her ears with her hands.

"Take her below," Jeremy told the boatswain, "and keep her there until the action ends."

Talbot obeyed with reluctance, unhappy because he would be missing the battle.

What followed, however, was no combat in the ordinary sense. The freebooter ships were manned by skeleton crews unable to return the strong enemy fire or even hoist anchor. The entrance to the lagoon was blocked, and all four of the vessels were helpless, forced to endure a ferocious cannonading.

The converted brig was the first casualty, listing heavily to port, then slowly sinking.

The barrage continued, and two of the remaining ships were set on fire.

Members of their skeleton crews tried to escape by jumping overboard and heading toward the shore.

"Bring some sharpshooters up to the main deck in a hurry," Jeremy told M'Bwana, "and tell them not to allow one of those swimmers to reach dry land. If just one of them makes his way up to the mountains and gives the alert, we'll have a far worse battle to fight."

Sharpshooters were summoned, and opened fire on the swimmers. The action was ruthless and cold-blooded, contrary to all of the prevailing rules of warfare, but Jeremy believed he had no choice. Obviously Lord Saunders felt the same way: Royal marines in green uniforms lined the deck of the *Porpoise* and were taking aim at the swimmers too. American and British casualties in the climactic engagement yet to be fought might be far lighter if the enemy was prevented from giving the alarm to the main body of buccaneers, who had retreated to their mountain stronghold.

The freebooter flagship was sturdy, and both the *Elizabeth* and the *Porpoise* fired round after round into her, puncturing her hull repeatedly and reducing her superstructure to kindling. But still she refused to sink.

Jeremy thought of sending a boarding party to put the torch to her. Before he could act, however, flames suddenly shot skyward amidship, and within moments the entire ship was burning.

The bombardment ceased, and the silence was punctuated only by the musket fire of the sharpshooters.

M'Bwana was watching through his glass. "Ah, we got one, the poor devil. Another, a score for Saunders' lads." He spoke calmly enough, but the experience shook him.

"Did any of them get ashore?" Jeremy wanted to know.

"Nary a one. A horrible way to die, but we've had no choice."

The *Elizabeth* and the *Porpoise* anchored near the entrance to the channel, effectively blocking it in the event that other buccaneer ships should arrive in the next few days. Jeremy and Admiral Saunders agreed that it was prudent to leave strong forces on board both ships so they could repel any attackers who might appear.

Then landing parties were organized, and one hundred men from each of the ships were rowed ashore, with each carrying his own musket, ammunition, and enough food to last for three or four days. Jeremy had hoped to leave M'Bwana in command of the *Elizabeth*, but he decided such a move made no sense. No one was better-equipped than the Bantu prince to lead the land expedition, which would be crossing terrain similar in many ways to the tropical world he had known in the African jungles. So one of the lieutenants took temporary charge of the ship.

Dolores went ashore in the commodore's gig, and Jeremy glared alternately at her and at Talbot. "Tell the woman I'll tolerate none of her female disturbances on this march. I'm making you responsible for her conduct, Boatswain, and I'll have your hide if she makes advances to any man."

"Aye, aye, sir," Talbot replied dolefully, and sighed. Never had a chief boatswain been given such a strange order.

Ten men from each of the ships were assigned to the vanguard, under M'Bwana's leadership. Dolores went with this party as a guide, attended by the dour Talbot. Jeremy and Dickie Saunders marched with the main body.

Within minutes of leaving the lagoon, Dolores removed her high-heeled shoes and made the march in her bare feet. Her stamina was limited, however, so the company's progress was slower by far than it would have been if the men had known where they were headed. In all, however, the girl proved to be less of a handicap than Jeremy had feared. She exchanged her blouse for a man's shirt, which she wore with the sleeves rolled up; she borrowed a pair of long trousers that made it easier for her to plow through bramble bushes and thickets; and she tied her hair at the nape of her neck with a ribbon.

The shelling of the buccaneer fleet had made her aware of the seriousness of the expedition, and she abandoned her flirtatious ways, but she was cheerful in the face of obstacles as she trudged beside M'Bwana, and even when her steps faltered she was reluctant to admit she was tired.

First they made their way through a rain forest where the odors of the tropics were almost overpowering. The purpose of the expedition was grim, but the attitude displayed by Dolores changed the mood of the men. She saw a pair of wild orchids growing, placed one in her own hair, and insisted that M'Bwana do the same. Thereafter no one minded the heat, the thorns, or the insects.

They camped that night in a forest clearing, and after Jeremy and the admiral ordered that no fires be lighted, they ate cold meat and parched corn, drinking water from a nearby brook.

Jeremy thought it might be wise to assign a special night guard to keep watch over Dolores, but M'Bwana unexpectedly solved the problem. The girl was performing a valuable service, he announced, and consequently was under his personal protection. Any man who molested her or approached her for any reason would be responsible to him.

The change in Dolores was remarkable. She was quiet now, her manner earnest, and she treated the men as comrades rather than as potential customers. Certainly the gravity of her own situation had a bearing on her approach. If the buccaneers learned of her participation in the expedition, she would be a marked woman in the future.

The next morning the march was resumed, and they left the forest behind as they moved into rolling hill country where the vegetation consisted, in the main, of knee-high grass interspersed with an occasional towering hardwood tree. In the distance they saw large herds of the wild cattle that roamed the interior of Hispaniola and for generations had been the main source of food for bands of freebooters. No one had ever known for certain who had first introduced the cattle to the island.

For all practical purposes, M'Bwana took active command of the company. From time to time he called a halt while he pressed an ear to the ground and listened intently. Occasionally he climbed a tree, moving with the agility of a monkey, and remained motionless for long periods in the upper branches. Only after assuring himself that no foes were in the area did he permit the company to proceed.

They moved steadily toward higher ground, covering a distance of about twelve miles, only half of what they might have done had they not been hampered by Dolores' lack of strength. By late afternoon they could see the towering peaks that marked the border separating Santo Domingo and Haiti. The line of demarcation had no significance, however, because no one lived in this wild region except freebooters.

That evening Dolores became jittery, apparently realizing that she was placing herself in danger. M'Bwana managed to calm her, however, stroking her hand and speaking to her at length in soothing tones while Boatswain Talbot translated for him. Eventually her incipient hysteria subsided, and she was so exhausted she fell asleep.

"I promised her," M'Bwana told Jeremy and the admiral, "that we'll leave her behind in a safe place tomorrow when we approach the buccaneer headquarters, and that we'll assign four men as her bodyguards. At the first sign that we might be defeated, they're to retreat to the ships, take her on board, and protect her from the freebooters with their own lives. Her courage has been greater than any of us have realized. She swears she'll be tortured to death if she falls into the hands of the buccaneers. She claims they're worse than savages, that they kill and torment people for the sheer joy of it."

Lord Saunders nodded. "I'm sure she doesn't exaggerate. Many of the tales I've heard about these pirates in the years I've been in the West Indies—and I'm speaking of stories that have been confirmed by people they've held as captives—have been blood-curdling."

"All the more reason for the world to be rid of them," Jeremy said, relieved that—so far, at least—his gamble on Dolores seemed to be paying off.

The march was resumed after an early breakfast of smoked meat and parched corn, and they headed into the mountains. The rocks underfoot became sharper, and they had to pause while M'Bwana, demonstrating remarkable skill, made thick, comfortable footgear for Dolores out of broad leaves of tropical grass.

There was no flirtatiousness in the smile of gratitude she bestowed on the Bantu.

By noon they had climbed high into the mountains, and when they paused for a light meal M'Bwana insisted that henceforth all conversation be held to a minimum. Again he placed his ear to the ground, then reported in pantomime to Jeremy and the admiral that they were no more than two miles from the buccaneer camp.

Talbot and three mature veterans were ordered to guard Dolores, to proceed no farther with her, and to take her back to the warships in the lagoon if serious trouble developed.

Muskets and pistols were loaded, swords were loosened in their sheaths, and the Royal marines affixed bayonets to their firearms. M'Bwana, who carried a brace of pistols in his belt, also had a leather container slung over his shoulder. From it he removed a dozen spears, each no more than two feet long, and taking a vial containing a pale brown liquid from a pocket, he dipped the metal tips of the spears in the solution. No one questioned him, but it was obvious that he was relying on weapons he had used in Africa, and that he had poisoned the spear tips.

The admiral gave the signal to resume the march.

Before the company moved off, Dolores went to M'Bwana and kissed him lightly. The gesture was that of a woman who was thankful for the help he had given her, and was completely lacking in sexual provocation.

Jeremy and Lord Saunders moved side by side behind the vanguard, at the head of the main column.

They proceeded for more than a mile without incident and began to make their way through a narrow pass no more than twenty or thirty feet wide, with a sheer cliff at each side.

A shot fired by a buccaneer sentry broke the silence.

Jeremy instinctively flattened himself against the stone wall of the cliff, and Lord Saunders followed his example.

But that was not M'Bwana's way. Long accustomed to wilderness warfare, he motioned his vanguard forward, then leaped behind a boulder, at the same instant firing a pistol. The body of the buccaneer sentry toppled at his feet.

Jeremy galvanized himself into action. Waving the main body forward, he followed the vanguard, running at full speed.

They made their way safely through the pass, which would have been a bottleneck, and found themselves on a broad mountainside littered with enormous boulders that made their tactics obvious.

"Spread out and take cover behind the rocks," Jeremy shouted, and the men obeyed.

The vanguard, imitating M'Bwana, had already done the same thing.

Suddenly the buccaneers roared down the mountainside, some carrying muskets and others brandishing swords. They were employing the same techniques they utilized when boarding a ship and rushed their foes en masse, which made them easy targets.

"Pick them off!" M'Bwana called.

American and British seamen proceeded to do just that, and within moments the mountainside was littered with the bodies of freebooters.

But the buccaneers still had a major advantage. They outnumbered their attackers by at least three to one, and in spite of the casualties they suffered, they continued to pour down the side of the mountain. Their tactics were questionable at best, but they were not lacking in courage, and soon they achieved their immediate goal, that of engaging in individual combat against most of their enemies.

Lord Saunders faced a bearded young giant who was only half his age and who wielded a double-edged sword with fierce abandon. The admiral excelled as a swordsman, but he was accustomed to the niceties of formal duels, and the freebooters observed no rules.

It became plain to Jeremy that his colleague soon would be overwhelmed, and he ran toward the admiral, but was too late. A vicious blow knocked Saunders' sword from his hand, and the freebooter's blade cut deeply into his side.

M'Bwana, who was on higher ground, ducked behind a boulder just as a freebooter took aim at him with a pistol. As he braced himself for his opponent's certain assault, he became aware of a danger below that Jeremy did not recognize.

Still running across open ground toward the fallen Dickie Saunders, Jeremy had made himself a perfect target for a freebooter who was armed with a musket.

M'Bwana had to make a rapid choice, that of saving himself or preserving the life of the friend whom his father had directed him to guard, no matter what the cost.

He drew a short spear from its container and hurled it with deadly accuracy. It struck the face of the freebooter with the musket, the poison did its work, and the man fell without making a sound.

But M'Bwana paid the penalty for his selfless act. A buccaneer bullet smashed into him, and he too crumpled to the stony ground.

The realization that both Dickie Saunders and M'Bwana had fallen drove Jeremy berserk. "Hold your ground!" he shouted repeatedly. "Kill without quarter!" Seizing the dead buccaneer's musket, he fired it, quickly reloaded, and fired again.

His example steadied the sailors, and the Anglo-American sharpshooters rallied, giving far better than they received. The buccaneers could not stand up to their deadly fire, and so many were killed that the remainder became panicky and fled. The battle ended as abruptly as it had started, and neither then nor later did anyone ever know how many of the buccaneers escaped, leaving their dead behind.

Lord Saunders was still breathing, but had lost consciousness, and by the time Jeremy reached him, a British seaman had managed to stop the flow of blood from a deep wound in his side.

M'Bwana was unconscious too, and it appeared he had suffered a somewhat less severe but nonetheless serious wound. As nearly as Jeremy could judge, a bullet was lodged in the lower part of the Bantu's shoulder.

Anglo-American casualties had been relatively light, with five sailors and one Royal marine killed and a dozen others injured; most of the wounded were able to make their way with minimal assistance. The buccaneers had paid a heavy toll, however, and their dead were strewn on the field of combat. Jeremy made no attempt to count the enemy casualties or to guess how many had escaped.

One task still remained, and Jeremy dispatched a lieutenant and a squad of men to attend to it. These sailors climbed higher into the mountains and, as expected, found the headquarters of the freebooters, located in a series of connecting caves.

Wasting no time, they demolished the lair. Private belongings were consigned to bonfires. Far more important, however, was the destruction of the buccaneers' weapons. Muskets, pistols, and swords were confiscated, as was ammunition. Gunpowder was consigned to the flames, which leaped high in the air.

By the time the squad returned to the main body, which was now ready to begin the long march back to the lagoon, nothing was left of what had been the pirates' mountain hideout. The still-burning fires gave evidence of that fact.

Litters were fashioned for Lord Saunders and M'Bwana, and the victors began the march down from the mountains. When they came to the place where Dolores and her guards were waiting, the girl was horrified by the wounds that the admiral and the American flag lieutenant had suffered, but she quickly rallied and insisted on tending both of them.

Whenever they halted near a stream, she washed their wounds and bathed their heads in water, and she walked between their pallets, keeping watch over them. That night M'Bwana regained consciousness for a short time and managed to grin weakly when he saw Dolores bending over him.

Jeremy was worried about both of his friends, and was somewhat relieved when they reached the lagoon, where the ships' surgeons awaited them. The bullet was removed immediately from M'Bwana's shoulder, and the American surgeon said that, thanks to his rugged constitution, he should recover in short order. When he was carried to his cabin after the operation, Dolores accompanied him, announcing through Boatswain Talbot that she intended to stay with him and assist him.

Admiral Saunders' condition remained grave. He had lost considerable quantities of blood, and there was little the British surgeon could do for him other than wash his wound in brandywine, the most effective disinfectant known, and then pack it with healing herbs.

Jeremy wasted no time in setting sail for Barbados, and twenty-four hours after leaving the Hispaniola lagoon, when he paid a visit to M'Bwana, he found his friend sitting up in bed, trying to teach Dolores the rudiments of English.

In spite of the language barrier, he had already learned a great deal about the girl. Deserted as an infant, she knew only that one of her parents had been black and the other white. Reared in a bordello, she had gone to work there as an inmate in her early teens, and had never known any other life.

Boatswain Talbot was summoned, and acting as her interpreter again, revealed that she had no desire to return to Santo Domingo. M'Bwana helped plan her future, and she decided she wanted to open a small shop of some kind in Barbados, where she would encounter no color barrier. The Bantu gave her a substantial sum of money for the purpose, and a grateful Jeremy, realizing the successful expedition could not have been launched without her assistance, matched his friend's gift.

The following day they anchored off Bridgetown, and Jeremy steeled himself for an ordeal he dreaded. Lord Saunders, who had regained consciousness for short periods, was taken ashore on a litter, with both Jeremy and the British surgeon accompanying him on the carriage ride to his estate.

Lisa was stunned when she came to the front door and saw her husband being carried into the house. She and Jeremy carefully avoided each other's gaze as she listened to the surgeon.

"I'm reasonably certain his lordship has passed the crisis and will survive," the surgeon said, "But I hesitate to predict how long it may take him to regain his health. He suffered a nasty wound, and I find it remarkable that he's still alive. He'll require constant attention—medical care and nursing—in the months ahead."

"He shall have it," Lisa said. "I'll devote myself to him—to the exclusion of all else."

Before Jeremy returned to Bridgetown, he had a few moments alone with Lisa, and forced himself to face her squarely. "For whatever consolation this may be to you," he said, "Dickie is a hero, and was responsible for our victory. I just wish he'd been spared. I'd have much preferred that I be the one to suffer the injury."

"I'm sure you feel that way." Lisa's voice was soft.

"I . . . . I hope you'll write to me and tell me of his progress," Jeremy said.

She shook her head firmly. "No," she said. "His condition changes everything. You and I must not be in touch with each other again, either in person or by letter."

Jeremy knew she was right, and bowed to the inevitable. "Very well. But if there's anything I can do, ever—for you . . . or for Dickie—you know I shall."

"Thank you." Lisa fought back the tears that threatened to fill her eyes. "Good-bye, my dearest dear." She turned away quickly and left the room.

Jeremy remained unmoving until she disappeared from sight, and then he walked quickly to the waiting carriage. A phase of his life had come to an end, and he had to put Lisa out of his mind and heart for all time. He and Lisa would have been forced to take such a step under any circumstances, he knew, but to his own dying day he would regret that the tragedy Dickie Saunders had suffered had forced them apart. Never would he recover from the shame of his betrayal, from the knowledge that he had sacrificed honor for the sake of his own desire.

When he reached Bridgetown he found that Dolores had already organized her new way of life. With the help of Talbot she had purchased a part-interest in a shop that sold bolts of cloth, and would be associated with a woman from Puerto Rico. She would live in quarters available above the shop, and had already purchased new clothes that made her appear less conspicuous.

Jeremy allowed her to pay a final visit to the *Elizabeth* so she could bid farewell to M'Bwana, whom she regarded as her principal benefactor. The surgeon had permitted him to leave his bed for a short time, and he was sitting in a chair when Dolores entered his cabin.

The ship was preparing for an immediate departure, Jeremy being anxious to rejoin his squadron in Jamaica, and Talbot's roars echoed across the decks as he sent crew members to their sailing stations.

Dolores used almost her entire English vocabulary. "Good-bye, my friend," she said. "Thank you." Then she leaned down and kissed M'Bwana full on the mouth before hurrying off to the boat that would take her ashore.

The *Elizabeth* weighed anchor and headed out to sea.

Jeremy had taken the watch himself, and a short time later, as they passed Indian Bridge, he deliberately turned away from the land so he would not see the Saunders estate. Lisa would not be standing on the beach to wave to him to-day—or any other time. Her husband's serious injury had terminated a relationship that could have harmed others, and it was urgent now to show the strength of character that had been lacking in the days prior to the encounters with the freebooters.

The voyage was uneventful, and before they reached Kingston Town Jeremy composed his report to President Monroe and the Navy Department. Most of the buccaneer ships had been destroyed, scores of pirates had been killed, and the rest of the band had been dispersed. But his victory was not yet complete, even though the joint operation with the Royal Navy had come to an end.

Consequently he intended to stay in the West Indies for as many more months as might be necessary to hunt down any freebooter ships that might have survived the recent operations. By the time his damaged vessels were repaired, M'Bwana would be sufficiently recovered to return to duty. Together they would scour the Caribbean Sea in their search for the buccaneers, and from time to time they would visit the secret lagoon on the southern coast of Hispaniola.

"I shall not rest," he wrote, "until I send the last of these scum to the bottom. I shall go anywhere in my quest."

That statement, Jeremy realized, was not quite accurate. Never again could he take the risk of returning to Barbados.

# Chapter 8

Life at Oakhurst Manor was tranquil, at least on the surface. Sarah Beaufort conducted the affairs of the plantation with an expertise born of long practice, and the enlightened efficiency of Lester Howard in dealing with the field hands produced bumper crops. Profits were greater than they had ever been.

Sarah's admiration for the overseer continued to grow. He was a naturally kind and thoughtful man, she realized, as was evidenced by the attention he paid to Jerry and Lance. He went out of his way to take the boys hunting and fishing in the absence of Jeremy and M'Bwana, teaching them how to handle firearms and knives, and sometimes organized overnight camping expeditions for them. Lance, who excelled in outdoor activities, followed him everywhere.

In his spare time Lester made several puppets, Kai fashioned costumes for them, and together they amused little Carrie, whose mother paid scant attention to her. In fact, Alicia Emerson was a never-ending cause for concern.

Her brother made it his business to ride out to Oakhurst Manor from Charleston every weekend, ostensibly for social purposes but actually to keep an eye on her. Scott no longer lectured her, however, because she paid no heed to his advice. Alicia slept late, then wandered aimlessly around the house in one of her silk negligees, and usually didn't bother to dress until it was time for dinner.

It was Kai, who brought Carrie to her one day when the baby was weeping and could not be consoled, who accidentally discovered Alicia's secret, and reported it at dinner to Sarah and Lester, who had formed the habit of eating the principal meal of the day at the mansion.

"I hate to say this," Kai said, "but as I came into her sitting room, Alicia was drinking from a bottle, and the whole place reeked of whiskey. She paid so little attention to the baby that I took Carrie back to my own quarters and finally managed to calm her. Alicia shoved the whiskey jug under a settee as I came into the room, but I saw it before she could put it away."

Sarah was deeply troubled. "Do you suppose she drinks fairly regularly?"

Kai shrugged. "All I know for certain is what happened today."

"Drinking would explain her erratic conduct," Sarah said, and instinctively turned to the overseer for his help and advice.

"I've suspected Alicia of secret drinking for many weeks," Lester said. "I've never been able to prove it, and what she does is none of my business, but I've often smelled liquor on her breath when she comes down to dinner."

"I can't understand why she should drink," Sarah said. "No one in the Emerson family ever had that problem, really, although Scott was sometimes a bit careless in his rakehell days."

"It must have something to do with Alicia's experiences in New Orleans," Kai said. "I've tried in various ways to urge her to talk about them, but she refuses to say a word."

"From what I've seen of drinkers," Lester said, "either they solve the problems that sent them to the bottle in the first place, or they grow constantly worse."

"We can't let Alicia throw away her life," Sarah said firmly. "Not only for her own sake, but for her baby's."

"I don't see how you can stop her," Lester said. "As for Carrie, Kai has pretty much taken charge of her."

"It's the least I can do," Kai said. "She's such a darling little girl that I can't bear to see her being neglected."

"Well, we can't allow matters to drift, and I won't," Sarah said. "Margot and Tom have invited Scott to Trelawney this weekend, so I imagine he'll stop off here on his way, and I'll have a talk with him. Perhaps we can find some solution."

They did not refer to the problem again, although it remained in their minds. That Saturday Scott Emerson arrived at Oakhurst Manor at noon, while Kai and Lester were entertaining Jerry, Lance, and Carrie with the hand puppets. Sarah, who had been working in her flower garden, immediately removed her gloves and conducted Scott to a sitting room.

"I'm relieved that you're here, because all of us have been badly worried," she said. "Forgive my bluntness, but I don't know of any other way to tell you this. But Kai, Lester Howard, and I all suspect that Alicia is a secret drinker."

The young attorney nodded, wrinkles creasing his forehead. "I'm not surprised, and what you tell me confirms my hunch. Sarah, Alicia isn't related to you, except indirectly, and there's no reason you should be forced to carry this burden. I'm going to insist that Alicia come to Charleston and move into my place."

"She'll refuse, Scott, and you know it!"

He sighed. "I'm afraid you're right, but Aunt Lorene and your father will take her in, and—"

"No!" Sarah was emphatic.

"But Aunt Lorene is immediate family—"

"You're forgetting Carrie," Sarah said. "Alicia takes no responsibility for her child, and that's the heart of the problem. No matter how good Aunt Lorene's intentions might be, and I'm sure she'd do anything in her power for all of us, she and Papa are simply too old to assume responsibility for a baby girl. They'd do their best, but they couldn't cope."

Scott tried to object.

But Sarah silenced him. "Our situation is different. Cleo is wonderful with children, as you know. I do what I can. And Kai is a godsend. She treats Carrie as though the baby were her own, and nowhere else would Alicia's daughter get all that loving attention. What's more, Lester Howard is marvelous with her, too."

"Quite a fellow, that overseer." Scott had no intention of being snide, but it was obvious that Margot and Tom had talked to him about Sarah's emotional involvement with Howard.

Sarah leaped to his defense without apology. "He cares as much for Carrie as Kai and I do, and he's just employed here, remember. I'm grateful for his interest, and you should be, too."

"You're right, of course," he admitted. "But this doesn't solve the problem of what to do about Alicia."

"I suggest you make one more attempt to have a talk with her, Scott. We must help her find and help herself."

"You never give up, Sarah. It's amazing. All right, I'll try again. Where is she?"

"I haven't seen her as yet today. I'll ask Cleo to tell her you're here."

The housekeeper was summoned, went upstairs, and returned to the sitting room, her face bleak. "Missy Alicia not here," she said in obvious disapproval. "No sleep in bed. Cleo find this." She handed Sarah a sealed envelope.

The message it contained was as brief as it was vague:

*Sarah, dear:*

*I've gone off to Savannah for a few days. Don't worry about me. I'll see you in a short time.*

> *Your loving*
> *Alicia*

Sarah was stunned, and Scott was bewildered. "What friends might she visit in Savannah?" Sarah asked.

"I have no idea. A number of families there were close to our parents, but she hasn't set eyes on any of them for years. What's more, all of them are the stodgy, conservative kind of people she professes to hate."

It occurred to Sarah that Alicia might have gone off for a rendezvous with some man, but she was too discreet to mention the idea.

Scott appeared to read her mind. "Has she had any visits? Or any letters?"

"Not to my knowledge."

"Then I suspect she's simply gone off to an inn where she can drink herself unconscious." Scott was badly upset. "The worst of it is that she's abandoned her baby."

"Not really. She knows that Kai and Cleo and I will look after Carrie."

"All the same," he said, "she shows no responsibility for her own child!"

"We'll see to it that Carrie doesn't suffer. That's one advantage of giving Alicia a home here."

She was right, of course, but Scott knew that the basic dilemma was as yet unsolved.

A smiling, seemingly unperturbed Alicia Emerson returned to Oakhurst Manor four days later, telling no one where she had been or what she had done. She carried several new gowns in her luggage, so it was safe to assume they had been made for her by a Savannah dressmaker, but she made no reference to them or to her journey. She resumed her indolent ways.

The days passed, and one morning, about two weeks later, Sarah was at work in her garden when a stranger on horseback rode up the long driveway to the mansion.

He was a tall, slender man of about forty, with a thin mustache and a long scar on one side of his face, and his appearance was striking. He wore a white suit with black trim, a black waistcoat trimmed in white, a pair of white boots, and a white hat of brushed felt, set off with a black feather. He dismounted with elegant ease, and Sarah noted that he carried a long, utilitarian sword.

She had not expected company this morning. Her housedress was limp, there were smudges of dirt on her face, and she felt grubby as she removed her gloves and walked to the portico.

The man's attitude was arrogant. "I assume this is Oakhurst Manor?" he asked.

She took an instant dislike to him. "It is," she replied curtly. "I am Sarah Beaufort, and this is my home."

His manner changed when she identified herself. He removed his hat, revealing a balding head, and bowed low. "Emile Duchamp of New Orleans at your service, Mistress

Beaufort. Forgive my lack of manners, but I've been on the road from Louisiana for many days. I hope I haven't made my trip in vain. I've been told that Alicia Emerson is a guest here, and I've traveled a long way to see her."

"Yes, she's staying with us," Sarah said, and knew that good manners required her to receive this stranger hospitably. She conducted him into the house, sent a servant to tell Alicia of his arrival, and after pouring him a glass of sack, which he was pleased to accept, she went off to her own suite to change.

The postman arrived with a letter from Amanda and Willie, which she had to read to Cleo. It contained the good news that Amanda had given birth to a daughter, whom she had named after her mother-in-law, and the ordinarily stolid and unemotional Cleo's eyes filled with tears. Sarah read the letter to her a second time, and they rejoiced together.

When Sarah finally returned to the sitting room, she found a heavily made-up Alicia, dressed as though she were attending an evening party, engaging in an intense, low-toned conversation with Emile Duchamp. They seemed to be arguing, and both appeared upset, but they cut their conversation short when the mistress of Oakhurst Manor came into the room.

"You'll stay for dinner with us, Master Duchamp?" Sarah felt she had to offer the invitation.

"With the greatest of pleasure, ma'am." Duchamp's broad smile revealed two rows of even, gleaming teeth. "In fact, if it's no imposition, I hope you have a spare room I might be able to use for a few days."

Sarah couldn't remember when a guest had asked to stay at the plantation, but it would have been rude to reject the request, so she acceded with as much grace as she could muster.

Alicia glowered but said nothing.

Duchamp, already at home, praised the manor house in detail, and it was obvious he had noted everything of consequence about the architecture, decor, and furnishings.

Lester Howard arrived for dinner, and reacted with even more reserve than usual when introduced to the guest. He bowed stiffly, and thereafter said very little, replying in monosyllables to direct questions.

The last to arrive was Kai, who looked lovely in a simple, full-skirted gown with a square-cut neckline.

She made an immediate impression on Duchamp, who studied her at length and thereafter made certain to include her in his voluble conversation.

Sarah couldn't be certain whether his interest in Kai was real or whether he was using her as a means of arousing the sullen Alicia's jealousy.

Whatever his motives, he proved to be a man of considerable charm. He told a number of stories about New Orleans and about shipping on the Mississippi River, he was conversant with current Washington City politics, and he knew a great deal about the operations of a plantation.

He was making an effort to be pleasant, and both Kai and Sarah responded in kind, although the latter could not rid herself of a sense of uneasiness. Perhaps the unexpected tensions at the table were responsible. Alicia remained surly, saying very little and gulping her wine, while Lester Howard remained stiff and uncommunicative, too.

After the meal ended, Duchamp made such an issue of taking a stroll with Alicia that she was forced to accompany him. Kai went off to make certain the children were taking their naps, and Lester followed Sarah into the library.

"What's that man's relationship with Alicia?" he demanded before she could question him about his own conduct.

"I haven't yet had a chance to speak with her alone," Sarah said, taken aback by his unaccustomed ferocity.

"Duchamp," he said, "isn't the sort you or Jeremy make welcome at Oakhurst Manor."

"You know him, Lester?"

"We met in New Orleans, although he has no reason to remember me. He's one of the most accomplished swordsmen in Louisiana, and it's been rumored he's killed several men in duels, although that's something I can't prove."

Sarah shared the overseer's dislike of dueling, but didn't regard that as sufficient reason to condemn Duchamp. She raised an eyebrow and waited.

"He gambles for large sums. I've seen him at the tables myself, so I know there's more to such stories than hearsay." Lester seemed reluctant to talk.

"Well," Sarah said, "if he can afford to gamble for high

stakes, that's his privilege. Are you insinuating that he's a professional gambler, Lester?"

"Not really. He's notorious as a slave trader, and he's stocked many plantations up and down the Mississippi with slaves."

She tried to be fair. "You and I may not approve, but slave trading is legal."

"If you must know," he said, "Duchamp also owns the fanciest brothel in New Orleans. He tries hard—a little too hard, if you ask me—to pose as a gentleman, but no decent man in Louisiana will associate with him. I hate to tell stories behind anyone's back, but I'd be derelict in my own duty to you if I kept silent." He bowed slightly and marched out of the library.

Sarah was grateful to him and wanted to call him back, but she refrained, realizing their own strains would be relieved if he returned without delay to his own work. She was disturbed by what he had told her about Duchamp, but after pondering for a time, she decided to take no action.

If Jeremy were here and ordered Duchamp to leave the property, it would be different. She could not allow herself to lose sight of the fact that Alicia's sense of balance was delicate, and an unpleasant scene involving the man who had traveled hundreds of miles to see her might create new complications. Perhaps it would be easiest to do and say nothing, and in a few days Duchamp would depart.

Sarah kept busy all afternoon, and at dusk happened to see Alicia and Duchamp return from their long walk. She was white-faced and silent, while he looked annoyed.

Returning to the master suite, Sarah changed for supper. Just as she was finishing dressing, a servant came to her with word that Mistress Emerson was indisposed and would not be coming downstairs for supper.

Determined to get to the bottom of the mystery, Sarah went at once to Alicia's suite, and found her sprawled on a divan in her sitting room. Contrary to Sarah's expectations, however, she had not been drinking.

"I'm sorry to place a burden on you this evening, Sarah, truly I am," Alicia said. "It's just that I . . . I'm so angry and upset I couldn't be civil to Emile tonight, and I don't want to make a scene."

"Would you prefer that I ask him to leave?"

Alicia shook her head. "No, he loves dramatic situations, and I don't want to give him the satisfaction of creating one for him. I'll be in complete control of myself by morning, I promise you, and when Emile sees that I won't weaken in my resolve, he'll go of his own volition in a day or two."

"Weaken in what resolve?"

"Emile wants me to come back to New Orleans with him," Alicia said, "but his wife is still alive, and he knows I've sworn to have no more to do with him until he gets a formal court order putting her aside so he can marry again."

It was obvious that Duchamp was the lover with whom she had lived in New Orleans and, in all probability, was Carrie's father.

"Yes," Alicia said bitterly, "he paid all of my expenses for several years after I made the mistake of falling in love with him. And the bigger mistake of believing that his invalid wife would die at any time. I'm sure she'll outlive all of us, just as I know that Emile uses her as an excuse to avoid a permanent involvement with anyone else."

Sarah didn't know how to reply to such frankness. "He must think very highly of you if he's come all the way to South Carolina to find you."

"Emile doesn't think highly of any woman," Alicia said harshly. "Other mistresses bore him once he's conquered them. I challenge him because I'm a lady—or I was before I got mixed up with him. He's never known anyone like me. Oh, he's generous enough, I suppose, and I've learned how to handle him so he doesn't make many of his outrageous demands on me. But I refuse—ever again—to live in the shadows."

Sarah had heard far more than she had wanted to know. She couldn't have imagined herself arguing in favor of Alicia's return to a lover, but there were many factors to be considered. "If he'll give your baby financial security, you might want to accept."

Alicia's face was stony. "You're a good woman, so you simply don't and can't understand. Because of Emile I . . . I despise that child!" Suddenly she laughed. "There, just saying it makes me feel better. Be kind tonight, Sarah. Tolerate Emile through supper, and I give you my solemn pledge to be on hand all day tomorrow. By the next morning he'll be gone, and all of us can forget him. Forever."

Sarah was convinced Alicia was still in love with him; that was the root of her problem. It was better to say nothing, however, so she took her leave.

She heard voices in the principal drawing room when she went downstairs, and it was something of a shock to see Emile Duchamp exerting all of his charm on Kai, who was spellbound by a story he was telling her. It occurred to Sarah that Kai, who was young, impressionable, and lonely during her husband's absence, was fair game for such a man. There had been no opportunity earlier to issue a warning, but now that she was armed with facts, she would seek the first opportunity to speak with Kai in confidence. He was the sort of man every intelligent woman avoided.

There was no denying his magnetism, however. He was exerting it to the full, and deftly drew his hostess into his circle even while concentrating his efforts on Kai. When the disapproving, still-silent Lester Howard appeared for supper, Duchamp ignored his snubs and chatted on, as though talking with an old friend.

Thanks to his charm, the meal proved to be less of a disaster than Sarah had anticipated. It was astonishing, she thought: she knew he was a brothel owner and slave trader, that he had hopelessly compromised and corrupted Alicia, and had sired her illegitimate baby. Yet she found herself listening avidly to the man's stories and laughing at his jokes.

As they were completing the main course, a servant came to the door and announced breathlessly that a silo filled with corn had caught fire.

Lester immediately excused himself, and Sarah felt it was her duty to accompany him. "Finish dinner without us," she said. "We'll be back as soon as we can."

Duchamp told the fascinated Kai the climax of a story about New Orleans, then added lightly, "You might want to visit my city one day."

Kai was guileless. "Yes," she said, "I hope my husband will take me there."

"When will he return home?"

"Not for many months. I had a letter only this week, and their operations in the West Indies will go on."

"In that case," Duchamp said, "you might enjoy the change of scenery in the near future. I'd be delighted to show you New Orleans, and I'm certain I could take you to every place of interest in the town."

"That's very kind of you."

He pretended that an idea had just that instant occurred to him. "I'm going straight back there when I leave here, so I could escort you. There's nothing that would give me greater pleasure." He was telling the truth. Not since he had first met Alicia had any woman struck him with such impact. In fact, he found himself wanting this girl so much that he wasn't bothered by Alicia's refusal to go back to New Orleans with him.

For the first time Kai began to discern his motives, and studied him quietly, her lids half-lowered.

Duchamp thought she was flirting with him, and jumped to the conclusion that she might be weakening. "My dear," he said, "a girl as beautiful as you should wear gorgeous gowns. I'll provide you with trunkloads of them. You should have jewels to set you off too, and I'll buy you many kinds. Bracelets and necklaces and earrings." He reached for her hand.

Kai instantly withdrew. "You're making a mistake, sir," she said. "I love my husband, and I don't care to have anything to do with any other man."

"You'd soon be the queen of New Orleans society," Duchamp said. "You're wasting your substance, hiding away from the world in this rural backwater!"

"This is my home and my child's home as well as my husband's home," Kai said with great dignity. "I'm willing to forgive your rudeness if you'll drop the matter permanently. Otherwise I'll be obliged to excuse myself and to absent myself from your society for the rest of your stay here."

He wasn't accustomed to such a reaction, which merely whetted his appetite. But he knew women, and realizing she meant what she said, he bowed his head in mock defeat. "I promise I won't say another word," he told her. "It will be enough if I look at you."

Kai was relieved beyond measure when the fire in the silo was extinguished and Sarah returned, although Lester stayed behind to supervise the cleanup operation.

They adjourned to a veranda for coffee, and the embarrassed Kai soon retired, pleading a headache.

Duchamp refused Sarah's offer of a liqueur. "I had a long journey, and I'm going to retire soon myself," he said. "Before I go, Mistress Beaufort, I beg you not to think too badly of me. I don't know what Alicia may have told you about the past, and I don't want to contradict anything she may have said. I have too high an opinion of her for that. All I ask is that you remember there are two sides to every question."

He bowed over her hand and was gone.

Sarah shuddered and rubbed the back of her hand on the fabric of her chair. Emile Duchamp was too clever for his own good, much less that of any woman, and she felt desperately sorry for Alicia, who deserved a better fate than that of falling in love with such a person.

At an early breakfast the next morning Kai made it clear that she disliked Duchamp, but she was still too embarrassed to discuss the advances he had made to her.

Sarah, for her part, was relieved, and saw no reason to break Alicia's confidences, so she made no mention of the visitor's background. Both women went about their day's business.

Later, as Sarah returned from her regular morning ride around the property with Lester, she heard Alicia's voice raised in anger. Not wanting to eavesdrop, she waited until quiet was restored before she went into the house.

Emile Duchamp was waiting for her, dressed in his traveling clothes. It was necessary for him to leave at once for New Orleans, he told her, and he thanked her at length for her hospitality.

Kai was in the yard, supervising the play of the children, and as Duchamp went to bid her good-bye, Sarah, who stayed inside the house, noted that he did not even bother to glance in the direction of Carrie. Certainly he knew she was his daughter!

Duchamp bent over Kai's hand. "If you should change your mind, you know where to find me. I won't forget you, and I swear we'll meet again."

She had to restrain herself from reverting to the ways she had known as a child on the Barbary Coast of North Africa and spitting in his face.

A red-eyed Alicia joined Sarah at the window. "I sent the bastard away," she said, "and I told him never to bother me again. Good riddance to him!" Without waiting for a reply, she headed up the stairs.

At dinner that day both Sarah and Kai were lighthearted, and they laughed far more than usual. Even the quiet Lester was in something of a festive mood. No one bothered to mention Emile Duchamp.

Alicia did not appear for dinner or for supper that evening. She stayed in her suite for the next two days and nights, and during that time she did not draw a sober breath.

Life at Oakhurst Manor resumed its even tenor, and even Alicia became more cheerful, curtailing her drinking and joining in various activities. Lester Howard was busier than ever during the spring planting season; new silos were constructed and the barns were enlarged.

Early in April Sarah received a letter from Jeremy that was a cause for rejoicing. His mission in the West Indian islands was coming to an end. He had transferred his flag to the *Louise*, and was sailing without delay to Baltimore so he could ride to Washington City and report in person to President Monroe. Then he would sail to Charleston.

M'Bwana had taken command of the *Elizabeth*, and with the smaller ships of the squadron was putting into Barbados for minor repairs. He too was coming home, and would arrive a few weeks after Jeremy reached Oakhurst Manor. Only now did Jeremy reveal that M'Bwana had been wounded many months earlier in the decisive land battle with the buccaneers, but he emphasized that the Bantu was completely recovered and had been restored to perfect health.

The women at the plantation began to count the weeks and days. But Sarah was disturbed. She and Lester Howard had formed a pattern in their relationship that was unique: they had formed a close bond and had become almost intimate, even though they took extraordinary care to avoid physical contact of any kind. That pattern would be broken or sharply altered when Jeremy came home.

Sarah was eager to see the husband she loved after his absence of almost a year. But at the same time she was reluctant to give up her ties with the overseer, who had given her so much comfort, sympathy, and help. She remained realistic in spite of her concerns, however, and she knew she would have to let the future work itself out in its own way. Experience had taught her that problems either dissipated themselves or grew so complex that it became necessary to take a strong stand. In spite of her discomfort, she warned herself not to anticipate trouble.

About a week before Jeremy was due to arrive home, however, unexpected trouble did erupt, creating a situation as mysterious as it was tragic.

Kai did not appear for breakfast one morning, and Sarah, thinking she might be ill, asked Cleo to find out if anything was amiss.

The housekeeper went upstairs, then quickly returned to the dining room. "Missy Kai not here," she said. "Gone."

Sarah hurried to the second-floor suite, and to her astonishment discovered that Kai had not slept in her bed the previous night. All of her clothes and other belongings were in place in wardrobes and cabinets, but she herself had vanished.

Lester Howard was summoned, and with members of the household staff helping him, he scoured the entire property, but in vain. No horses were missing from the stables, and Kai had left no note. No one had seen her leave or had any idea where she had gone. The overseer continued his search.

In midmorning he came to Sarah, his face grim. "I went out to the road just beyond the plantation boundary," he said, "and I found this." He handed her a small lace handkerchief.

"This is Kai's," she said. "She bought several like this when we went shopping in Charleston two weeks ago."

"There's more," Lester said. "There was a shower last night, and only a few feet from the spot where this handkerchief was lying I saw carriage tracks. There's no doubt that a carriage was parked at the side of the road last night."

"But not one of our carriages. I can't imagine where Kai could have gone, or why. This is peculiar."

"Maybe she didn't go voluntarily."

"I'm sure of it. She wouldn't just go off and leave Lance behind. She loves her son too much for that."

"But who would want to take her off somewhere against her will? Could she have enemies we don't know about?"

"I can't imagine anyone hating Kai or wanting to harm her," the alarmed Sarah said.

The sheriff was notified, and Tom Beaufort joined Lester in a hunt that extended to the boundaries of the county and beyond. Word was sent to Charleston, and while Isaiah Benton went to work with the local constabulary there, Scott Emerson persuaded the state militia to extend the search to every part of South Carolina.

No clues were discovered. Kai seemed to have vanished from the face of the earth.

Sarah was frantic, and the atmosphere at Oakhurst Manor was so depressing that Alicia began to drink again, spending the better part of each day behind the closed doors of her suite.

"Perhaps Jeremy will know what to do when he comes home," Sarah said, speaking without conviction. "All I know is that we've got to find Kai before M'Bwana returns!"

Kai was in a daze, and could recall only brief snatches of the nightmare she had been forced to endure for day after endless day.

The terror at the very beginning had been the worst, the most sinister. Intending to retire when she had returned to her suite at Oakhurst Manor, she had found two men hiding there. Before she could scream or escape, they had seized her, expertly gagged her, and bound her. Then, waiting until the whole household had settled down for the night, they had carried her down the driveway and deposited her in a carriage, where a third man had been stationed. Then, as they had driven off with her, they had removed her gag and forced her to drink an evil-smelling potion that had caused her to lose consciousness.

The rest of the long journey on which they had taken her was a blur. She remembered vaguely that they had halted at inns every night, and she recalled that one of the men explained to the proprietors of these places that she was his wife, who was ill.

Her meals were brought to her in the privacy of her bedchamber in these inns, and although she had no appetite, she forced herself to eat. She had no idea why she had been abducted or what might be in store for her, but she knew she had to keep up her strength if she wanted to survive.

The flame of life burned bright and clear within her. For the sake of M'Bwana and Lance she intended to survive and somehow return to them.

The worst of her travail was that her captors kept her drugged day and night. Whenever she began to recover from the last dose of the potion they fed her, they insisted on giving her another. A few times Kai resisted, but on these occasions one of the men held her mouth open while another poured the nasty-tasting concoction down her throat. Gagging and spitting, she found herself helpless, and thereafter she conserved her strength by meekly drinking the substance whenever they offered it to her.

So most of the journey was fuzzy. She recalled seeing brief snatches of countryside and now and again driving through towns. But none of these memories were clear or reliable, and whenever she asked where they were taking her, the question was received in stony silence.

She had no privacy, either. One or another of her guards kept watch over her throughout the night when they stopped at inns. She would see him sitting in a corner of the room when she drifted off to sleep, and would find him still there when she awakened in the morning. In spite of her fears, however, all three of her captors treated her with the utmost respect, and none tried in any way to molest her. This attitude seemed so contrary to human nature that her fears for the future became all the more intense.

On the last night of the long journey, Kai was given an even stronger dose of the potion, and the following morning, still sound asleep, she was carried to the waiting coach for the final stage of the journey.

When she awakened, she was alone for the first time since her abduction. She found herself in a canopied four-poster bed, wearing a delicate nightgown of silk she had never before seen. The bedchamber itself was large and ornate, and beyond it, through an open door, she saw a handsomely furnished sitting room.

One of the windows was open, but the shutters outside it were closed and locked, and those that covered the other windows also were closed, making it impossible for her to look outdoors. She heard street sounds below, and the heavy traffic convinced her that she was in a city of some consequence, but she had no idea what it might be.

Lying in the bed, a mound of silken pillows beneath her head, Kai gradually began to identify sounds within the building too. She could make out feminine laughter and giggles, occasionally punctuated by the deeper notes of men's voices. These sounds struck a familiar chord in her memory, and at last she recalled where she had heard something similar.

She was reminded of the harem in Algiers in which she had spent her formative years. Sometimes her master had come to the harem in the evenings, accompanied by friends to whom he had turned over some of his concubines. The sounds were identical.

There were no harems in America, so Kai was puzzled. Then she remembered, on trips to Charleston, that she had driven past houses of prostitution, and a terrible fear gripped her. Had she been brought to such a place as an involuntary inmate?

Her alarm made no sense, however. Her abductors had gone to great expense and trouble, and had brought her a very great distance. Surely she hadn't been plucked from a South Carolina plantation to be made into the American equivalent of a harem inmate. There had to be some other reason.

A key turned in the lock of the sitting-room door, and a young, attractive black girl came into the suite carrying a tray. She brought it to the bed, deposited it without speaking a word, and then departed again, carefully locking the door behind her.

A meal rested on the tray, and looked delicious, which it proved to be. There were chunks of pink and green melon that had been soaked in wine, a clear broth with a strong, delightful flavor, an omelet that had been perfectly cooked and that had mushrooms and bits of ham in it, a crisp salad of Italian greens flavored with an oil-and-vinegar dressing, and a cup of cold sherbet with the flavor of black raspberries. A huge cup of black coffee was the best Kai had ever tasted, and helped clear the remaining cobwebs from her mind.

Apparently her abduction had entered a new phase. At

least she felt better fortified for whatever ordeal might await her.

Again the door was unlocked, and a handsome mulatto woman in her mid-forties entered, followed by several younger girls, one of whom carried a large tub.

"I am Maria," the woman said, "and I bid you welcome. I regret the discomfort you have been caused, but now we shall make it up to you."

The girls began to pour water into the tub from cold pitchers and steaming kettles, one of them testing the heat with her elbow.

"After your long and unpleasant journey you will enjoy the chance to cleanse yourself," Maria said. "I invite you to bathe."

Kai hesitated.

The woman nodded to her subordinates. Two of the girls seized the astonished Kai and held her, suppressing their giggles, while the third removed her nightgown.

Rather than submit to further indignity, Kai stepped into the tub and immersed herself in the hot water. As much as she hated the sense of compulsion, she had to admit that she relished the feeling.

At a signal from Maria one of the girls opened a small glass vial and poured its contents into the tub. Immediately the whole bedchamber was filled with a spicy-sweet scent.

Then, while Kai soaked in the tub, one of the girls brushed her long hair, taking particular care to fashion one thick strand into a fat curl.

"There has been enough of the bath," Marie said.

Kai was so cowed she stood and stepped out of the tub.

The girls dried her, then sprinkled her body with a scented powder, finally dressing her in knickers as fragile as a cobweb, dark stockings of fine silk, and a pair of sandals with almost absurdly high heels. The upper portion of her body remained bare.

Maria seated her in a chair and began to apply cosmetics to her face. Not even in the Algiers harem had Kai been aware of such meticulous preparations. First a thin substance that dried quickly was applied to her entire face. A violet-tined jelly that matched her eyes was smeared on her lids, which were lined in black, and something shiny was added to her lashes. Her lips were rouged, as were her cheeks, and a glittering beauty patch was affixed to one cheekbone.

Another was pasted onto a breast, no more than an inch above her nipple.

Then the girls helped her into a dress of gossamer-thin silk, a gown with a high slit on one thigh and a daring neckline that left her breasts half-exposed. The curl was brought forward over her shoulder and dropped, with careless artistry, over her breast.

Kai had never worn any clothes on the upper part of her body until she had married M'Bwana and Jeremy Beaufort had taken charge of their destiny, so she was not particularly bothered by her provocative near-nudity. But she had lived in the United States long enough to know that nowhere in polite society did any woman dress as she was attired at this moment, and fright gripped her again. Perhaps her abductors were transforming her into an American version of a harem concubine.

In spite of her fears, however, she had to admit to herself that the overall effect of her appearance was dazzling. Never had she looked so feminine, so alluring, so ravishing.

Maria put long diamond hoops in her ears, clasped a diamond bracelet around one slender wrist, and slipped a sparkling ring of cluster diamonds onto a finger.

Then the woman stood back to judge the results, and nodded in satisfaction. "I knew you were pretty enough when they brought you here, sleepy and dusty from the road. But it is true that you are lovely beyond compare. I should have known. The master's taste is impeccable, as always."

She and the girls withdrew, taking the tub, kettles, and pitchers with them.

Kai stood frozen as the key turned in the lock, again reminding her that she was a prisoner in this strange place. The master, Maria had said! So this place was a harem, and she was being forced to become a concubine.

She looked at the reflection of the provocative creature who stared at her from the pier glass, and wondered if the years she had spent as M'Bwana's wife had been only a dream. She had been reared in Islam, where a woman counted as nothing and only a man and his desires were important. Perhaps it had been her kismet—her fate—ever since birth to exist only as an outlet for male pleasures. Perhaps she should submit now to that fate.

No!

She loved M'Bwana, who was kind and generous and thoughtful, always placing her welfare ahead of his own, always sensitive to her wishes and eager to fulfill them.

Above all, there was Lance. Her son was no ordinary child. Granted that he was Jeremy's son, so Beaufort blood flowed through his veins. He was also M'Bwana's son, and consequently he had a doubly proud heritage.

Lance meant more to her than life itself. For his sake she would not only survive, but she would find some way to return to him. He needed her, and she would not fail him. No matter what the cost, she would be reunited with him.

A key grated in the lock of the outer door, alerting Kai, and she turned away from the pier glass.

A man came into the sitting room, splendid in a suit of black-trimmed white. Emile Duchamp.

He bowed to her, dazzled by her beauty, his eyes devouring her. "Welcome to New Orleans, dear Kai," he said. "I hope to make you very happy here."

A fiery volcano erupted within her. "You dared to do this terrible thing to me!"

"You fulfill my dream of a lifetime," he said, sniffing a scented handkerchief. "I knew when I first saw you that I had to have you. Here. Looking as you look at this very moment."

"I demand that you release me instantly!" Kai said.

His smile was a trifle rueful. "Dear Kai, you're safe here from the entire world. This place is a house of assignation that I happen to own. Armed sentries are everywhere, and the presence of another beautiful girl causes no excitement in the town. Never fear, I have no intention of turning you over to the customers—unless you refuse to cooperate with me. But there's no way you can leave without my express permission. You needn't take my word. The girls who work here will confirm the truth of what I say."

"You seem to forget I'm a married woman!"

"Your husband is sailing in the West Indies, I believe."

"He'll soon return home."

Duchamp shrugged. "Then he'll mourn your loss, and being a man, he'll marry again someday."

"I am also a mother."

"Give yourself to me as joyously as I want to take you, and I give you my word that you'll be reunited with your son. I'll send some of my people for him this very week."

"This is no place for Lance," Kai said contemptuously.

He shrugged. "Then you'll have to learn to live without him. I wonder if you realize how much time and effort, not to mention expense, it required for me to bring you here. I spent weeks working out every detail."

Her rage continued to mount. "Release me this instant!"

Duchamp chuckled. "This isn't the most savory part of town, and if I let you go now, looking as you do, you'd be raped before you could walk more than a few feet."

"Then return my own clothes to me." She heard her voice faltering, and hated her weakness.

"Every stitch you wear belongs to you. In the months and years ahead, you'll have a wardrobe that queens would envy. The jewels you wear belong to you too, and they are just the start. I'm a man of means, dear Kai, and you may accept my word that you'll own rubies and sapphires and pearls. All that money can buy to enhance your beauty."

She knew enough about men to fear that he would become ugly if she rejected him too strenuously, and only that knowledge prevented her from tearing off his diamonds and throwing them at him.

"Please listen to me," she said, speaking slowly and with great dignity. "I did nothing to attract you when you came to Oakhurst Manor. Everything you see in me springs from your own mind—"

"You're wrong," Duchamp interrupted. "My imagination and the reality are one. You need only look at yourself in a mirror and you'll be forced to agree that I'm right. Maria has seen scores of pretty girls in the years she's worked for me, and she said to me just now that she's never known one with your aura." An unpleasant smile lighted his face. "Come to think of it, if you believe you're too good for me, I'll turn you over to Maria for a time, and by the time she's finished with you, I assure you that you'll be glad to be loved by a man. Any man."

Kai shuddered.

"But I don't want to threaten you," Duchamp said. "That isn't my way. Give yourself to me freely, and you shall have anything in my power to bestow."

She made no reply.

"I'm in no hurry, and I'm willing to be patient," Duchamp said. "Your journey was difficult and tiring, so you need time to rest, time to become acclimated to your new surroundings. I want you to feel at home here, and you shall have servants of your own to wait on you. If there are any special dishes you crave, they'll be prepared for you. In the days ahead, your new wardrobe will be delivered to you as rapidly as the dressmakers finish sewing clothes to your measurements, which Maria took while you were asleep. One of your problems, you see, is that you've been unaware of your beauty, and you need time to experiment."

"Experiment?"

"With clothes and cosmetics and hair styles and jewelry. You'll want to try new ways to make yourself even more attractive. Soon you'll delight in ways to stun me when I visit you."

He was mad, she thought, and truly intended to transform her into the kind of brainless concubine she had known in Algiers. She had always felt contempt for the creatures whose greatest delight was sitting in front of a pier glass, primping, rearranging their hair, and trying on different clothes. Now Duchamp was proposing that she accept such a life. And worst of all, he was leaping to the conclusion that she would actually like it.

Obviously he couldn't understand the joys of motherhood, the joys of leading a free life, the joys of loving a man and being loved in return.

Kai looked inscrutable, but something of what she was thinking brushed off on the slave-trader/brothel-owner/gambler who had gone to such extremes to abduct her and bring her to New Orleans. "There are many women who don't find me repulsive," he said, "and I'm certain you'll learn to appreciate me when you stop resenting me. As I intend to prove to you, I'm far more expert in the art of lovemaking than any man you've ever known."

Not waiting for her reply, he moved toward her, his half-smile confident as he lightly brushed her almost-bare breasts with his hands before he took her in his arms.

Kai felt like retching, and had to curb the desire to spit in his face.

Duchamp kissed her, forcing her lips apart.

She submitted because she had no real choice. If she clawed him with her fingernails and drove her knee into his groin, as she so badly wanted to do, he was certain to react in kind. There was a vicious streak in this man, and she knew she would arouse it at her peril.

So she allowed him to kiss and fondle her, trying desperately to think of something else when a hand dipped inside the front of her absurdly low-cut gown and he began to toy with her breasts.

Her passivity was too much for Duchamp. One of her qualities that most appealed to him was the fiery, savage nature he sensed beneath her calm facade, and he wanted her to challenge him, to provide him with an excitement that was lacking in his relations with most of the women he knew.

He released her so suddenly that she almost lost her balance.

"I was premature," he said. "Forgive me. I'll come back tomorrow, and the next day, and the next. Learn to accept me on my own terms, and you'll have everything I can give you, including the company of your son. Refuse me, and you'll regret it."

Was he threatening Lance? Kai didn't know, and tried her utmost to conceal her new fear. Duchamp was ruthless, a man without conscience, and she realized he would do anything to bend her to his will. She had no intention, if she could possibly help it, of giving him an additional means of breaking her spirit.

She had already discovered that passivity was an effective weapon in the war of wits he was forcing her to fight. So be it. She might be his prisoner, but she could still beat him at his own game. Ultimately she would find a way to escape. Or she might be rescued. Certainly Alicia Emerson would guess what had become of her, and might summon the courage to tell Sarah Beaufort, so help could be on the way at any time.

Until then, perhaps she could stall.

Emile Duchamp bent over her hand, with only a hint of mockery in his eyes. "Good night, dear Kai," he said. "Sleep well. And dream of me. Until I return tomorrow."

# Chapter 9

By order of the Navy Department the four ships of Commodore Jeremy Beaufort's squadron were decommissioned, and he and his officers and men were returned to civilian life. At a White House dinner President Monroe thanked Jeremy for his services and emphasized that his countrymen were in his debt.

After returning to Baltimore from Washington City, Jeremy sailed for Charleston on the *Louise*, and during the voyage made his long-range plans. Having been absent from home for a year, he intended to return to Oakhurst Manor and stay there. The invention of the cotton gin by Eli Whitney meant that plantations were returning far larger yields on the principal crop, and he was looking forward to the growth of his holdings.

His shipping interests were a major investment too, and their future was equally bright. After M'Bwana returned from Barbados he would transfer the Bantu to the command of the *Louise*, and would give the more experienced Captain Ned Slocum the *Elizabeth*. What mattered most was that his crews had been tested in the crucible of war, and had learned to work together in efficiency and harmony. He could afford to pay higher wages than other shipowners in the South, and consequently most of his sailors would sign on with him again after taking a well-deserved shore leave. Men like Boatswain Talbot, he reasoned, were worth every penny they received.

The *Louise* reached Charleston in mid-evening, too late for Jeremy to make the journey to Oakhurst Manor. Wearing civilian clothes for the first time in a year, he went directly to the Benton house, where Isaiah, Lorene, and Scott Emerson were just finishing dinner. They were delighted to see him, but their mood was somber.

Lorene best expressed their mutual feelings when she said, "Thank God you're back!"

"What's wrong?" Jeremy asked, steeling himself for bad news.

They told him about the disappearance of Kai.

He was stunned. "But this makes no sense. M'Bwana had a letter from her shortly before I sailed, and she sounded happy. Certainly she was looking forward to his return."

"We're fairly positive that she didn't leave voluntarily," Scott said, and filled him in on the details.

"M'Bwana will be here in about a month, no more," Jeremy said. "We've got to locate her and bring her home before then, or he'll go wild."

"Neither the constabulary nor the state militia have picked up any clues," Scott said. "We've had a lot of time to think about this terrible tragedy, and I've been developing some thoughts of my own that I'd rather not mention out loud just yet. But if you don't mind, I'll ride out to Oakhurst Manor with you in the morning."

"I wish you would," Jeremy replied. "We've got to do something, and do it fast."

Scott went back to his own house for the night, and the next morning at dawn he returned to the Benton home to pick up Jeremy. Few people were yet abroad, so they made good time, and arrived at Oakhurst Manor in less than two hours.

Sarah was still sitting at the breakfast table, going over manifests with Lester Howard, when her husband walked into the room.

He took her in his arms, and she clung to him, feeling

safer and more secure than she had in all the months he had been away. At the same time, her heart ached for the missing Kai, and Scott's presence told her that Jeremy had already learned the unhappy news.

Seeing Jeremy and the overseer greeting each other with great warmth gave Sarah a strange sensation. There was no question in her mind that she loved her husband; never once in the trying period that had passed had her love wavered. He alone was paramount in her life.

At the same time, however, Lester continued to occupy a special place in her mind and heart, a secret place that she could confide to no one. Even at this moment, seeing the two men together, she knew she would always be faithful to Jeremy, but in spite of her fidelity she would keep wishing she could develop a still closer relationship with Lester.

At the very least she could understand that Jeremy was drawn to Lisa Saunders. He hadn't mentioned Lisa in his letters, so she had no idea whether he had seen her during his year in the West Indies, and she was too proud to ask. All she knew was that Admiral Lord Saunders had been severely injured, and she felt sorry for his wife. When she saw the troubles that other couples were encountering, she knew she and Jeremy were fortunate.

Jeremy and Scott hadn't eaten breakfast, but the meal was delayed when Jerry and Lance raced down the stairs. As a special treat the boys were permitted to eat with the adults, so conversation on serious matters had to be postponed until after breakfast, when the children went off with Lester on his morning rounds. Jeremy was delighted to see that both boys were riding unassisted; Lance looked as though he had been born in the saddle.

Ultimately the Beauforts were alone with Scott, who asked Sarah for another mug of coffee. "I hate to spoil your reunion," he said, "but I want to talk to Alicia. In your presence. In spite of all the changes in her these past few years, I still think I know her fairly well, and I find it strange that whenever we talk about Kai she goes to great pains to change the subject."

"I'll fetch her myself," Sarah said, and went upstairs.

To her surprise, she found Alicia drinking coffee in her sitting room. She had been awakened by the commotion caused by Jeremy's return, and was already wearing her customary heavy makeup, although still dressed in one of her revealing peignoirs.

"Don't bother to get dressed," Sarah said, deliberately refraining from mentioning that Scott had ridden out from Charleston too. "Come down and say hello to Jeremy before he gets too busy."

As a guest in the Beaufort home Alicia had no choice, and accompanied her to the dining room. There she greeted Jeremy with a kiss that was more affectionate than propriety warranted, but she stiffened when she saw her brother, and barely nodded to him.

They chatted about inconsequentials for a few minutes, and Jeremy told them about the climactic sea and land battle that had broken the power of the buccaneers.

Scott waited for a lull in the flow of conversation, and then, displaying the shrewdness that was winning him a state-wide reputation as an attorney, he took the plunge. "Alicia," he said, "when Jeremy landed last night, I told him immediately about the disappearance of Kai."

"I just don't want to talk about her," Alicia murmured. "It does no good, and everybody gets upset all over again."

Scott looked hard at her. "I have reason to believe you may know what's happened to her."

"That's ridiculous!" Alicia retorted, then smiled at Jeremy. "I swear, you look as though you acquired a permanent suntan in the Caribbean."

"Tell us what you know," Scott said. "Now."

Her petulant sigh was a shade too long-drawn.

"M'Bwana will be coming home soon," he told her, "and he'll be less patient than the rest of us.

Alicia returned his stare, but all at once she buckled. "I . . . I don't actually know anything. All I have to go on are my own ideas, and I can't prove any of them."

This was something new, and Sarah caught her breath.

"I'm sure you remember when Emile Duchamp came here to see me some weeks ago." She addressed her remarks to Sarah rather than to Scott or Jeremy. "He was very angry because I refused to go back to New Orleans with him. But even though he came here just to see me, he was attracted to

Kai. He's that sort of man. I could tell that she fascinated him. I know all the signs."

"Who is this Duchamp?" Jeremy asked.

"A disgusting man," Sarah said.

"He is not!" In spite of herself Alicia felt compelled to defend him.

"He's a New Orleans slave trader who has a reputation as a duelist," Sarah said, ignoring the interruption. "Alicia will tell you what she wishes about her relations with him."

Alicia fell stubbornly silent.

"I've made it my business to investigate the man," Scott said quietly, "and I've learned that he's also the proprietor of the fanciest bordello in New Orleans, probably the fanciest in the whole country. Now, then. What connection do you believe he may have with Kai's disappearance, Alicia?"

His sister's last defenses crumbled. "If Emile wanted Kai, he'd get her. And he wouldn't let anyone stand in his way."

Jeremy leaned forward in his chair. "Are you suggesting that he may have returned to Oakhurst Manor and abducted her?"

"Not personally. But he's very wealthy, and there are unscrupulous men on his staff."

"Would he have taken her to his home?" Jeremy demanded.

"Never." Alicia became bitter. "His invalid wife is there. Not even I ever saw the inside of Emile's house."

Jeremy and Scott exchanged a long, knowing look.

Sarah touched her husband on the arm as she gazed at him inquiringly.

"Scott and I are wondering," he said, "whether Duchamp might have hidden Kai in his brothel."

Sarah gasped.

"It isn't as bad as you seem to think," Alicia said, a hint of contempt in her voice. "I had my own quarters there for a long time, a lovely suite. I came and went as I pleased, and I had nothing to do with the . . . the commercial activities on the lower floors. If Kai is there, you can be sure Emile is taking good care of her. Emile is the sort who would give her lovely clothes, beautiful jewelry, servants to wait on her, even her own carriage to take her shopping."

Again Jeremy and Scott looked at each other. Then the

master of Oakhurst Manor turned to his wife. "Sarah," he said, "I'm afraid my homecoming must be delayed. I'm leaving for New Orleans as fast as I can pack a saddlebag and order a strong mount sent from the stables."

"Order one for me, too," Scott said. "And if I may, I'll borrow some clothes from you. As well as a brace of pistols."

Sarah conquered her disappointment, knowing Kai's safety was of paramount importance. She and Jeremy had the rest of their lives to be together. "May God ride with you," she said.

"If Kai is there," Alicia said bitterly, "don't be surprised if she refuses to return with you. Emile has a very special way with women."

"We'll take that chance," Scott told her curtly.

Jeremy hurried to the master suite, and while he was packing a saddlebag for the long ride and Sarah was finding spare items of clothing for Scott, Jerry and Lance returned, racing into the bedchamber.

Both boys clamored for Jeremy's attention, wanting him to play with them.

"He can't," Sarah said gently. "He must go away again this very morning."

"Where?" Lance asked.

"Papa Beaufort is going to find your mother and bring her home," Sarah said.

Lance absorbed the information in silence, his expression reflecting hope, loneliness, and fear. All at once he looked determined. "I go, too," he said.

Jeremy chuckled. He tried to think of Kai's son as M'Bwana's, and most of the time he succeeded But he could not forget that he had sired this sturdy child. It was no accident that Lance displayed both courage and independence. "I reckon that'll be all right," he said.

Sarah was horrified. "He's too young, and you may run into trouble—"

"I'll sit him on my horse, so we won't lose time," Jeremy replied. "I'm sure that between us Scott and I can see to it he isn't hurt. He wants to go, and it's his privilege. After all, it's his mother who is missing."

Sarah still thought he was wrong, but felt she was being excluded, so she had no adequate reply. In spite of her own efforts to think of M'Bwana as the boy's father, she could not ignore the fact that this was Jeremy's son. She had no right to interfere in a matter than concerned Kai, and she felt as though a wall had been erected between her and those she loved.

"Don't agree so quickly," she said. "Travel with a boy this small won't be easy."

"Just pack a saddlebag for him," Jeremy said, "and leave the rest to me. I promise you that no harm will come to him, and he won't be a hindrance. He has the right to come with us."

"I want to go, too," Jerry said.

His father shook his head. "Your mama is here, safe and sound. Lance is coming with me to find his mama and help her."

Sarah left the room without another word and busied herself preparing a travel kit for Lance.

A half-hour later the rescue mission departed, with Lance mounted in front of Jeremy. Anyone who saw them would know instantly that they were father and son.

Sarah stood on the portico, an arm raised in farewell until they disappeared at the far end of the driveway. Then, but only then, did she retire to the privacy of her dressing room and weep. Her tears accomplished no useful purpose, she knew, but her need for release was desperate.

The squadron dropped anchor in the Bridgetown harbor, and M'Bwana went ashore immediately. He would take on supplies for the homeward voyage in the next twenty-four hours, and in the meantime many errands would keep him busy.

His first stop was a small shop in the business district, and there, as he had hoped, he found Dolores. She was standing on a ladder, storing bolts of cloth on shelves, and he had a chance to study her before she saw him.

Women in the Americas were like those he had known in Africa, M'Bwana thought. An individual's nature did not change, regardless of circumstances. Dolores was no longer attired in the low-cut blouse and slit skirt of the Santo Domingo harlot, but she continued to wear snug-fitting clothes and still used cosmetics with a lavish hand. He wouldn't be surprised to discover that she augmented her income by accepting money from men.

Dolores heard him clear his throat, saw him, and leaped down to the floor, her long earrings jangling. Her delight was genuine as she embraced and kissed him.

M'Bwana was embarrassed by her fervor. "Well, now," was all he could say.

"Dolores knew you would come back." Her command of English was remarkably good.

"I'm just here for a little while," he said, "and then I'm sailing home to my wife and son."

Dolores appeared not to hear his mention of his wife and child. All that mattered was that her benefactor had returned to Barbados. Locking the door of her shop, she insisted that he accompany her to her private quarters upstairs, and there she insisted that he accept food and drink.

It was too early in the day for either, but M'Bwana did not want to hurt her feelings, so he took two fingers of rum, then carefully filled the glass with water. Most of the furniture in her sitting room was new, he noted. "I see that you're prosperous," he said.

"Dolores make much money," she replied happily. "Sell much cloth, have many friends."

It was wise, he reflected, not to make inquiries about the identities of her new friends. "I just dropped in to see if you needed any help."

"Dolores need nothing," she told him proudly. "But want to thank the one who save her." She went to him, sat on his lap, and curled her arms around his neck.

She was very attractive and it would be all too easy to become aroused, but M'Bwana had no desire to create complications for himself. Not when he was sailing for home the next morning to rejoin Kai. What was more, he realized that Dolores knew of only one way to express her gratitude; her whole background made it impossible for her to think of life in other terms.

Lifting her to her feet as he stood, he kissed her gently to indicate that he wasn't trying to avoid her. "I didn't help you because I wanted to take you to bed," he said gruffly. "We'll have a better friendship if we don't."

Such treatment was new in the girl's experience, and she

looked at him with shining eyes. "M'Bwana is truly the friend of Dolores," she said, and retreated abruptly to her own chair.

He stayed for another half-hour. Her life was not one he would have chosen, he thought, but she was successful and contented. She would spend the rest of her life in Barbados, she told him, and had no desire to return to Santo Domingo.

She deserved her happiness, M'Bwana reflected as he departed. Only her cooperation had made it possible to smash the buccaneers who had terrorized merchant shipping in West Indian waters. He meant every word when he assured her that he would not forget her.

After leaving Dolores' shop, he went to the open-air market, where his quartermaster was buying supplies that would be loaded on board the ships later in the day. He inspected the meats and fish, fruits and vegetables, and satisfied with the efforts of his subordinate, he hired a carriage for the trip to Indian Bridge.

The majordomo at the estate of Admiral Lord Saunders admitted M'Bwana to the house, and a few moments later Lady Saunders came into the room.

There were smudges beneath Lisa's eyes, but otherwise she looked as she had the last time he had seen her. She was still ravishingly beautiful, and he could understand why Jeremy was infatuated with her. Not that Jeremy had mentioned his attachment, but M'Bwana had known.

Lisa was delighted to see him, and not until she asked a delicate question did she hesitate. "Has your whole squadron come to Barbados?"

"All but the ship that took Commodore Beaufort home last month," he replied.

Her face became blank.

"His mission has ended, so he went off to report to the president and then return home. I'm sailing for South Carolina myself tomorrow morning, so I came to pay my respects to the admiral, if he's well enough."

"He sees few visitors," Lisa said, "but it will do him good to have a visit with you. Don't spend more than a short time with him, because he tires so easily. And if you're shocked by his appearance, try not to show it."

"He's that bad off, ma'am?"

"He'll never recover his health," Lisa said, her manner indicating no feeling. "He knows it and I know it, but we never discuss the subject."

She led him to a solarium, where Lord Saunders was sitting in a wheelchair, a robe across his lap.

M'Bwana was stunned, even though he had been warned. The man with white hair and a lined face bore little resemblance to the vigorous fleet commander he had known.

He saluted, and when he shook the admiral's frail hand, he could feel almost no flesh on the protruding bones.

Dickie Saunders recognized him, but after inquiring about his health and Jeremy's, seemed to lose interest in his immediate surroundings and his mind appeared to wander.

M'Bwana made a few painful attempts to converse with him, but had to give up. When he took his leave, the Admiral's farewell wave was vague.

"May I offer you something to drink?" Lisa asked as she walked through the house with him. "I don't want to be inhospitable."

He thanked her, but declined. "Is Lord Saunders . . . always this way?"

"Always," she said. "Many doctors have seen him, including the personal physician to the prime minister, who was here on a holiday a few weeks ago. He had known Dickie and his family in England, so he made a point of paying a professional visit. He confirmed the diagnosis of all the others. There's nothing that anyone can do for him."

"What about you, ma'am?"

"I look after him," Lisa said simply.

M'Bwana didn't want to press too hard, but knew Jeremy would want to learn every detail. "Are your spirits holding up?"

Lisa's smile was courageous. "I suppose you might say I'm paying for all the sins I've ever committed. I do what I must, and I make no complaint."

When they reached the front door, he took a deep breath. "May I give your greetings to Jeremy?"

"If you will, please, I'll be in your debt. And give them to Sarah, too."

War, M'Bwana reflected as he drove back to Bridgetown, was not a romantic experience, and there was little glamour in the life of a sailor or soldier. Not only was the once-hearty admiral reduced to a pitiful shell, but his lovely wife was compelled to waste her substance, too. Life was unfair, and he knew Jeremy would be unhappy when he learned of the existence Lisa Saunders led.

There was no escape, and Kai knew it. The entrance to the lavish suite remained locked at all times, with a sentry stationed outside the door. And she knew it would do no good if she smashed the shutters that covered her windows and called for help. No one would answer such a summons from a bordello.

The worst of her situation was that she was helpless. When she objected to the outrageously revealing clothes that Emile Duchamp had ordered made for her, and refused to wear them, the girls who obeyed Maria's commands dressed her in them against her will. In fact, they seemed to delight in giving her an even more provocative appearance. When she grew tired of daubing her face with cosmetics, the girls enjoyed strapping her to a chair, and then Maria herself made up her face, using exaggerated amounts of makeup.

Kai could no longer even look at her reflection in the pier glass. She hated her silken sheets, her carefully groomed hair, even the potent scents that Maria and the girls poured over her body. The years seemed to roll away. It was almost as though she had never known Jeremy, never been married to M'Bwana, and was still an inmate of the hated harem in Algiers.

Duchamp, however, relished her appearance. He visited her every day, usually in the early evening, and remained persistent in his attempts to bed her. He begged, cajoled, threatened, one night warning her that he would turn her over to the brothel's customers unless she gave in to him, then presenting her with an expensive necklace or bracelet the next night.

Kai didn't know how much longer she could hold out against him. She was coming to know this man well, and she realized he was both ruthless and determined. The longer she refused him, the more his inflated vanity demanded that she belong to him.

Sometimes she felt like ending the torture by yielding to

him, but on these occasions her pride inevitably intervened. She loathed him too much to give him the satisfaction.

So far her only protection was inertia. On the occasions when he kissed and pawed her, she remained motionless, offering no protest and refusing to respond. Each time, Duchamp had become disgusted and had stamped off. But his frustration was increasing, and Kai didn't know how much longer her technique would be effective. She could not allow herself to forget that he was dangerous. Or that she was completely under his control.

One afternoon, after she had been forcibly attired in a flimsy, semitransparent dress that she regarded as absurd, Duchamp came to her unexpectedly early.

He had been riding, so there was a film of dust on his boots and he still carried a riding crop. His face was flushed, his eyes were bloodshot, and when Kai realized he had been drinking, she knew she was in for trouble.

Duchamp was courtly, as he always was at the beginning of a session. "Dear Kai," he said, bowing to her, "you look adorable."

In her own opinion she looked ridiculously underdressed, but she smiled and made no reply.

He stalked out of the sitting room, went into the bedchamber, and beckoned.

She joined him, walking as slowly as she dared and wondering how to end this agony.

"I've been very kind and patient with you," Duchamp said. "I've given you more gifts than either of us can count—"

"Except the freedom you took from me."

He paid no attention to her interruption. "Now the time has come for you to show your gratitude. Remove your clothes."

Kai's heart sank, but she stood motionless.

Duchamp's face became scarlet, and, his eyes blazing, he threw her onto the bed.

She sprawled there, facedown, terrified by his rage.

He cursed her, then raised his riding crop and struck her full force across the back.

As a slave girl in Algiers, Kai had been forced to endure whippings, and she told herself that this occasion was no worse than all the others.

Again and again the leather riding crop landed on her back and shoulders. The pain was so excruciating that she wanted to scream, but she refused to give him the satisfaction. Biting her lip, she buried her face in the bedclothes. Sooner or later he would grow tired.

The exhausted Duchamp hurled the riding crop across the room, cursed the girl again, and stamped out.

Kai was afraid she would lose consciousness.

After a time—she had no idea whether it was minutes or hours—Maria and her helpers came into the suite. Not speaking to her, they stripped her with the expertise born of long practice, then smeared a cooling, soothing salve on her back and shoulders before they departed.

As she drifted off to a pained, troubled sleep, it occurred to her that she wasn't the first one Emile Duchamp had abused.

The next day Kai saw in the pier glass that long welts crisscrossed her back and shoulders. That morning the women applied the unguent again, and did the same later in the day. To her infinite relief, Duchamp did not appear.

She was treated the same way the next day and the next, and it finally dawned on her that her kidnapper had no intention of visiting her again while her beauty was marred. Well, she could be thankful for that much.

Kai lost count, and five or six days passed before the welts disappeared. That same day she sensed that a climax was at hand.

More perfume than usual was poured into her bath, and she was ordered to soak there for such a long time that she almost gagged on the scent. Still more perfume was brushed into her hair; the brushing seemed to last forever. Then Maria made up her face with great care, and grinning broadly, added rouge to her nipples.

Finally they attired her in a transparent gown of thin silk, and did not even give her a robe or peignoir to wear over it. She didn't know whether to laugh or cry, but realized that Duchamp was shrewd. By forcing her to appear virtually nude before him, he would break down the last of her defenses.

Kai did not have long to wait. He sauntered into the suite, his eyes lighting up as he looked at her, and there was no mockery in his bow.

To her astonishment, however, he made no attempt to touch her. Instead he sat in a handsome Louis XV chair and waved her to another, opposite it.

She sat, conscious of her near-nakedness and filled with foreboding. The change in his attitude meant that he intended to use new tactics, and she knew she could not match his sly cleverness.

She was tempted to run into the bedroom, retrieve the riding crop she had hidden after he had left it, and strike him with it. But such a gesture would be worse than futile. He could overcome her physically, and well might do her real harm.

Duchamp chatted with her for a time, casually, even pouring her a small glass of sack while he himself drank a concoction of gin and lemon juice. He seemed to be pretending that she was fully dressed and that this was an ordinary social occasion. Certainly he was enjoying himself.

Finally he leaned back in his chair and plucked a nonexistent thread from the sleeve of his handsome silk coat. "Dear Kai," he said, "you've been very obstinate for many days. I've tried all my usual methods of persuasion, and all have failed. But you've whetted my appetite for you, and I refuse to be denied. Now, at last, I've found a means of persuading you to give yourself to me voluntarily. Are you willing to believe that?"

She looked at him, bracing herself, but made no reply.

"My employees are very talented," he said. "They spirited you away from Oakhurst Manor without anyone being the wiser. What was done once can be done again. Grant me the privileges I demand, or your child will follow you into imprisonment."

Kai turned cold. "You wouldn't dare!"

"I beg you not to challenge me. I'm prepared to send a group of my best men off to South Carolina this very evening, and I promise you they'll bring your son to me. Here."

She knew he was capable of fulfilling his threat. Under no circumstances could she allow Lance to be abducted and made a hostage for her future conduct.

The man had played his trump card and won the game.

Kai stood, slowly removed the sheer silk gown, and let it fall to the floor. "You may do what you please with me," she said, speaking with as much dignity as she could muster. Then, turning, she walked into the adjoining chamber and stretched out on the bed.

Duchamp was grinning as he removed his own clothes and joined her. He had needed time to find the key to this stubborn woman's fortress, but he had found it, and nothing else mattered.

Kai had only one weapon left in her arsenal, and she used it as her captor smothered her in a close embrace and began to kiss her passionately. Now, more than ever before, she remained completely passive while allowing him to do as he pleased.

His hands roamed and his mouth was busy as he caressed, explored, and tried to arouse the body he had craved.

But there was no response. Kai remained limp, unfeeling, and uncaring.

Duchamp's ardor increased, and his lovemaking became more insistent.

Kai continued to lie still, her eyes closed and her breathing regular. She might as well have been asleep.

Even when Duchamp took her, she made no move, and her expression was unchanged.

Exhausted and bewildered, his satisfaction only a fraction of what he had expected, he rose from the bed and looked down at her. Uncertain whether she was as cold as she seemed or whether she had been playing the ultimate game with him, he knew only that his vanity was bruised. Never had he tried harder and achieved less. The goddess had been lifeless.

Surely his own prowess wasn't declining! Surely he wasn't the one who had failed! The very thought alarmed him.

He'd have to find out. There were other girls in this place, attractive girls for whom wealthy men paid large sums. Later tonight—and perhaps tomorrow night, too—he would experiment. The worst of it was that such girls were accustomed to simulation, so he might not really learn whether his powers were declining.

Duchamp dressed quickly, then hurried out of the suite.

Kai, who had been pretending to be asleep, made no move. She realized he was badly upset, but her victory was minor.

He had penetrated her defenses and had forced her to have relations with him.

She was too sick at heart to weep.

She couldn't blame herself for what had happened, and she knew M'Bwana wouldn't blame her, either. Assuming she won her release someday and was allowed to return to Oakhurst Manor.

At this moment she knew only that she despised herself for being weak. In Algiers she had known a concubine who had plunged a knife into her heart rather than allow herself to be sold to a new master whom she loathed. Kai told herself that, somehow, she had to acquire the courage to perform such a deed. Perhaps, if she could kill Duchamp, too, she could find the strength.

The journey was arduous, but passed without incident as the two men and the boy rode westward through South Carolina, then traveled southward through Georgia and Alabama to avoid the mountains. They pushed their horses, and the superb mounts responded to the challenge.

Lance, riding in front of his father with Jeremy's strong arm steadying him, caused no delays. Not once did he complain, even when they were forced to ride for a full day in a driving rainstorm. Even when he was hungry he remained silent until they reached an inn where food was available. Sometimes he napped in the saddle, but never lost his poise. Aware of the gravity of the mission, he curbed his playful impulses and did not pester the men.

Jeremy was proud of him, and wished he could acknowledge the child's paternity.

Perhaps Sarah had been right. Perhaps he shouldn't have given in to sudden impulse and brought Lance on this journey. On the other hand, regardless of the outcome, he would treasure this experience.

When they reached Mobile they rode straight to the waterfront. Luck was with them, and they booked passage on a coastal sailing ship to New Orleans, giving Lance and the horses an opportunity to rest. The overnight voyage was pleasant, and they reached the mouth of the Mississippi the next morning. After a hearty breakfast they docked beside a barge that had carried produce down the great river.

One of the largest and busiest cities in the United States, New Orleans was by far the most cosmopolitan. Some of her citizens spoke French, some Spanish, and some English. Elegantly attired gentlemen rubbed shoulders with raw frontiersmen in buckskins. The architecture was that of the Old World, the atmosphere very much that of the New.

Jeremy and Scott knew the place well, and were in no state of mind for sightseeing. They engaged a suite at an inn, ordered a meal for Lance, and, while the boy ate, plotted their next moves.

Careful inquiry, concealed in casual conversation with the proprietor of the inn, indicated that the place was located only a few city blocks from Duchamp's bordello, so Jeremy and Scott decided to walk there and stabled their horses. They assumed that the brothel would not open its doors until noon, at the earliest, so they planned to go there in midafternoon. It was preferable to confront Duchamp there rather than at his home, because he might try to have Kai spirited out of the bordello unless they were on the scene themselves.

Neither man was hungry, and as they waited for Lance to awaken from his nap, they cleaned and loaded their pistols. There was little conversation, but they felt no need for talk. Regardless of Duchamp's reputation as a duelist, both were confident of their own abilities. Jeremy had been a crack shot since boyhood, and Scott long had rated only a shade behind him.

When Lance awakened, Jeremy gave him careful instructions. "I don't want you to say anything when we go to this place," he said. "Uncle Scott and I will do all the talking. Just stay close to me."

"Will we bring Mama home?" the child asked.

"We hope so," Jeremy said, and his manner was grim.

Passersby stared covertly at the heavily armed men, but no one halted or interfered with them. Firearms and swords were commonplace in New Orleans, one of the few major cities in the United States where dueling, although officially forbidden, was still permitted by the authorities, who looked the other way.

The bordello was a building of stone and wood, built in the French Creole style and standing four stories high, the top floor resembling a rather large garret, at least from the street.

The uninitiated inevitably thought of it as another of the city's elegant mansions.

Jeremy took Lance's hand, and Scott raised the highly polished brass knocker.

Maria answered the summons, and smiled at the pair. "Welcome, gentlemen," she said, then looked in surprise at Lance. "Isn't the boy a little young for a visit here?"

They did not reply until they entered the ornately furnished entrance hall and stood at the bottom of a marble staircase. "We've come to see Emile Duchamp," Jeremy said.

Their manner made her uneasy. "He hasn't arrived yet, but we expect him shortly. May I tell him who you are?"

"We'll tell him ourselves," Scott said.

Taking note of their pistols and swords, the woman conducted them to a small sitting room off the entrance hall and left them there, taking care to close the door behind them.

Scott promptly reopened the door, and they sat down on the plush-covered furniture to wait.

After a few minutes a pair of burly men, both carrying short, ugly clubs, came to the door and stood on the threshold. "What's your business here?" one of them demanded.

Jeremy rested his hands on the butts of his pistols. "I take it that neither of you is Emile Duchamp," he said.

Scott, too, was ready to draw his firearms at the first sign of trouble. "Our business is with him," he said.

It was obvious to the guards that these determined strangers were prepared to become thoroughly unpleasant if anyone tried to interfere with them. Perhaps it would be best to let Duchamp himself deal with them. A brawl or a shooting would mean an immediate visit from the city authorities, and business inevitably would suffer. Duchamp wasn't on the best of terms with New Orleans officials, who would not hesitate to close the establishment if serious unpleasantness developed.

The guards came to the conclusion that discretion was the better part of valor, and withdrew.

During the next half-hour a number of curious young women came to the door and peeked inside, drawn by the novelty of Lance's appearance. All were heavily made up, a few wore revealing evening gowns, and the rest were dressed in equally alluring negligees and peignoirs. Several tried to flirt with Scott and Jeremy, but received no encouragement in return, and two or three who started to engage in conversation with Lance changed their minds when they saw the unsmiling faces of his guardians.

At last the dapper Emile Duchamp came into the room. It was apparent that he had been forewarned, because he, too, wore a brace of pistols in his belt.

His visitors rose but did not bow.

"I'm told you have business with me," he said, his manner superficially pleasant.

"My name is Emerson, and I come from Charleston," Scott said. "I understand you're rather well-acquainted with my sister."

Duchamp's eyes widened for an instant, but his smile remained fixed.

"I'm Jeremy Beaufort of Oakhurst Manor." Jeremy was as unyielding as his friend. "You paid a visit there during my absence from the country, and I have reason to believe that my hospitality was abused."

Duchamp looked distressed. "There must be some misunderstanding," he said. "I stayed for only a short time at your home, but I had a most pleasant visit with Mistress Beaufort ... and with Mr. Emerson's sister."

Jeremy had no intention of prolonging the conversation. "Where is Kai?" he demanded.

Duchamp's stare was blank. "Ah, a lovely young lady I met at your plantation. Has something happened to her?"

"We have reason to believe she's here," Scott said, "and that she's being held against her will."

"Your information is mistaken," Duchamp said. "There's no such girl here. I can't imagine how anyone could have thought that she'd come here."

Obviously the questioning was producing no results.

Lance decided to take matters into his own hands, even though he was disobeying Jeremy's specific instructions. Suddenly he moved forward and snatched a pistol from Duchamp's belt. Cocking it, he pointed it at the man.

"I want my mama," he said.

Duchamp paled. "My God! That dueling pistol has a hair trigger! Take it away from him!"

Jeremy saw the fear in the man's eyes, and realizing he

was a coward in spite of his reputation as a fighter, immediately decided to take full advantage of Lance's unexpected action. "The boy has been using firearms since he first began to walk," he said. "He can handle them."

There was no humor in Scott's smile. "I advise you to pay close attention to Lance's request," he said. "It would be unfortunate if he fired, but I can't imagine any judge or jury convicting a child that young."

The last of Duchamp's bravado crumbled. "Come upstairs with me," he said. "But for God's sake take that pistol away from him."

Lance continued to aim the weapon at him.

"I suggest that you lead the way, and we'll follow," Jeremy said, drawing his own pistols.

Duchamp was trembling. "If the boy stumbles on the stairs—"

"You won't live long enough to know it," Scott interrupted, and removed the man's remaining pistol from his belt. "This is a distasteful business, so let's have it over and done quickly. Take us to Kai."

For an instant Duchamp reached out to the nearest wall for support. Then he turned, and not saying a word, started slowly toward the staircase.

Lance had accomplished a miracle, but it was taking too great a risk to expect more from him, and the danger that the pistol might go off on the stairs was very real. So Scott gently took the weapon from him.

Jeremy winked at the child to reassure him.

Lance grinned broadly and returned the wink.

They started up the stairs in silence, with Maria and the maids gaping at them and the inmates of the bordello crowding the landings to watch in stunned surprise.

The two burly guards appeared, but Jeremy waved them away. "Stay out of this if you know what's good for Duchamp," he said.

The men hesitated, then vanished.

The climb to the top floor seemed endless, but at last they reached the landing.

Duchamp made a final attempt to pull himself together, but failed. Resigned to the inevitable, he took a key from his pocket and unlocked the door.

Kai stood in the sitting room of the suite, braced for Duchamp's next appearance. She loathed the outrageous gown in which Maria and the women had attired her, a dress with high slits on the sides of the skirt and a neckline so wide and low that her breasts were in danger of being exposed. She stood erect, but she was weary, and the strain of what she had undergone during her imprisonment was beginning to show.

"Mama!" Lance shouted, and ran across the room to her.

For an instant Kai was afraid that her son had been kidnapped, as Duchamp had threatened. But at almost the same instant she saw Jeremy and Scott, both armed, and realized she was being rescued.

Tears streamed down her face, smudging her makeup, as she gathered her son to her and smothered him with kisses.

The door of the sitting room closed and was locked from the outside, although none of the participants in the drama realized it.

"You're safe now, Kai," Jeremy said. "We're taking you home with us."

She rose slowly from her knees, releasing Lance. Then, still weeping, she went off to the bedchamber, returning a moment later with the riding crop in her hand.

Duchamp backed away as she approached him, raising a hand to protect himself.

Kai silently slashed him across the face with the leather crop.

The pain was so intense that Duchamp screamed.

She struck him again and yet again. All of the frustration and humiliation she had been forced to endure welled up in her, and, her fury mounting, she continued to beat him on the face, head, and shoulders.

Duchamp's face was swollen and bleeding, but there was no escape from the enraged woman who had taken justice into her own hands. He backed into a corner, but she followed him, the riding crop whining as it cut through the air and found its target.

Jeremy and Scott did not interfere.

Lance watched, too, his eyes wide as the scene engraved itself indelibly on his memory.

At last the exhausted Kai's arm fell to her side, and the riding crop dropped to the floor.

Jeremy went to her and placed an arm around her shoulders before she crumpled. "This man abducted you?" he asked.

She nodded, but was too tired now to speak.

"Then we'll bring formal charges against him. At once," Scott said. "There are corresponding attorneys with whom I work here, and they'll go into court immediately."

Kai gathered her remaining strength. "No," she said. "I'm satisfied now. For Lance's sake I want no scandal that will follow him for the rest of his days. I . . . I never want to see this creature again."

Duchamp was crouching in a corner, moaning and holding his hands to his battered face.

"Take me home," Kai said.

Scott went to the door and found it locked from the outside.

Jeremy exchanged a quick glance with him.

Not hesitating for an instant, Scott placed the muzzle of a dueling pistol against the lock and squeezed the trigger.

The sound of a shot echoed through the entire house.

Scott opened the door, saw the hall crowded with retainers, and pointed the still-smoking pistol at Maria. "Fetch a cloak for the lady," he ordered.

The woman hurried away.

Neither the inmates nor any of the staff members made any attempt to approach Duchamp, who was writhing in pain.

Maria returned with the cloak.

Scott placed it around Kai's shoulders, concealing her obscene gown.

With Jeremy in the lead and Scott bringing up the rear, both carrying pistols, Kai walked out of her prison, holding her son's hand. She did not look back at the suite, and she did not hear the moans of the man responsible for her torment.

She had been faithful to her husband in spirit if not in deed, and that act had been beyond her ability to prevent. In a strange, inexplicable way, the beating she had administered to Emile Duchamp had cleansed her, given her a new start and new hope. She could put him out of her mind for all time, never again thinking of him, never dwelling on the nightmare she had undergone.

When they reached the street and Kai knew for certain that she was free, she laughed aloud, joyously and without restraint. Then she looked down at Lance and impulsively hugged him again.

Jeremy and Scott replaced their pistols in their belts, and the little group walked to the inn with light steps. Passing pedestrians stared at the lovely girl whose face was streaked with makeup, but Kai didn't care. She was free, and never had she valued liberty so much.

When they reached the inn, Kai and Lance went into one chamber for a private reunion. Jeremy, still taking no unnecessary chances, insisted that the doors be locked.

Then he and Scott went off to perform the unfamiliar and uncomfortable task of buying a wardrobe in which Kai could travel. It was virtually impossible to purchase ready-made clothes for a lady, so rather than wait several days for a dressmaker to fashion new attire for her, they bought her men's boots, breeches, and shirts, as well as a heavy sweater and a short jacket similar to those worn by sailors.

Kai, her face scrubbed clean, was delighted with her new clothes. At last she felt respectable again, she said, and with her hair pulled back she looked like Lance's older brother.

Scott went off again to obtain passage the following day on a sailing ship to Mobile, and bought a mare for Kai to ride on the rest of the journey.

They dined in their suite that night, with Jeremy and Scott taking the precaution of keeping their weapons close at hand. "You owe your freedom to Lance," Jeremy told Kai, and for the first time she learned of the key role her son had played in her rescue.

"I predict a great future for that lad," Scott said.

Lance enjoyed their praise, but was far more interested in the pecan pie with praline filling, a New Orleans specialty, that he was eating for his dessert.

Later that evening, after the boy had been put to bed by his mother, Kai told Jeremy and Scott the full story of all that had happened to her, sparing no details.

They listened in grim and horrified silence, which Jeremy

finally broke. "What you may choose to say to M'Bwana when he comes home in the next few weeks is strictly between you and him," he said. "But I give you my solemn pledge that I'll repeat none of this to any person. A story this lurid should be buried for all time."

"You have my promise, too," Scott said. "I'd have preferred that you bring charges against Duchamp in the hope that we could send him to prison—"

"No," Kai said. "I'm afraid that even in a court of law I wouldn't be able to control myself and would fly at him again."

"I understand," Scott replied, and fell silent.

Jeremy knew at once why he was brooding.

It took Kai a little longer, and then she reached out and touched Scott's hand. "You're thinking of Alicia," she said. "And of little Carrie."

"After I saw the girls in that rotten place and saw what Duchamp did in his attempt to change you," Scott said, "I realized why Alicia is so transformed. She's still trying to live up to an image that Duchamp created, and I'm afraid she hasn't seen the last of him. He still has a terrible hold over her."

"I can't speak for Alicia, and I don't pretend to know what she'll do or why she finds that awful man attractive. But you and Jeremy have saved my life and my sanity, so there's one promise I can make to you in return. I missed Carrie as much as I missed Lance, and I swear to you that no matter what may become of Alicia, I intend to cherish and protect Carrie as though she were my own."

The determination in her voice, the expression in her clear eyes, were the only rewards that Scott wanted.

They left New Orleans early the following morning, and not until their coastal brig moved slowly down the muddy waters of the Mississippi delta did Jeremy and Scott relax their vigil.

The rest of their trip was a holiday. They reached Mobile without incident, and then took to the road, Lance sometimes riding with Kai and sometimes with Jeremy.

More than ever before, Jeremy wished he could tell the whole world that he was Lance's natural father. His pride in the child was unbounded, and he was filled with admiration for the boy's courage and resourcefulness. He knew, however, that he was indulging in a daydream. M'Bwana was Lance's father, and that was that. The fact that Beaufort blood flowed in the boy's veins was irrelevant.

As they made their way toward South Carolina across the rich plantation country of Mississippi and Alabama, the thought occurred to Jeremy that he was paying the penalty for giving in to temptation so long ago, deep in the African jungles. Kai had been a slave girl then, and had offered herself to him because it had been expected of her. He had succumbed to a momentary weakness, and now the world would never know that Lance was his son.

After several days on the road they came to the hills of South Carolina. That night they stayed at the plantation of Emily and Ted Grainger, with whom Jeremy and Scott had grown up when the Graingers had been neighbors in the Charleston area. Emily, as charming and flirtatious as she had been as a girl, leaped to the conclusion that Kai and Scott were married and that Lance was their son. Too many explanations would have been required to tell her the truth, so they allowed her to assume whatever she pleased.

At dawn the next day they were on the road again, and shortly before sundown that night they turned onto the familiar driveway of Oakhurst Manor.

King N'Gao, Jeremy's huge mastiff, raced toward them, barking a greeting, and Lance insisted on jumping to the ground so he could hug the dog.

Tears filled Kai's eyes, and her nightmare faded rapidly from her memory. "We're home," she said softly.

# Chapter 10

The arrival of M'Bwana at Oakhurst Manor less than two weeks after the return of Kai and Jeremy was a cause for celebration, and the Beauforts gave their first major party in more than a year. Then Jeremy quietly granted his good friend a six-month leave of absence, enabling him to become reacquainted with Kai and Lance.

M'Bwana's news about the poor state of Admiral Lord Saunders' health was disquieting, and Jeremy's heart ached for Lisa. How she must be suffering, he thought, devoting all of her time, attention, and energies to the nursing of a man she had never loved. He took care, however, to write only to the admiral, leaving it to Sarah to send a letter direct to Lisa. Never again could he and Lisa be in touch with each other. Even a simple letter was too much, and might set off new sparks.

Old, familiar ways were resumed at Oakhurst Manor, and the plantation prospered. With Sarah still handling the books and Lester Howard in charge of the field staff, Jeremy was required to spend only a portion of his time attending to Oakhurst Manor business. Consequently he spent two days a week in Charleston, where his shipping interests continued to grow. Gradually he acquired a fleet of eight merchant vessels, and became a major figure in the coastal and West Indian ~~trade.~~

Sarah settled into the routines she knew and loved, but her happiness was marred by her continuing yearning for Lester Howard. Her life with Jeremy was satisfactory in every way, and she frequently scolded herself. She had everything in life a woman could want, and her occasional restlessness made no sense. Perhaps, she decided, she was influenced by the knowledge that Lester was in love with her. Not that he ever said a word or made an improper advance, but she could tell by his expression in the odd moments when he lowered his guard, by the special tone that sometimes crept into his voice.

Under no circumstances, however, would anything ever allow them to become more than friends. Her high sense of morality was unimpaired—and unimpairable. Her heart and body belonged permanently to Jeremy.

Sometimes, she knew, her son caused her uneasiness. As the children grew, she couldn't help comparing Jerry and Lance, and her own child came off second best. Lance was increasingly dependable, a bright student who also excelled at sports. Jerry frequently whined when he failed to get what he wanted, and was developing a tendency to blame others, particularly Lance, for his own shortcomings.

Perhaps Lance was doing so well, Sarah thought, because Kai excelled as a mother. Not only was she doing a superb job of rearing her own child, but for all practical purposes she was acting as the mother of Carrie, who grew more lovable every day.

The one dark cloud in the Oakhurst Manor sky was formed by Alicia. Moody, erratic, and unpredictable, she sometimes remained in her suite for days at a time, occasionally going off on unexplained trips to cities as distant as Richmond. She continued to ignore Carrie, and although Sarah and Jeremy agreed with Scott that something had to be done about her, no one could decide what steps to take.

The family was overjoyed when Amanda and Willie wrote from Boston that they now had a second child, a son whom they named Paul in honor of the father of Jeremy and Tom.

It happened that Isaiah and Lorene Benton were making a trip to Boston for purposes they revealed to no one, and when they insisted that Cleo accompany them so she could see her grandchildren for the first time, the indomitable housekeeper finally gave in and agreed.

M'Bwana went back to sea, spending three months as master of the *Louise*, then returning to Oakhurst Manor for an eight-week furlough. He soon established this routine as a regular practice.

In 1821 the territory of the United States was expanded again when negotiations for the formal acquisition of the Floridas were completed with the government of Spain. General Andrew Jackson, who had conquered the Floridas in a whirlwind campaign, was named governor by President Monroe.

Jeremy, who had become acquainted with the general in the course of several business trips, when he had gone to the Floridas to buy timber, sent him a letter of congratulation. The prompt and ever-cryptic Jackson sent him a reply by return mail, in which he said: "It is my hope, Commodore Beaufort, that I can soon call upon you to perform a small service for your country and for me. I shall communicate with you again after the season's holidays."

Isaiah and Lorene returned, bringing Cleo with them, and Sarah was the first to notice a change in the housekeeper.

"Cleo is mellowing," she told Jeremy. "Not only does she carry miniature portraits of her grandchildren with her and show them to everyone who inquires about the babies, but she's become far more lenient with Jerry and Lance. Carrie, too. She was always so strict with them, but now she lets them get away with murder."

The family gathered at Oakhurst for Christmas, and two days before the holiday M'Bwana returned from sea, bringing gifts for everyone. Kai received sapphire earrings so lovely they reduced her to tears, and he brought Sarah a length of cloth woven by the Carib Indians of Santo Domingo. Jeremy received a French pistol, its handle pearl-inlaid, that came from Martinique. And Lance and Jerry were given sets of small spears, similar to those that M'Bwana himself used, which had been made to his specifications for the boys in Jamaica.

There was a gift for Alicia, too, but on the day of M'Bwana's arrival she departed abruptly, saying she was going to spend the holidays with friends in Asheville, North Carolina. It did not occur to her to take Carrie with her, and her attitude was the only sour note in the season.

The children helped decorate the spruce tree that Lester Howard cut down in the woods near the swamps. Sarah and Cleo devoted themselves to the Christmas feast. The meal began with a clear, strong chicken broth, in which tiny liver dumplings were scattered, and was followed by baked, deviled crab, which simmered in the oven for hours. There were roast geese and turkeys, complete with dressing, potatoes, and vegetables, and then came a smoking joint of beef, served in the old style on slabs of fresh-baked bread that sopped up the gravy. Desserts included peach and apple pies and a traditional English plum pudding.

A new penny was hidden in the pudding, and Sarah saw to it that the appropriate portion was given to Carrie, the youngest present. The little girl was elated, more pleased than she had been with any of the numerous gifts she had received. Jerry sulked, but promptly subsided when his father glared at him.

After dinner Jerry and Carrie went off to play with their new toys; Lance, however, preferred to go outdoors and practice with his spears, M'Bwana having set up a target for him in the yard behind the mansion.

The adults repaired to the formal parlor, which was used only on holidays and special occasions. There, after toasts were offered with champagne that M'Bwana had brought with him from Guadeloupe, several surprises were revealed.

"I've decided to retire," Isaiah Benton said. "I'm turning over my practice to Scott, who is well able to handle it in addition to his own. And now I'll tell you something else. The reason Lorene and I went to Boston was to reoccupy the house in which Sarah and Margot were reared."

"You're moving back to Boston, Papa?" the incredulous Sarah asked.

Lorene replied for her husband. "For part of each year, dear. Your father is a New Englander, remember, and I spent many years in New York; the summers here are too warm for us. We plan to go to Boston for the warmer months and divide our winters between Oakhurst Manor and Trelawney."

"We'll miss you for those six months," Sarah said.

"But you're right to do it," Margot added.

Jeremy was thoughtful. "Does this mean you'll sell the house in Charleston, Isaiah?"

"I'm afraid so," the elderly attorney replied. "It's far too large and expensive for part-time use."

"In that case," his elder son-in-law replied, "Sarah and I will be glad to buy it from you. As you well know, I'm spending a great deal of time in the city now, and Sarah could come with me more often, especially as we have more entertaining to do there."

"Splendid," Isaiah said. "We were hoping we could work out that arrangement. You and I can discuss details later."

Margot laughed. "Papa, you and Lorene aren't the only ones who have news. Tell them, Tom."

The younger of the Beaufort brothers looked both pleased and troubled. "Margot and I have been wanting to see more of the world," he said, "and we've had the feeling that our daughter would benefit by spending at least some of her formative years in a city far from home. Well, thanks to Secretary of War Calhoun, I've been offered a post by the State Department. As a permanent member of our legation staff in Paris."

There was an excited buzz, and everyone offered congratulations.

"Wait," Margot said. "We haven't decided whether to accept."

"It's a mite complicated," Tom explained. "I've repaid Jeremy the loan he made me, so I own Trelawney free and clear now. But I don't believe in absentee ownership. And there's a question of money. Government jobs don't pay much, and I'd need the cash from the sale of Trelawney to augment my income."

"If that's all that bothers you," Scott said with a grin, "you'll soon be on your way. Trelawney belonged to the Emersons for a long time, and I've had a strong hankering to own it again. I could even commute into Charleston most days. So I'd be happy to buy it from you, Tom. For many reasons."

Sarah and Kai exchanged a quick glance. Both knew that one of Scott's reasons was the hope that Alicia could be persuaded to return to her childhood home and, once there, would behave reasonably and responsibly.

"Thanks, Scott," Tom said. "This could solve a lot of our problems."

"But we still need time to make up our minds," Margot declared. "It's a huge step. It excites us, but it scares us, too."

"How soon must you give the State Department your answer?" Jeremy wanted to know.

"We have another ten weeks," Tom said, and smiled at his wife. "I reckon we'll be sitting up late a good many nights weighing the pros and cons."

All at once Sarah felt bereft. "Oh, dear," she said, "our family is breaking up."

She sounded so forlorn that Jeremy rose from his chair, went to her, and kissed her.

For the rest of the day it was difficult to talk about anything but the Benton move to Boston and the possibility that Margot and Tom might live in Paris.

As Sarah became accustomed to the idea, her mind raced. It would be good for her to spend several days of each week in Charleston, she thought. Kai could act as temporary mistress of Oakhurst Manor in her absence. Of far greater importance, she would see less of Lester Howard, and therefore might find it easier to put him out of her mind.

Two days after the beginning of the new year, an aide to Major General Andrew Jackson, governor of Florida, arrived at Oakhurst Manor with a letter for Commodore Beaufort from his superior. The general hoped the commodore had the time and inclination to perform a vital service that, however, would require little effort.

The aide, who had been well-briefed, enlarged on the theme. "The Spaniards settled along the coastlines of the two Floridas," he said, "but much of the interior has never been explored, thanks in part to the ferocity of the Seminole Indians."

"Well, General Jackson has tamed them now," Jeremy said with a smile.

"That he has, sir. So what he proposes to you is very simple. We know almost nothing about a wild region known as the Everglades. There are rivers there, and many miles of jungles and swamps. What General Jackson is anxious to learn is whether those rivers are navigable, and whether the area could be settled. Provided the jungle growth was cleared away."

"In other words," Jeremy said, "he wants me to make a journey through the Everglades."

"Right, Commodore. He can give you a special commission for the purpose, but he can't pay you much, if anything—"

"I want no pay," Jeremy replied. "I can well afford to finance such a mission myself. How detailed a survey does General Jackson want?"

"Just enough to give him the broad outlines of the area. If the land is rich and there are outlets by water, he'll try to interest President Monroe in opening the whole region to homesteaders. If not, he wants to forget the idea."

"In other words," Jeremy said, "I'd be spending anywhere from one to three weeks in the Everglades country."

"No more than that, Commodore."

"Then I accept with pleasure. I'll give you a letter of acceptance to give to the general, and tell him that I'll report to him in person on my way to the Everglades."

Later that same day, after the aide had departed, Jeremy discussed the idea in detail with M'Bwana, both men taking it for granted that the Bantu would accompany him. They were excited by the prospect of exploring a little-known wilderness region, and their enthusiasm soared as they discussed the project. They would be taking a holiday in what was strictly a man's world.

Neither could remember, subsequently, which of them first proposed that they take Jerry and Lance with them. It was enough that both men approved heartily.

Sarah was not pleased, however, when Jeremy broached the plan to her that night after they had retired to their suite. "Jerry is too young," she said.

Her husband grinned at her. "With all due respect to you, my dear, that's nonsense. He can handle a pistol, a rifle, and a knife. What's more, he's learning to use that set of little spears M'Bwana gave him for Christmas."

"But there must be terrible dangers in the wilderness."

Jeremy shook his head. "I think not. General Jackson has

knocked the fight out of the Seminole, and they won't attack us. You're forgetting that M'Bwana and I will be along to shield the boys if some unknown danger arises. I look on this as a chance to take an unusual fishing trip, with some hunting thrown in on the side."

He looked so boyishly eager that Sarah relented. "Very well," she said. "I suppose I'm foolish to worry. If you and M'Bwana can't offer protection to the boys, no one can."

Kai accepted the plan without a murmur. No harm could come to the boys in the presence of M'Bwana and Jeremy, the most courageous and resourceful men she knew.

Jerry and Lance learned of the scheme the following morning at breakfast, and each reacted in a typical way. Jerry asked a score of questions, wanting to know where the party would sleep, what they would eat, and what wild animals they would encounter.

Jeremy replied to each inquiry with a shrug or a gentle "We'll see when we get there, son. Part of the fun of a trip like this is not knowing what to expect."

Lance remained silent, but his eyes glowed with pleasure.

Jeremy threw himself into the project, and on his next visit to Charleston he bought small pistols for the boys, as well as knives he believed they could handle. Each would be provided with his own pack, small enough to be carried on his back. And because General Jackson's aide had indicated that there were many swamps in the Everglades country, new knee-high boots were made for the boys, then soaked in oil to make them reasonably waterproof.

A week after Jeremy had accepted the offer, the little party set out, riding south through South Carolina and Georgia and making a detour around the swamps near the Florida border. The boys were riding their own horses, the pace was leisurely, and each night they stayed at an inn, so they were forced to endure no hardships.

The journey was uneventful, and at last they came to Pensacola, the temporary capital of the territory of Florida. For all practical purposes, they discovered, they had entered a Spanish town: most of the two to three thousand residents spoke only that language, and signs on streets and buildings were printed only in Spanish. After asking directions repeatedly, they came to the Plaza Ferdinand VII, in the center

of the town, and there they saw a large, somewhat dilapi-
dated two-story building of pink-and-white stucco that they
identified as the governor's "palace," because the American
flag was flying from a pole in the unkempt yard and a nine-
pounder cannon sat near it.

A sentry in buckskins, armed with a long frontier rifle,
lounged against the wall, and replied to Jeremy's inquiries in
a Tennessee twang. "Yes, siree, this here is Old Hickory's
house. Mosey on in and you'll find him somewheres, prob'ly
signin' papers in a room down the long corridor to the left."

The lack of formality was astonishing.

The interior was unguarded, and the little group followed
the sentry's directions, coming at last to a small cubicle domi-
nated by a battered desk on which papers, pamphlets, and a
variety of other documents were piled in disorder. Seated behind the desk was a man who, at first glance, did not look
like America's greatest military hero since George Washington.

Major General Andrew Jackson, the conqueror of the
British at New Orleans and of the Spaniards in Florida, the
leader who had defeated Indian foes throughout Tennessee
and Alabama, was working in his shirtsleeves and smoking an
old, foul-smelling pipe. Middle-aged and thin, with a receding
hairline and sharp features, he looked up through spectacles
balanced precariously on the bridge of his nose, and most
nearly resembled the Nashville lawyer he had been before entering government service.

As soon as Jeremy and M'Bwana introduced themselves,
he shoved aside his papers, leaped to his feet, and welcomed
them with a warmth and simplicity that were unfeigned. He
shook hands with the boys, too, treating them as equals and
rummaging in his desk until he found some sugar-ball candies
for them.

He shouted for an aide, who took Jerry and Lance off to
see a pet bear lodged in a shed behind the "palace," and then
he conducted his adult guests to a sitting room cluttered with
furniture that ranged from the elegant Spanish tables and
chairs of his predecessors to a broken-down easy chair.
Jeremy knew instinctively that this was the general's favorite.

"I'm grateful to you for helping me out, boys," Jackson

said as he poured stiff drinks of whiskey and water. "I want to get things in shape here before I leave."

"You're not staying on as governor, sir?" Jeremy asked.

Old Hickory grinned as he raised his glass in salute. "This job drives me crazy. I'm no paper-pusher, and I can't stand the bickering that goes on with the State and War departments. I'm resigning so I can go home to my wife and tend to my crops."

Jeremy understood how he felt. At the same time, however, he had heard Jackson might enter politics, but it wasn't his place to comment.

"You'll stay overnight with me," the general said, "and you'll share my barbecue and roasted potatoes at dinner, which is all my infernal cook knows how to fix. I'll have a ship ready to sail you south to the entrance to the Everglades country first thing in the morning, and the crew will wait to bring you back here. It's the fastest and easiest way to get there."

After they finished their drinks, they sauntered down to the little harbor, General Jackson still in his shirtsleeves and Jerry and Lance playing tag. Occasionally they passed small groups of American soldiers in buckskins, and the general greeted each of them by name, asking about the head cold of one and if another had yet received word from home as to whether he had become a father. Jackson's memory was phenomenal.

The sloop that would sail down the west coast of Florida was small but seaworthy, and was also manned by members of the general's army of Tennessee and Kentucky militiamen. On the main deck was a canoe fashioned of thick but lightweight bark, large enough to carry at least eight men. The general explained that it had been obtained for the explorers from a sachem of the nearby Ocala tribe.

M'Bwana examined the craft and shook his head. "This will leak if it stays in the water for more than a few hours," he said, "and it'll fall apart if we hit an underwater rock or root."

When they went ashore, he studied the trees in the area, most of them unfamiliar to him, and finally found a grove that satisfied him. "Lads," he told Lance and Jerry, "you're going to work with me."

While Jeremy went back to headquarters with General Jackson, M'Bwana remained behind, and with the assistance of the two boys he took a thick gum from the trees, boiled it until it became sticky, and then coated the entire exterior of the canoe with the substance. By morning, he said, it would be sufficiently dry for the canoe to be returned to the deck of the sloop, and twenty-four hours thereafter it would be hard enough to be used.

The meal served that evening was as simple as General Jackson had indicated, and consisted of beef that had been cooked for hours over a smoking fire, served with potatoes and sweet corn roasted in the coals. The bread was so hard it had to be moistened with ale to make it palatable, and the dessert consisted of a local melon with yellow meat.

Jerry and Lance ate heartily, the former drifting off into daydreams as the adult conversation swirled around him. Lance listened carefully to the talk of the men, however, and although he maintained the respectful silence expected of children, he missed nothing that was said.

Everyone retired early, as was the custom under Andrew Jackson's roof, and before they went off to bed the general had a private word with Jeremy. "I like the looks of your younger son, Commodore," he said. "If I'm any judge of character, that boy has a bright future ahead of him."

Jeremy, who privately agreed with him, was embarrassed, and was glad that no one else heard the comment. Lance looked so much like him that it would have been absurd for him to offer the explanation that the child was not his son but M'Bwana's.

The next morning, after a hearty breakfast of grilled fish, leftover smoked beef, and more stale bread, the adventurers took their leave, with militiamen returning the canoe to the deck of the sloop. Winds were favorable, and with the permission of the captain M'Bwana took command on the quarterdeck so he could teach Jerry and Lance the rudiments of sailing. Jeremy did not interfere, and was pleased to observe that M'Bwana himself had become a master mariner. Ultimately, he thought, he would give the Bantu his own flagship, the *Elizabeth*.

The weather stayed fair, sleeping arrangements were

cramped but comfortable, and the following afternoon the anchor was dropped.

"We'll come back for you in about ten days," the captain said as the canoe was lowered into the water.

"Fair enough," Jeremy told him, "and if you aren't here, we'll wait for you."

The men paddled ashore, then carried the canoe across the dunes, with Jerry and Lance responsible for their own packs and weapons. After a walk of about an hour they came to what looked like an inland waterway, and floated the canoe.

"We have a few hours of daylight left," M'Bwana said. "So we may as well get started."

The only food supplies they had brought with them were several bags of dried corn, and Jerry was troubled. "What will we eat for our supper?"

The men laughed, and his father replied, "Our adventure has begun. If we don't want to go hungry, we'll have to provide our own food."

They started off down the waterway, with the boys required to do their share of the paddling. Grass appeared on both banks as they left the sandy seacoast behind, and gradually they moved into a jungle where trees ranging from stately royal palms to stunted palmettos seemed to be everywhere.

The channel grew narrower, the water grew muddy, and the foliage on the banks became thicker, with branches, shrubs, and vines forming a bower overhead. The dampness became all-pervading, so that a thin film of water formed on all of the packs and weapons. This condition would persist and remain constant the entire time the party remained in the Everglades.

"Don't trail your hands in the water, boys," M'Bwana cautioned as he sat in the prow. "There are snakes hereabouts."

"I don't see any," Jerry said.

Lance made no reply, but followed the example of the men and peered into the muddy water, concentrating hard. At last he pointed quietly.

Jeremy nodded in confirmation. A snake four or five feet long and at least two inches in diameter was wriggling under the surface a short distance from the nearer bank. Lance, he thought, had the eyes of a hawk.

The foliage became so thick as the channel continued to grow narrower that it impeded their progress. So M'Bwana took a long, curved knife with a double-edged blade from his pack, and wielding it with deft, swift strokes, cut away the underbrush as the canoe continued to push forward. Branches, leaves, and vines cut off the light, making the area as dark as midnight, and the stench of rotting vegetation was almost overwhelming.

The boys were fascinated, and Jeremy took careful note of their surroundings, calling the attention of Jerry and Lance to the sounds of animals in the underbrush on both sides of the waterway.

M'Bwana was in his element. He had known similar terrain in the jungles of Africa, and he wielded his knife tirelessly for more than an hour while Jeremy, sweat soaking him, paddled through the thick, slimy waters.

There was no place to land in the vicinity so they could make camp for the night, and the men were thinking of turning back and trying again in the morning when the waterway unexpectedly became wider and the foliage began to thin. M'Bwana picked up his paddle again, and the canoe gained speed.

Suddenly the Bantu raised his hand in warning, and Jeremy responded instantly, slowing to a near-halt.

They came to a narrow branch of the channel, and floating on the water was a flock of large geese.

M'Bwana removed a short spear from his quiver and in a continuous, smooth-flowing motion sent it singing through the air. The single shot killed a goose, and the rest of the flock took flight.

Hauling the carcass aboard and retrieving his spear, M'Bwana grinned. "Here's our supper for tonight," he said.

A short time later they saw higher, dry ground off to the left, and there they made camp for the night. The boys collected dry wood, and then Jeremy made a fire.

"We'll use this to cook our meal," he said, "but it has another purpose, too. We have no idea what animals may be lurking in the Everglades. Some of them may be dangerous, but the fire will help keep them at a distance."

M'Bwana prepared the goose as Jeremy built up the fire and Jerry continued to gather wood. Lance silently went back to the water. Less than a half-hour later, he returned with a string of fat, speckled fish, each about six inches long.

Jerry, not to be outdone, climbed onto higher ground and came back with his hat filled with juicy berries.

"How do you know whether they're edible?" M'Bwana asked him.

"I . . . I guess I don't," the boy said.

"Show me where you found them, and I'll tell you," the Bantu said. "You come, too, Lance."

They walked a short distance, with M'Bwana carefully cutting a path through the waist-high, coarse grass. "You took a bad chance, Jerry," he said. "This is snake country, so you always want to know where you're stepping."

Soon they came to a thick patch of bushes where the boy had gathered the berries, and M'Bwana studied the branches for a few moments.

"Edible berries," he said.

Jerry felt compelled to challenge him. "How can you tell?"

"Look at the berries still on the bushes," M'Bwana said. "You'll see that some have been partly eaten by birds. It's a fairly safe wager that what birds eat, humans may also eat."

That night they feasted on fried fish, roasted goose, and berries.

The next morning, after extinguishing their fire following a breakfast of more fish, they resumed their travels. Before long they came to a freshwater lake so large they couldn't even see the far shore. For the next seventy-two hours they made their way around the perimeter of the lake and saw that although many small streams ran into the lake, none were navigable for any craft larger than a canoe.

Another phenomenon was that trees had vanished, as had bushes. As far as they could see on somewhat higher land and in the endless marshes that were extensions of the huge lake, there was no vegetation but thick, coarse swamp grass, which sometimes grew four to five feet high. Food was no problem, however. The lake teemed with fish, which the boys caught; there were freshwater shrimp and crab near the banks; and they varied their diet with an opossum that Jeremy shot and a large rabbit that M'Bwana snared.

On the fifth morning, after they had broken camp, returned to the canoe, and were ready to get under way,

M'Bwana silently called a halt and pointed to the bottom of the canoe halfway between the boys.

A large black snake was curled up there. It was at least six feet long and three inches in diameter, and, awakened by the approach of humans, it began to slither.

"Spear it, boys!" M'Bwana commanded, his tone urgent.

Jerry was too frightened to move, and was frozen.

But Lance responded instantly to the order. Removing a short spear from its container, he let fly.

His aim was true, the spear landing just below the creature's head. But the blow did not finish off the snake, and it started to glide forward.

M'Bwana himself completed the task, killing the snake with a spear that landed directly between the eyes.

"That's a water moccasin," Jeremy said as M'Bwana removed the spears and heaved the carcass overboard. "One bite from those fangs, and it would have been the end of you lads. Good work, Lance."

"Good," M'Bwana said, "but not quite good enough. In the future, boy, remember one thing. When it's a question of your life or that of an enemy, make sure your aim is true. Never maim. Always kill."

Lance nodded, and it was plain that he would remember the lesson.

The trembling Jerry scarcely heard the instructions.

In the next two days they explored several waterways leading from the lake that looked promising, but each time the channel narrowed, the mud and silt were so thick that the canoe could be propelled only with difficulty, and they turned back.

On the seventh night, as they were hauling the craft to higher ground prior to making camp, Lance saw what appeared to be a water-soaked log near the bank, and his instinct led him to move around it.

Jerry, however, seemed intent on stepping on the log.

M'Bwana dropped his end of the canoe, snatched the boy into the air, and removed him from danger.

"That," he said, "is a crocodile. A beast that can tear off your arm or leg."

The wide-eyed Jerry stared at the unmoving crocodile. "Let's kill it!"

M'Bwana shook his head. "No, he does us no harm, and if we don't go near him, he'll avoid us. What's more, where there's one there are sure to be others, and we'd be begging for trouble if we killed one. The meat is too tough to eat, so killing would serve no good purpose."

At Jeremy's suggestion they returned the canoe to the water and went on for another half-hour. It would have been foolish to camp near a place where crocodiles made their home.

Three more days passed without incident. Jeremy and M'Bwana agreed that although the soil beneath the waters of the swamps was marvelously rich, there was no way it could be utilized by farmers. The Everglades were not fit for human habitation, and the waterways were unsuitable for easy entrance and egress.

On their last night they feasted on a large creature, a fish that sometimes floated on the surface for long periods and breathed air. The Seminole, Jeremy said, called it a manatee.

Jerry gathered more berries for their supper, and Lance experimented with several different kinds of root he had unearthed, boiling them to see which were edible. His judgment was good, and one thick, bulbous root that tasted a little like wild onions proved to be delicious.

After the meal they cleaned up, then settled down for the night near the fire. The humidity was intense, as usual, causing them to perspire, but they had discovered that if they stayed near the fire, where there was less dampness, they were somewhat cooler.

Jerry slapped absently at a mosquito.

Lance yawned and looked off into space, reluctant to stretch out for his last night of sleep in this strange wilderness. Never had he had a better time.

Suddenly he was alert, his whole body tensing. Something or someone was watching the party, concealed in the high grass. The boy wondered if his imagination was playing tricks on him, but the grass was swaying slightly, and there was no breeze.

Saying nothing to anyone for the moment, Lance reached for his container and quietly drew out a spear.

Now. As he rose to his feet, he saw a pair of glittering, yellow-green eyes staring at him, and he made out the head and body of a very large brown cat. As large as King N'Gao.

Lance didn't know the animal's breed, but that didn't matter. The big cat was stalking its prey, and that prey was human.

If the boy gave the alarm, he was afraid the animal would attack before he could finish his cry. There was only one thing he could do.

He remembered M'Bwana's instructions: "Never maim. Always kill."

Lance braced himself, then closed his eyes for an instant so he could see more clearly in the dark, a trick he had learned from M'Bwana. Then, taking careful aim, he threw the spear with all of his strength.

The animal leaped high in the air, making a screaming, almost human sound before it collapsed onto the ground, the spear deep in its throat.

Jeremy and M'Bwana reached for their pistols as they jumped to their feet. But there was no need for them to fire. They advanced cautiously, then saw the beast was dead.

"My God, a cougar," Jeremy said in wonder, and turned to Lance. "Lad, you actually killed a full-grown cougar with a spear."

"And with one shot." M'Bwana hugged the boy.

Then it was Jeremy's turn. "We'll skin the carcass for you, so you'll have a souvenir to take home."

"Why didn't you warn us and let us deal with the animal?" M'Bwana asked. "You don't take chances with cougars."

"There wasn't time," Lance said. "I was afraid he'd attack first. So I just got a spear. And I threw it."

"Incredible," Jeremy said. "M'Bwana, this boy is a natural outdoorsman."

No one noticed that the neglected Jerry was sulking. His face was averted, which was fortunate, because at that moment his sullen, gleaming eyes resembled those of the cougar.

# Chapter 11

Richard Viscount Saunders, rear admiral in the navy of his Britannic Majesty and the holder of seven decorations, died quietly in his sleep at his estate in Barbados. A visiting bishop of the Anglican Church, who was on holiday in the West Indian islands, conducted the funeral services and told the dry-eyed widow that her husband's death had been a blessing.

Lisa was forced to agree. Dickie had known no pleasure since he had been wounded in the battle with the buccaneers on Santo Domingo, and since that time he had merely existed from day to day, a wretched man burdened by constant pain and weighed down by the knowledge that he had been a burden on others.

The brunt of that burden had been carried by Lisa, but now she was free, although she didn't yet realize it.

The Royal Navy gave the departed commander of the West Indies fleet a full military funeral. A contingent of marines fired a thirteen-gun volley in final salute, and the flag that draped the admiral's coffin was carefully folded and handed to his widow. Dressed in black, with a black veil over her face and head, she stood alone, refusing assistance.

Later, at her Indian Bridge estate, the governor-general and his lady led the callers, who included admirals and captains, prominent local civilians, and many visitors from England. Everyone remarked on Lady Saunders' courage. She accepted the sympathies of friends and acquaintances, but she wanted no pity. Her husband had lived a useful, valiant life, she said, and no man could have asked for more. Her one regret, which she did not voice aloud, was that she had been unable to give him a son to carry on his name. His title now went to a distant cousin who lived in London.

Several people tried to persuade Lisa to go to England, but she demurred, not bothering to explain that the Caribbean was her real home and that London was a city she had visited a few times and scarcely knew. She wanted to rest, think, and take stock of herself.

Certainly her own long-range future was anything but tragic. She was still in her twenties, still ravishingly beautiful. She had a noble title and a large estate, and Dickie had left her enough cash, real estate, and securities that she had no financial worries.

As the weeks passed and turned into months, others took an interest in the lovely Lady Saunders' situation, too. Two local planters, one a widower and the other a bachelor, were frequent callers at the Indian Bridge mansion. So were a Royal Navy captain who had never been married and a commodore, recently arrived from the home fleet, who had lost his wife two years earlier.

Lisa treated her guests graciously and was charming with everyone. Gradually she returned to an active social life, and was inundated with more invitations than she could accept or cared to accept. Every hostess wanted her to attend dinner and supper parties, and the bachelors and widowers clamored for the right to be her escort.

One by one her suitors began to pay active court to her, but she discouraged them without hurting their feelings. Never aloof, she nevertheless managed to hold them at a distance. Someday she might remarry, she told them, but that day was still far distant.

The better part of a year passed before it dawned on Lisa that now she was truly free. She had the social stature and the financial security she had craved as a girl, and she was grateful for them, but she was in a position to take them for granted. She had expiated the sin of her affair with Jeremy Beaufort by taking care of Dickie as no one else could have done, looking after him day and night, and she no longer felt guilty for a relationship that had been unavoidable, that she had been powerless to prevent.

Very well, now she was free. What would she do with her freedom?

A visit to London didn't appeal to her at the moment, and a visit to the United States was tempting. All too tempting. America meant seeing Jeremy again, and she couldn't take that risk. She owed it to him and to his wife to avoid him, no matter how great the cost. She knew what would happen if she saw him again. There was no doubt of it in her mind.

She didn't dare even write to Jeremy. Or to Sarah. On at least a dozen occasions she sat down and composed a note to one or the other, telling them of Dickie's passing. But she lacked the courage to post any of the letters, and consigned all of them to the fire in her sitting-room hearth.

Jeremy would be tempted, too, she knew all too well. And it would be so easy for him, as the owner of a whole fleet of merchant ships, to find an excuse to make a voyage to Barbados. Once they saw each other, they would explode together, as they had done in the past. In an affair that would lead nowhere and would cause nothing but fresh grief.

No, Lisa could not recreate a hopeless triangle and cause anguish for Sarah Beaufort. It was far better to curb her natural desires and impulses. She suffered a constant, dull ache, to be sure, and Jeremy was always present in her mind, but she was learning to live without him.

Now she had to convince herself that she would have to spend the rest of her life without him.

Occasionally she wanted to drink too much at a dinner party or plunge into a reckless affair, but common sense held her back. Lisa, the nobody of Liguanea Hills, Jamaica, might have behaved with impropriety when she became so frustrated she thought she would go mad. But Lisa, Lady Saunders, widow of a distinguished Royal Navy officer, was discreet and kept her head. There was no other way.

A few of her suitors lost heart and gave up, but more and still more appeared. One day, while visiting a shop in Bridgetown where she was buying cloth for a wardrobe that needed refurbishing, Lisa fell into conversation with the proprietress, an attractive girl names Dolores, who spoke with a strong Spanish accent.

"Milady," the girl said, "everybody talks about you."

"Oh?" Lisa was amused. "What do they say?"

"They wonder what man you will marry," Dolores said with a giggle, "and they make wagers. Even my new friend, who owns a small plantation across the island, makes wagers and begs me to find out who you will marry so he will earn a large sum."

"Tell your friend to save his money, Dolores," Lisa said. "I'll tell you a secret. I don't intend to marry anyone."

That was the truth, Lisa reflected as she returned to Indian Bridge, packages of cloth half-filling her carriage. She liked seeing people, entertaining and being entertained, and she had to admit to herself in all candor that she enjoyed the attentions of men. Her vanity demanded it, she supposed. But an affair for its own sake would be meaningless, and marriage to anyone she knew would be hopelessly dull.

Jeremy Beaufort, she realized, had spoiled her for any other man. She couldn't have him, now or ever, and consequently there was no one else she wanted.

Someday she might meet another man to whom she would spark, although she doubted it. But she was in no hurry to find him. She had no need for romance, and her day-to-day existence was far less complicated without it.

She was lonely, of course, but she had been lonely most of her life. She had to live in the present rather than speculate on the future, enjoy small pleasures and stop dreaming of a lost love who was beyond her reach.

It sounded so easy.

Tom and Margot Beaufort finally reached a decision: he would accept the position that had been offered to him in the United States legation in Paris.

They immediately launched into a round of frantic preparations, which were complicated by the fact that Isaiah and Lorene Benton were leaving for their Boston home at the same time. Somehow everything was accomplished.

Scott Emerson made his old friend a fair offer for Trelawney and Tom was delighted to sell it back to a man whose family had owned the plantation for generations. Scott would take good care of the property, ensuring its prosperity, and it was wonderful to know that the traditional friendship between the proprietors of Oakhurst Manor and Trelawney would continue.

As soon as the negotiations were completed, Scott rode over to Oakhurst Manor and confronted his sister.

"Trelawney belongs to us again, and I want you to come home. I want to give Carrie a permanent home, too."

Alicia's smile was weary. "I appreciate your offer, Scott, truly I do. But what you can't understand—what you won't understand—is that I've always hated life at Trelawney. Just as I hate it at Oakhurst Manor. Plantations are dull, dull, dull!"

He tried to speak.

But Alicia gave him no chance. "As for Carrie, I don't even think of her as my child anymore. Kai looks after her so much that she goes to Kai now instead of to me. She won't even miss me."

Her brother stared at her, his eyes hardening. "What does that mean?"

She became evasive. "I'd rather not say. But I can promise you I have no intention of staying on here. I don't aim to turn into a maiden aunt."

"There's no chance of that," he replied wryly.

"Well, I've got to live my own life. In my own way. I've suffered for mistakes I've made, and I'm prepared to pay again. Don't lecture me."

"Surely you aren't thinking of going back to that loathsome Duchamp!"

"You don't understand Emile," Alicia said. "Few people do, and I refuse to discuss him with you. Just leave me, please."

Two days later Alicia disappeared from Oakhurst Manor, leaving a brief note behind on her pillow:

*Sarah, dear,*
   *Never will I be able to thank you and Jeremy enough for giving me your home and your sympathies at a time when I needed help so badly.*

*Now I feel strong again, and with so many changes in
the air, the time has come for me to do what I feel I
must, too.*
*I know what I'm doing.*
*Ask Carrie not to hate me too much.*
*Ever your loving*

*Alicia*

Sarah wanted a search conducted, but Scott refused, and
Jeremy agreed with him. "Sure as all hell she's gone off to
New Orleans to join that confounded Duchamp," Jeremy
said: "We can't go off there again, not to rescue a woman
who refuses to be rescued."

Sarah gave in with a heavy heart.

"There's one thing in all this that strikes me," Scott said.
"Carrie is an Emerson, so I ought to take her off to Trelawney, get a governess for her, and bring her up there."

"You'll do no such thing, sir. And if you mention the very
idea to Kai, she'll scratch your eyes out. Carrie has a real
mother in Kai, someone who cherishes her, and you simply
can't part them. I won't permit it, and neither will Kai!"

When the subject was broached to Kai, she was even more
vehement. "Thank God, Alicia didn't try to take that baby off
to New Orleans. I'd have done something violent rather than
let Carrie go to that dreadful place. She's my little girl now,
and I swear to you that I'll kill anyone who tries to take her
from me!"

That was that, and Scott had to reconcile himself to the
idea of paying frequent visits to Oakhurst Manor so he could
visit his niece.

As for Carrie herself, she seemed unaware of the departure
of her natural mother. For all practical purposes she had become Kai's daughter, and was content. She was so pretty that
every visitor to Oakhurst Manor commented on her appearance. Carrie was a laughing child, bubbling with good humor,
and marvelously natural, even though everyone spoiled her.

Jeremy planned a special going-away gift for his brother
and sister-in-law. He made arrangements to send the *Louise*
to France with a cargo of cotton and tobacco, and at Brest
the ship would pick up a load of silk to take to the French
West Indian islands. This was a longer voyage than any of his

ships ordinarily made, so he and M'Bwana handpicked a crew, with Talbot assigned to the post of chief boatswain.

Tom, Margot, and their daughter would be the only passengers, and M'Bwana offered to give up his own cabin to them, but Jeremy would not permit the sacrifice. The captain would continue to occupy his own quarters, but some of his officers would bunk together so the passengers would be able to enjoy comfortable accommodations.

The Bentons and the younger Beauforts made plans to go their separate ways on the same day, and forty-eight hours earlier Sarah and Jeremy gave a farewell party for them at Oakhurst Manor. The food, punches, and wines were up to their usual standard, and Cleo outdid herself in her preparations. The service was impeccable, as always, the lanterns in the gardens created a romantic aura, and the music provided by three fiddlers from Greenville was lively. The guests, members of three generations, enjoyed themselves thoroughly.

Sarah, who was wearing a full-skirted gown with multicolored petticoats, had never looked lovelier. She wore the brilliant diamond ring that had been fashioned for her after Jeremy's return from Africa, and her diamond earrings, and she put up a vivacious front all evening. In actuality, however, her gaiety was tinged with sadness. Never had she been separated from her father and sister for any appreciable length of time, and now both of them were going elsewhere.

She consoled herself with the thought that her father and Lorene would return to South Carolina in six months and make their home at Oakhurst Manor for the next half-year. Now that Isaiah was retired after a lifetime of hard labor, he deserved the opportunity to spend the rest of his days as he chose, and she was happy for him.

But it would be a long time before she and Margot saw each other again, so she tried not to dwell on their separation. At least she did not envy her sister's new life. As a young girl she had dreamed of visiting faraway places, but she had found her true home at Oakhurst Manor and was content to remain here. It would be quite enough to take on the full responsibility for the house in Charleston, too. Perhaps someday in the distant future she and Jeremy would pay a visit to Paris, and might go to London, too, but she no longer felt the desire to travel.

The last of the guests left the party shortly before midnight. Isaiah and Lorene had already gone to bed. Sarah and Jeremy went into the library for a last drink of champagne with his brother and her sister, and the master of Oakhurst Manor raised his glass in a toast. "Until we four meet again," he said.

"May God bless and keep you," Sarah added.

"And you," Margot and Tom echoed.

In spite of the pleasant evening, this was a solemn moment, and they sipped their drinks in silence. Then the younger Beauforts left to spend their last night at Trelawney before going in to Charleston to make last-minute purchases the following day.

Sarah smiled at her husband but felt weary as they started up the stairs to their suite. All at once she became so dizzy she couldn't stand; she reached for the railing but missed it and began to fall.

Jeremy caught her and held her in his arms. "What's wrong?" he asked anxiously.

The moment passed. "I . . . I'm all right now. For a second I thought I would faint, but the feeling passed as quickly as it came over me."

"You're sure?"

"Very sure." She returned his hug and stood by herself, then resumed her walk up the stairs.

Jeremy said no more, but kept a close watch on her. Perhaps the brief spell had been no more than an emotional reaction to the pending departures of her father and sister. On the other hand, there might be more to the incident than even she suspected. She had grown so pale, and when he held her in his arms she had been trembling violently, even though she appeared not to realize it.

He thought of how much she meant to him, and a terrible sense of fear gripped him. He was just being morbid, he told himself, and angrily shook off the feeling. He and Sarah had a lifetime of happiness still ahead.

She awakened at her usual early hour the next morning, thereafter was her normal, cheerful self. That afternoon they drove into Charleston with Kai and M'Bwana, and the captain of the *Louise* had himself rowed out to his ship so he could make a presailing check.

That night Kai and M'Bwana joined Isaiah, Lorene, and the Beauforts for a quiet dinner, and then Jeremy and Sarah took formal possession of the Charleston house. This consisted only of a twin ceremony: Jeremy was given a deed and Sarah was handed the keys. The entire household staff would be kept, and Lorene was leaving all of her furniture and houshold goods behind, the house in Boston being already fully furnished. Sarah, who admired her stepmother's taste, had no desire to make any immediate changes.

Everyone was awake at dawn the next morning to bid fare-well to Isaiah and Lorene, who promised they would return to Oakhurst Manor in six months to the day. Meantime Lorene and Sarah promised to keep in touch.

Jeremy accompanied M'Bwana to the *Louise* to make an inspection of his own, and a couple of hours later Sarah and Kai followed with Tom, Margot, and their baby.

Margot, as excited as a young girl, was enthralled by the brig, and her enthusiasm caused Sarah and Kai to exchange smiles. The water didn't attract either of them, perhaps because they were married to seafaring men. They were happy to remain at home and let others see the world.

M'Bwana was notified by a midshipman that the tide was beginning to turn. "All visitors ashore," he said, and kissed his wife.

After a tumult of kisses, handshakes, and hugs, Sarah, Kai, and Jeremy boarded a launch that remained in sight as the *Louise* weighed anchor and slowly made her way out of the Charleston harbor, beginning the first leg of her long voyage.

Margot and Tom stayed on deck waving until they could no longer make out the figures in the launch.

An era had come to an end, Sarah thought as she watched the brig grow smaller in the distance, and the thought was truer than even she knew.


The supper party had been lively, the table companion of Lisa, Lady Saunders, had been more interesting than anyone she had met in months, yet she had been bored. Lethargic but wide-awake after returning home, she took her time un-dressing. She thought of taking a late swim but decided she was too lazy, so she amused herself by dabbing on some perfume and donning one of her more attractive semisheer nightgowns.

Sleep did not come easily, but it never did anymore, and she tossed for a long time. But she had learned the trick of making her mind blank and relaxing her body, so at last she drifted off.

The door burst open with a crash that awakened Lisa instantly, and she saw three burly men in worn sailors' garb, weapons in their hands, coming into the room.

She sat bolt upright in bed, pulling the sheets and blankets around her, and tried to scream. But she was so terrified she could make no sound.

"There she be," the bearded member of the trio said. "You know what to do, but be careful, and no shenanigans. Hawk wants her as is."

The other two advanced swiftly toward the bed.

Lisa found her voice and screamed.

The sound was cut off abruptly as one of the men stuffed a gag into her mouth.

She tried to fight them off, scratching, kicking, and striking at them as best she could, but she could not match their far greater strength.

"Easy, now," one of them said with a dry laugh. "We don't want to hurt you none."

Lisa could not prevent them from binding her ankles and wrists, and then one of them threw her over his shoulder as though she were a sack of meal and started down the stairs with her.

In spite of her fear, every element of the scene below registered in her mind, and her horror deepened.

A number of similarly dressed men—perhaps six, possibly as many as a dozen—were systematically going through the room, stripping paintings and tapestries from the walls, scooping silver, bric-a-brac, and other valuables into burlap bags.

Lisa's majordomo was sprawled on the floor of the entrance hall. His throat had been cut, and he was dead. Nearby lay the principal maid, the front of her night robe stained with blood; she, too, was dead.

Lisa's captor paid no attention to the activities in the

house. Heading straight for the dunes, he carried his helpless victim to a small boat hauled up on the shore. His two companions launched it, and he waded into the water, then dumped her into the bottom. A moment later all three began to row.

Unable to free herself or cry out, Lisa at last struggled to a half-sitting position and saw that the men were rowing toward a nondescript but sturdy ship with dirty sails that was anchored beyond the coral reef. The men knew what they were doing, and eased the boat over a place where the water covering the reef was deep enough to let them pass.

One of them hailed the ship.

There was an answering shout, and a basket was lowered.

Lisa was unceremoniously dumped into it, and while she was being hauled to the deck, the bearded sailor climbed a rope with the agility of a monkey. He picked her up, and like his companion, carried her over his shoulder, with her head dangling.

He walked aft, and with his free hand he pounded on the door of a cabin.

The door opened and another bearded man with blond hair stood inside. He appeared to be in his mid-thirties, no older, and was as brawny a giant as Lisa had ever seen. His arm and shoulder muscles bulged through his open-necked shirt, and there was so much hair on his chest and arms that she was revolted.

He captor dumped her on the floor. "Here ye be, Hawk," he said. "The boys will be along soon as they finish claiming their share of the reward."

"Thanks, friend," the man addressed as Hawk said in a deep baritone. "Now, get out."

There was a broad grin on the man's face as he obeyed.

Paying no attention to the bound captive lying on the floor of the spacious, well-furnished cabin, Hawk took his time locking the door, pouring himself a drink of rum and water, and tidying the cabin.

Then suddenly he seemed to become aware of the young woman's presence, and nudged her with his foot. "Well, milady," he said, "I bid you good evening."

The gag in Lisa's mouth prevented her from speaking.

Pretending to become aware of her problem for the first time, he bowed with mock deference and removed the gag.

"What's the meaning of this . . . this outrageous insanity?" Lisa demanded.

"Now, now. Keep a civil tongue in your pretty mouth or you'll lose all your teeth. Speak to me nicely, and you'll find out all you need to know."

Well aware that she was helpless, completely at the ruffian's mercy, and realizing, too, that she was scantily clad, Lisa forced herself to speak civilly. "I'm unaccustomed to being awakened so rudely and dragged off in the middle of the night. I hope you'll be good enough to explain."

"Gladly. Would you like a drink?"

Her long experience with men told her she had no choice, and she knew it was better to pacify him than anger him. Besides, he might release her bonds. "I believe I'd find anything preferable to being trussed on the floor."

He laughed, moved toward her, and loomed above her. Removing a knife with a bone handle from his belt, he looked down at her, then swiftly slashed her nightgown from top to bottom and hauled it from her body. "Sometimes I like my wenches naked," he said, "and this is such a time."

Incongruously, she found herself trying to identify his accent. She was nude now in the presence of this muscled stranger, but all she could do was wonder about his speech. Perhaps that was merely her way of preventing herself from weeping in fright or even fainting. But she wasn't the fainting kind. Ah, she had it now. He was Welsh.

Hawk bent down again and cut her bonds. Then, turning his back to her, he went to the table against the bulkhead on the far side of the cabin and mixed her a rum and water.

It occurred to Lisa that he was testing her, first cutting her loose and then ignoring her in the possible hope that she would spring at him. Common sense told her not to engage in so quixotic a gesture. There were other men, many of them, on board this vessel, and still others on shore. Even if she managed to make her way to the rail and jump overboard, there were sharks in the waters outside the coral reef. Her chances of reaching the beach were virtually nonexistent, and even then it would be easy enough for a party of men to capture a lone, unclad young woman.

Long ago she had put her career as a courtesan behind her, but it stood her in good stead now. Pretending to a calm she was far from feeling, she walked shakily to the nearest chair, sat in it, and waited, her seeming poise as great as if she had been fully dressed.

He turned, and his quick smile indicated that he appreciated her show of courage. Handing her a glass, he lifted his own.

She did the same, and sipped her drink. It was abominable rum, and very strong.

"Once," he said, "I was a lieutenant in his Majesty's navy. My name doesn't matter, although you'll find it posted on the rolls of deserters." He paused.

Lisa made no comment.

"Wouldn't you like to know why I deserted? Thanks to Rear Admiral Lord Saunders, who hated me from the day he first saw me and threatened to ruin me. Well, I'm still alive and he isn't." He laughed boisterously.

"You've abducted me because you hated my late husband?" Lisa was incredulous.

"That's one reason. But you yourself are another, milady. I wanted you the first time I ever saw you, and I continued to want you all this time." He looked her up and down slowly, his small, pale eyes taking in every line, every contour of her nude, lovely body. "Now I have you."

"So it would appear." Lisa's playacting was superb, and her pretended calm was remarkable. "Perhaps you'd be good enough to introduce yourself."

Again he laughed. "I'm called Hawk."

"I gathered that much."

"Surely you can guess the rest, milady."

"You're a buccaneer—"

"The direct successor to Morgan and Kidd. The organization was ruined by Saunders and the Americans, so I've been able to take over, little by little, and now I'm ready to set up my empire!" He gulped half of his drink. "I've avoided British dependencies because I'll be hanged if I'm caught, but I had to have you. And I promised this crew, the best I have, that they can keep all the booty they can take from your house. Clever, isn't it?"

"Abominably clever." Lisa actually needed another swallow of the vile liquor.

"Now there are things you need to know. You're my wench, mine alone, as long as you behave yourself and as long as you please me. Make a fuss, and I'll turn you over to my crew right this minute, as naked as the day you were born, and you know what they'll do to you."

She concealed a shudder.

"By pleasing me you'll earn your clothes. A skirt, shoes, whatever. Day by day. Then you'll be given earrings and all the other little trinkets that women so enjoy. But you'll earn them, too. I have an appetite for wenches, so I'll keep you busy, and I'll expect you to keep me amused. In your spare time you'll keep house and cook for me."

"You make your requirements clear," she said.

His grin indicated his appreciation of her wry humor. Then, as they heard the sounds on deck of the landing party returning from shore, he went to the door. "I'll be back after we've sailed. Don't go away." He left, locking the door behind him.

Looking around for the first time, Lisa realized that the cabin undoubtedly had been the quarters of the ship's master before it had been confiscated by the freebooters. It was furnished in good taste, and was comfortable though unkempt. Miraculously, there were clean sheets on the large bed, presumably in honor of her anticipated arrival, so the man who liked to call himself Hawk wasn't completely lacking in finesse.

A flickering light drew Lisa's attention, so she went to one of the square windows overlooking the stern. Flames were leaping high in the air on shore, and she was stunned anew when she realized that the marauders had set fire to her home.

Of course. By burning the place to the ground they would not only destroy the evidence of their raid and the murder of her household staff members but also provide a perfect cover for her disappearance. It would be assumed by everyone on the island that she had died in the fire.

For a long moment Lisa covered her face with her hands. The long years she had worked to provide herself with social standing and financial security were gone, along with her home, her wardrobe, and her jewels. Within a short time her securities and real-estate properties would be inherited by Dickie's cousin.

Lady Saunders had vanished for all time.

In her place had been created a buccaneer chieftain's wench.

In spite of her horror and revulsion, Lisa knew there was literally nothing she could do to turn back the sweeping tide that was so drastically altering her life.

But she was determined to survive. She had fought in the past after suffering severe blows, and she would do it again.

Hawk had promised her jewelry if she did his bidding. Very well, she would begin again. Ultimately she would accumulate a new nest egg, and no matter how dire her circumstances, she would find a way to escape. No matter how desperate her situation, she would overcome it.

"Beloved Jeremy," she murmured aloud, "this is my last farewell to you."

She heard the sounds of the anchor being hauled up, and a few moments later the ship was in motion. Again she looked out of the window at the fire that was consuming the safe, pleasant world she had known.

When she turned back into the cabin, she stood erect, her firm breasts outthrust. Fate had decreed that she become a freebooter's woman, so she would make the best of her sordid lot. She would become all that this vile man wanted, and a great deal more.

A quarter of an hour later Hawk returned to the cabin, and was astonished to find his captive stretched out on the bed, with pillows propped behind her. She hadn't bothered to cover herself with the sheets. A fresh drink rested on the table beside her, and she had refilled his glass, too.

He had expected hysteria, at the very least, and had been certain she would even put up a physical struggle. Her attitude so confused him that he became wary.

"Here," he said, dropping a sack on the table. "I had one of my men brings your rouge pots, crayons, and suchlike. You'll have a use for them."

"That was very thoughtful of you," Lisa said. "I do thank you."

He continued to stare at her, his eyes narrowing to slits. "If you're mocking me . . ."

"Hardly," she said, and her smile was beguiling. "Lover, you waste too much time in talk." Crooking a finger, she beckoned him.

He wasted no more time.

He might regard himself as a hawk, Lisa thought as he gathered her in a smothering embrace, but he was more like a bear, and even his foul breath was animallike.

He proved to be a demanding lover with an almost insatiable sexual appetite, as he had told her. But she was able to handle him, just as she had handled others when she had been a courtesan in the Liguanea Hills. She was passive when his vanity required it, active when his energies flagged, and she needed no lessons in the fine art of simulating passion.

For the present she might be the victim of this crude and vicious boor, but eventually she would bend him to her will and enslave him.

Two days later, as the ship approached the secret cove on the north shore of Santo Domingo that was the new hiding place of the buccaneer fleet, Lisa came into the open for the first time. The crew gaped at her as she made her way to the quarterdeck.

A scant sixty-five hours earlier the charming Lady Saunders, widow of the commander of the British fleet in the West Indian islands, had been carried on board, a helpless prisoner.

Surely the young woman with copper-colored hair whom they saw now was a different person. Her makeup was heavy, her lips a bright scarlet, the beauty patch high on one cheek emphasizing her green, kohl-rimmed eyes. She was clad in the "uniform" of the Santo Domingo harlot, a snug blouse open to the waist, a tight-fitting skirt slit high on one thigh, a wide belt that called attention to her tiny waist, and absurdly high-heeled sandals. Her long silver earrings moved back and forth hypnotically, and several bracelets of thin silver jangled on one wrist. Even her hips swayed sensuously as she walked.

Paying no attention to her audience, she went straight to Hawk on the quarterdeck, her bewitching smile indicating to his men as well as to him that she was entranced by him. She cuddled close to him, and he slid his arm around her. Then his hand dropped to grasp her buttocks, and she actually snuggled still closer.

Lady Saunders? This wench actually *was* a Santo Domingo harlot—far more attractive, flashier, and more provocative than any other.

# Chapter 12

Sarah and Jeremy spent a full week in Charleston, moving into the master-bedroom suite of their new house. While Jeremy attended to business matters concerned with his still-growing shipping empire, Sarah began to relish being the mistress of the home that had belonged to her father and stepmother. It was spacious without being too large, quietly elegant without being ostentatious, and before they returned to Oakhurst Manor she gave a small supper party for some friends who lived in the city.

"I have everything I've ever wanted," she told her husband after they returned to the plantation.

The next morning, after they had breakfast with Kai and the children, she worked for a time on her ledgers, then went out to weed in the rose garden that was her great pride.

There Lester Howard found her an hour later, unconscious and crumpled in a heap.

Unable to rouse her, he sent a servant to find Jeremy, who was inspecting the tobacco fields about a mile away.

Jeremy returned at a gallop, and while he carried Sarah upstairs to bed, Howard rode off to fetch the new physician in the area, Dr. Jenkins.

When they returned together an hour later, Sarah had not regained consciousness. Her breathing was regular, but she was very pale, and her pulse rate was high. The physician spent a long time examining her, and then joined her anxious husband, who was pacing up and down in the sitting room.

"I must be honest with you, Mr. Beaufort," Dr. Jenkins said. "Some of her symptoms are abnormal. In fact, they're rather alarming. But I'm afraid I don't know what's wrong with Mistress Beaufort. I'm unable to make an accurate diagnosis."

Jeremy's throat was dry. "Then she's . . . seriously ill?"

"So it appears. This case calls for someone with more experience than I've had, and I suggest that you bring Dr. Francis Marion, the general's nephew, out here from Charleston."

Lester Howard rode off to the city at a gallop, and covered the ground in an hour and a quarter.

By noon he was back with the middle-aged physician, generally regarded as the best in the state.

Dr. Marion conducted an even longer examination than his younger colleague had made, and when he finally came to Jeremy in the sitting room, his face was grave.

"I've seen four or five similar cases, Jeremy, during my years of practice. All are fatal."

Too numb to react, Jeremy swallowed hard. "Are you telling me there's no hope for her, Francis?"

"If my diagnosis is accurate, as I'm afraid it is, all you can do is pray."

"But there must be something . . ."

"Some patients go quickly, and they're fortunate. They awaken for a short time, and then they're gone. Those who linger gradually become paralyzed, and they appear to suffer a great deal. According to a theory advanced at the Edinburgh Medical School, a mass of some sort presses on the brain, but still too little is known to permit surgery."

"Isn't there some treatment . . . ?"

"I know of none," Dr. Marion said. "I'll stay on through the crisis, if you wish, but I feel like a charlatan, because there's so little I can do."

Jeremy tried to steady himself. "Is Sarah in pain?"

"To the best of my knowledge, she isn't, and if she goes

quickly, her suffering will be very slight. But I can make no predictions if she takes a slow turn for the worse."

Jeremy nodded, went into the bedroom, and stayed there. He stationed himself in a chair, strategically placed so he could observe Sarah at all times, and there he remained for the next thirty-six hours, leaving only when he had to relieve himself. Occasionally he took brief catnaps, and in spite of the urging of Kai and Cleo, he ate only a few token bites of food.

On the second night of his vigil he was still wide-awake when Sarah opened her eyes for the first time.

He went to her instantly.

"I'm going to die," she said, her voice barely audible.

"You mustn't say that," he replied fiercely as he covered her hand with his.

"It's true, and I know it." There was no fear in Sarah's eyes, and she appeared serene. She intended to die as courageously as she had lived. "Don't argue, please, and listen to me, because I have no breath to spare."

Jeremy fell silent, trying hard not to weep.

"Don't grieve for me too long," she said. "We've had a wonderful life together, a wonderful marriage, and it must not be spoiled by sorrow."

He bent down and kissed her hand.

"Help Jerry and encourage him. He needs it. He isn't as strong as he might be."

She confirmed his own feelings about their son, and again he nodded.

"Someday, perhaps, you can acknowledge Lance as your son. I don't know how you can manage it, but if the chance comes, don't hesitate." Sarah gasped for breath, then steadied herself. "He's a wonderful child, and I wish he were mine. I wish Carrie had been mine, too."

"I'll do everything in my power for both of them," Jeremy said.

"And don't stay single, dear Jeremy. Some men enjoy a bachelor life, but you aren't one of them."

"I want only you." The cry was wrung from his heart.

Her smile was tender. "If you're able, marry Lisa Saunders."

"No!"

"I've known from the day I first saw her that you were intimate with her, and long ago I forgave you for it."

Jeremy bowed his head.

"Don't feel guilty, I beg you. I don't understand the force that drew you to each other, but I recognize it and I sympathize with it. Don't be ashamed of it."

"I love you, Sarah, with all my heart," he said.

"As I love you. Good-bye, beloved Jeremy."

Again he bent over her, and as he kissed her on the lips she breathed her last.

The members of the buccaneer band had to admit that Hawk had a way with women. It was almost impossible for any member of the company to recall that their leader's wench had been Lady Saunders, the widow of an admiral.

It was obvious that she was infatuated with Hawk. When he toured the caves or met with his men, she invariably joined him, kissing and caressing him, rubbing her body against his and climbing into his lap. When he amused himself in the presence of others by dipping a hand inside her low-cut blouse and fondling her breasts, it was apparent that she became aroused, and she felt no shame when she squirmed in delight at his touch.

Sometimes, when he drank to excess or was in a foul mood and cuffed her, she actually enjoyed being beaten by him, and her ardor for him became all the more pronounced. She worshiped him, and in her eyes he could do no wrong.

It was true that Hawk spoiled the woman, saving the most choice pieces of jewelry from their loot for her after a raid, but they couldn't blame him. She was the most dazzling trollop they had ever seen, and her loyalty to him was absolute.

When they were particularly successful in one expedition, capturing three ships and gaining fifty new recruits from their crews, Hawk allowed them to celebrate by bringing a score of harlots from Santo Domingo City to the caves in the mountains for a week of sport. Their presence emphasized the difference between them and Hawk's wench. She was superior to them in every way: she was far prettier, had an infinitely superior figure, and was so much more provocative that every man in the company still wanted her.

Hawk even went so far as to grant her the privilege of carrying a knife in her broad belt, and the wiser members of the band approved, even though it seemed inconceivable to most that any woman should be allowed to bear arms. There were too many who coveted her, and she needed to protect herself during Hawk's absences from the stronghold.

As always, Hawk was right. He and most of his followers spent the better part of a week at the secret harbor, preparing the ships of his growing squadron for a new expedition. His wench, naturally, remained behind. Only a handful resented the fact that she had never even learned to cook, and automatically joined the men twice each day for their barbecued beef and wildfowl.

At meals she was friendly enough, but always kept her distance, and invariably retired without delay to the cave she shared with Hawk. Several of the group swore they would take her before the leader returned, claiming she would never dare to use her knife and would be too cowardly to admit to Hawk what had happened to her.

Several hours before his expected return with the bulk of the band, Lisa ate her customary meal with the guards, taking her usual care to remain apart from them and to speak only when directly addressed. Removing her upper garment, she sat near the cave entrance, where she could take advantage of the daylight, and began to prepare for Hawk's return. First she rouged her nipples, a touch that delighted him, then made up her face, using cosmetics far more lavishly than she had ever done previously. Holding a mirror in one hand as she worked, she kept her mind totally blank, a condition that became easier to achieve each day.

By now, she estimated, she had accumulated jewelry worth two or three thousand English pounds sterling, perhaps ten thousand dollars in American money. It was a good start, but not nearly enough for her purposes. She would need at least five times that amount before she could make a break for freedom, flee to some place where the buccaneers could not find her, and then begin a real life again in safety and solitude.

She thought nothing, she felt nothing, and she satisfied Hawk's every whim, behaving as he expected her to behave and giving him even more than he wanted. So far she had managed to preserve her sanity, and she was determined to hang on, living only for the day when she would be free again.

Suddenly, in the mirror, Lisa saw a member of the band slowly creeping up the slope that led to the cave entrance.

She recognized him immediately. He was one of the newcomers, a wiry French seaman who spoke no English. Perhaps the language barrier was partly responsible for his inability or refusal to realize what Hawk would do to him if he molested her. But Hawk wasn't here.

Pretending to study her makeup, Lisa drew her knife from her belt, gripped the handle firmly, and waited. Never in her life had she used a weapon, but she felt no nervousness, no trepidation. Her attitude remained what it had been since the time of her abduction: she would do what was necessary. In this instance it was essential that she incapacitate her wouldbe attacker. Otherwise Hawk would be convinced that she had cooperated willingly.

The man moved closer.

Lisa was alert and ready, but still felt blank.

She continued to wait, knowing a premature move would be disastrous.

The Frenchman came nearer, then stood. Brushing his hands on the sides of his breeches, he appeared ready to pounce.

Now!

Lisa whirled, jumping to her feet, and before the Frenchman could grasp her, she struck at him wildly with the knife, using all of her willpower to prevent herself from closing her eyes.

Desperation improved her aim, but she was still luckier than she knew. Her slashing stroke found its target, and in one blow she slit the attacker's throat.

The Frenchman collapsed at her feet, blood pouring from his wound as he died.

For a long moment Lisa stared down at his body. A wave of nausea almost overcame her, but it passed. She had actually killed a fellow human being, but her mental discipline was so great that she refused to dwell on the matter.

She wiped the blade of her knife on the Frenchman's shirt, then returned it to her belt. Next she took the precaution of donning her blouse, which afforded her minimal covering.

Gazing down at the body again, she gave in to a rare impulse and stamped on the man's face with a high heel. "Hawk," she said aloud, "your time will come, too."

Recovering her poise, she moved into the open and uttered a high, piercing scream that would be sure to summon the other guards.

For several weeks after Sarah's funeral Jeremy was in a daze, but work was his salvation. He labored from early morning until after dark, eating little in spite of the coaxing of Kai and Cleo, and in addition to his other duties he took charge of the ledgers that Sarah had kept for years.

It occurred to Jeremy that Lester Howard's grief was intense, and he wondered fleetingly whether the overseer had loved Sarah, too. Probably. He couldn't blame Lester, believing that every man who had known Sarah had to have loved her.

Whenever Jeremy went into Charleston on business for several days at a time, Kai now accompanied him, taking Lance, Jerry, and Carrie with her. His only pleasure in life now, it seemed, was playing with the children for an hour every evening before they went off to bed. Then he returned to the parlor, and Kai, after trying in vain to converse with him, respected his long silences.

After one such trip Jeremy found a letter from Isaiah Benton awaiting him. There had not yet been time for Sarah's father to receive the news of her passing and reply to it. Instead, Isaiah told of yet another tragedy.

Willie and Amanda were dead, Isaiah wrote, killed by a bigot who had set fire to their house. The man, a cabinetmaker like Willie, had been jealous of the success the black man had enjoyed, and obtained revenge in his own insane way.

The public had been revolted. The murderer had already been tried, and was sentenced to be hanged.

The sad tale had one bright element. The two small children of Willie and Amanda, Cleo and Paul, had been saved by an alert neighbor. Isaiah and Lorene had taken in the youngsters immediately, and were giving them a home.

They intended to bring Cleo and Paul to Oakhurst Manor with them when they themselves returned.

The stunned Jeremy sat down at once and wrote a brief reply. The two children used the name of Beaufort, because Willie, prior to being granted his freedom, had known no surname of his own and had followed the custom of using his master's name. So it was particularly appropriate, Jeremy wrote, that two more Beauforts would be coming home.

Willie had been as close to him as his own brother in their formative years, and the fresh tragedy was crushing. Nevertheless Jeremy steeled himself as he went to tell Willie's mother the sad news.

Cleo was at work in the kitchen outbuilding, as usual.

Jeremy sent her helpers away, then read her the letter.

They looked at each other, and as they embraced, Jeremy and Cleo wept for the first time since Sarah's funeral.

Early that evening Jeremy retired to his own suite and stayed there for two days, seeing no one but the children, who came in to play with him as they always did.

Not even the arrival of Scott for his usual weekend visit tempted Jeremy to come downstairs.

"I'm worried about him," Kai said at dinner. "He's so active that this isn't at all like him."

"He must be allowed to grieve in his own way," Scott said. "But he'll be all right. After all, he's a Beaufort."

"I'm not sure I know what you mean."

"I've known them all my life, as well as I know my own family," Scott said, "and all Beauforts have an inner core of tempered steel. Especially Jeremy, who is stronger than any of them. Don't pity him openly, and if you pamper him, don't let him know you're doing it."

"I'll do my best," Kai said.

"Which means you'll succeed. Jeremy is far more fortunate than he knows to have you acting as the mistress of Oakhurst Manor."

"Don't flatter me too much, or it will go to my head and I'll get nothing constructive done."

"I don't believe you for a moment. You can do anything when you set your mind to it." Scott couldn't help envying M'Bwana. Kai was one girl in a million.

The transatlantic voyage to France was pleasant and uneventful. Winds from the west were brisk, the sea was calm for the better part of the trip, and both Tom and Margot had the time of their lives.

The counselor of the American legation awaited them in Brest, and M'Bwana went off to Paris with them for a few days before returning to the *Louise* and supervising the loading of cargo. He set sail for the Caribbean a full week ahead of his planned schedule.

The fair weather was too good to last, and a series of heavy squalls, combined with stronger than usual headwinds, slowed the westward passage to the West Indian islands. M'Bwana not only lost all the time he had gained previously but dropped behind by an additional week as well.

He was unworried by the developments, it being customary for a merchantman to allow at least an extra month on a voyage of such long duration. One minor problem developed, however, when his water supplies ran low. So he studied his maps, and rather than sail all the way to Martinique, he decided to make a short detour.

Sailing by way of the Virgin Islands chain, he put into a snug harbor of a small, unoccupied island due south of Virgin Gorda. There were fresh water springs there, as well as citrus fruits and coconuts that grew wild.

He anchored in the harbor, vaguely aware of a large schooner with dirty sails in the distance that was heading in his direction, but he paid scant attention to the ship. Merchant shipping invariably was heavy in Virgin Island waters.

Leaving only a few men on board the *Louise*, M'Bwana had all of his boats lowered and took virtually his entire company ashore. After spending six weeks at sea the men were eager to stretch their legs on land again.

While some filled the water casks at the spring, M'Bwana and the rest of the company wandered farther inland through the grove of coconut palms, intending to cut down some of the ripe coconuts later. Their immediate goal was the small forest of lemon trees where the thick-skinned yellow fruit had just ripened in the sun. Like all sailors, they craved fresh fruit after being at sea for an appreciable period of time.

The men sucked the juice of lemons as they dropped large quantities of the fruit into baskets, and M'Bwana relaxed, too. He found a large, succulent lemon, plucked it, and cut it open with a small pocketknife.

The juice was delicious, precisely what he had wanted, so he cut a second, then a third.

He was aware of footsteps in the coconut stand behind him, and assumed that the men who had been filling the water casks were joining the rest of the party.

Instead, a large company of shabbily dressed sailors came into the clearing, all of them heavily armed. They were led by a blond, bearded giant who held a cocked pistol in each hand.

Buccaneers.

Too late M'Bwana realized that he and his crew had left their own weapons on board the *Louise*. Perhaps he had been negligent, but there had been no reason to bring arms ashore.

"Raise your hands high in the air!" Hawk ordered.

One of the Americans was tardy in obeying, and a musket shot in the forehead felled him instantly.

"Do what you're told," Hawk said amiably as he surveyed his captives. Suddenly he caught sight of M'Bwana, and his eyes lighted. "Aha! So you're the black sea captain men have been talking about for years. Your days on the quarterdeck are ended, my friend."

One of the freebooters raised a musket, intending to shoot the Bantu.

But Hawk intervened quickly. "Put down your gun, you goddamn idiot!"

"But we always kill the captains," the man said.

"Not this one. His carcass is worth nothing, but alive he'll bring us a small fortune. He's a husky, healthy specimen, and they'll pay the top price for him in the slave markets."

The infuriated M'Bwana leaped at the blond giant, indifferent to the pistols he was holding.

But one of the buccaneers was too quick for him. Wielding his musket like a club as he grasped it by the barrel, the man brought the butt down on the back of the Bantu's head with full force.

M'Bwana sprawled on the ground unconscious.

The American first mate sprang to his master's aid.

Hawk coolly took aim and shot the officer through the heart.

"If the rest of you have any thoughts of fighting, now is the time to tell me," he said.

The stunned American seamen stood still, their hands still held above their heads.

"Nothing rash now, lads," Chief Boatswain Talbot said. "There's been enough killing."

"Ah, a wise man." Hawk nudged the unconscious M'Bwana with a booted toe. "Truss him, take him aboard the schooner, and throw him in the hold. Make sure you keep him tied."

Two of his subordinates hastened to obey.

The buccaneer leader surveyed his captives. "Seeing we've taken possession of your ship, I'm in a good mood today," he said. "There are some open places in our band of brothers, and any who want to join us are welcome. We can always use experienced sailors. You'll obey me in all things at all times. And when we take loot, you'll get your fair share. Those who want to come with us stand forward."

There was a long silence.

Then Boatswain Talbot took two steps forward. He felt only contempt for freebooters, but he knew what would become of those who refused to join the band. Later, when the opportunity presented itself, he would part company with these cutthroats. In the meantime, his instinct for survival was too strong to permit him to take any other action.

After a moment's hesitation he was followed by a half-dozen others.

"So you're the boatswain," Hawk said.

"Aye, sir, that I be."

"And you're English, from the sound of you."

"That I be, Captain."

"Splendid. I'll have special use for your talents, you can be sure. I'll have words with you after we return to the ships. I'll want you on my schooner, not on the prize."

"Aye, aye, sir," Talbot said, and forced himself to salute the murdering villain.

"As for the rest of these Yanks," Hawk said, "tie them up!"

The freebooters obeyed with alacrity, and soon the rest of the Americans were trussed.

"One way or another," Hawk said, "you'll work your way free of your bonds in due time. But by then we'll be long gone across the horizon. And you'll be left here to rot with the coconuts and lemons. The hurricane season is about to begin, which means there will be no more shipping in these waters, so I doubt you'll be able to attract the attention of any passing vessel. Ah, well, it's your choice."

He marched off at the head of his company, and there was no sound in the grove but the thud of retreating bootsteps.

When the *Louise* was six weeks overdue on her return to Charleston, Jeremy became concerned. The *Elizabeth* was sailing on one of her regular voyages to the Caribbean, and although her primary destination was Jamaica, he asked Captain Slocum to call at the French West Indian islands to find out whether the smaller ship had arrived there and, perhaps, was delayed because she was undergoing repairs.

Another ten weeks passed, and Captain Slocum finally returned with bad news. There had been no sign of the *Louise* at the French islands of Martinique and Guadeloupe, and she had not been seen, either, at Santo Domingo, Puerto Rico, or Cuba.

Jeremy intensified his search, writing to other American shipowners, as well as to the proprietors of English, French, and Spanish vessels. After an agonizing wait of another four months he finally received a letter from an English company that did nothing to improve his peace of mind. The *Louise* had last been sighted, only slightly behind her regular schedule, about three hundred miles off the Virgin Islands in the open Atlantic. At that time she had been moving under full sail as she headed westward, and had been in no apparent difficulty.

Kai displayed a remarkable calm. Even though she, like Jeremy, couldn't imagine what had become of the ship, she continued to feel confident that her husband would return to her. M'Bwana was indestructible, she declared, the most resourceful man on earth, and one of these days he would bring the *Louise* safely into her home port.

Under the law a ship was declared lost at sea one year after she failed to make an appearance, and her officers and men were pronounced dead. The dreaded anniversary loomed ahead, but Kai refused to lose faith. "M'Bwana will come home," she said repeatedly.

She passed the time in useful activities, and her stature

seemed to grow. She acted as mistress of Oakhurst Manor and the house in Charleston, and after Jeremy's time of mourning for Sarah came to an end, she entertained for him, giving small dinner and supper parties, and on several occasions inviting large numbers of guests to the plantation. When the Bentons appeared with the housekeeper's grandchildren, she took charge of little Cleo and Paul, too. She had already engaged a tutor for Jerry, Lance, and Carrie, so she hired another, and regular classes were held daily at Oakhurst Manor, with Kai supervising the activities.

Sometimes she fumbled, but she never made the same mistake twice. Her self-confidence expanded, and she became exceptionally confident in her management of affairs. Her basic attitude was unyielding, and she refused to admit even the possibility that she might be a widow.

In spite of her stand, however, others believed that ultimately she would be forced to face the reality of her unfortunate situation. When that day came, friends and neighbors were confident, she and Jeremy would marry. In their opinion such a union would be a natural outgrowth of their present relationship.

But the friends and neighbors were mistaken, as were Isaiah and Lorene Benton, who shared the same view. It was true that Jeremy and Kai relied on each other, leaned on each other, and helped each other, but neither felt romantically inclined toward the other. They were the best of friends, united by their memories of many shared experiences, but the spark that welded a man and woman and made them one was missing.

Perhaps their separate memories of Sarah dampened any ardor that otherwise might have developed. Even more important, however, was their mutual loyalty to M'Bwana. The shadow of the missing Bantu loomed large, and certainly it was a major factor in keeping Jeremy and Kai apart.

Only one person was aware of the real extent of Kai's loneliness, possibly realizing it even more than she did herself. Scott Emerson made it his business to bolster her feelings, to act as her partner at various social functions, and to help her keep up her spirits. He told himself it was the least he could do for her in return for the love she was giving his niece.

When she came into Charleston with Jeremy, sometimes bringing the children with her, Scott sometimes took her to the theater, the most active in America, or to lectures. He invited her to dine with him at various of the city's eating places, and she enjoyed herself thoroughly on these occasions. He saw to it that she went to the most fashionable dressmaker and the best shoemaker, and as an attorney, after M'Bwana was officially declared dead, he advised and helped her in the handling of her financial affairs.

It took Scott a long time to realize what Jeremy had begun to suspect, that he had fallen in love with Kai. Gradually it dawned on him that his feelings for her had changed when he and Jeremy had gone to New Orleans and rescued her from the imprisonment she had suffered at the hands of Emile Duchamp. That had been the beginning of something new.

Recognizing his love now, Scott had to cope with it. He knew that Kai remained faithful to M'Bwana, so he would not and could not allow himself to take advantage of her loneliness or intrude on her privacy. He went to great lengths to conceal the state of his feelings from her, and played the role of the faithful friend who asked nothing for himself, who wanted only her happiness.

Kai was no fool. She and Jeremy were bound together by many ties, ranging from their mutual close association with M'Bwana to the inescapable fact that Jeremy had actually sired Lance. By dwelling under the same roof, each served many useful purposes for the other, and they had achieved a balance that prohibited physical intimacy.

But her relationship with Scott was far different. His devotion to her was as sincere as it was obvious, and she sometimes wondered why he did so much for her without asking anything in return. Sometimes she guessed he might be in love with her, but he gave no sign of it in word or deed. Never did he allow himself to make advances to her. Even when they dined together by candlelight in a cozy corner of an inn, sitting before windows that overlooked the sea, his friendly demeanor remained unchanged.

Now and again it seemed to Kai that Scott's expression was guarded, that he was exercising care in his approach to her. Then he said something that made her laugh, or gave her sage advice that solved some problem with which she was wrestling, and her moment of doubt passed. She knew less about men than she realized, and she satisfied herself with the interpretation that he was simply a dear friend who had a genuine interest in her welfare.

Kai knew, too, that she did not dare look too deeply into Scott's motives. She found him enormously attractive, but her loneliness made her vulnerable, so she refused to open her mind and heart to the possibility that he loved her. M'Bwana still came first, and not until she received positive proof that he was no longer alive would she allow herself to think of her future in other terms. Her position was not easy to maintain, but her fidelity to M'Bwana was so great that it sustained her in her time of trial.

One evening, in Charleston, she and Scott returned to Jeremy's house from an outing with friends that both had enjoyed, to find that Jerry and Carrie were suffering from mild stomach upsets. Kai went upstairs immediately to see the children, and Scott joined Jeremy for a drink in one of the sitting rooms, the latter having just come home from a business meeting.

"You had a splendid day," Jeremy said as he handed his old friend a mug of ale.

"How did you know?" Scott asked.

"By the look on your face. It tells me about your day . . . and a great deal more."

"Does it show that much?"

"Not to most people, maybe, but we've known each other a long time," Jeremy said.

Scott's smile faded. "I spend most of my professional life as a lawyer advising other people," he said. "But I'm afraid I have no advice to give myself."

"It's that difficult?"

"Worse than I could have imagined. Between us, Jeremy, and to be repeated to no one, I'm desperately in love with Kai."

"I can't blame you. She's a wonderful girl. She's highly competent as well as beautiful and charming, and she's a superb mother. Her devotion to Jerry and Carrie, as well as to Willie's and Amanda's orphans, is as great as her love for her own son."

"There's nothing I can do about it," Scott said. "My hands are tied."

"She has no idea of how you feel?"

"I do my damndest not to let it show. No, I don't believe she knows."

"You understand she's convinced M'Bwana is going to come back. I'm afraid nothing will persuade her that the *Louise* sank in an accident of some sort and that all hands were drowned. She listens to her heart, not to logic, just as my Sarah did in all those years that I was missing and everyone else had given me up for dead."

"I think that knowing your story is what gives Kai courage. That and the admiration she always felt for Sarah. So you can see the position that I'm in, Jeremy. If I reveal to her that I love her, she'll not only reject me but she'll think I'm being devilishy unfair. Any feeling of warmth and friendship she may have for me will be dissipated, and that's a chance I don't care to take. I'm grateful for any crumbs I get from her, and I'm not brave enough to take the risk of losing that little."

"You can't, Scott," Jeremy said. "You're quite right. I've got to be very careful in my own dealings with Kai. I never come out in so many words and say that in my opinion M'Bwana has been drowned. She simply wouldn't accept it."

"Then what shall I do?"

"Nothing," Jeremy said. "Absolutely nothing. If she's worth having—"

"She is!"

"Then you've got to be patient. Wait. Treat her as you've been doing. If M'Bwana should come home—and the odds in favor of it are almost nonexistent—you can retreat gracefully into the background again. If he doesn't show up, as he almost assuredly won't, the time will come when Kai is ready to accept reality. I'm sure you'll recognize the change in her attitude when it takes place, probably without her knowledge. Then you'll be in a position to take action accordingly. Until then, Scott, you'll simply have to love her in silence. There's no other way."

Lisa couldn't remember when she had been so tired. It was only dusk, but her body craved rest, so she stretched out on the thick pallet at the rear of the cave, high in the mountains of Santo Domingo, but sleep wouldn't come. Her mind, unfortunately, remained alert and refused to be silenced.

It was no wonder that her body was weary. She had been forced to engage in another long session in which she had served the sexual needs of Hawk, and as always, she was disgusted. The man's gluttony and crudeness were almost beyond credence, and she didn't know how much longer she could tolerate him.

She had transformed herself into a buccaneer harlot, even cutting her long copper hair to shoulder length. She had deadened her soul. She cavorted, dressed, and made up as Hawk wished, but his appetites were insatiable, and often she was in despair.

Granted that she was accumulating jewelry, thanks to the gifts she wheedled out of him after he returned from a raid. Little by little she was approaching the goal that would then enable her to make a break for freedom. By that time, however, she was afraid that she herself would be too coarsened and callous to start the new life she craved.

If she had the courage, she would kill herself, but hope kept her alive. Hope for the future, combined with her recurring dream. Someday she would plunge her double-edged knife into Hawk's flesh, all the way to the hilt. She would watch the blood spurt from his wound, and as he died she would laugh. She envisioned the same scene again and again, asleep or awake, and it sustained her, enabled her to go on.

At least she had managed to put Jeremy Beaufort out of her mind. Almost. He was totally beyond her reach now, so she no longer thought of him, at least when she was awake. It was different when she slept and had no control over the workings of her mind. Then he appeared before her, loving and protective and strong, and often she awakened with tears streaming down her face.

"Lisa! Damn your soul, woman, where are you? Come here!"

The grating voice of Hawk aroused Lisa from her reverie.

Not bothering to patch her makeup or run a comb through her tousled hair, she donned a silk dressing gown he had brought her from his last expedition, slipped into a pair of the absurdly high-heeled slippers that were the only footgear she owned, and made her way to the front of the cave.

There, sitting around a fire built near the ledge of a steep precipice, were Hawk and a number of his lieutenants. A ship commanded by a renegade Frenchman had just returned to Santo Domingo after a voyage, so Lisa assumed he had been successful and that the meeting had been called to divide the loot.

Of all members of the freebooter community, she regarded the Frenchman as the most loathsome. He was known as the Hangman because of his unpleasant habit of choking captured merchant captains and their officers to death with a long thong of thin leather that he always carried in his belt. Even now, as the Hangman looked up at her, lust and avarice in his small, hard eyes, he was playing with the leather thong, threading it between his fingers.

Lisa knew why she had been summoned, and required no instruction. She tapped a barrel of confiscated rum, filled stolen pewter mugs with it, and added token quantities of coconut milk or fruit juice to the strong liquor. Then, making her way around the fire, she served the mugs to the dozen men who were gathered there.

But her duties were far from completed. After serving the drinks, she went to Hawk, sat on his lap, and curled an arm around his neck. As always, he began to grope, reaching under her thin robe as he pawed and caressed her.

Now it was her place to simulate great pleasure. She squirmed and wriggled beneath his touch, pretending to become aroused, aware that the chieftain's subordinates were jealous of him and impressed by his seeming prowess.

To the best of her ability she blocked out the conversation.

"The galleon I captured was a Spanish merchantman," the Hangman said. "The better part of her cargo was grain, so we'll all have plenty of bread for the next few months. She also carried gold bullion worth a half-million *dólares,* and even after we've paid my officers and crew their shares, there will be plenty left for us."

His colleagues murmured their approval.

"As for me," the French captain said, "I'll assign my share to Hawk and the rest of you."

They were astonished.

"Why the generosity?" Hawk demanded.

The Hangman's crooked smile revealed two rows of yellow, irregular teeth. "I'd rather have a quarter interest in all the galleon earns in the future."

Hawk was elated. "I accept," he said. "And I hope the rest of you will follow his example after future raids. I've been trying to make deals like that with all of you." He picked up his pewter mug and thrust it in front of Lisa's face.

She took the mug from him and swallowed a substantial quantity of rum, even though she loathed the drink. She had learned that Hawk always had a purpose in mind when he gave her liquor, and she suspected she was in for another long session of sexual play with him. Perhaps the rum would anesthetize her and blur the edges of her memory, so she took another swallow.

"The Hangman deserves a special reward," Hawk said.

Before Lisa quite realized what was happening, he stood abruptly, almost toppling her from his lap. He grasped her so she wouldn't fall, and in almost the same motion he stripped off her robe.

She stood nude before the gaping buccaneer captains and lieutenants.

Some moistened their lips, some rubbed their hands together, and all stared hungrily at her.

Only the Hangman sat motionless.

Lisa was too stunned to react. Now, less than ever, she failed to appreciate Hawk's humor. But he had whisked her robe out of reach, so she was unable to cover herself, and she could only stand unmoving, afraid he intended to take her in the presence of his subordinates.

"How do you like my wench, boys?" Hawk boomed. "I'll wager you've never seen a woman her equal, eh?"

Their eyes indicated that every man present wanted her.

Lisa wondered if she had the courage to throw herself off the lip of the precipice.

"The Hangman deserves a reward," Hawk said, "so I'm lending him the wench until morning."

Lisa was shocked to the marrow.

The freebooter captain leaped to his feet, profusely thanking his superior. Then, wasting no time, he turned to Lisa and beckoned.

She felt paralyzed, unable to move.

Using a chopping motion, the Hangman slashed her on her bare buttocks with the edge of his hand. Then he dropped his leather thong around her neck and tugged.

The buccaneers cheered, and the laughter of Hawk could be heard above the voices of all the rest.

Lisa had no alternative, and was compelled to follow the Frenchman to his own cave a short distance down the mountainside. She felt sullied and degraded beyond compare, knowing this incident was only the beginning. Hawk intended to use her as bait for all of his senior lieutenants, and her transformation into a harlot was complete.

She didn't care what the Hangman did to her body, because it was no longer her own.

# Chapter 13

M'Bwana was convinced his nightmare would never end.

Stripped and chained by wrists and ankles, he was taken to a slave market on an island that no one identified for him, and was sold into slavery. No one listened to him when he protested that he was an American sea captain who had served in the war against the buccaneers, an American citizen and a Bantu prince by heritage. The more he talked and complained, the more he was beaten into silence.

In the slave pens at the market and again after he was sold, he was lashed with a whip until his back and shoulders were laid open repeatedly. He could tolerate physical pain greater than most men could endure, but his captors, determined to break his spirit, whipped him until he lost consciousness, then began again when he awakened.

His wounds festered and became infected. He ran a high fever and scarcely could remember being thrown into the hold of a small inter-island ship, where he was chained to the bulkhead. He recalled nothing of the ship's voyage.

M'Bwana awakened to find himself in a small, primitive hut, one of many in a compound, and through the open entrance he could see fields of sugarcane as endless as his nightmare.

His head was clear now, and his back was improving, thanks to a greasy, foul-smelling salve that was smeared on it. Beside him on the hard-packed ground was a gourd of water and another of coarse food, a mixture of grain and fish. Fastened to his ankles were heavy chains that made it impossible to move. He was wearing a loincloth now.

Realizing he was both hungry and thirsty, he wolfed down the food and drank the water. His situation called for patience and a cool head, he decided as he settled back to await further developments. He was at the mercy of his captors, and had learned it was useless to protest too loudly against the fate that had made him a slave.

He would find out all he could before he made his next move. For Kai's sake and for Lance's he intended to live, and one way or another would return to them. He had another motive for staying alive and winning his freedom, too. He would not rest until he obtained vengeance against the buccaneer named Hawk. The very thought of killing the man gave him strength.

In the days that followed, M'Bwana was able to piece together various elements of his situation. His hut was located in the slave quarters of a sugar plantation somewhere in the West Indian islands. His fellow slaves, most of them newly arrived from Africa, spoke no English and had no idea where they were. In fact, M'Bwana had to communicate with them in Bantu or Watusi, tongues he had not used in years.

His meals were brought to him twice daily by an elderly slave fluent in Watusi, who was reluctant to say too much. By coaxing and biding his time, however, M'Bwana learned more from him than the man realized he was saying.

The newcomer would be a field hand, one of fifty on a large sugar plantation. The proprietor lived in a town elsewhere on the island, and came to the plantation only on weekends. Directly in charge of all operations was a black overseer, more demanding and vicious than any white man.

When the master came out on weekends, he usually brought with him a supply of grain, salt fish, and smoked meat. This was the staple fare of the slaves, who were allowed to augment their diet with bananas, coconuts, and breadfruit, which they grew themselves.

All of the slaves were men in their prime, the master believing that the presence of women among the field hands created problems. The overseer worked a man until he dropped, and when he died, he was replaced by a newcomer purchased in a slave market.

When M'Bwana recovered his health, he would go to work in the fields, too, and if he behaved properly, his leg chains would be removed. If he tried to escape, however, he would be beaten to death; that was the inviolable rule.

The old slave urged him to submit. There was no place on the island where a runaway slave could hide, and no place to go even if he succeeded in reaching the sea.

M'Bwana had his own ideas on the subject, but kept them to himself. Since the place was an island, there were ships and boats here, and he could sail anything that floated. But he had to prepare his escape with care. First he had to regain his strength. Then, while accumulating weapons and supplies, he had to learn all he could about the island, and most important of all, he had to ascertain where he could find and steal a boat. He needed time.

M'Bwana's knowledge of navigation stood him in good stead, and a study of the stars convinced him he was being held on an island in the easternmost end of the Caribbean. He had no instruments to help him, so he couldn't pinpoint the location, but his estimate was close enough for his present purposes.

The days became weeks, and M'Bwana lost count of time, but the calendar was of no significance. He had a mission to accomplish.

One day the overseer, a tall, thin man who scowled perpetually, came into the hut and prodded M'Bwana's back with the butt of his long rawhide whip. "You are well enough to work," he said in Watusi. "You will begin tomorrow. If you are lazy, you'll suffer for it. If you disobey me, you'll regret it. If you please me, you will be rewarded. Your leg chains will be unlocked, and each week you will be given two large gourds of *n'hoy.*"

As M'Bwana well knew, *n'hoy* was a drink made of fermented raw sugar, and both slaves and poverty-stricken freemen throughout the islands drank the potent concoction to forget their troubles. So far so good. He would accumulate quantities of *n'hoy,* and subsequently would use it as barter for his own purposes.

At dawn the next morning M'Bwana was roused and sent off into the fields. Hampered by his leg chains, he hobbled to his post, and there was handed a machete, a thick sword with a double blade. He went to work with a vengeance, realizing he had to build up his strength for the escape ordeal that lay ahead.

He was spurred, too, by the singing of the overseer's whip. The man was merciless, and any slave who paused to rest without being granted permission, any slave who failed to work rapidly, received a slash across the back.

M'Bwana was too wise to engage in heroics for their own sake, without purpose. He could endure great pain and vast quantities of punishment without flinching, but saw no useful purpose in arousing the overseer's ire. On the contrary, he wanted to lull the man's suspicions so escape would be easier and simpler to accomplish at the appropriate time.

Therefore he labored harder than any of the others, never pausing until a brief respite was granted at noon. In spite of his great endurance, he was exhausted when sundown came and the machetes were collected before the slaves were marched back to their huts. Not once that day had the whip touched him.

Even though the overseer was hard-driving and ruthless, he was a man of his word. At the end of a week M'Bwana's leg irons were removed and he was given two gourds of *n'hoy.*

That night the other slaves became intoxicated and for a few hours put their troubles out of their minds. M'Bwana carefully dug a hole with his bare hands in the ground inside his hut and buried his liquor there. After covering his cache and tamping it down again, he sat cross-legged outside his hut and resumed his study of the stars.

He felt no sense of impatience, no restlessness. His love for Kai and Lance gave him great endurance, and the prospect of breaking Hawk's neck filled him with fierce joy.

The weeks passed, and it was two months later, as the slaves worked their way up a hill, that M'Bwana caught his first glimpse of the Caribbean Sea. Continuing to labor so he wouldn't feel the whip, he was nevertheless elated and made a careful study of the immediate area.

It was his good fortune that the plantation stood near the water, a fact he hadn't realized previously. There was a long stretch of sandy beach, and about two hundred yards offshore he saw a natural breakwater.

For the next two weeks, as the slaves worked within sight of the Caribbean, M'Bwana continued to observe the breakwater critically. He believed it to be a coral reef, and if he was right, he saw a slit of some kind in it, perhaps fifteen feet wide, at a spot where the beach curved. It was wide enough for a small boat to slip through, which was all he wanted to know at present.

During those two weeks he saw a number of ships passing back and forth anywhere from a half-mile to a mile at sea. All were merchantmen, so he knew that the island, whatever it might be, engaged in a lively commerce. Of far greater importance to him, however, were the fishing boats that put out to sea every morning and came back every evening. Many were sturdy craft, capable of sailing considerable distances. All seemed to be based somewhere to the left as he faced the beach, out of sight beyond a knoll. Never mind, he was making progress.

Ultimately M'Bwana was given an even greater reward. His good conduct won him the privilege of distributing the machetes to his fellow slaves every morning, then collecting them every night and returning them to the storage barn, where the overseer counted them. At the appropriate time he would steal a machete.

Even now there was something he could do to further his cause. Grain was stored in the barn, too, and the overseer laughed when he saw M'Bwana eyeing the corn. "Help yourself to a sack," he said.

M'Bwana took one before the man changed his mind. Wrapping it in several layers of burlap to protect it, he borrowed a shovel and then buried it in the ground under his hut, too.

At last he put his hoarded supply of *n'hoy* to good use. The old man who was allowed to stay alive because he cooked for the other slaves was very fond of the liquor, so it was no trick to trade him a considerable quantity for a cask of smoked beef.

The old man was somewhat upset, however. "I hope you don't have foolish ideas of trying to escape. If you aren't caught before you can leave the island, you'll drown at sea."

"I have no intention of drowning, I promise you," M'Bwana said, and the old man was reassured.

The cask joined the other supplies in the ground under the hut. Now all that remained to be done was to obtain empty casks for fresh water, take a machete, and—the most difficult task of all—steal a boat.

None of the other slaves had any inkling of what he had in mind, and M'Bwana took care to conceal his thoughts. The task was simplified by the attitude he had adopted from the beginning. He spoke to the poor wretches only when necessary, and even on the nights when they drank too much, he refrained from fraternizing with them. They made few attempts to become friendly with him, either, as they were in awe of his prodigious strength and regarded his aloofness as a sign of surliness.

He had seen the main house of the estate only from a distance. So he was surprised, when the slaves went to work in a field that adjoined the main driveway, to see that it was much smaller than he had imagined, only a fraction the size of Oakhurst Manor.

Oakhurst Manor meant Kai. And Lance. M'Bwana clenched his teeth and renewed his vow that nothing would prevent him from returning to them.

One morning, as M'Bwana was slashing cane with his machete, a small carriage appeared and moved up the driveway toward the house. Holding the reins was a smartly dressed man, apparently the proprietor of the plantation, who was busy lighting a *cigarro*.

Beside him sat a stunning young woman with café-au-lait skin, her blue-black hair cascading down her back, a tiny hat with a long feather protruding from it perched on the top of her head. Her gown was made of rich, embroidered silk, and the snug-fitting bodice made no concealment of her slim but rounded figure. She turned, glanced idly at M'Bwana, then stared at him in shocked disbelief.

Dolores!

The hissing of the overseer's whip forced M'Bwana to resume his cane cutting.

His mind seethed. There was no question in his mind that Dolores had recognized him. He had no idea whether she was the wife or the mistress of the plantation owner, but he felt reasonably certain—at least he hoped—that she would help him in some way.

Her presence on the island indicated the probability that he was being held in Barbados, although it was possible that she had moved elsewhere. If this was indeed Barbados, there were people in high places who could assist him. Lady Saunders lived here. So did high-ranking Royal Navy officers who had known him when he had held a brevet commission in the United States Navy. For the rest of that day he worked harder than ever.

Then came the letdown. There was no sign of Dolores, who appeared to be making no attempt to get in touch with him. He realized she faced possible difficulties, that it might be a delicate matter for her to explain to her husband or lover that she had an interest in a slave who was working as a field hand. He tried not to lose hope.

Gradually, as the days passed, that hope dwindled. M'Bwana decided that Dolores, like most people, was interested only in feathering her own nest. She seemed to have a short memory, and preferred not to help someone who had befriended her when she had been in need.

Very well, then. He would act on his own initiative. First he would have to make certain that this island was Barbados. Then he would have to acquire a shirt and trousers, at the least, as he would be sure to be apprehended if he tried to make his way to Bridgetown clad only in a loincloth. The problems were complex and couldn't be solved overnight.

The better part of a week passed. The excitement caused M'Bwana to lose his appetite, but he forced himself to eat, knowing he had to keep up his strength. One night, after the slaves were served their supper around an open-pit fire, M'Bwana retired to his hut, as usual. The others went off to their quarters, too, and soon the compound settled down for the night.

M'Bwana heard the light sound of cautiously approaching footsteps before they reached his hut.

Dolores crept in, badly frightened, and embraced him. "I was sure it was you," she whispered, "even though I couldn't believe it. I came out this weekend a day ahead of my friend, and I bribed the old man so he would show me where you slept."

M'Bwana wasted no words. "Is this island Barbados?"

"Of course."

"Slaves aren't told much," he said bitterly. "Please, Dolores, go to Lady Saunders. Tell her I was captured by buccaneers and sold into slavery."

"Lady Saunders is dead. She was killed in a fire that burned down her house. Many months ago."

He was shocked, but his self-preservation depended on his ability to keep his head. "Then go to the Royal Navy base and speak to the new commander there——"

"The base here has been closed. All operations have been moved to Jamaica because the British are no longer at war."

"The governor-general——"

"A new one has just been sent here from London."

A wave of despair swept over M'Bwana, but he tried to steady himself.

"I would buy you from my friend if I could," Dolores said. "But he wouldn't understand, and I am sure he would order me to leave him."

Escape was the only resort left. "Is there some way you could get me a boat, Dolores?"

The girl thought, then nodded. "I think so. I will tell my friend I want it for my own pleasure. I will tell him I wish to go fishing and sailing. In some ways he is very kind, and I believe he will indulge me."

A feeling of sudden relief eased M'Bwana's depression. Now, perhaps, he would have a fighting chance. "Do you know the beach at the end of this plantation?"

"Of course," she said. "I swim there every Saturday and Sunday."

"Good. Anchor the boat there, inside the reef, where it will be safe. If you can, fill several casks with water, and store them in the boat. Could you get me any weapons?"

Dolores looked puzzled.

M'Bwana changed his mind. The mere fact that a girl might be trying to obtain pistols and ammunition could create comment and cause complications. "Never mind," he said. "Just get me the boat and the water, and leave the rest to me."

She smiled up at him.

"How soon can you make the arrangements?"

Again Dolores was lost in thought. "It will take me a few days. This is Friday. You may rely on it that I will have the boat waiting for you by next Friday night."

He caught hold of her arms, his eyes blazing. "I'll never forget you for this," he said. "I just wish there were some way I could thank you."

"Perhaps there will be a way," she replied. Before he could question her, she kissed him, then departed as silently as she had come to him.

The next week passed so slowly that M'Bwana was in agony. Constantly refining and changing his plans, he finally decided not to steal a machete from the plantation storehouse. The overseer kept a close count, and if he discovered that one was missing, he well might order all of the slaves placed in leg irons until he recovered it.

M'Bwana didn't like the idea of being totally defenseless, but common sense told him not to take the risk. So he made up his mind to carry only his hidden sack of grain and the cask of smoked meat. He would be short of supplies, but that didn't matter. Freedom was worth a few hunger pangs.

At last the night of his planned departure came, and he prayed that Dolores had done her part and had the boat waiting for him. He ate heartily at supper, knowing the meal would be the last filling one he would eat for many days. Then he waited until the slave compound grew quiet before he dug up his meat and grain.

Slinging the sack over his shoulder and carrying the cask in his other hand, he sneaked out into the open. There was no sign of life anywhere other than the chirping of a cricket in the underbrush.

A lizard scurried down from a tree and crossed M'Bwana's path, causing him to smile. According to an old Bantu superstition, the lizard would bring him good luck.

He started to run, making almost no sound as he balanced his weight on the balls of his bare feet. As he neared the far end of the compound, he sensed rather than saw the presence of someone else in the open, so he flattened himself against the outside of the last hut in the row, holding his breath.

The old man loomed in front of him. "You are stupid, my son," he said. "If you are caught, you will be beaten to death. If you swim out to sea, the sharks will devour you. Stay here and live. There are worse fates, and even a sour life is sweet."

"I thank you for your kindnesses, Grandfather," M'Bwana said. "May the gods of the African jungle watch over you for the rest of your days." He sprinted toward the high brush.

Growing cane provided him with cover, and he ran for a half-mile, slowing his pace only when he reached the cover of a coconut grove. In spite of his high hopes, he began to suffer doubts, and not until he reached the dunes overlooking the beach and saw a small boat riding at anchor inside the reef did he breathe more easily.

The craft was frail, no more than ten feet long and perhaps half as wide. Amidships was a small mast, with a furled sail in place. The boat was barely adequate, but he was in no position to ask for better.

He made his way down the dune, then halted abruptly. Someone was lurking below, and he was afraid he had walked into a trap. Well, if that was the case, he would fight here and now until he drew his last breath. It was better to die in a battle than tied to a stake while allowing his enemies to flay him until he expired.

Dolores stepped out of the shadows.

M'Bwana could only gape at her. She was dressed in a gown with swirls of braid on it, and looked as though she had just left a dinner party.

"I'm coming with you," she said.

He had no time to explain to her that the request was impossible to grant. He carried inadequate supplies for one person, much less for two, and the boat was too small for him to carry a passenger. "It can't be," he said.

Dolores was prepared for his resistance. "If you don't allow me to come," she said, carefully staying beyond his reach, "I'll scream and scream. The overseer and his guards will hear me, and you'll never get away safely."

In his exasperation M'Bwana wanted to choke some sense into her.

Giving him no chance to protest again, Dolores walked down to the water's edge, removed her high-heeled shoes, lifted her skirts, and began to wade out to the boat.

Every moment was precious, and M'Bwana knew that if he wasted more time arguing with her he might be discovered. She was giving him no alternative, so it appeared that it was his fate to take her with him.

He stalked out to the boat, passing her in the water, and after depositing his meat and grain, he hoisted her into the craft, assisting her to a seat in the prow. Then, still standing in the thigh-deep water, he hauled in the small anchor, shoved the boat toward the reef, and began to swim, pushing it ahead of him. He had committed every inch of the topography to memory and found the slit in the coral reef without difficulty. He pushed the craft through it, climbed in, and unfurled the sail. With the lines in one hand and the tiller in the other, he negotiated his way into the open Caribbean.

Dolores sat quietly, her expression serene, and looked like a young lady attending a garden party as she trailed one hand in the water.

Even though she had kept her word to him, her presence on this hazardous voyage was an insupportable burden, and he could not speak civilly to her. "Unless you want to feed the sharks," he said gruffly, "take your hand out of the water."

She hastily folded her hands in her lap, her back rigid, her smile vanishing.

M'Bwana studied the stars, then headed westward into the Caribbean. The boat was too small for him to venture into the open Atlantic Ocean, even though the route to the United States would be shorter. He would have to sail as far as he could through more placid seas, and when possible, go ashore on uninhabited islands.

No more than a quarter of an hour after leaving Barbados, a small sloop appeared around a bend in the island and seemed to be heading straight toward the tiny craft.

M'Bwana knew he could not avoid the vessel, which could achieve a speed far greater than his, so he remained on course.

A half-dozen men stood at the rail, peering across the water at the little boat.

M'Bwana sucked in his breath. The sloop could overtake him with ease, and he had no weapons with which he could defend himself. This could be the end, for Dolores as well as for him.

The girl's instinct saved them. She smiled at the men on the deck, then waved to them as though she had no care in all the world. She was a girl in a party frock, enjoying an evening's sail with a friend.

The men returned her wave, several smiled, and the tension was broken. The sloop neither slowed its speed nor tacked in the direction of the smaller boat.

M'Bwana sailed on. "I'm in your debt again," he said, praising her with reluctance.

Dolores' expression was demure.

"Now," he added, "I'll repay you by killing you."

She was too startled to reply.

"There's almost no chance we can survive this voyage," he told her. "The risk would have been enormous if I'd been alone. The odds against two of us are almost too great to bear."

"Wherever we go, we'll go together," she said, "and while I'm with you, I know I'll be safe."

Her logic was faulty, but he saw no reason to quarrel with her. "Sleep while you're able," he said. "It will be far more difficult after the sun comes up."

Dolores obediently curled up in the prow and dropped off to sleep.

He tried to see the bright side, and told himself that at least she obeyed instructions.

All through the night and the following day M'Bwana remained at the tiller, frequently manipulating the sail in order to coax the boat to achieve its maximum speed. He rationed food and water with care, but did not mention that the supplies would not last for more than four or five days.

Dolores remained cheerful and offered no complaints. She relieved herself over the side of the boat without embarrassment, and when her voluminous skirt proved to be cumbersome in such close quarters, she removed it and sat happily in her petticoat.

When M'Bwana seemed preoccupied, she kept silent for hours at a time. But when he appeared more relaxed, she encouraged him to talk, and listened to every word as he told her about his early life in Africa, his more recent experiences in South Carolina. She made no comment when he extolled the virtues of Kai, but her reserve indicated her conviction that she intended to become the principal woman in his future.

After sundown M'Bwana taught her the rudiments of navigation, instructing her how to use two stars as guides. Then, after letting her practice at the tiller, he finally rested. He slept for an hour or two at a time, awakening long enough at intervals to correct their course.

By dawn Dolores was exhausted, and he took charge again.

A pattern was established, and for five days and nights they followed it. Occasionally they saw an island in the distance, but M'Bwana took care to avoid it. They were still too close to Barbados, and by now word could have spread to other islands to the effect that a slave had escaped, taking with him the mistress of a planter.

On the fifth day they used the last of their food, and although small quantities of water remained, they had no more to eat. Of necessity they fasted for the next seventy-two hours.

It was obvious that Dolores suffered severe discomfort, but still she made no complaint.

"If you can," M'Bwana told her, breaking a long silence, "remove the braid from your skirt."

She obeyed, asking no questions, and the task required hours to perform.

He tested the braid, hoping it would be strong enough to suit his purposes. "Now," he said, "please give me a pin from your hair."

She handed it to him, and he bent it into the shape of a crude hook.

"Also your medallion."

Dolores' hand flew to her throat. The disk she wore there was fashioned of solid gold and was her most prized possession.

"If I can," M'Bwana said, "I'll retrieve it for you. But I must have it. I need it as a lure."

She removed it, slipped it from its chain, and handed it to him.

A few moments later he threw his primitive fishing line overboard, and it trailed behind the boat.

For more than an hour nothing happened. Then a fish struck, but a few moments later it slipped away.

Another hour passed under the blazing sun, then another. Suddenly the line grew taut.

The calm of M'Bwana's voice could not conceal his excitement. "Take the tiller," he said. "Hold the boat on course, and make certain the wind keeps the sail filled. No matter what happens, don't let us slacken speed."

The girl scrambled to the stern and took his place.

By now he had taken the end of the braid in both hands and held on as best he could. The fish at the other end was trying to break free, and was putting up a ferocious fight.

"Full speed!" M'Bwana commanded.

Dolores had to utilize all of her newly acquired skill in seamanship to obey.

Weakened after eight days in the boat, M'Bwana could feel the braid cutting into the flesh of his hands. Suddenly there was a flash of silver off the starboard stern, and he guessed the fish weighed between sixty and eighty pounds. He hoped he had the strength and stamina to survive the struggle.

The fight continued through the day. M'Bwana's arms became so weary he was certain they would be pulled from their sockets. Again and again he thought the fish was getting away, but he tightened his grip on his makeshift line, desperation giving him added vitality.

They were off course now, but he had no opportunity to give Dolores instructions.

Finally, shortly after sundown, M'Bwana felt the fish weaken for the first time. Laboriously but quickly he pulled in his line, hand over hand.

All at once the squirming, leaping fish appeared.

M'Bwana grasped it with both hands, barely able to hold the wriggling creature, and killed it by smashing its head against the hull.

Dolores had closed her eyes and looked ill.

"We'll eat now," M'Bwana said, and began to tear flesh from the fish with his hands.

"I . . . I can't," Dolores said.

He began to eat, then repeated his offer to her.

Her hunger overcame her fastidiousness. She took a chunk of the raw meat, closed her eyes again, and ate slowly, almost gagging every time she swallowed. Then her nausea passed, and she began to eat more rapidly.

The meal was filling, and they had consumed only a portion of the fish.

M'Bwana took the tiller again and tried to put them back on the course he was trying to follow. By now, however, dark clouds were filling the sky, obscuring the stars.

"Quickly," he said, "take off your clothes, all of them, and spread them out."

For the first time since the beginning of their adventure, Dolores was too startled to obey.

"Stop wasting time," he told her impatiently. "Tropical squalls come up in a hurry, and we need the water!"

Now she understood. Removing her clothes, she spread them on every square inch of space available on the crowded boat.

She was none too soon. The rain came down in torrents, soaking them. Visibility was reduced to a few feet, so M'Bwana made no attempt to remain at the tiller, and instead squeezed Dolores' garments and the sail, emptying the precious water into their casks and the container that had held the smoked beef.

The rain ended as abruptly as it had started, and for the first time in days they had enough to drink. The rain had cleansed them, too, lifting their spirits, and they laughed aloud together.

Less than a half-hour later M'Bwana made out a smudge in the distance and headed toward it.

When they drew closer, he saw an island, scarcely larger than an atoll, with a clump of coconut palms and a tangle of bushes standing behind the beach area.

"There's more food ahead," M'Bwana said. "We're going ashore."

He threaded his way past rocks and coral reefs, his ability to see in the dark little short of astonishing. When they reached the shallows, he lowered himself overboard, and a moment later Dolores followed his example. Both of them naked, they pushed the craft ashore, assisted by a pounding surf, then dragged it high on the beach.

Dolores' clothes were still too wet to wear, and M'Bwana's skimpy loincloth was even more useless.

A cool, stiff breeze was blowing out of the west in the aftermath of the squall, and M'Bwana rubbed his arms. "Wait for me here while I investigate the island," he said.

Dolores nodded, too cold to reply. The rain had soaked her, the surf had given her another bath, and the winds felt icy.

A quarter of an hour later M'Bwana returned in triumph. "The gulls have a nesting place on the other side of the island," he said, "and I saw eggs by the hundreds. Turtles' eggs farther down the beach, too, if I'm right. There are ripe coconuts at the top of the hill, and the berries on the bushes look edible, too. I thought I heard the sounds of a spring in a thicket, although I couldn't be certain, but I'll find out for sure in the morning. We may stay here for several days, building up our strength and gathering fresh supplies before we go on."

"By that time I'll have frozen to death," Dolores said, and her teeth were chattering.

M'Bwana realized he was thoroughly chilled, too.

He looked at the girl, and she returned his gaze. He had told her with great emphasis that he loved Kai and wanted no other woman, but nature offered him and Dolores only one way to grow warmer. Unless they took it, they could fall ill, and with no medicines available, a sickness could prove fatal.

With survival at stake, M'Bwana did not hesitate. He took Dolores in his arms, and they stretched out together on the scrub grass, their bodies providing mutual warmth.

In spite of the mental barriers M'Bwana had erected, he found it impossible to resist the appeal of this willowy, attractive girl. Many months had passed since he and Kai had last slept together, and in that time he had suffered frustrations, humiliations, and physical torment. Now he was being offered balm.

Dolores enjoyed a moment of private ecstasy. She had known from the outset that if she demonstrated enough patience this man whom she had wanted for so long would belong to her alone. Now her fondest wish was coming true.

They made love with a reckless abandon inspired by the circumstances in which they found themselves. They had faced danger together and had lived, but their future was dubious, and nothing mattered beyond this moment.

M'Bwana was as virile and passionate as Dolores had imagined, and she responded in kind.

But something was missing. If she knew nothing else on earth, Dolores understood men and was familiar with every nuance of lovemaking. When M'Bwana took her, she was reminded of sailors she had known long ago in Santo Domingo, men whose arousal was mechanical and who cared nothing about the woman.

No, she wasn't being fair. M'Bwana wasn't that remote. He was considerate and gentle, taking care to ensure that her enjoyment was as great as his own.

All the same, the spark she felt, the thrill of intimacy that almost consumed her, was missing in him.

What he had told her was true, then. The wife whom he never tired of praising was his one love, and he could feel nothing in depth for another.

Dolores told herself she had to be satisfied with whatever he offered her.

Ultimately they spread her clothes and his ragged loincloth on the hard-packed sand high on the beach to dry when the sun came up in the morning. Then M'Bwana took the girl to the far side of the island, and they ate a "supper" of raw gulls' eggs. Finally they went to the top of the hill, where the little coconut grove was located. Embracing again for warmth, and weary after their long ordeal, they fell asleep locked in each other's arms.

Alien sounds awakened M'Bwana, and when he opened his eyes he saw that the sun was already rising. He must have been tired to sleep so late.

Instantly alert as the sounds continued, he crawled to the edge of the foliage and looked down. Anchored in a tiny cove where the water was calm, he saw a sailboat, about twenty-five feet long, that had anchored there.

Turning closer, he saw a sight that wrenched his stomach. Two men were studying his frail boat, looking at Dolores' clothes spread out on the ground, and grinning slyly, were nudging each other.

The elder of the pair appeared to be about thirty, and was a husky man with a barrellike chest. He carried a short sword and wore a pistol in his belt. The other, about a decade younger, was short and slender, with a long scar disfiguring one side of his face. He carried a pistol and a knife.

M'Bwana knew that he and Dolores were in desperate straits. These men, heavily armed, looked like ruffians, and it wasn't difficult to guess what they would do when they discovered a naked, attractive girl on the little island, her only protector an unclad, unarmed man.

At any moment the pair would begin a search for the owner of the clothing, so there was no time to lose.

M'Bwana awakened Dolores, holding a hand over her mouth so she wouldn't speak aloud and gesturing for silence with the other.

The girl awakened quickly, fear in her eyes.

M'Bwana put his lips close to her ear and explained their perilous situation.

Her fright was so great she seemed on the verge of losing consciousness.

He shook her, then whispered again. "I want you to do exactly as I tell you. Walk slowly down the hill, very slowly. At the bottom, where the beach begins, there is a large rock. Stand beside it. No matter what happens, stand only in that one place. And pay no attention to me. No matter what I'm doing, no matter where you see me, pretend I'm invisible. I'm going to use you as a decoy so they won't notice me."

"When they see me undressed like this," she replied, "they'll rape and kill me."

"No," he replied firmly, "they will not. Trust me."

"I do," she said, and stood, her fear dissipating somewhat.

Using all of her self-control, Dolores began to walk slowly down the little hill. Following M'Bwana's instructions to the letter, she ignored her companion.

One of the coconut trees grew in an arc, so it extended beyond the hill, its fronds and fruit hanging directly over the beach at the hill's base. M'Bwana began to climb that tree.

The younger of the pair on the beach was the first to see Dolores, and said something to his friend in a guttural language that neither the girl nor M'Bwana understood.

Both stared at her as she made her way down the hill.

She returned their gaze, as conscious of her nudity as they were, and for good measure she smiled at them.

They began to move toward her, their good fortune so great they could scarcely believe it.

Dolores saw the rock that M'Bwana had indicated and halted beside it, her heart pounding so hard she thought it would break through her rib cage.

The attention of the two men was riveted on the naked girl, so they remained unaware of M'Bwana's proximity.

He climbed the coconut tree with ease, making no sound, and reached the relative shelter of the fronds near the top.

The two men halted, conversing in low tones.

Dolores stood very still, continuing to play her part, and her smile felt as though it was pasted on her face.

Again the pair came closer, and again they halted. Apparently they had reached an understanding of some sort, because the younger now moved alone toward the waiting girl, a lascivious grin covering his face.

M'Bwana poised himself and waited, carefully gauging the distance to the ground below.

He continued to wait until the young man came within arm's reach of Dolores. Then he jumped, hurtling twenty-five feet or more to the ground.

His aim was perfect, as it had to be, and he landed with full force on his victim, instantly bearing him to the ground. The impact was so great that the young man's neck was broken and he died on the spot.

For an instant M'Bwana was stunned, but as he felt the body beneath him grow limp he just had time to snatch the knife from the dead man's belt.

The older man had drawn both his sword and his pistol, but not realizing his friend was dead, he hesitated before using firearms at such close quarters.

Instead he thrust his sword at the wild creature who had appeared out of nowhere.

M'Bwana barely managed to roll out of the path of the blade. Never losing his balance, he regained his feet.

At that instant the terrified Dolores screamed at the top of her voice.

For a second the sound distracted the burly stranger.

M'Bwana knew he had to act at once, before the man

could fire at him. He had been testing the knife ever since he had taken it, and he threw it now with all his might, his aim as accurate as it was when he wielded one of his short, deadly spears.

The knife lodged in the man's throat, and he crumpled to the ground, life ebbing from him.

Dolores began to tremble violently.

M'Bwana put an arm around her shoulders to steady her. "They're dead," he said. "You have nothing more to fear."

For the next few hours he was very busy. He removed the clothes from the corpses, and was pleased to discover that the smaller man's shirt, breeches, and even his boots fitted Dolores reasonably well. She had to overcome her repugnance, however, before she could wear them.

Although M'Bwana was husky, the larger man's clothes were somewhat too big for him, but he didn't care. After wearing only a loincloth for months, he was glad to be fully dressed again.

Using a small rowboat to go out to the sailing vessel, he and Dolores examined the contents with care, and were elated when they found casks of salt fish and smoked beef, sacks of parched corn, and several large containers of water. There was a net for fishing, as well as several strong lines and hooks. And M'Bwana now had two pistols, a sword, and a knife. The situation was radically changed for the better.

Dolores was elated when she found a sand pit on the aft deck with a frying pan and a small kettle beside it. Now, when they resumed their voyage, they could eat cooked food.

They returned to shore and gathered as many gulls' eggs as they could carry. M'Bwana climbed the trees again, and after he cut down every ripe and near-ripe coconut he could find, they piled these in the rowboat, too.

They made several trips to the fishing vessel, loading the deck with firewood, gathering still more eggs from the far side of the island, and finally taking their own clothes and the few belongings from the frail boat that had brought them this far. M'Bwana took care to remove its sail and lines, too.

The water that bubbled up in the spring at the top of the hill had a slightly brackish taste, but it was better than no water, so they filled every empty container with it, even using coconut husks that had fallen open for the purpose.

In all of their activity, Dolores took care to avoid the bodies of the two men. "Shouldn't we . . . bury them before we leave?"

"It would take too long to dig a grave for them," M'Bwana said. "If they knew of this island, others must visit here, too, and we want to leave as quickly as we can." He did not call her attention to the flock of vultures circling overhead, patiently awaiting their departure. It wouldn't be long before the two men were reduced to skeletons.

The sun stood directly overhead before they were ready. Leaving their own frail boat high on the beach, M'Bwana rowed them out to the fishing vessel with the last of the water and firewood. They took it on board, hauled the tiny rowboat onto the deck, and M'Bwana weighed anchor.

Dolores continued her search as they put out to sea, and in the small cabin located forward she found two mattresses and several blankets. "This is a real luxury ship," she said.

M'Bwana smiled wryly. "You may think otherwise if we run into any storms. I can think of ships I'd far rather sail from here to the United States, but I'll grant you it's better by far than what we had."

A tinderbox and flint were in the cabin, so Dolores made a fire in the sandbox and spent several hours hard-boiling the gulls' eggs in seawater, then storing them carefully.

After they were under way in a brisk wind, M'Bwana threw two fishing lines overboard, and during the course of the afternoon caught a fish on each of them.

When Dolores finished her other work, she searched the small, cramped hold, where she found ammunition and powder for the pistols, as well as a cask of ale and a score of bottles filled with wine.

That night they dined on grilled fish, hard-boiled gulls' eggs and, somewhat recklessly, shared a coconut and its milk. "We'll save the wine and ale for a time when we may want or need it," M'Bwana said.

At midnight he turned the boat over to the increasingly proficient girl and slept for a few hours, following his previous practice of awakening from time to time to reset their course.

The next day M'Bwana sailed north, still avoiding major populated islands. If they came to another atoll where they could obtain water at some future time, he wouldn't mind going ashore again, but he figured that, with luck, he could reach the United States now with the supplies they had on board, augmented by the fish they could catch.

That afternoon they were becalmed for several hours, just as they were finishing a midday meal of parched corn and smoked beef. Since they had nothing better to occupy them, Dolores insisted that they drink a bottle of wine. Thereafter it seemed only natural for them to make love again.

M'Bwana was as virile, passionate, and considerate as he had been on the little island, but Dolores again had the feeling that something was missing. No matter. She would accept all the love he would give her, for as long as he elected to give it to her.

They lost count of the days as they sailed toward the northeast, and M'Bwana was tireless, his seamanship superb. When the winds were high, the seas rough, and the skies threatening, he remained at the helm for as long as forty-eight hours at a time, nursing his sails and guiding the vessel through mountainous seas. When rain fell, which it did on five separate occasions, they followed their previous practice of spreading clothes and sails to catch the water, although now they took the precaution of keeping one set of clothing dry.

The change that took place in Dolores on the long voyage was so gradual that M'Bwana was scarcely aware of it. She had no cosmetics, and didn't miss them, and she tied her long hair at the nape of her neck with a bit of line. Her dress was too cumbersome and awkward for life on board the little boat, so she wore only man's attire, and was in no way self-conscious. She forgot to act flirtatiously, she never pouted or complained, and she did her share of the work cheerfully.

M'Bwana began to think about her future. Increasingly confident that they would reach their destination, he was determined that she would not resume the life of a prostitute or be forced to depend on a protector for her living. He had no idea how to guide her or what to suggest to her, but Jeremy would know, and so would Kai.

Just thinking now about Kai, and about Lance, thrilled him and kept him awake when he should be sleeping. His sexual experiences with Dolores were as natural as eating when they were hungry and drinking when they were thirsty, so he did not dwell on them and felt no sense of guilt. At heart, he guessed, he was still an African, and had not completely acquired the American belief in monogamy.

Certainly he had never asked Kai about her experiences in New Orleans when she had been taken there as a captive, and he didn't want to know them. By that same token, he was sure she would accept his relationship with Dolores.

Gradually the weather turned cooler as M'Bwana sailed due north, and late that afternoon he pointed to a smudge on the horizon. "There's the coast of Florida," he said. "We're no longer in danger of being captured by freebooters, and there's little chance that I'll be sent back to the fields. I intend to keep within sight of land from now on, and if the weather holds, we should be home in a week."

That evening, after they had eaten, Dolores came and sat close beside him at the tiller. "I wonder what I will do when I reach America," she said. "It has been much on my mind."

"Mine, too. My wife will help you, and so will my friend, the man who owns the plantation where we live. Commodore Beaufort."

Dolores relaxed. "That is good," she said, "because one thing I have decided. Never again, no matter what becomes of me, will I sell my body to any man."

Six days later, early in the evening, they reached Charleston, and M'Bwana tied up at the Beaufort wharf. The long and arduous voyage had come to an end.

A short time later he and Dolores reached the Beaufort house, where Jeremy, Kai, and Scott were just sitting down to a quiet supper.

Kai stood as her husband came into the room, and the presence of his pretty companion, the girl in man's clothing, was irrelevant.

M'Bwana came straight to her and took her in his arms.

Dolores, whom Jeremy scarcely recognized as the prostitute from Santo Domingo who had guided his expedition to the buccaneers' hideout, averted her face so no one could see the tears that came to her eyes. For M'Bwana's sake she rejoiced. He had suffered a long and terrible ordeal, and he deserved the happiness he had more than earned. Perhaps it didn't matter that she felt bereft.

Then Jeremy smiled at her. "Welcome," he said.

Dolores recognized him immediately, although she had never known his name. He was a kind man, she knew, a tower of strength, and although a sense of loneliness continued to envelop her, she realized that under his sheltering wing she would be safe. For the moment she could ask for nothing more than that.

# Chapter 14

The return of M'Bwana, seemingly from the dead, was celebrated by everyone at Oakhurst Manor, but the Bantu wanted no party held in his honor. It was enough, he said, that he was reunited with Kai and Lance and could resume his close friendship with Jeremy. He had much on his mind, but was not yet ready to talk about these matters. For the present he was content to enjoy a respite from care.

Jeremy grieved when M'Bwana told him Dickie Saunders had died, and was shocked to the marrow when he learned that Lisa had been killed in a fire that had destroyed her home. He found it almost impossible to accept the hard fact that this loveliest and most desirable of women was no more. Perhaps, since the loss of Sarah, he had been sustained by the secret hope that Lisa someday might be his. Now she was gone, too, and never, anywhere, would there be another like her. His world was bleak, his personal future grim.

He did not suffer alone. Scott Emerson's hope that someday Kai would consent to marry him was destroyed. For her sake he was happy that M'Bwana had returned, and he participated in the family celebrations without reservation. Relieved that he had never spoken to Kai of his feelings, he realized that the great love of his life had been thwarted. Like Jeremy, he lost himself in his work.

The most pressing problem at Oakhurst Manor was what to do about Dolores. An outsider in a strange land, she seemed like a lost soul, and was both timid and withdrawn. She trusted Jeremy, but could not relax totally in his presence, and only in M'Bwana's company did she come truly alive.

The color problem was no help. She was a free woman, of course, but as a mulatto it was difficult for her to meet guests as a social equal. M'Bwana had been accepted, but his situation was unique, and Dolores stood outside the pale.

Kai was determined to find the right place for the girl from Santo Domingo. M'Bwana owed his life and freedom to Dolores, and Kai accepted full responsibility for her. It wasn't difficult to guess that her husband had slept with the girl, but Kai didn't care, M'Bwana had returned to her and still loved her. What was more, Dolores had offered him comfort during a trying, grueling period, just as he had sustained her, so there was no room in Kai's heart for jealousy.

All she knew for certain at the moment was that under no circumstances could she send the girl away. Dolores, who insisted on dressing primly and wore no cosmetics, would land in trouble in a city, even if given funds to support her, but there seemed to be no way she could fit into the patterns of Oakhurst Manor.

It was Lester Howard who unexpectedly provided a possible solution.

Kai followed the late Sarah's practice of conferring with Cleo each morning after breakfast, then making a tour of the slave quarters with the overseer. One morning, after they had made their rounds, Lester pushed his broad-brimmed hat onto the back of his head. "You got an extra minute?"

"Of course," Kai said.

"I've been having a few quiet talks with Dolores the last couple of days," he said.

"I'm worried about her," Kai confessed.

"Well, I have the start of an idea, if you and Jeremy approve," Lester said. "The only time that girl is natural is when she's with the children. Lance likes her, and so does

Carrie. Little Cleo and Paul go running to her the minute they see her. Jerry stays apart for a while, the way he always does, but even he joins in eventually."

Kai clapped her hands together. "I see it! You're suggesting that she become the children's governess!"

"Exactly, if you don't think the idea is too farfetched. I know her background isn't all that reputable—she told me about it herself. But she's reformed and wants to lead a decent life."

"We could give her a house of her own and pay her wages that would make her self-sufficient. This could be perfect, Lester. I'll have a word with Jeremy right now, and then I'll talk to Dolores. Thank you."

She found Jeremy in the library, undergoing the regular drudgery of keeping the books. He heard the proposal, and approved heartily. "That would solve a lot of problems," he said. "Be sure you pay her enough to make the plan appealing to her."

Soon thereafter Kai closeted herself with Dolores in a sitting room.

Always ill-at-ease, particularly in the presence of M'Bwana's wife, the girl tugged nervously at a lace-edged handkerchief, the first she had ever owned.

"I'm afraid you aren't happy with us," Kai said, "but your happiness means a great deal to all of us, and we want to help you."

"I do nothing all day," Dolores replied. "I feel useless."

Kai outlined the scheme, stressing that the girl would live in her own house and would be paid a substantial sum each month.

Dolores was radiant. "The money does not matter!" Suddenly her face fell. "You would trust me to take charge of the children?"

"I trust you with my husband," Kai said quietly. "If it weren't for your help, he'd be dead."

In spite of her timidity, Dolores was not lacking in courage. "There are things you do not know about M'Bwana and me."

"I prefer not to know them," Kai said. "It's enough that he's come home to me."

"But you are not familiar with my past. It may be that you will think I am not suited for the position."

"I do know your past," Kai said, "and it isn't too different from my own. In this country everyone has the right to make a fresh start, to lead a new life. You have that privilege, just as I had it."

"Then I will do it!" Dolores said, tears of joy filling her eyes. "My prayers are answered!"

The arrangements were made the same day, and the delighted children demanded the right to give a party of their own in honor of their new governess.

Only Jerry held back. "Nobody asked me if I wanted that woman as my governess," he said.

Jeremy, who was about to go into a meeting with M'Bwana and Captain Ned Slocum, made short work of his son's protests. "If you want to sulk," he said, "do it alone, in your own room. Don't spoil the party for everyone else."

The boy decided to attend the party after all.

Jeremy closed the door of the library behind him and turned to Captain Slocum, who had just returned the previous day from a voyage on the *Elizabeth*. "You're looking hale, Ned," he said to the elderly sailor. "I gather you had no problems?"

"None this voyage," Slocum said, "and I don't aim to have any in the future. I'm going to sea just once more before I retire, and I'm damned if I want to be sent to the bottom. I want guns—plenty of them—before I go off to the West Indian islands again."

M'Bwana smiled bitterly.

"The buccaneers are becoming that active again?"

"Yes, and they're smarter than they were a few years ago. They've reorganized, Commodore. They use a smaller fleet now, and they hit fast and hard. They empty a merchantman's hold, then send her to the bottom with all her crew on board. This new crowd is really the scum of the earth."

"I know them," M'Bwana said, "and I have taken a vow to destroy them. I don't care what becomes of me, but I want to end the threat of piracy in the Caribbean for all time."

"It's either that," Captain Slocum declared, "or Commodore Beaufort will lose every last ship in his fleet, and so will a lot of other owners. The British have other fish to fry, the French have lost their naval strength, and the Spaniards have been too weak for decades. The other European powers are too small and have too little shipping in West Indian waters to care."

Jeremy had been listening with care, and reached a decision. "That leaves it up to the United States to clean out the bastards. Ned, you'll have all the guns you want for your farewell voyage. Meantime, I'm sending off a letter to the new president, and I reckon you and I will go up to Washington City to see him, M'Bwana."

The Bantu's face was grim. "Good," he said. "I have rested long enough, and my time of vengeance is at hand."

Every member of the buccaneer band wanted Hawk's wench, who was so much more attractive than the trollops they sometimes brought to their mountain hideout from Santo Domingo City. They knew, too, that she sometimes spent a night with one or another of the chieftain's lieutenants, and that knowledge whetted their appetites.

But they had to exercise great care in the wench's presence, and were more afraid of her temper than they were of Hawk's anger. She might be a harlot, but she permitted no ordinary seaman to make advances to her.

No freebooter would forget what had happened to the Dutch boatswain's mate who had approached her from behind one night as she had walked through the compound and had grabbed her from behind. Not hesitating for an instant, the wench had drawn her knife and slashed the Dutchman's hand so severely that he had lost three fingers. Unlike most women, she had appeared unmoved by the incident and had calmly gone about her own business.

Then there had been the incident with a recent recruit, a young and impressionable Dane. He had accosted her one day, and after telling her he loved her, he had tried to embrace her. Showing no pity for his youth, she had cut him across his face, leaving him scarred for life.

Fighting between members of the company was strictly forbidden, but Hawk had been amused by the wench's ability to protect herself, and on both occasions had roared with laughter. It was even said he had rewarded her with expensive gifts captured in recent raids.

So the freebooters stood back when she came down the path from the upper caves carrying a bucket she intended to fill at the spring. Her heavy makeup emphasized her features, yet somehow concealed her expression. The gaze of every man lingered on her half-seen breasts, her tiny, supple waist, the high slit in her skirt that revealed so much of her thigh, the provocative walk that whetted appetites.

Those who were acquainted with her greeted her from a distance, and the others pretended to be occupied with various tasks. No one could afford to forget the knife so prominently displayed in her belt.

Then, to the astonishment of those who saw the incident, Chief Boatswain Talbot of the Hawk's own flagship came up to her. He was old enough to have more sense, the men decided as they retreated even farther.

"I wonder if I could have a word with ye, ma'am," Talbot said.

Instantly alert, Lisa fingered the hilt of her knife and looked at him disdainfully.

"I mean ye no disrespect, ma'am."

"That's good," she said, and waited.

"I've heard it said ye come from Barbados, and I'm sure in my own mind I either knew ye or saw ye there. But I can't rightly place ye."

Her eyes were cold, her voice icy. "I don't remember living anywhere before I was brought here. Now, be good enough to stand aside." She began to edge past him.

But Talbot held his ground, even though he was watching the slender hand that grasped the knife hilt. "One more word, ma'am. Please."

Something in his attitude made Lisa curious. If he intended to make advances to her, he was being uncommonly clumsy, and she would do to him what she had done to the young Dane. When she used her knife, she discovered, a little of the rage bottled up within her was released for a short time.

Talbot lowered his voice so the other men couldn't hear him. "They brought me here, too," he said. "I had to join these pigs or die. I hate them more than I ever hated any people in my life, so I can guess how you must feel."

A gleam of sympathy appeared for an instant in Lisa's clear green eyes.

"It don't matter none to me who ye were in the world outside. I just want you to know you ain't alone. Me and my friends—shipmates who were forced to come here, too—stand ready to help anytime ye say the word. Offhand, I don't know what we could do, but we crave to cut out the hearts of these pigs."

"So do I," Lisa said, and to the astonishment of those who were watching from a distance, she actually smiled. "I don't believe anyone can do anything for me, but I'm grateful for your offer, and I'll remember it."

Talbot instinctively raised his hand in salute, then moved aside to let her pass.

Lisa walked on to the well, her hips swaying in the manner she had employed for so long that the motion had almost become second nature to her. More shaken than even she herself knew, she realized that the chief boatswain was the first person she had encountered since the beginning of her nightmare who had treated her with kindness, the first man who had thought of her as other than a wench whom he wanted to bed.

She had told him the truth, to be sure. He and his friends might be filled with all the goodwill in the world, but there was nothing they could do for her. She had no future, and would be kept here until she died of violence or Hawk tired of her and gave her to the company, in which case she would kill herself.

All the same, the chief boatswain had kindled a tiny spark of hope within her, and for the first time in months her feeling of despair was eased.

James Monroe had retired from public office at the end of his second term, and the atmosphere in the White House was changed. President John Quincy Adams—like his father before him, President John Adams—was an austere, reserved man who thought carefully before he spoke and, with New England parsimony, uttered as few words as possible. His few intimates swore it didn't occur to him that he gave the impression of being chilly.

Jeremy Beaufort's self-confidence was sufficiently great that he could relax in the company of almost anyone, but he addressed the president succinctly as he and M'Bwana sat in

John Quincy Adams' office. There was no need for him to talk about his previous expedition to the Caribbean, since Adams had been secretary of state under Monroe and consequently was familiar with the details of that adventure. Instead he dwelt exclusively on the new situation that had arisen, and described the travail to which M'Bwana had been subjected in just a few words.

The president nodded and fingered the gold chain on his waistcoat.

"On my own behalf and that of more than sixty other shipowners whose signatures I bring you, Mr. President, I petition you to send a new expedition to the West Indies so we can get rid of these buccaneers once and for all."

"You aren't the first who has come to me, Commodore. The navy has been after me for many weeks."

"I volunteer my services, Captain M'Bwana's, as well as my flagship and her veteran crew," Jeremy said.

"What do you want from me?" Adams, as always, was blunt.

Jeremy was prepared for the question. "Two frigates small enough to maneuver in West Indian waters. Two sloops of war and a bomb ketch. An arrangement with the British that will make it possible for us to use the facilities at the base they've closed in Barbados. We'll need an operations center."

"You and the navy must be working together in this," the president said with a faint smile. "Your requests are identical. And just today Secretary of State Clay told me he's certain the British will grant us the right to utilize their Bridgetown base. A remarkable coincidence."

Jeremy couldn't help grinning. He and M'Bwana had done their groundwork thoroughly during the week they had spent in Washington City prior to this meeting.

President Adams had a better understanding of human nature than his critics believed. "I anticipate no problem in granting your requests, Commodore," he said. "In fact, the orders calling you and Captain M'Bwana to active duty are already being processed. What else do you want?"

"A company of one hundred marines, Mr. President. I want to rid the Caribbean of pirates for all time."

"You shall have them," the mild-mannered John Quincy Adams said. "All I ask of you is that you remember an expanding America depends increasingly on her foreign trade. Make the West Indies safe for our merchantmen."

The squadron mobilized at Charleston, one frigate sailing there from Savannah, another coming from Boston, the sloops and the ketch arriving from other ports. Ned Slocum having retired, Jeremy gave the command of the *Elizabeth* to M'Bwana, and they stayed in Charleston for several weeks, preparing for the expedition and returning to Oakhurst Manor only on weekends.

Jeremy gave power of attorney to Scott Emerson, authorizing his friend to supervise the affairs of Oakhurst Manor during his absence. He also made out a new will, leaving one-third of his estate to Jerry, one-third to Lance, and the remainder to be divided equally among Carrie, little Cleo, and Paul.

Kai brought the children to Charleston to watch the squadron's departure, with Dolores in attendance. On the night prior to the sailing, the youngsters ate supper with the adults, and Jeremy addressed a few remarks to them, explaining the purpose of the mission.

"Papa Beaufort," Lance said, "I want to go with you and Papa."

"Me, too," the angelic Carrie chimed in.

Paul indicated that he wanted to go too, and then little Cleo added her voice to the clamor.

M'Bwana laughed aloud.

Jeremy tried to restrain himself as he turned to his elder son. "What about you, Jerry?"

"Somebody has to stay behind with Uncle Scott and take care of Oakhurst Manor," the boy said. "I'd rather do that."

Jeremy didn't know why he felt disappointed.

Early the next morning they drove down to the docks. Jeremy kissed Kai and the children, said good-bye to Dolores, and shook hands with Scott. "Look after everyone until I come back, old friend," he said, "and you'll know what to do if I don't return."

"You will," Scott told him. "You're indestructible."

The commodore's gig was waiting, and Jeremy was rowed out to the waiting ships for a final inspection.

M'Bwana waited for the better part of an hour before he

climbed into his gig. He and Kai, who was trying hard not to weep, had said their farewells in private, so he hugged each of the children. Then he kissed Dolores lightly, and she would have clung to him had she dared.

He embraced Kai again, fiercely but briefly, and then he said a last good-bye to Scott. "If anything happens to me," he said, "see that no harm comes to Kai."

"Never fear," Scott said, "she'll be safe."

The large crowd that had gathered at the wharves was disappointed because no bands played and there were no farewell ceremonies. "This is not a time for celebration," Commodore Beaufort had said. "We'll set off fireworks when we come home."

Jeremy boarded his flagship soon after the new captain of the *Elizabeth* arrived, and joined him on the quarterdeck.

"Be good enough to notify the squadron to set sail," he said, and retired to the far rail so he wouldn't interfere while M'Bwana gave the necessary orders. It was difficult to hold such high rank when he didn't command a ship of his own.

As they sailed out of the familiar harbor, Jeremy stood motionless, ignoring the bustle around him. Never had he felt so desolate, so isolated, and only the mission on which he was setting out gave him a sense of purpose. Oakhurst Manor was highly profitable, his merchant ships were earning still more money, and he had no more private worlds to conquer.

In a few more years Jerry would become a man and would no longer need him. Lance, whom he privately favored, was known to the world as M'Bwana's son. Carrie had Kai, her Uncle Scott, and Dolores to look after her. Cleo and Paul relished the affection of their doting grandmother, and in a few more years would return to Boston to continue their education. No man lived for his children or for those of other people.

What, then, was the purpose of his existence? Sarah, whom he had cherished, was gone. Lisa, for whom he had yearned and about whom he still dreamed, was gone. No other woman whom he knew or might meet would be endowed with the loyalty of Sarah, the electrifying magnetism of Lisa.

Jeremy realized he had to reconcile himself to the inevitable. He was still in his early thirties, with a long life ahead, but he would live that life alone. He could not settle for sec-

ond best; there would never be another Sarah or another
Lisa. But it was wrong to feel sorry for himself. He had
known the love of two extraordinary women, so he was more
fortunate by far than most.

Looking through his glass, Jeremy saw that the ships of his
squadron were falling into line in perfect order: the frigates
followed the *Elizabeth*, the sloops of war came next, and the
squat bomb ketch brought up the rear. Present operations
were mechanical, and his captains were competent to carry
them out without suggestions or directions from him.

He turned away abruptly and went off to his own quarters,
where he remained in isolation for the rest of the day and the
night. His orderly brought him his meals there, his door remained closed, and no one disturbed his privacy.

He did not appear on deck again until the following morning. Only M'Bwana, who saw the shadows beneath his eyes,
could guess the private torment he had just endured.

The voyage was uneventful, the weather remaining perfect,
and two and a half weeks later the squadron put into the harbor at Bridgetown, dropping anchor offshore. While the captains and their quartermasters went about the business of
obtaining fresh provisions and the crews were granted shore
leave, Jeremy paid a courtesy visit to the new governor-general, accepting a supper invitation for the following evening.

Then, renting a carriage and dismissing his aide-de-camp,
he drove out on the familiar road to Indian Bridge, the
memory of which had haunted him for so long. He had
braced himself, but the reality of what he saw nevertheless
was shocking.

The manor house in which he and Lisa had enjoyed their
bittersweet idyll was gone. The burned-out shell had been
demolished, and green grass grew now where the house had
stood. Dickie's cousin, who had inherited the property, had
recently sold the land to the owner of a neighboring estate,
and even the summer house had vanished. Only memories remained.

Jeremy hardened his heart, returned to the harbor, and established his headquarters in the old fort. There he remained
for the next ten days, leaving only to sleep on board the *Elizabeth* and to attend the obligatory social functions required
of his position. He spent virtually all of his waking hours in-

terviewing the masters of merchant vessels, questioning them closely.

After a week and a half there were still gaps in the information he required, but he assumed the buccaneers had spies in Bridgetown who were keeping tabs on him, so he didn't want to tarry too long. He gave orders for the squadron to make ready for sea duty, then summoned all of his officers to a council of war at the old fort.

"Gentlemen," he said, "our enemy performs according to two predictable patterns. Some of his ships roam the Caribbean singly and in pairs, pouncing on merchantmen, robbing them, and sinking them. These instances are relatively isolated."

He signaled to his aide, who unrolled a map and placed it on a wall.

"The real danger area," Jeremy said, using his sword as a pointer, "is the Mona Passage that separates Hispaniola and Puerto Rico. Those of you who accompanied Captain M'Bwana and me there some years ago will well remember those waters. Any merchantman that sails in the passage is in danger. The buccaneers appear out of nowhere and attack."

"Sir," one of the frigate captains asked, "how many ships do the freebooters use?"

"No one is certain," Jeremy said. "But I've sifted the evidence as best I'm able, and it's my guess they use five or six ships in their operations."

The officers exchanged satisfied glances: the two sides were evenly matched.

"Three masters who managed to escape from the pirates all tell me the same thing," Jeremy said. "They're convinced that the enemy makes his base on the north shore of Hispaniola, where there are only a few villages and where access to the mountains is easier than elsewhere. So I've conceived an operation in two stages. First, we'll meet the enemy in the Mona Passage and sink as many of his ships as we can. Second, if any escape, we'll follow them to their base on the north shore and dispose of the remaining ships."

Major Richard O'Brien, the commander of the marine contingent, jumped to his feet. "Suppose they run off to their hideout in the mountains, Commodore?"

"I sincerely hope they will," Jeremy said, "because we'll

follow them there, and then you'll have your work cut out for you, O'Brien."

All of the officers joined in the laughter.

"My basic tactics are very simple," Jeremy said. "I've bought a small brig, and we'll man it with our own people. That merchantman will be our decoy. While the squadron remains in hiding in a harbor on the Hispaniola coast, the brig will pretend to be in trouble in the Mona Passage. She'll loiter there until the buccaneers appear. Then we'll sail out and put in some target practice with live ammunition."

"How will we know where to follow them if they run, Commodore?" one of the frigate commanders asked.

"I was just coming to that," Jeremy said. "Captain Allen!"

The commander of a sloop of war stood.

"Your ship is the fastest in the squadron, so I have a special assignment for you. If the buccaneers cut and run, you'll follow, remaining at a safe distance so they can't resume the engagement. You won't fight them again, no matter how great the temptation. You'll learn the location of their harbor and then lead the squadron to it."

"You mean I can't fight in the battle, sir?" The young officer could not conceal his disappointment.

"Oh, you can mix in for a time, but you'll take no chance of becoming disabled. The Hispaniola coast is tricky, and if the enemy gives us the slip, we'll fail in our mission."

Allen understood, and was somewhat mollified.

"Gentlemen," Jeremy said solemnly, "this is no ordinary campaign. The rules that govern warfare at sea shall not apply. If an enemy ship raises a white flag, his surrender will be ignored. If an enemy ship is disabled, it will not be regarded as having left the action. All enemy ships shall be sunk. Any individual pirates who jump overboard will be shot, and our marines will shoot to kill. By the time this mission ends, every living freebooter will be dead. Without exception. If just one of them survives, I'll be obliged to report to President Adams that we have failed. I trust I make myself clear, gentlemen."

The orders were so harsh that the officers were stunned.

"I believe Captain M'Bwana can shed some light on the reason we have adopted this position," Jeremy said.

M'Bwana stood and in clipped tones related his own experience with the buccaneers. "If any of you show them mercy," he concluded, "rest assured that I won't. They're thieving murderers, and I won't rest until we kill every last one of them."

There was a long silence, and every officer present at last understood the gravity of the mission.

"You'll receive your written order of battle instructions later this evening, gentlemen," Jeremy said. "You're dismissed!"

The operation began smoothly, with the decoy brig, her armaments carefully concealed beneath tarpaulins on her decks, leaving Bridgetown two hours before the squadron set sail. If the buccaneers had spies keeping watch on the movements of merchant shipping, a possibility that Jeremy kept constantly in mind, they would see no connection between the brig and the activities of his own warships.

Acting under strict orders, the brig's captain dawdled as he headed northwest into the Caribbean Sea, giving the enemy ample opportunity to prepare for a seizure. Meantime the squadron crept across the water under reduced sail, too.

Three days passed before they reached the Mona Passage separating Puerto Rico and Santo Domingo. The little merchant vessel took up a position less than a mile from an uninhabited section of the latter, and the warships moved into a cove that concealed their presence. A lookout stationed in the crow's nest on board the *Elizabeth* kept watch, and as a double precaution, it was also arranged that the captain of the brig would send up flares if and when the freebooters should appear on the scene.

The watch was maintained throughout the long day, but nothing happened. Tensions on board the warships relaxed, and the men became bored. Even some of the senior officers privately questioned the wisdom of the tactics the commodore had elected to employ.

At dawn the next morning, while the brig continued to wallow in a slight sea, the midshipman who had just gone aloft to the crow's nest gave the warning.

"Sails to the north, bearing down on the brig!" he called. "There are at least two ships, but there may be more. I can't make them out yet."

Jeremy, who was eating breakfast in his cabin with M'Bwana, immediately ordered an alert sounded. The squadron was to make ready to sail when he gave the word, but he intended to hold back until the last possible moment so the buccaneers would commit themselves and be unable to turn away.

"Three ships, sir!" the lookout called. "No, I'm wrong! They're bearing down with four!"

Jeremy ordered his ships to strip for action, even though they were not under sail as yet. He was reversing the usual process, but wanted to waste no time when the battle began. Gunports were lowered, shot was heated, and the cannon crews were ready at their battle stations.

"They're closing in, sir!" the lookout shouted.

Jeremy understood the purpose of the enemy's maneuver. If possible, the freebooters hoped to capture the brig intact, without firing their cannon. In that event they would sail alongside her and send boarders to dispose of her crew.

The captain of the brig was a senior commander who had served in battle during the War of 1812 on the *Constitution*, and subsequently had seen action on the *Philadelphia* in the war against the Barbary Coast pirates of North Africa. A cool, levelheaded veteran, he undoubtedly was aware of the enemy's intent, too, and he played his role to perfection, waiting until the last possible moment before he sent up his warning flare.

Jeremy's order to his signals lieutenant that sent the squadron into motion was virtually superfluous. The moment the American captains saw the flare, they weighed anchor, hoisted their sails, and left the cove.

The *Elizabeth* was first in the order of battle, followed by the two frigates and one of the sloops, with the other sloop already beginning to edge toward the north, where she would be in a position to follow in the event the enemy retreated. The bomb ketch brought up the rear; she was too small and her armaments were too weak to enable her to participate in a major action. Her turn would come later.

The four buccaneer ships were bearing down on the supposedly helpless brig when the vessels of the squadron appeared, and they had a clear choice: they could either stand and do battle or they could run.

"Lieutenant," Jeremy said quietly, "be good enough to notify all ships they may fire at will."

M'Bwana was not losing a single second, and even as the signal flags were hoisted, the *Elizabeth*'s twelve-inch cannon roared, her nine-pounders soon adding to the din.

The frigates joined in with a will, but the sloops, mounting smaller guns, had to hold back for the present.

The buccaneers knew they had been tricked, and watched in dismay as the decoy merchantman suddenly came to life, sailing for safety behind the *Elizabeth* and the frigates. Regardless of Hawk's faults as a man, he was no coward, and the appearance of his black-and-white flag flying from the yardarm of his schooner indicated that he would fight.

His ships had not anticipated such an action, however, so several precious minutes passed before the four buccaneer ships were ready to reply to the fire of their foes.

In the meantime the *Elizabeth* and the frigates subjected them to a merciless bombardment. Each carried forty-eight guns, and their portside cannon, seventy-two in all, were fired as rapidly as the Americans could reload.

The squadron remained in motion from a distance of no more than a half-mile, and there was no way the pirates could escape. Heated cannonballs crashed into their hulls, raked their decks, and smashed through their rigging. Not one escaped damage.

Hawk's schooner took a beating, but one of his converted brigs was already badly crippled and could not get under way again.

"Captain M'Bwana," Jeremy said, "stand to, if you please, and send that ship to the bottom. Signals Lieutenant, ask the squadron to tack and open fire with their starboard guns."

While the other American ships smartly executed a turn and raked the enemy with their starboard cannon, the *Elizabeth* halted, disdainful of the target that a stationary ship presented, and engaged in a slugging match with the buccaneers.

When her cannon became so overheated they were in danger of exploding, their crews threw buckets and pails of seawater over them to cool them. The noise was so loud that conversation of any kind became impossible.

The freebooters' converted brig began to burn, and, her

hull peppered with holes, it appeared that she was settling i
the water.

Hawk tried to come to her aid by directing his own fire ex
clusively at the *Elizabeth*, but his gunners were far less accu
rate than those of the U.S. Navy, who were demonstratin
that they had no peers.

When a cannonball from the schooner finally landed on
forward section of the *Elizabeth*'s main deck, sending up
shower of splinters, Jeremy knew the time had come to alte
his tactics. He ordered M'Bwana to take evasive action, the
tack and open fire with his starboard guns.

Meantime he sent his eager sloop of war to finish off th
converted brig.

The frigates by now had virtually demolished a second en
emy schooner. Flames leaped high above her decks, witherin
her sails, and an explosion in her magazine chamber sent de
bris flying in all directions, causing the seagulls circling hig
overhead to take themselves elsewhere.

That's two of them, Jeremy thought grimly as the smalle
schooner vanished in sheets of hot flames, continuing to bur
fiercely even as she went down.

Hawk's schooner and the other remaining vessel of hi
fleet, a miniature frigate, continued to fight doggedly. Bu
they were no match for the Americans, and at last the buc
caneer commander was compelled to withdraw.

Jeremy's second sloop had its opportunity now, and as th
two freebooters fled toward the north, the swift American fol
lowed, peppering them with fire that made it difficult fo
them to regain their balance.

The time had come for Major O'Brien's marines to do
their grisly work. Lining the decks of the *Elizabeth* and the
frigates, they fired their rifles at any moving bodies they saw
in the water. Emptying round after round at any buccaneers
who had survived the sinking of their ships, they completed
the slaughter. The commodore's orders were being followed
to the letter: there were no survivors.

This phase of the operation lasted no more than a half-
hour, and then the entire squadron joined in the chase of the
retreating buccaneers, with the second sloop speeding forward
to join her sister ship in harassing the enemy.

Jeremy went alone to his quarters, and while he ate a hasty

meal he weighed the situation. So far the operation had been an unqualified success. He had sunk two of the enemy's major vessels, and had been fortunate enough to suffer no casualties. His own ships had endured only minor damage, and it was obvious that the freebooters were badly outclassed.

What had been done up to this point, however, was only the beginning. Two of the pirate ships were still afloat, with their crews more or less intact. If the intelligence information he had gleaned in Barbados was correct, the buccaneers had at least one more ship in their possession that had not taken part in the battle. If he ended his campaign here and now, the freebooters still had the strength to stage a comeback, to capture more merchantmen, increase the size of their fleet again, and resume their reign of terror.

The previous campaign that he and Admiral Lord Saunders had waged had taught him lessons he had no intention of forgetting. The buccaneers were running away because they faced a superior force, which was sensible. But they were victims of a strange mentality: instead of scattering until the danger ended and then regrouping, it was likely they would retreat into the mountains of Hispaniola in the hopes that they would be able to hold their pursuers at bay and turn them back.

Very well, Jeremy would follow them wherever they went.

As soon as he finished his simple meal, he summoned Major O'Brien to his cabin. "I want all of your marines and navy auxiliaries on board the *Elizabeth* and the frigates to be prepared for a landing on short notice. We'll move fast, without a wagon train as a backup, so every man will have to carry his own ammunition and supplies."

"For how many days, Commodore?" the marine commandant wanted to know.

Jeremy shrugged. "Four days to a week, roughly. I'm anticipating a march into Hispaniola's highest mountains, Major."

"Forgive me if I seem impertinent, sir," O'Brien said, "but why don't we sink those two ships that are left and be done with it? We outnumber them, we have the firepower, but we're dawdling behind them, giving them a chance to mount a land campaign."

"Precisely. They may have other ships. They undoubtedly have a nucleus of other men awaiting them at their mountain headquarters. I want to clean them out completely and permanently. If as many as a dozen of them survive, they'll build up their company again. And this entire operation will have to be repeated in a few more years. I'm using the buccaneers on those two ships that are limping along ahead of us right now as stalking horses. They'll lead us to the rest, and we'll be done with them once and for all. Four or five years from now I'll be too old to conduct yet another campaign."

The marine officer understood, and his smile was tight. "I fought at Tripoli, Commodore, and the odds on land are no worse now than they were then."

"Our chief problem," Jeremy said, "is that we don't know the location of the enemy hideout in the mountains, and we can't afford to spend weeks searching for it. That means we'll have to follow them ashore and stay close behind them while they lead us there."

O'Brien frowned. "What you're saying, sir, is that my men may have to march without rest for several days and then plunge into battle before they have a chance to gain their breath."

"I'm afraid so. You've been sifting through the navy rosters, O'Brien. How many men do we have—including your marine contingent—who are capable of taking part in this march?"

The major was prepared for his question. "One hundred and seventy-five, sir. Another fifty, maybe, if we content ourselves with a slower pace."

Jeremy shook his head. "I want only those who can push themselves to the utmost."

"In that case, Commodore, a maximum of one-seventy-five."

"All right. Organize them, and keep them on alert. I have no idea when the enemy intends to land, so we've got to keep breathing down his neck, and we can't give him the chance to get away."

In midafternoon the disabled pirate ships turned westward, sailing along the north shore of Hispaniola. Hawk proved himself a worthy opponent, twice feinting in attempts to fool his enemies, but the U.S. Navy sloops refused to be fooled and continued to sail close behind him and his smaller ship.

The full squadron followed doggedly.

At sundown Jeremy ordered the gap separating his ships and those of the buccaneers shortened so there would be no opportunity for the enemy to give him the slip. Tensions on board the American vessels ran high.

A bright half-moon came up, aiding the pursuers and making it more difficult for the freebooters to disappear.

Hawk's situation became increasingly desperate, and he could escape only by going ashore and marching to his hideout. Perhaps he could rally his forces there and disperse these men who refused too abandon their pursuit.

Around midnight the two buccaneer ships tacked sharply, then headed toward the shore.

The entire squadron followed, and as the ships sailed into a horseshoe-shaped harbor, Jeremy saw two medium-sized ships riding at anchor there. The reports he had gleaned were true. The pirates had commanded a total of six ships.

He knew what had to be done, and his orders were crisp. The entire squadron was directed to bombard the two anchored ships as well as the disabled freebooters. When they were too crippled to return the fire, the bomb ketch would close in and sink them.

That, however, was only the first phase of this final operation.

"O'Brien," he said to the marine commandant, who stood beside him on the *Elizabeth*'s quarterdeck, "be good enough to instruct your landing party to be ready to go ashore at a moment's notice."

The appropriate signals were sent to the frigates, and boats were lowered.

Meantime the bombardment of the buccaneer ships began, and the quiet harbor was transformed into an inferno.

The freebooters put up only a token resistance. Hawk had already reconciled himself to the loss of his ships, and most of his men were hurrying ashore by boat.

"Landing parties away!" Jeremy ordered, and started down the quarterdeck steps.

M'Bwana halted him. "I'm coming with you," he said. "I've turned over the *Elizabeth* to my first lieutenant."

Jeremy started to protest, but fell silent when he saw his friend's face.

"I'm not forgetting what they did to me," M'Bwana said. "I have a private score to settle."

# Chapter 15

---

Desperation gave the buccaneers greater stamina than they ordinarily possessed, and they marched through the night, maintaining their rapid pace all through the following day. They halted only for brief periods, and thanks to Hawk's efforts they managed to maintain discipline in their ranks, so their retreat at no time turned into disorganized flight.

Their American pursuers dogged their footsteps. Twice the freebooters tried to delay their advancing foes, but the expert marksmen of the marine vanguard blistered them with such accurate fire that they gave up the attempts.

Jeremy, flanked by M'Bwana and Major O'Brien, marched at the head of the main body. They made their way across gradually rising plateaus as they headed toward the cloud-capped mountains, and he was satisfied with his party's progress.

The coarse tropical grass grew high, particularly in the vicinity of the rivers, and occasionally they saw herds of wild cattle in the distance. But there were no jungles in this area, no dangerous animals or snakes with which to contend, and few rocks underfoot. The marines and sailors were able to keep up with their enemies.

In the foothills of the mountains, which they reached around noon, the terrain suddenly changed for the worse. Now there were boulders everywhere, and footing became difficult on shale. But the buccaneers had to slow their pace, too, and were just as tired as the weary Americans behind them. Late in the afternoon the freebooters reached heights that Jeremy estimated at six to seven thousand feet, and then seemingly vanished on narrow trails along the edges of precipices, some of them only inches wide.

Too late Jeremy realized why the buccaneers hadn't made a more determined effort to turn back their foes. The pirate hideout was a natural redoubt, a fortress that nature had made, and from the heights above, the pirates could control any approach to their stronghold.

A spray of musket fire forced the Americans to halt, and Jeremy ordered his party to take cover behind boulders.

The men were glad enough to halt, and many of them removed their boots while they rested.

"I don't care in the least for this situation," Jeremy said to M'Bwana and Major O'Brien. "We can't get at them up yonder, but they can hold us down here indefinitely with a fire screen. No wonder they didn't resist harder on the march."

"Maybe we'll have to lay siege to them, Commodore," the marine said.

"Maybe." Jeremy looked dubious. "The only trouble is that we carry food for only a few days, and they must have ample supplies in their redoubt to last much longer than that. It's obvious they hope to wear us out here until we run out of food, and then we'll have to leave. I'm afraid I didn't give them credit for being this clever."

M'Bwana pondered at length. "It seems to me," he said at last, "that we'll have to storm their positions."

Jeremy shook his head. "No. Not only does their stance appear to be impregnable, but we're outnumbered. So, even though our marksmanship is superior, the odds are against us, and our casualties would be too high."

"Then what will we do?" his friend demanded angrily. "Just sit here?"

"Yes, until morning, anyway. It's too dark now to see the terrain clearly, and we may be able to work a plan of attack that isn't suicidal after we have a chance to study the paths, ledges, and passes in daylight. O'Brien, set your picket lines and establish a sentry schedule. We can't go up there tonight, the enemy sure as hell won't come down, so the men can get a night's rest. They need it."

Sentry outposts were set up, and the Americans ate a meal of the inevitable field rations of parched corn and smoked beef. Then they settled down for the night, every marine and sailor sleeping with his rifle close at hand.

Rest did not come to Jeremy. He was forced to admit to himself that the enemy had outsmarted him, and he was deeply chagrined. It would have been far better, he now realized, to have disposed of the buccaneer force and allowed however many might have been at the redoubt to escape. Instead he and his men were in dire danger of being driven off, and the buccaneers soon would flourish again.

Not until the early hours of the morning did he drop off, and even then he slept uneasily.

He was awakened a short time later by a young marine lieutenant, who dropped to one knee beside him.

"Sir," the officer said, "we've captured an enemy deserter. The men were going to run him through with their bayonets, following your orders to take no prisoners. But he's been making an awful fuss, and he claims over and over that he knows you and has to speak to you. So I figured I'd best check with you before we do him in."

Jeremy sat up wearily. "I reckon it will do no harm to see him."

The lieutenant saluted and hurried away in the dark.

A few moments later everyone in the vicinity heard the hoarse, angry voice. "Belay there! Take your filthy hands off me and show some respect for rank!"

"I'll be damned," Jeremy said as he recognized Chief Boatswain Talbot.

"I knowed you was here, Commodore," Talbot said, "because I saw you earlier from a lookout place up the mountain."

M'Bwana came forward incredulously. "You're a buccaneer now, Talbot?"

"Aye, sir, in a manner of speaking. Me and six of the lads from the *Louise* joined these murderous scum, not wanting to be killed. Better if they'd hanged us, but here we be. It took me three hours to work my way down here, and your sentries near chopped off my head."

"The circumstances are extraordinary, but I'm glad to see you, Talbot," Jeremy said. "You do manage to turn up everywhere. How many men are in that redoubt?"

"Two hundred and fifty. Maybe a few more than that."

Jeremy exchanged glances in the dark with M'Bwana and Major O'Brien. Their force definitely was outnumbered.

"There's just two ways you can take them, Commodore," Talbot said. "One is with cannon."

Jeremy became testy. "We've been engaged in a hot pursuit up the mountains, so we could carry no artillery with us."

"I know that, sir, and so does Hawk."

"Who?"

"The head of the buccaneers. He's sitting in front of his cave right now, gloating, while his wench brings him drinks. He thinks he's beat you and that you'll have to leave."

"He may be right," Jeremy said.

"I told you there was two ways, Commodore, and you ain't heard the second one. Hawk would stay sober if he knowed what I know." Talbot grinned, enjoying himself thoroughly.

Jeremy controlled his temper. "Just what is it you know, Talbot?"

"There's a path off to your right there. Follow it to the top, and it leads you right into the middle of the buccaneer compound, which is a little plateau with caves all around it."

"Surely the buccaneers can defend that path?"

"If they don't have other problems that make them put their minds and attention elsewheres." Talbot had been waiting a long time for this moment, and was relishing it.

M'Bwana was about to strike him, and had to be restrained.

"It's like this," the former chief boatswain said. "Me and the lads from the *Louise*, all seven of us, have been wanting to get our own back from the murderers. We've been talking about if for hours tonight, and we see our chance. This way, Commodore. When you see the first crack of dawn in the sky, send your men in single file up that path. They can go about seventy-five feet. Then they're to stop."

Major O'Brien's expression indicated that he feared a trap.

But Jeremy's instinct told him the man was faithful and could be trusted.

"We'll time your climb, me and the lads from the *Louise*," Talbot said. "As best we're able. When we think you have enough men up the path to rush the buccaneer compound, we'll create a diversion."

"What kind of a diversion?" the skeptical marine commandant wanted to know.

Talbot grinned at him. "My last summer in the United States, I was in Charleston on Independence Day. My, what grand fireworks shows they put on in the harbor! Well, Major, I figure we can set off some gunpowder explosions and fire enough pistols and muskets to make the buccaneers think they're being attacked from the rear. The won't be fooled for long, but there ought to be enough time for your lads to reach the plateau and start some fireworks of your own. Then my friends and me can really stage an attack on the buccaneers from the rear."

The scheme was risky, but Jeremy saw no real alternative. "It just might work," he said.

"We've fought in a lot of battles together, sir, and I ain't never let you down yet. I won't today, either. Not with the score I have to settle with Hawk and his scum."

"We'll do it," Jeremy said, and extended his hand.

Talbot gripped it hard.

"There's just one question," Major O'Brien said. "If that path is so well guarded, are you sure you can get back to the compound without being detected?"

Talbot laughed. "I came down the mountain, didn't I? I never yet met a boatswain who got lost."

Before anyone could reply, he vanished in the dark.

The members of the expedition prepared for the assault in almost complete silence. The men ate a light meal, then checked their weapons, and the marines affixed bayonets to their rifles.

Jeremy asked for volunteers to participate in the initial attack up the path, and M'Bwana insisted on leading the party. Ordinarily a senior officer would have been refused the assignment, but Jeremy knew that no man was better qualified than the Bantu, whose early training in the African jungles enabled him to see better than others in the dark and made him as surefooted as a cat.

M'Bwana stripped off the upper portion of his uniform so the gold braid wouldn't call undue attention to him, then discarded his hat, too.

The vanguard consisted of twenty marines, a group sufficiently large to establish a bridgehead. With M'Bwana in the lead they crept approximately seventy-five feet up the path, then halted, and the main body formed behind them.

Everyone watched the sky, which seemed to grow darker.

Then a faint pencil of light showed off to the east.

At that moment an infernal racket erupted above. Musket and pistol fire cracked, and there was a flash of light, followed by a deafening roar as a barrel of gunpowder exploded. Talbot and the former crewmen from the *Louise* were doing their part.

M'Bwana and the vanguard needed no urging and raced up the path, which was momentarily left unguarded, and reached the plateau before the sentries quite realized what was happening.

The noise of the explosion and gunfire aroused the entire freebooter company, and the men poured into the open from the caves.

"Fire at will!" M'Bwana shouted, and the marine sharpshooters began to mow down the disorganized buccaneers.

By the time Hawk arrived on the scene and tried to rally his followers, the marines were using their bayonets with a vengeance.

Then the main American party, led by Jeremy and Major O'Brien, reached the plateau and joined in the battle.

The buccaneers recovered sufficiently to start returning the fire of the attackers.

But the marines were superb in close-quarters combat, and gave far better than they received.

Suddenly M'Bwana went berserk. His memories of having been sold into slavery and then abused for months suddenly erupted, and not bothering to reload the rifle he carried, he used it as a club, grasping it by the barrel and laying about with demonic force, cracking skulls and virtually decapitating a number of freebooters.

The rifle slipped from his grasp, but his blood lust was not yet satisfied. He drew his sword, and emitting a piercing, high-pitched scream that the enemies of the Bantu would have recognized, he continued on his rampage, maiming and killing indiscriminately.

He inspired the rest of the Americans, who were firing methodically at their foes. The ranks of the buccaneers broke, and those who tried to flee were shot down.

M'Bwana's luck was too good to last. In spite of the precautions he had taken, he had called attention to himself, and as the buccaneers tried to retreat, several took aim at him simultaneously.

He went down under a hail of bullets, the last shots the pirates fired, and lay dead on the ground.

Jeremy saw him fall, but there was no time now to mourn for his friend. For the present he had to concentrate on his mission to the exclusion of all else. "No quarter!" he shouted.

The marines and sailors went on with their deadly work, killing every member of the band who came into their line of fire. The carnage was devastating.

Too late the surviving members of the buccaneer company realized that Chief Boatswain Talbot and the six Americans who had been recruited with him were fighting on the other side. Their aim was as accurate as that of the marines, and they needed no urging to refuse the enemy quarter.

The ranks of the freebooters broke, and what little remained of their discipline was dissipated. Men who were bullies by nature and fought best when the odds were strongly in their favor became badly confused and frightened when the tide turned against them. They were felled without mercy as they tried to flee from the scene.

Only one man managed to get away. Hawk's instinct for survival was strong, and he hugged the inner side of the precipice, flattening himself against the mountainside as he surreptitiously crept higher in the direction of the upper caves.

His retreat did not go unnoticed, however, and a half-dozen marines under Major O'Brien's direct command followed him cautiously, keeping him in sight on the twisting path as best they could, but unable to fire at him because the angles were bad.

Jeremy saw what was happening, and realizing from the retreating buccaneer's expensive dress that he had to be a member of the top freebooter echelon, he left the final phase of the operation below to subordinates, and he followed, too, at a distance.

When Hawk gained the top level, a young woman rushed out of the cave. Attired in the vulgarly revealing costume of the Santo Domingo harlot, with makeup heavy on her face and laden with jewelry, she threw herself into Hawk's arms.

He was quick to utilize her sudden presence to his advantage, and as the marines approached, he shifted her position so she stood between them and him as she continued to cling to him.

"Fire at me," he called, "and you'll hit the wench!"

The Americans were nonplussed, and held their fire.

At that moment the young woman snatched a double-edged knife from her belt and drove it deep into Hawk's body.

He staggered and fell to the path only inches from the lip of the precipice.

She dropped with him, landing on top of him and still clutching the knife, which she continued to press into his body.

The marines broke into a run, as did Jeremy, and they saw the woman holding the knife in place.

Hawk writhed, bleeding badly, but lacked the strength to push the wench away or remove the knife.

She shifted her position so she straddled him, with her knees resting on the ground, and continued to hold the knife in place. None of the blade was visible.

Hawk's efforts to free himself became more feeble, but he was fully conscious as he looked up into her cold eyes.

"Die, you bastard," she said, her voice icy.

The marines were so stunned that no one moved forward to drag the wench away.

Hawk died as he had lived, by the sword, with the knife still protruding from his body.

The young woman wrenched herself to her feet, ran into the cave, and emerged again a moment later carrying a large, ornately carved wooden box. When she opened it, the onlookers saw sparkling gems set in gold and silver.

Before anyone could stop her, she hurled the box over the side of the precipice. The bracelets, earrings, and necklaces stolen by the buccaneers from merchant ships crashed to the bottom of the ravine several thousand feet below. The area there was virtually impassable, so the jewelry could not be recovered.

"Unclean," she muttered, "unclean." Ripping bracelets from her arms and tearing a necklace with a diamond-encrusted brooch attached to it from her neck, she threw them over the ledge, too.

Not yet satisfied with her efforts, she pushed the body of Hawk over the side, and his lifeless form dropped to the base of the inaccessible ravine.

Then she took a deep breath as she poised at the ledge, and it was obvious that she intended to jump to her own death.

Jeremy intervened before she could kill herself, and caught her just in time. .

At that instant he recognized her.

Lisa!

For a moment he was too astonished to realize that she was actually still alive, that he wasn't dreaming.

In that same instant she knew him too, and struggled to free herself so she could jump to her death. "I'm unclean, too," she murmured. "Let me die."

Jeremy tightened his grip. He couldn't yet guess or figure out how Lisa had survived the destruction of her Barbados home by fire or how she had appeared in the buccaneer hideout looking like a Santo Domingo harlot, but those details didn't matter. She was alive, and he accepted the miracle.

Lisa tried to free herself from his grasp, but in vain, and suddenly she went limp.

Jeremy saw that she had lost consciousness, and it occurred to him that she was suffering from a high fever. Tropical diseases sometimes killed with little warning, and he prayed he would not lose her again so soon after finding her.

While the marines scoured the interior of Hawk's cave, where they found large quantities of gold and silver, Jeremy carried Lisa back down to the plateau.

There a litter was prepared for her, as well as for the bodies of M'Bwana and the others who had been killed in the assault. A dozen Americans had been wounded, but most of the injuries had been minor, and the men were able to walk under their own power.

The buccaneer company had been totally destroyed. A total of two hundred and thirty-nine bodies were counted, and although it was possible that a handful might have escaped, they were minor members of the company, incapable of reorganizing and starting again.

Lisa remained unconscious on the day-and-a-half march back to the waiting ships. Jeremy tried repeatedly to rouse her, and she stirred when he spoke to her or touched her, but did not awaken.

She was lodged in the cabin that had been M'Bwana's on board the *Elizabeth*, and both the surgeon and his assistant looked after her, both saying her fever was very real but that they were unable to diagnose her ailment.

The American ships put out to sea, and after they reached open waters clear of the Mona Passage a burial service was performed. Jeremy watched from his quarterdeck, his expression bleak as the flag-draped body of M'Bwana was lowered over the side, and he knew that a significant period of his life had come to an end. Without his good friend, his existence would never be the same.

Chief Boatswain Talbot, who had been restored to full standing, as had the other Americans impressed into the buccaneer company, wept openly. So did many others.

Through sheer ability a black man had surmounted the odds that handicapped his race at a time when prejudice was virulent, and had won high honors. Now he had made the supreme sacrifice for his country and his friends.

For the rest of the day Jeremy remained alone, and even when he paced his quarterdeck his subordinates took care to avoid him, knowing the commodore had to grieve alone.

Thirty-six hours later the surgeon told Jeremy that Lisa's fever had broken and that she would recover. He offered a long prayer of thanks to God for her safety.

But he waited another day before paying her a visit, wanting to give her a chance to recover at least a part of her strength before they saw each other.

Jeremy was surprised to discover that he felt strangely nervous as he tapped at the door of her cabin.

"Come in," she called in a firm voice.

She was sitting up in bed, her face scrubbed clean, her body concealed beneath one of Jeremy's nightshirts, which was many sizes too large for her. Her expression was polite, but when she saw him she stiffened and scowled.

"It's you," she said. "I thought it was a yeoman bringing me something to eat."

"If you wish," Jeremy told her, "I'll ask the cook to prepare a tray I can bring you."

Lisa was in no mood for his humor. "Why did you force me to live when I wanted to die?"

"Because you didn't know what you were doing and have every reason to live."

"But you don't understand what I went through in the mountains of Santo Domingo."

"I can guess. The buccaneers abducted you and made it appear that you died in a fire."

"Yes, a fire they set. But that was only the beginning. Hawk was a former Royal Navy officer who bore a grudge against Dickie Saunders. He not only compelled me to look like a harlot, but forced me to act like one. When I wasn't sleeping with him, I had to have relations with one or another of his lieutenants. I came to know many of them. Intimately. I not only played the part of a strumpet. I actually became a strumpet."

"That's in the past now, and it doesn't matter." Jeremy tried in vain to stop pacing up and down the length of the cabin.

"I beg you," Lisa said, "put me ashore somewhere, and I'll manage."

"I don't think you're cut out for the life of a harlot," he said mildly. "It doesn't become you."

"I have nothing else to offer to anyone," she replied with great bitterness.

"Forgive me if I happen to think otherwise."

"I could have been wealthy enough if I had kept the jewelry Hawk gave me. But it was tainted, discolored by the blood of innocent people he had murdered, so I had to get rid of it."

"For your sake as well as for mine, I'm glad you did," he told her. "You didn't need it."

"Well, I've sold my body so many times that doing it again shouldn't be all that difficult." Her voice broke.

Jeremy looked hard at her, then went to her.

"Don't come near me!" Lisa cried, panic in her voice as she shrank to the far side of the bed.

He ignored her protests. Sitting beside her, he drew her to him and kissed her.

The magnetism that had sparked them at the beginning of their long and tortured relationship had not lessened over the years. The cabin swam before them, and for a long, breathless moment they were aware only of each other.

Barely in time Jeremy remembered that Lisa was still convalescing and managed to pull back.

The last of her defenses had been destroyed. "That was unfair, but you win. You know very well I can't resist you, that your touch turns me to jelly. All right, Jeremy. Set me up as your mistress somewhere, and I'll accept any terms you offer me. My destiny, it seems, is to sell my body to men."

"That isn't what I had in mind," he said quietly.

"What, then? You can't take me back to Oakhurst Manor and torture your wife with my presence, even though I'd accept even that if you insisted."

"Sarah's last wish," Jeremy said, speaking slowly and distinctly, "was that I marry you if the opportunity ever offered itself to us."

Lisa's huge eyes widened. "Sarah is . . . ?"

"I've been a widower for three years," he said. "Never consciously allowing myself to think of you because I believed that Dickie Saunders was still alive."

For a long moment Lisa remained motionless. Then she looked at him, her smile tremulous.

Again he kissed her, and she responded so willingly, so eagerly that both of them were breathless.

"We're putting in to Nassau for repairs and provisions before we sail back to Charleston and the squadron is disbanded," Jeremy said. "I have no doubt we'll find a clergyman there who will be happy to perform a marriage ceremony for us."

"No!" Lisa was emphatic.

"Now what?" Jeremy asked wearily.

"The only clothes I own are that horrid strumpet's blouse

and skirt. I refuse to be married wearing them. It would be obscene, a travesty of a wedding!"

He didn't share her concern, but knew from her manner that she wouldn't be budged. So he thought hard for a few moments. "All right. The moment we reach Nassau, I'll send a dressmaker to you, a half-dozen of them, if you like. I daresay we'll be there for ten days to two weeks, so they'll have ample time to make a complete new wardrobe for you, and there will be no need for you to set foot outside this cabin until you have it. We've waited this long to be married, so a few more days won't matter."

Lisa looked at him, her expression radiant. "That leaves only one thing to be settled."

He had no idea what might be coming next, and braced himself.

"No woman, no matter how battered and bruised, wants to be taken for granted. She wants a formal proposal."

He was quick to overcome the error. "Dear Lisa, will you marry me?"

"Yes, with all my heart, darling Jeremy."

# Chapter 16

Lisa Beaufort, the new mistress of Oakhurst Manor, brought the old plantation to life again. Overseer Lester Howard approved of her compassionate treatment of the slaves. The white-haired Cleo, who had been reserved when Lisa first arrived, soon cooperated with her in all things, and they enjoyed a perfect rapport at their daily conferences.

The children were ecstatic. Lance made no secret of his great admiration for Lisa, Carrie imitated her walk and manner of speech, and little Cleo and Paul delighted in accompanying her as she went about her chores.

Dolores admired her, too, and soon confided in her. Lisa respected her secrets, and refused to tell even Jeremy the substance of their conversations.

Lisa made a point of welcoming Isaiah and Lorene Benton, treating the late Sarah's father and stepmother as though they were her own blood relatives. They, too, endorsed her without qualification. "You're a fortunate man, Jeremy," Lorene said. "Lisa is warm and wise as well as lovely."

Scott Emerson felt the same way. "Some men have all the luck," he said. "I wish I'd known her first."

In their private relations Jeremy and Lisa enjoyed complete

contentment. The tensions of the past were forgotten, and they put out of their minds all that they had suffered. Separations of only a few hours bothered them, and after Jeremy spent even part of a day inspecting the plantation, he and Lisa greeted each other with a passionate yearning that most couples reserved for reunions after long partings. Lisa accompanied her husband to Washington City when he went there to receive the thanks of President Adams for the success of his expedition against the buccaneers, and she always accompanied him to Charleston.

Her previous marriage to Lord Saunders had accustomed her to managing an estate, and she handled day-to-day existence at Oakhurst Manor and the Charleston house with smoothness and finesse. Her suppers and larger parties were brilliant successes, and she soon achieved wide popularity in the area, even among those who had been Sarah's good friends and, at first, were inclined to resent her successor.

There were only two clouds on Lisa's horizon. The first was Kai, who was stunned by M'Bwana's death in battle. For months she grieved alone and in private, refused to be consoled, and rarely ventured from her suite.

But Lisa persisted in her attempts to be helpful, as did Scott Emerson, and little by little Kai began to emerge from her shell. There were smudges beneath her eyes and furrows in her brow, but gradually the shadows disappeared and the lines were smoothed away. A year after the return of Jeremy and Lisa to Oakhurst Manor, she was beginning to return to normal. Her future was very much on her mind, and one day she offered to leave the plantation.

"Jeremy and I won't hear of it," Lisa said firmly. "This is your home. As much as it was when M'Bwana was still here, and we won't hear of your going elsewhere."

Tears of gratitude appeared in Kai's eyes.

Scott Emerson had exercised great caution for a year, but now he began to pursue his suit of Kai more openly.

"I'm almost positive," Lisa told Jeremy one morning as they were dressing, "that Kai will marry him."

"I'm inclined to doubt it," he replied, pulling on his boots. "She's suffered so much that it wouldn't surprise me if she remained a widow for the rest of her days."

Lisa kissed him. "Darling Jeremy, trust a woman's intuition."

"Especially yours," he said with a grin. "I'd be the last to argue with you, of course, and I know that Scott has loved her for a very long time. There's no finer man anywhere, and a marriage would be grand for both of them, but from what I've seen, Kai doesn't love him."

"Not yet," Lisa said, and looked smug.

Jeremy was bewildered.

"Kai is lonely and vulnerable," she explained. "Scott is a wonderful person. Kind and thoughtful and attentive, so she can't help responding to him. Love will come later, after they're married. And she'll never regret it. Take my word for it."

"I take your word in everything." Jeremy gathered her in his arms and kissed her.

The air seemed to crackle with electricity, and both were badly shaken when they drew apart.

"Enough of that," Lisa said, "or we'll go straight back to bed."

"That's the best idea I've heard today," Jeremy said, reaching for her again.

She managed to evade him. "Later, darling, you have a busy morning ahead, and so have I."

They went to breakfast arm in arm, and there they were confronted by their major problem.

Jerry.

The heir to Oakhurst Manor was in his teens now, and his inability to get along with his peers was even more marked than it had been when he'd been younger. His moods were mercurial, shifting from effusiveness to sullen withdrawal, and no one could predict his behavior.

Only in the presence of his father was he careful to mind his manners. Jeremy tolerated no nonsense, no misconduct, and was quick to reprimand him, sometimes boxing his ears when he failed to obey with alacrity. He was rude to Isaiah and Lorene, his grandfather and step-grandmother, and he made it his business to ignore Kai when he dared. He was jealous of Lance, but had to exercise caution in the presence of the younger boy, who was bigger and stronger, and who did not hesitate to thrash him when he stepped out of line.

When no one else was around, he teased Carrie unmercifully, and at all times he treated little Cleo and Paul with disdain because they were black.

Most of his hatred was reserved for the woman his father had married, the woman who had taken his mother's place as the mistress of Oakhurst Manor. In Jeremy's hearing the boy was polite and rather subdued, but when alone with Lisa, Jerry treated her with an exaggerated courtesy that was almost ludicrous.

Lisa did her best to win the boy's affections and persisted in her attempts, but her efforts were to no avail. Jerry continued to regard her with such malevolent scorn that she sometimes felt uneasy in his presence.

She put him out of her mind, however, when Kai and Scott Emerson finally came to her and Jeremy with the news that they planned to marry in the immediate future. Lisa gave a supper party to celebrate their betrothal, and the affair was brilliant, attended by everyone in the neighborhood and many friends from Charleston, too.

Lisa, wearing a gown of pale green chiffon, tried hard not to put the guest of honor in the shade, but nevertheless looked entrancing. Kai was lovely, too, in a pink satin dress with a hoop skirt, a style that was just becoming popular.

The company enjoyed a banquet, many of the dishes being Caribbean specialties with which Lisa long had been familiar. There were lightly smoked oysters, served with crisp bacon crumbled on them, a rich pumpkin soup with a beef base, fish baked in clay, and a roast with a spice-laden crust. As a surprise dessert, star apples from Jamaica were served, the *Elizabeth* having just returned from the Caribbean with a crate of them.

Star apples had a special meaning to Jeremy and Lisa, and sitting at opposite ends of the long table, they silently toasted each other.

Jeremy looked somewhat preoccupied, and Lisa assumed he was concerned because Jerry had elected to absent himself from the festivities. It developed, however, that he had other matters on his mind.

After the guests had departed, he asked Scott and Kai to join him and Lisa in the library for a nightcap. The ladies accepted glasses of a mild wine, and Jeremy poured whiskey for Scott and himself, then closed the door.

"There's something I've had on my mind for a long time," he said. "If M'Bwana had lived, I never would have brought it up, but I feel it must come into the open now. I'm speaking of Lance."

Kai looked faintly distressed, but Lisa and Scott seemed undisturbed.

"I don't want to embarrass you, Kai," Jeremy continued. "But we do Lance a disservice if we keep silent now." He paused, then turned to his wife and his friend. "It's an open secret in the whole state that Lance is my natural son. M'Bwana adopted him, and had my dear friend lived, that would have been the end of the matter."

"I'm prepared to adopt him, too," Scott said. "There's no finer lad anywhere."

"I have no intention of standing in your way, Scott," Jeremy told him. "All of us are interested in Lance's welfare and want only what is best for him. Certainly I know he'll move to Trelawney, as will Carrie, when you and Kai are married. All the same, I've been wondering if there isn't some way—legally and without a lot of fanfare that will cause gossip—that I can acknowledge him as my son so I can make him one of the principal heirs to my estate."

Scott pondered the problem.

Kai was overwhelmed.

Lisa was so struck by her husband's thoughtful generosity that she reached for his hand.

"Lance is thirteen now," Scott said, "so it won't be too many years before he reaches his majority. You're far wealthier than I'll ever be, Jeremy. You could buy and sell me ten times over. In good conscience, I can't stand in the lad's way."

"If you acknowledge him," Kai asked, "would that mean he'd stay at Oakhurst Manor when I become mistress of Trelawney?"

Scott reassured her with a kiss. "Not at all. He'll move in with us, just as Carrie will. For all practical purposes, I'll act as his father. But he'll be known legally as Lance Beaufort. Naturally, he can come here to visit as often as he pleases. And someday he'll come into a very substantial inheritance."

Jeremy nodded in agreement. His friend had analyzed his own wishes to perfection.

"I've lived here only a year," Lisa said, "so I'm not all that familiar with American ways. But I do know human nature, and even though this legal acknowledgment is handled privately in a closed court, the news is almost certain to leak out. So there will be a certain measure of gossip, I'm afraid."

Kai straightened. "No one will say what hasn't already been said. There's a portrait of Jeremy in the front parlor that was painted when he was in his early teens, and I'll wager I've been asked a thousand times if it isn't Lance. A legal action will only confirm what everyone already knows. I'm not afraid of gossip, and for the sake of a few whispers I won't block my son's financial future."

"Nor will I," Scott said firmly. "I'm happy to draw up the legal papers tomorrow and take them to court. So that's settled."

"Not quite. There are two other steps to be taken first." Jeremy turned to Lisa. "You've been hurt enough in this world, and I won't subject you to fresh anguish. What do you want done?"

"I insist that you acknowledge Lance as your son," she said without hesitation, "and the gossips be damned."

She was so unselfish, so sincere, that Jeremy embraced her.

"Now," he said as he straightened, "that leaves Lance himself. He's old enough to have some voice in all this, and I don't think anything should be done without his consent."

The others were in agreement.

"I wonder if he's gone to bed yet," Kai said.

"Hardly," Scott replied with a grin. "There are piles of cold meats and bread left from supper, and seeing that he and Carrie hadn't eaten anything for at least a couple of hours, they were hungry again. As we came in here I saw them heading out to the kitchen to make themselves some sandwiches. That might possibly prevent them from starving between now and tomorrow morning. I'll fetch him."

"Let Carrie come, too, since she's a member of our family," Kai said.

Scott hurried off to the kitchen outbuilding, and soon returned with the two youngsters, both holding oversized sandwiches of ham, turkey, tongue, and cheese. Lance, who looked mature for his years, was almost as tall as Jeremy, although still slim. Carrie, wearing her first evening dress of white linen, with her dark hair streaming down her back, gave every promise of being a great beauty.

Both continued to eat as they came into the library. The door was closed behind them again.

Kai explained the situation, with an occasional assist from Scott.

Jeremy, feeling ill-at-ease, waited until they were finished before he entered the conversation. "If you wish, Lance, I'll tell you the story of how I happened to sire you when there was no love between your mother and me. All I want you to know and believe is that I hold her in the highest respect and admiration."

The boy stood ramrod straight and tall, his eyes clear. "I know it already, Papa Beaufort," he said. "I know the whole story, too."

All four of the adults were dumbfounded.

Lance exchanged a glance with Carrie, in whom he had obviously confided. "Papa M'Bwana told me everything before he went off on his last voyage. I think he knew he wasn't coming back. He had a premonition. A long time ago he taught me that people who are close to nature sometimes sense what will happen in the future. Anyway, I don't blame you for anything that ever happened, and I don't blame Mama. I'm grateful to both of you for loving me and taking care of me, and now I can tell you that I love you, too."

Jeremy embraced him, even though he was afraid the boy would be embarrassed by the intimate gesture.

Instead Lance grinned. "Now that everything is coming out into the open," he said, "I don't mind saying that as far back as I can remember, I've known that I'm your son."

"How have you known?"

"The way you've looked at me. The special tone in your voice when you've spoken to me. And I'd have to be blind not to see the special resemblance when I look in a pier glass. I look much more like you than Jerry does. That's why he hates me so much, I guess."

"I don't think he hates you." Jeremy's protest was feeble.

Again Lance glanced at Carrie, but preferred not to pursue the point and shrugged.

"Then you wouldn't mind being recognized as my son?" Jeremy asked him.

Lance's eyes were bright. "It'll make me very proud," he said. "I just hope I can live up to the Beaufort name."

Jeremy was pleased, as were Lisa and Kai.

"But I intend to be loyal to Papa Emerson, too," Lance added, turning to Scott. "He's been wonderful to Mama, as well as to Carrie and to me."

Scott, deeply touched, hugged him, too.

Something Lisa had said a few weeks earlier came into Jeremy's mind. Lance's attitude toward Carrie was fiercely protective, and he was determined that no harm come to her. They had been reared as brother and sister, even though they were unrelated, and their fierce mutual loyalty reminded Jeremy of his own boyhood relationship with his brother. Close family ties, he believed, were of paramount importance in an indifferent and often cruel outside world.

The immediate issue was settled, with complete understanding and amicability on all sides. Scott promised to draw up the appropriate legal documents the following day, and later in the week Jeremy would go into Charleston for a private hearing before a judge, who would formalize his acknowledgment of Lance as his son.

Lance and Carrie finished their sandwiches, and when the celebrating adults poured themselves one last drink, the youngsters decided to go off to bed.

As Lance opened the door, he saw someone move in the shadows outside the library, and he knew instantly that Jerry had been eavesdropping, listening to the entire conversation. Rather than say anything to Kai or Jeremy, which would have spoiled the mood of the occasion, the boy remained silent.

His eyes met those of his half-brother for a moment, and Jerry's glare was baleful, filled with suppressed hatred. Suddenly he turned away and vanished into the far recesses of the house.

Lance shrugged and dismissed the incident from his mind. He knew, of course, that Jerry disliked him, but the feeling was mutual and grew more intense with each passing year. Jerry knew better than to cross his path or make trouble for him. Fists, as Lance had discovered, could speak far louder than words.

After the marriage of Kai and Scott Emerson, the population of Oakhurst Manor was reduced. Dolores had only little Cleo and Paul as her charges now, but she devoted herself to them with the same loving care she had shown the older children.

Lisa and Jeremy Beaufort had more time to themselves, and they relished every moment of it. The promise of their early relationship was more than fulfilled, and they lived in almost complete harmony, rarely quarreling, even though both had had quick tempers.

"You grow more beautiful every month of every year," Jeremy told his lovely wife, and he spoke the truth. A half-dozen artists clamored for the privilege of painting her portrait, and it was accepted as a fact that she was the most attractive woman in South Carolina.

Lisa quietly made certain that the late Sarah's portrait stood beside her own in the vast entrance hall, and occasionally guests regarded the twin display as bizarre. Only a few dared to question her, but to them she always gave the same reply. "My husband loves me and I'm proud of his affection," she said. "But he loved his first wife, too, and I had the good fortune to know and admire her. She won't be forgotten at Oakhurst Manor."

The nightmare Lisa had been forced to endure during her year and a half of captivity at the buccaneer hideout in Santo Domingo was rarely mentioned. From time to time she made a passing mention of the period in private conversation with her husband, but gradually the terrible time faded from her mind.

Scott Emerson brought up a more important issue. Inasmuch as Lisa was very much alive, she was entitled to inherit various properties and securities that Lord Saunders had left to her, which, at the time of her presumed death, had been claimed by his cousin. But Lisa had no desire to recover them.

"I'm mistress of Oakhurst Manor," she said, "I have the house in Charleston, too, and Jeremy gives me far more than

I need. Let Dickie's cousin think I'm dead, and let the past remain buried."

She and Jeremy made a trip to Paris so they could visit Tom and Margot Beaufort, and for sentimental reasons they traveled on board the *Elizabeth*. The whole journey lasted six months and they enjoyed themselves thoroughly.

After their return, however, Jeremy gave in to his wife's wishes and offered her his solemn pledge that he would never go to sea again. He loved life on the quarterdeck, but he loved her more, and she was so apprehensive when he went off to sea on a commercial venture that he contented himself with ruling his fleet from his Charleston headquarters. Under no circumstances, as he told her, would he knowingly cause her anguish.

Lisa repaid with all of the vast attention and care she was capable of giving him. Virtually every man she met was attracted to her, but she had eyes only for Jeremy.

Her one major burden was eased when Jerry was enrolled at the College of William and Mary and went off to school. Lisa realized she had no concrete grounds for feeling as she did about him, and hoped she wasn't being unfair. She had never been forced into a direct confrontation with him. On the contrary, he had gone to great pains to avoid her when she had tried to talk with him, and only her instinct told her that he despised her.

In another year Lance would go off for a higher education, too. Jeremy and Scott held long discussions, and finally decided the most suitable school was the College of New Jersey, in Princeton, which was attended by the brightest and most talented young men in the South. Scott wanted him to become a lawyer, while Jeremy planned to have him take over the Beaufort shipping interests. Both men had the good sense to defer a decision until Lance could make up his own mind.

Cleo, the elderly housekeeper, died in her sleep one night, and was mourned by everyone. Neighbors and friends of the family rode long distances to pay their last respects to her at her funeral. Jeremy, who had regarded her as a mother, wept without shame at her graveside.

A few weeks later Isaiah and Lorene Benton, who were returning North for their regular six-month sojourn in Boston, took little Cleo and Paul with them. These children were growing up, too: Cleo had expressed a desire to teach, while Paul wanted to be a physician. But their opportunities were limited in the South, and Jeremy, enthusiastically supported by Lisa, was eager to see them advance. He set up trust funds for both to ensure that they received a higher education.

The departure of little Cleo and Paul created a crisis at Oakhurst Manor. Dolores had become a first-rate governess, but now no children remained at the plantation.

Lisa, who had heard the young woman's whole story from her husband, was only temporarily nonplussed. "Dolores lacks the experience to succeed Cleo as our housekeeper, but I'll find something for her to do that's useful and that will make it possible for her to keep her pride. I know how a woman feels when she's forced to live as a harlot, and I promise you, darling Jeremy, that Dolores won't be reduced again to that extreme!"

A few days later the problem unexpectedly resolved itself. Lisa and Jeremy were sitting over a second cup of coffee in their dining room when Lester Howard came in, followed by a shy and reserved Dolores.

The overseer wasted no words. "We were sorry to see Paul and Cleo go back to Boston," he said, "but their leaving has simplified a great many things. Dolores and I aim to get married."

Lisa jumped to her feet and kissed the future bride and groom.

Jeremy offered his congratulations too, but became thoughtful after asking them to sit. "Lester," he said, "you have the right to marry anyone you please, and so has Dolores. But not in this state or anywhere else in the South. For a marriage to be sanctioned under the law, a white is forbidden to marry anyone who is more than one-thirty-second black."

"I told him it would be much easier for us to live together," Dolores said, "but he won't listen to me."

"That's right. I sure as shooting won't," the overseer said. "You're going to be my wife, and our children will be legitimate."

"Apparently you have something specific in mind," Jeremy said.

"Yes, sir. I do." Lester drew in his breath. "The years I've spent at Oakhurst Manor have been the happiest I've ever known, but I can't stay on here. Dolores and I aim to settle out West, where folks don't give a damn about race or color."

"Good for you!" the delighted Lisa exclaimed.

Jeremy approved too, but was more cautious. "Conditions in the West are more liberal than they are here, of course, but there's prejudice everywhere. How far do you plan to travel?"

"All the way to the Colorado country," Lester said.

Jeremy's eyes widened.

"I realize it isn't even a part of the United States yet, but the day is coming when we'll incorporate it into the Union. Meanwhile, we can start our own life there. I've been saving my wages, and I'm hoping we'll have enough to build a house and buy ourselves a herd of cattle."

"It seems to me," Jeremy said, "that after all your years of service at Oakhurst Manor, the least I can do is give you a wedding present of two thousand dollars."

"But that's a fortune," Lester said.

Dolores was stunned.

"It's the least I can do for you," Jeremy said, "and I know Sarah would have wanted me to do it."

How much did the master of Oakhurst Manor know or suspect about his first wife's unfulfilled romance with the overseer? Lester realized that question never would be answered.

Jeremy had no intention of dwelling on the matter in his own mind. It was enough that Sarah would have been pleased by his generous gesture.

Certainly Lisa did not question his motives. In her opinion he could do no wrong.

"That's settled, then," Jeremy said crisply. "We wish both of you the best of everything good."

A member of the staff was promoted to housekeeper, with Lisa assuming more responsibilities herself until the newcomer learned to handle her position. And after Lester and Dolores left the plantation, a temporary overseer was hired, giving Jeremy time to find the right person for the post.

The Beauforts and the Emersons exchanged frequent visits,

maintaining a tradition that had gone on for generations, and both families saw Lance off to college.

In one way, at least, it was just as well that he had gone North, Kai told Lisa in a private conversation. Carrie was maturing rapidly, and of late Lance's expression when he looked at her had not been that of a brother. "The separation will be good for both of them," Lisa said.

Developments in Jeremy's shipping interests made it necessary for him to visit Boston, New York, and Washington City. He took Lisa with him, as usual, mixing business and pleasure. They traveled on one of his brigs and enjoyed themselves so much that they extended their stay at each stop, and more than six months passed before they returned home.

A series of shocks awaited them at Oakhurst Manor. Jerry had come back to the plantation to stay, and not only had taken supervision of affairs into his own hands, but had ordered the temporary overseer to whip the slaves in order to increase the production of cotton and tobacco.

"Not in my time, my father's, or my grandfather's has a whip ever been used at Oakhurst Manor, and it won't be used now," Jeremy said, and directed that the practice be halted at once.

The atmosphere at the supper table was tense that night, and Lisa felt uneasy. Now that Jerry was maturing, he was turning into a thoroughly unpleasant young man. She hated it when he looked at her insolently, studying her figure, and she was disturbed by his badly concealed lack of respect for his father.

Jeremy saw no reason to be diplomatic. "Why have you left school more than a year before you were scheduled to win your degree?" he asked bluntly.

"If you must know," his son said, "the college's rules on drinking and gaming are ridiculously old-fashioned."

"So you were expelled?"

"Not technically. I quit before they could throw me out." Jerry seemed pleased with himself.

Don't intervene, Lisa thought. Stay out of this.

Jeremy was deeply disappointed. "I hope we can find another college that will accept you."

"Not for me!" Jerry was emphatic. "You may as well

know that I can't stand school, any school. Spending night after night just reading is my idea of a dull waste of time."

"There's no other way to gain an education," Jeremy said, and was pained.

"Lots of planters hereabouts don't have college degrees," his son said.

Jeremy sighed.

Lisa's heart ached for him. She knew how much he wanted for the young man, but she realized, as he was just beginning to glean, that Jerry would never live up to his expectations.

"Suppose you don't return to school," Jeremy said. "What will you do?"

"We have enough money so I wouldn't have to do much of anything." There was little joy in Jerry's laugh. "But I'm not lazy. I wouldn't mind taking the job of permanent overseer."

His father shook his head. "It isn't as simple as it might appear to you. In the first place, you know virtually nothing about farming. After a few years as an apprentice, you might learn. And in the second place, you'll need to learn how to handle people. I won't have my slaves abused and beaten. Not by anyone."

Jerry fell silent as he went into one of his customary sulks, and seemingly devoted his attention exclusively to the food on his plate.

But Lisa caught him glancing at her, and there was such malevolence in his gaze that a chill shot up her spine.

The damn bitch, Jerry thought. She lords it over me while she twists Papa around her little finger. She's succeeded Mama as mistress of Oakhurst Manor and shares Papa's bed with him. She even dares to sit in Mama's chair at the table.

I know she persuaded Papa to recognize that bastard Lance as his son and cut me out of a part of my inheritance. May she rot.

Not that Papa needed much encouragement. He's always preferred Lance to me.

Lisa saw the young man glower surreptitiously at his father, and she felt afraid for Jeremy. Her reaction was absurd, she realized, but she could not get rid of it. There was a greater menace in Jerry than anyone had ever recognized.

The meal limped to an end, and Jeremy went off to the library to look at the ledgers that had been kept during his absence by a hired bookkeeper.

"We'll discuss your situation again," were his parting words to his son.

Lisa went up to the master-bedroom suite to supervise the unpacking of the many leather clothing boxes she and Jeremy had taken on their long journey.

Jerry poured himself a generous portion of brandywine, lighted one of his father's *cigarros*, and wandered out to the portico. Gazing across the cropped lawns in the moonlight, he told himself fiercely that Oakhurst Manor was his. Only his.

Never would he share the plantation, the shipping business, or any of Papa's other interests with Lance, who now used the Beaufort name as though it belonged to him.

Even Carrie—who was no blood relative—would inherit some portion of his father's estate. So would Cleo and Paul, through the trust fund that had already been established for them. Well, there was nothing he could do about that trust. As for Carrie, he'd take care of her in due time. Maybe she'd turn into a whore, like her mother, and then he'd have her declared unfit to share in the estate.

A sense of rage built up within Jerry until it seemed to consume him.

It was a familiar feeling, and in a strange way it comforted him, making him feel stronger and more sure of himself. The rage had always been a part of him, even when Mama had been alive, although he had always gone to great pains to conceal it from her. Like all women, she had been too inclined to make a fuss when she had thought something was wrong.

But there was nothing wrong with his rage. It soothed him and made him feel whole. Even more than that, it gave him a sensation of being omnipotent.

Thoughts that had been in Jerry's mind for months began to crystallize. That damn bitch would have to go. God, how she relied on her beauty to bend Papa to her will. She made him sick.

Papa, with his old-fashioned ideas and strict morality, couldn't be allowed to live, either. Give him half a chance, and he'd hand out more and more of his estate to outsiders, leaving nothing to his elder son, the one person entitled to inherit everything.

Jerry went into the house for another glass of brandywine, then returned to the portico. It was remarkable how liquor clarified his thinking, and when combined with his rage, made him infallible.

He had no specific plan yet, and he had no intention of rushing things. In due time everything would fall into place. He'd find a way to get rid of Papa and Lisa so no hint of suspicion fell on him.

Ah! Suppose he found a double-barreled solution and could pin the blame on Lance? Perfect! If his half-brother went to the gallows, he alone would gain possession of Oakhurst Manor, the shipping business, and Papa's large portfolio of securities and cash. He wouldn't even begrudge Carrie the piddling sums she inherited, although he'd prefer to gain control of her share, too.

The fever began to burn. Jerry knew the signs all too well, and gulping the rest of his brandywine, he hurried upstairs to bed before he became incapacitated. The rage, as long experience had taught him, always ended in fever.

But it didn't frighten him. Nothing did. No more Papa, no more Lisa, no more Lance. He would become the sole master of Oakhurst Manor and would do with it as he pleased.

This was more than a dream. It was the ultimate reality, and somehow he would achieve it.

## Other Big Bestsellers from SIGNET

☐ **CRAZY LOVE: An Autobiographical Account of Marriage and Madness** by Phyllis Naylor.  (#J8077—$1.95)

☐ **EUGENIA** by Clare Darcy.  (#E8081—$1.75)

☐ **HARMONY HALL** by Jane Meredith.  (#E8082—$1.75)

☐ **TWINS** by Bari Wood and Jack Geasland.  (#E8015—$2.50)

☐ **THE RULING PASSION** by Shaun Herron.  (#E8042—$2.25)

☐ **CONSTANTINE CAY** by Catherine Dillon.  (#J8307—$1.95)

☐ **WHITE FIRES BURNING** by Catherine Dillon.  (#J8281—$1.95)

☐ **THE WHITE KHAN** by Catherine Dillon.  (#J8043—$1.95)*

☐ **KID ANDREW CODY AND JULIE SPARROW** by Tony Curtis.  (#E8010—$2.25)

☐ **WINTER FIRE** by Susannah Leigh.  (#E8011—$2.25)*

☐ **THE MESSENGER** by Mona Williams.  (#J8012—$1.95)

☐ **FEAR OF FLYING** by Erica Jong.  (#E7970—$2.25)

☐ **HOW TO SAVE YOUR OWN LIFE** by Erica Jong.  (#E7959—$2.50)*

☐ **HARVEST OF DESIRE** by Rochelle Larkin.  (#E8183—$2.25)

☐ **MISTRESS OF DESIRE** by Rochelle Larkin.  (#E7964—$2.25)*

\* Price silghtly higher in Canada

**THE NEW AMERICAN LIBRARY, INC.,**
P.O. Box 999, Bergenfield, New Jersey 07621

Please send me the SIGNET BOOKS I have checked above. I am enclosing $_____(please add 50¢ to this order to cover postage and handling). Send check or money order—no cash or C.O.D.'s. Prices and numbers are subject to change without notice.

Name_____

Address_____

City_____State_____Zip Code_____
Allow at least 4 weeks for delivery